ALSO BY JOHN GILSTRAP

Fiction

High Treason

Damage Control

Threat Warning

Hostage Zero

No Mercy

Scott Free

Even Steven

At All Costs

Nathan's Run

Nonfiction

Six Minutes to Freedom (with Kurt Muse)

Collaborations

Watchlist: A Serial Thriller

Praise for John Gilstrap

DAMAGE CONTROL

"Powerful and explosive, an unforgettable journey into the dark side of the human soul. Gilstrap is a master of action and drama. If you like Vince Flynn and Brad Thor, you'll love John Gilstrap."
—**Gayle Lynds**

"Rousing . . . Readers will anxiously await the next installment."
—*Publishers Weekly*

"It's easy to see why John Gilstrap is the go-to guy among thriller writers, when it comes to weapons, ammunition, and explosives. His expertise is uncontested."
—**John Ramsey Miller**

"If you haven't treated yourself to one of John Gilstrap's Jonathan Grave thrillers, you need not deprive yourself any longer. *Damage Control* is riveting, with enough explosions, death traps, and intrigue to fill three books."
—**Joe Hartlaub**, *Book Reporter*

"The best page-turning thriller I've grabbed in ages. Gilstrap is one of the very few writers who can position a set of characters in a situation, ramp up the tension, and yes, keep it there, all the way through. There is no place you can put this book down."
—**Beth Kanell**, Kingdom Books, Vermont

"A page-turning, near-perfect thriller, with engaging and believable characters . . . unputdownable! Warning—if you must be up early the next morning, don't start the book."
—*Top Mystery Novels*

"This addictively readable thriller marries a breakneck pace to a complex, multilayered plot. . . . A roller-coaster ride of adrenaline-inducing plot twists leads to a riveting and highly satisfying conclusion. Exceptional characterization and an intricate, flawlessly crafted storyline make this an absolute must-read for thriller fans."
—*Publishers Weekly* **(starred review)**

NO MERCY

"*No Mercy* grabs hold of you on page one and doesn't let go. Gilstrap's new series is terrific. It will leave you breathless. I can't wait to see what Jonathan Grave is up to next."
—Harlan Coben

"The release of a new John Gilstrap novel is always worth celebrating, because he's one of the finest thriller writers on the planet. *No Mercy* showcases his work at its finest—taut, action-packed, and impossible to put down!"
—Tess Gerritsen

"A great hero, a pulse-pounding story—and the launch of a really exciting series."
—Joseph Finder

"An entertaining, fast-paced tale of violence and revenge."
—*Publishers Weekly*

"No other writer is better able to combine in a single novel both rocket-paced suspense and heartfelt looks at family and the human spirit. And what a pleasure to meet Jonathan Grave, a hero for our time . . . and for all time."
—Jeffery Deaver

AT ALL COSTS

NATHAN'S RUN

JOHN GILSTRAP

END GAME

PINNACLE BOOKS
Kensington Publishing Corp.
www.kensingtonbooks.com

PINNACLE BOOKS are published by

Kensington Publishing Corp.
119 West 40th Street
New York, NY 10018

All Kensington titles, imprints, and distributed lines are available at special quantity discounts for bulk purchases for sales promotions, premiums, fund-raising, educational, or institutional use. Special book excerpts or customized printings can also be created to fit specific needs. For details, write or phone the office of the Kensington special sales manager: Kensington Publishing Corp., 119 West 40th Street, New York, NY 10018, attn: Special Sales Department; phone 1-800-221-2647.

ISBN-13: 978-0-7860-3021-7
ISBN-10: 0-7860-3021-6

First printing: July 2014

10 9 8 7 6 5 4 3 2 1

Printed in the United States of America

First electronic edition: July 2014

ISBN-13: 978-0-7860-3022-4
ISBN-10: 0-7860-3022-4

For Joy

CHAPTER ONE

The pounding on the front door meant trouble, a staccato beat delivered by a heavy hand. It bore the urgency of a neighbor with news that the house was on fire. In the living room, just fifteen feet away, the pounding ripped Jolaine's attention away from her computer search for the best business schools. In one year, her life would look a hell of a lot different than it did now.

She uncurled her legs from beneath her, placed her laptop on the end table, and edged toward the foyer. It was, after all, her job to answer the door, just as it was her job to deal with the emotional turmoil that defined fourteen-year-old Graham, who was supposed to be steeped in homework by now—homework that she knew he wouldn't be doing because he was one of those kids whose four-oh average came with zero effort. He ranked among the biggest reasons why next year would look so different.

Her heart hammered at least as loudly as the fist on the door as her bare feet crossed from carpet to marble. She considered ignoring it. At nearly ten o'clock, was there really an obligation to answer? The fact that she was separated from her nearest weapon by two flights of thirteen stairs didn't help at all. Why hire a bodyguard and then forbid said bodyguard to be armed in the house?

The pounding continued. "Bernard!" a voice yelled from beyond the door. "For God's sake, let me in!"

Jolaine had nearly reached the door when Mr. Mitchell—Bernard—barked, "No!" He'd appeared on the steps behind her.

Startled by the sharpness of his tone, she whirled and was even more surprised to see that he'd armed himself with a tiny MAC-10 automatic pistol. Dressed in the kind of pajamas that she'd seen only in old television shows—light blue with dark blue piping—he held the weapon at the ready, but with the muzzle pointed at the ceiling, his finger clear of the trigger guard. His apparent familiarity with the firearm startled her.

"Step away, Jolaine," he said as he hurried down the stairs. "I'll get it." By the time he reached the foyer, Sarah, his wife, had started down behind him. Her nighttime attire consisted of gray sweats.

Nothing about this was right. Mrs. Mitchell never appeared downstairs after nine. Jolaine took two giant steps backward, into the living room archway.

As the pounding grew more desperate, Bernard Mitchell slowed his gait.

"Bernard!" the visitor yelled. "There's no time!"

Bernard cast a glance back at Sarah. From Jolaine's angle, she couldn't see his face, but the reaction he got from his wife was at once heartbreaking and terrifying.

It was a look of surrender, of inevitability. Jolaine fought the urge to ask because in just a few seconds, she would see for herself.

The man on the outside was still pounding when Bernard pulled open the door without even a peek through the peephole. With his MAC-10 pressed to his shoulder, he looked ready for war. Jolaine calculated her escape route.

The instant the door separated from the jamb, a little nothing of a man spilled inside onto the marble floor. Dressed in shorts and a T-shirt, he had a mop of gray hair, but all Jolaine saw in the first seconds was the blood. The front of his clothes shimmered in it, and as he collapsed onto the stone, spatters dotted the tiles.

"Gregory!" Bernard yelled. If Jolaine was any judge, this was not the man that he'd been expecting.

On the steps, Sarah made a yipping sound and glided to the foyer as Bernard cleared the man's legs from the threshold and closed the door.

"God, what happened?"

"They know," the man gasped. "I'm so sorry. They know." Jolaine detected an Eastern European accent, and as he spoke, he passed a bloody slip of paper to Bernard. "Here it is, Bernard. I'm so, so sorry."

Mr. Mitchell's hands trembled as he lifted Gregory's shirt, presumably to find the source of the bleeding. Jolaine looked away. She'd seen enough bullet wounds to recognize the damage at a glance, and she didn't care to see any more.

"Call an ambulance," Mr. Mitchell commanded.

Jolaine spun around and hurried toward the phone in the kitchen.

"No!" Sarah said. "Jolaine, go upstairs and get Graham out of the house."

Jolaine froze. She understood the words, but they made no sense. To get him out meant to take him somewhere, and she hadn't a clue where that might be.

"Gregory needs a doctor," Bernard said. His voice broke.

"He needs an undertaker," Sarah corrected. She fired a look at Jolaine. "Graham. Now."

"Tell me what's happening," Jolaine said. She heard the stress in her own voice—the borderline panic—and the sound upset her. This was not the time to lose control.

"Not your concern," Sarah snapped. Her face was a mask of something awful. If Jolaine had encountered the same expression in Jalalabad, she would have assumed the presence of a suicide vest. "Do your job, Jolaine. Take my son to safety."

Jolaine wanted to ask for more details, but realized that they were irrelevant, at least for now. Everything about this screamed urgency of the highest order. Graham had to be roused and dressed. That was step one, and given his personality, it was a *big* step. Step two and beyond were for later.

The man on the floor was doomed; of that, Sarah was correct. His skin looked like gray construction paper with hints of blue around his nose and mouth. As Jolaine passed him on her way to the stairs, she made a point of not stepping on the blood.

She was living a nightmare. *The* nightmare. This was what she'd been hired to do, and this was why they ran all their emergency drills, though Bernard had never said why, and Jolaine had always sensed that it was all about an overinflated sense of self-worth. She'd never really bought into any of it.

Her job was to protect Graham while at the same time never cluing him in to the fact that he needed protection. She had a hard time believing that he'd never caught a glimpse of her weapon as she drove him to and from school, or wondered why he needed an au pair at his age, but he'd never said anything—at least not to her—so she'd assumed him to be as clueless as he pretended to be. He had a hell of a surprise in store. First, she had to haul his skinny, cranky ass out of bed and get him dressed.

The silver light of the television disappeared from under Graham's door as Jolaine approached. It was, she knew, anything but a coincidence, and she wasn't the least bit surprised to see him sprawled on his stomach, feigning sleep. She slapped the wall switch and right away missed the days of the incandescent lightbulbs with their instantaneous illumination.

"Graham!" she barked. "Get up. Get dressed."

He made a grumbling sound, and Jolaine realized that she'd misplayed her hand. If she'd ordered him to go to sleep, he'd have leaped out of bed. She didn't have time for this. *They* didn't have time for this. She grabbed the sheet at the line where it draped beneath his bare shoulders and stripped it down to his ankles. Given his recent adolescent obsessions, she felt relief when she saw the flash of blue boxer shorts.

"Hey!" He whirled to face her. "What the hell—"

"We need to leave. Now."

"Get out of my room! You can't just—"

Jolaine planted her hand on his chest and pushed him down into the mattress. "Listen to me, Graham," she said. "A man has been shot and is dying downstairs in the foyer. Your parents are terrified. You and I are leaving this house in one minute. You can be dressed and cooperative or naked and unconscious. I don't care which." She bounced him once to emphasize the point, and then she left for her own room on the third floor.

Her space in the attic had been converted into the nicest apartment she'd ever lived in. The stairway terminated in the middle of what she thought of as her living room. Two gabled windows provided an impressive view of rural Indiana. Her living room led to a tiny yet fully functional kitchen, beyond which were the bathroom and bedroom. Paranoid of being photographed in her sleep or in the shower—Graham was a budding photojournalist—she kept the doors locked all the time.

This was a bugout, and as with all such things, clothing didn't count. Only weapons and ammo counted. She pulled open the nightstand to reveal her daily carry weapon, a reduced-size Glock 27 chambered in .40-caliber Smith & Wesson. In a single motion, she stripped off her Indiana University T-shirt—when in Rome, right?—and stretched her elastic Kangaroo holster around her rib cage. Having done it a thousand times, her hands knew exactly what to do. Five seconds later, when the two straps were secured, she holstered the pistol under her left armpit and shoved two spare ten-round mags into their designated pockets at midline. With the T-shirt back on, no one would know that she was armed.

She moved to her closet. Ignoring the temptation of

the suitcase and clothes, she instead reached to the top shelf, where her Colt M4 lay snug in its case. She pulled it down, swung it to the floor, and worked the zipper. The aroma of gun solvent and oil enveloped her and brought an odd sense of calm. She lifted the carbine by its pistol grip and eased the charging handle back to reveal the ass end of the bullet she already knew was there. That round, combined with the others in the curved magazine, ensured a full load of thirty 5.56 millimeter bullets.

Reaching back into the bag, she grabbed two more thirty-round mags, leaving another five in the bag for later. She zipped up the gun bag and stood, slipping the two mags into her back pockets, then reached back to the top shelf for her bugout bag—a tactical vest festooned with pockets that held still more ammo, plus some rudimentary first-aid supplies, a flashlight, two knives, a thousand dollars in cash, and the kind of stuff that she figured she might need if she needed to keep Graham and herself alive for a couple of days on the run.

Jolaine shrugged into the vest without fastening it, battle-slung her M4 across the front of her body, then lifted the gun bag and headed back downstairs for Graham.

He'd managed to find a pair of jeans, but he remained shirtless and barefoot. "Come on," she said. "We're going."

"But I'm not—what the hell are you wearing?"

"Your one minute is up," Jolaine snapped. "Grab something for your feet. We're getting out of here."

"Just another minute—"

Jolaine grabbed his biceps and pulled. This was about survival. If she had to beat him senseless to save his life, she was perfectly willing to cross that line.

"Let me go!"

Jolaine ignored him, just as she ignored the distant sense of satisfaction that came with hurting him a little. Adolescent angst and anger had hit Graham with staggering force over the past twelve months, turning him into a monster.

Not quite five-nine, the kid weighed nothing, so when Jolaine pulled, he followed. She worked out, he played video games.

Why was she being such a bitch?

Okay, Jolaine was always a bitch, but that was part of her job, and at some corner of his brain, Graham realized that he brought that side out of her, but this was at a whole new level. He yelled as her fingernails stuck into the soft, sensitive flesh of his armpit, but she didn't seem to care. As he dug his heels into the carpet to slow her down, she merely squeezed tighter and pulled harder. He had no idea that she was that strong.

"Are you serious?" he asked. "Are we really leaving?" And what was with all the military crap she was wearing?

Graham wasn't even sure his feet touched the stairs as he more or less flew to the first floor. That's when he saw the blood. That's when it all became real. The man on the floor writhed in agony. "They know," the guy said. "Oh, God, they know, they know . . ."

Mom and Dad were arguing about something—they seemed really angry—but if Graham could hear the words beyond the thrumming of fear in his head, he couldn't understand them. They came out as random sounds: *fight, die, kill.* He even heard his own name in the mix. He tried to pull away from Jolaine, to be with his parents, but her grip was like iron.

"Mom!" he yelled.

Sarah's head snapped up, but her face wasn't the face he was used to seeing. Her eyes had a dead set to them, like a doll's eyes, and her mouth was set in a tight little line. "Get out," she said. "Go with Jolaine."

"Where?"

"I love you, Graham. Never forget that."

That was the line that triggered the panic in his gut. So simple, yet so final. Of course she loved him. She was his mother. Why would she think that he would assume anything else? Her words had a finality about them that made him want to cry.

He started to say, "I love you, too," but before the words could form, the front door burst open, as if propelled by explosives, and a bunch of men dressed in black flooded into the foyer. His dad shot one of them in the head at point-blank range, and the air turned red.

At the sound of the bursting door and the gunshot, Jolaine pushed Graham to the ground and planted a knee in his back to keep him there while she brought her M4 to bear. The collapsed stock plate found her shoulder and her finger found the trigger without thought. She popped one of the invaders with a shot to his chin that all but sheared his head from his shoulders. It always sucked to be one of the first people through the door.

Then the enemy adapted and the shooting started in

earnest. Sarah and Bernard both dove for cover as the front wall and windows exploded in the fusillade of incoming rounds. Within two seconds, Jolaine realized that she needed to leave while there was still some chance of getting out alive. If they hadn't done so already, the attacking forces would soon surround the house, making escape impossible.

Do your job.

Easing the pressure on Graham's back, Jolaine grabbed the nape of his neck and pulled him first to his knees and then to his feet. "We're going out through the kitchen," she said softly into his ear.

"But what about—" The rest of his question was lost in the next volley of gunfire.

Jolaine focused on the solution, not the problem. That was the secret to surviving any emergency. What was done, was done. Her only chance for mission success was to push all of that away, and concentrate on the single goal of guiding Graham to safety. Everything else, including her own survival, was secondary.

The focused commitment calmed her. The cacophony of the gunfight became so much background noise as she focused on their exit. The car keys were on the peg beside the garage door, just where they were supposed to be. She snatched them up with her right hand and switched them to her left to keep her dominant hand free.

The door to the garage opened with a thump and a hollow echo as she pushed it open. She noted in an instant that the exterior doors were still closed, but scanned the area for threats anyway before pushing Graham through the opening. "Get in the Beamer," she said, gesturing to the late-model BMW 740Li that sat in the closest bay of the three-car garage.

"We can't leave them," Graham objected.

"Would you rather die with them?" Jolaine heard the words before she'd considered them, and regretted the coldness of her tone. She closed the door behind them. In case Graham had any designs on changing plans, Jolaine kept her left hand on his shoulder as they negotiated the four steps down to the concrete floor of the garage, steering him toward the car. Her right hand stayed clasped to the grip of her M4 as she moved backward and sideways to keep the muzzle trained on the door she'd just exited. "Climb in the backseat and get on the floor," she said.

Graham tried to wriggle free. "They're killing my parents!"

"Your parents are fighting back," Jolaine snapped. "And they want you out of here. You heard that your-self from your mother." She turned her attention from the door and the threats that seethed behind it and fo-cused on Graham. In the silver light that passed in through the windows in the garage doors, his eyes glimmered with tears. She felt her heart skip as she considered what he was going through.

Jolaine tried to adopt a less threatening posture. "We need to get out of here. It's my job to keep you from getting shot. By any means possible. Now get in the backseat and lie on the floor." As an afterthought: "Okay?"

Graham swiped at his eyes with his forearm and shook his head no. Then he opened the door and climbed inside.

Jolaine unslung her M4 and put it into the car first, then slid into the driver's seat and pressed the start button.

"You forgot the garage door," Graham said.

Actually, she hadn't. Whatever lay beyond those doors was a mystery of the deadliest kind. The last thing she needed to do was give the invaders notice that they were fleeing. With her foot pressed on the brake, she dropped the transmission into reverse and ran the RPMs up high. When the tachometer needle nearly touched the red line, the kitchen door flew open, revealing Sarah in the doorway. Her shirt was wet with blood and her posture showed that she'd been wounded.

"Mom!"

Jolaine released the brake pedal and the Beamer shot backward like a bullet. The garage door blasted from its tracks and collapsed in a twisted tangle onto the driveway. As the car passed over the wreckage, Jolaine winced at the sound of metal on metal as the broken door tore at the undercarriage.

"No!" Graham yelled. "We can't leave her!" He threw his door open and prepared to jump out.

Jolaine jammed the brakes and reached back for him, "I told you—"

He was already out, rolling on the ground to find his feet. Outside, she saw a black van parked in the grass near the house, its doors open, but with no lights on. At first glance, she saw no people. A heartbeat later, a silhouette appeared at the front door. Jolaine saw the man beckon to his friends.

"Graham, get back here!" He ignored her. "God-dammit." Jolaine snatched up the M4 from the passenger seat and wielded it like a pistol to fire four rounds through the passenger side window in the direction of the guy on the stoop. The bad guy ducked back inside. She had no idea if she'd hit him, but that wasn't really the point. She was buying time.

While Graham dashed back toward the garage, Jolaine shouldered her door open and stood. Forming a solid base with her feet spaced wide, she extended the stock with a quick tug, tucked the butt plate into her shoulder, and switched the firing selector to full-auto. She fired a three-round burst toward the front stoop just to keep their heads down, and then pivoted her aim to the four vehicles that were clustered in the front yard. She fired long bursts—five or six rounds—into the fenders and hoods of each, hoping to take out tires or engine blocks, or maybe both. She'd take any advantage she could get.

The bolt locked open when the magazine went dry, and she never broke aim as she fingered the mag release with her trigger finger. She pulled a fresh one from her pocket, slid it into place, and smacked the bolt release to recharge the weapon. Total elapsed time for the change was less than five seconds. Jolaine was astonished at how quickly her skills had returned.

Sarah Mitchell met Graham halfway, stumbling over the wreckage of the garage door and lurching her way toward the BMW.

"Quickly!" Jolaine yelled. The fact that the bad guys were no longer trying to come through the front door told her that they had developed a different plan. Once they got their shit together, the limits of her firepower would spell the end.

Jolaine fought the urge to run forward to help them. Now that they were all exposed, her job was to lay down covering fire.

As the Mitchells closed to within a few feet, Jolaine knew that Sarah was in trouble. Her face was ashen. She was bleeding out somewhere. Graham's chest was bloody as well, but from the ease of his movement, she could tell that the blood was not his own.

They were out of time.

"In, in, in!" Jolaine yelled. Fifteen seconds ago, she'd never have believed that they could survive this long. Now that they were on the verge of getting away, time had slowed to an agonizing crawl.

Graham pulled the front door open for his mother. "Be careful," he said.

"Be careful my ass," Jolaine said. "Sarah, sit down and close your door. Graham, get on the floor of the backseat and keep your head down."

She saw movement in the darkness on the near side of the house and she reacted without looking, raking the area with a ten-round burst. This business of keeping heads down burned a hell of a lot of ammunition. Thank God there were no neighbors to get caught in the crossfire.

When the family was inside, Jolaine ducked back into the driver's seat. With the M4 jammed awkwardly across the center console, she didn't bother to close her door before she pulled the shifter into reverse and stomped on the gas.

The Beamer launched backward across the lawn for thirty feet. She shifted to drive. She heard shots being fired at them, and she felt a couple of rounds thunk into the car somewhere, but no warning lights came on, and no one yelled in pain.

They were on their way. To somewhere.

CHAPTER TWO

The emptiness of the Indiana cornfields swallowed the headlight beams, revealing nothing but miles of darkness. "Graham, are you okay?" Jolaine shouted over the wind noise from the shattered passenger window. When he didn't respond, she wrenched her body around in the driver's seat to look in the back. The boy was still on the floor, his head wrapped in his arms. "Graham!"

"Make it stop!" he yelled.

"Are you hurt?"

"Why are they doing this?"

"Are you *hurt?*"

"No! I'm not hurt! Why are they doing this?"

"I don't know," Jolaine said. "Mrs. Mitchell? Sarah?" She could smell the blood.

"We can't go to a hospital," Sarah said. Her voice was soft. Jolaine didn't know if it was because she was weak or because she didn't want Graham to hear.

"How bad are you hit?"

Sarah shook her head. Jolaine saw it as a shift in her silhouette. "It's not good. I'm hit in my middle."

"So we *do* need to go to a hospital."

"No. That's where they'll be looking. The doctors will have to call the police for a bullet wound."

"Yeah!" Graham said from the back. "We need to call the police."

"Not for this, sweetie," Sarah said. "We don't want the police involved."

"Where's Dad?"

Sarah shot a look to Jolaine that said it all. But she didn't respond.

"Mom?"

"Dad's staying behind," Sarah said.

"But he's okay? He'll be joining us?"

Silence.

"Mom?"

"Let's talk about this later, okay, Graham?" Sarah asked.

"Is he okay?"

"*Later,* Graham." That tone cut the conversation off at the root.

Jolaine said, "What's going on, Sarah? Tell me why this is happening."

With effort that seemed to trigger a spasm of pain, Sarah stretched her leg out to gain access to the front pocket of her jeans and went fishing for something.

"Mom?" Graham said. "Why aren't you answering?" His voice trembled in a combination of anger, fear, and sadness.

Sarah was holding herself together pretty well, especially with her bullet wound. Since she hadn't bled out already, and clearly no bones had been clipped, Jolaine had hope for her. But she needed a doctor, and she needed one now.

"I'm sorry, Graham," Sarah said. "I'm okay, really.

I've just got a lot of things going through my mind right now."

"So, are we going to the police?"

"No, not tonight."

"A hospital, then," Graham said. "You're hurt. You've been shot."

Sarah's hunt through her pocket produced a cell phone. Jolaine was hoping for something else. She wasn't sure what, but some kind of a solution would have been nice.

"You're going to make a phone call?" Jolaine said. "How about you answer my question? We're all in danger here, you know. Not just you."

Again, Sarah ignored her. The smart phone's screen bathed her in a silver-blue light that highlighted her pallor. As she swiped at the screen, she left bloody streaks.

"What are you looking for?" Jolaine insisted. Ahead, the twisting country road was an opaque black ribbon.

"I found it," Sarah declared. She pressed a button and brought her phone to her ear. Whoever she was calling had better be of calm temperament, Jolaine thought. Ten-thirty at night was late for anyone.

"Doctor Jones, please," Sarah said into the phone. "This is Mrs. Smith."

Ah, Jolaine thought. *They're spooks. I should have known.*

"Four seven four bravo," Sarah said after a pause. "Gunshot. Serious." After another pause, Sarah said, "I'm sorry, but I'll never remember all of that. Let me hand you over to someone who will. Yes, a trusted source." With that, she handed the Droid across the center console to Jolaine. "This is Doctor Jones," she said.

Sure it is, Jolaine didn't say. She brought the phone to her ear. "Hello?"

"What's your name?" the voice asked from the other side.

"What's yours?"

"Don't trifle with me, missy. You already know my name. I am Doctor Jones."

"Fine," Jolaine said. "My name is Doe. Jane Doe. Don't trifle with me, either, Doc. The last few minutes have been really, really intense. I've got a seriously injured woman sitting next to me who needs help, and you want to do small talk. Seriously, Doc, who's trifling whom?"

Five seconds of silence convinced Jolaine that she'd either made her point or driven the doc to hang up. "You sound like you're part of the Community," Jones said.

"On the periphery," Jolaine confessed. "A contractor, never official."

"I see. How bad are her wounds?"

"I don't know. I haven't seen them. There's a lot of blood. She's pale but she can talk, and she seems to have it together cognitively."

"*Cognitively,*" Jones mocked. "That's a high-dollar word for a grunt."

"Why did you want to speak with me?" Jolaine pressed. She didn't have time for bullshit, and she figured the best way to avoid it was to stay away from the bait.

"I want you to bring Mrs. Smith to my clinic. We can care for her here."

Translation: the Company had a contract with a

quick-quack that would keep serious injuries off the grid.

"How do I know I can trust you?"

The doctor laughed. It sounded like genuine amusement. "Well, Jane, you don't. You can't. But let's be honest. You have no option."

Jolaine didn't answer.

"All right, then," Jones said. "I'm going to give you an address. Do you have a GPS system to punch it into?"

"I have my phone."

"Are you ready to copy the address?"

"Stand by," Jolaine said. Then into the rearview mirror: "Graham, listen up. Are you listening?"

"To what?"

"Just listen."

"Who's Graham?" Jones asked.

"He's the patient's son."

"He can't stay here."

"Let's do that later," Jolaine said. "Let's have the address."

Jones gave an address in Defiance, Ohio, and Jolaine repeated it. "Got it, Graham?"

"Yes," he said. The kid was blessed with perfect recall—literally, he remembered every word said to him and everything he read.

Jolaine asked the doctor, "How far is that from Antwerp, Indiana?"

"Worst, worst case, thirty minutes."

Jolaine clicked off, whipped the BMW onto the right-hand shoulder, and hit the brakes.

"What are you doing?" her passengers asked in unison.

"I'm figuring out where we're going," she said. "Recite back the address, Graham." As he regurgitated the house number and street, she entered them into the phone's navigation program. Good news: fifteen miles, seventeen minutes.

She bet that she could make it in thirteen.

With an utter disregard for speed limits, it actually took twelve. Doctor Jones lived slightly north of nowhere, off a road that was marked only with a caduceus.

"What is this place?" Graham asked.

Jolaine resisted the urge to extinguish her headlights to provide less of a target. To do that would be to commit them to total darkness, which could mean driving into a ditch or a tree.

"It's the doctor's house, sweetie," Sarah said. Her voice had become breathy, and there was a grunt of pain between "house" and "sweetie." "He's going to make me all better."

Sarah often spoke to her son as if he were three years old, and the tone made Jolaine wince.

"Dad's dead, isn't he?"

"Don't talk of such things," Sarah said. In those words, Jolaine caught the hint of the Eastern European accent that Sarah worked so hard to camouflage. Jolaine thought it was a sign that the woman was becoming weaker.

Jolaine also noted the absence of an answer to the boy's question. That could mean any number of things, but in Jolaine's mind, it only meant one: *Yes, Graham, your dad is dead.*

If there was a paved roadway in here, Jolaine couldn't

see it. Navigating—if that was indeed what she was doing—was mostly a matter of not hitting the surrounding foliage. By default, the road was where a bush or a tree was not.

Judging distance was an exercise in futility, as was assessing the passage of time. After what felt like several long, whole minutes, she saw another caduceus just like the previous one, but this one was underlined by a reflective arrow that pointed to the right. Jones hadn't mentioned the driving gauntlet during their telephone conversation. Spooks thrived on mind games. She'd known a lot of spooky people when she was tromping through the Sandbox, and most made her want to take a shower after speaking with them. Even "hello" needed to be treated with suspicion.

Finally, the driveway opened up, and she saw a house in the distance. Barely discernible in the dark, it would have been invisible had a single coach light not burned in the front.

"How sure are you that this is a good idea?" Jolaine thought aloud.

"How many other options can you think of?" Sarah responded. The accent was even thicker.

As Jolaine cleared the woods, with fifty yards or more separating them from the house in the distance, she cut the lights. The risk of getting raked by gunfire from the building trumped any worries about wrecking the car.

"I'm scared," Graham said.

"I am, too," Jolaine said. The words were out before she could stop them. She wished she had a plan. Back in the day, she and her comrades from Hydra Security would never have made an approach like this out in the open. Of course, she would not have been the only operative wielding a weapon, either.

They were open and exposed—targets to anyone who wanted to take them out.

"I'm not liking this," Jolaine said.

No one answered, and that was fine.

As they closed to within one hundred feet of the house, a rectangle of light appeared in the center of the structure. It grew to reveal the silhouette of a man standing in the opening. From his posture, he might have been holding a pistol or he might not have. Jolaine reached under her shirt and drew her Glock from its holster.

"Do you know this guy?" Jolaine asked.

"No," Sarah said.

"Then how do we know—"

"We know," Sarah said, cutting her off. "The system works. Trust it." She reached across the console and grasped Jolaine's arm. "And trust your training. All of it."

Jolaine jammed the brakes and the transmission, threw open her door. Shifting her Glock to her weak side—her left—she brought it to bear on the figure in the doorway, using the structure of the car for cover.

"I'm not armed," said a male voice from the doorway. He sounded a lot like the voice she'd spoken to on the telephone. "Put your firearm away, please. We have a patient to treat."

With that, the man approached. The farther he moved away from the light of the doorway, the more invisible he became, but he kept his hands to his sides, his fingers splayed. She broke her aim and lowered her weapon, but she did not re-holster it. Not yet.

"Where is she?" the man asked.

"Are you Doctor Jones?"

"I think we both know that I am not," the man said. "The real name is Wilkerson. Doug Wilkerson. I'm a good guy." Even in the dark, Jolaine saw him smile. "I'd shake your hand, but you look like you might shoot me."

Wilkerson had a youthful look about him. He had thick dark hair that could have used some serious combing at this hour, and a thin face that looked as if it hadn't smiled in a while. His voice had a reedy, almost adolescent quality to it.

"I very well might," Jolaine said. She tried to keep her tone light, but she was stating the truth. She'd done a lot of shooting tonight. One more wouldn't hurt a bit.

"So, since you have the firepower, tell me what you want me to do."

The passenger-side door opened, startling both of them. "I've been shot," Sarah said. "Forget what she wants. Patch me up before I bleed to death."

Wilkerson acknowledged her with a glance, but otherwise, his eyes remained locked on Jolaine. "And who are you?" he asked.

"I'm Jolaine Cage," she said. "And I think this is Sarah Mitchell."

"You *think?*"

She shrugged with one shoulder. "On a night like tonight, I assume that I don't know anything. The boy in the backseat is Graham Mitchell. That I know for sure."

Illuminated now by the BMW's dome light, Jolaine saw the doctor's face darken. "Ah, the boy."

Graham opened his door. "Right here," he said.

Wilkerson glowered at Sarah. "You didn't say anything about children."

"I thought we agreed to talk about that later," Jolaine said.

"I don't want children here."

"I'm pretty sure he doesn't want to be here, either," Jolaine said.

"Do you think this is a good time for humor, Ms. Cage?"

Jolaine didn't understand the dynamic of what was going on. "We need to get Sarah inside," she said. "I'll help."

She holstered her pistol, then reached back into the car for her M4, which she slung over her shoulder, muzzle down. She walked around the front of the car to join the doctor. Graham climbed out, too.

"Stay in the car, kid," Wilkerson said. "You're not coming in."

"We're not having this discussion now," Sarah said. "Not while I'm bleeding to death."

Jolaine was prepared to push Wilkerson out of the way if it came to that—the guy had a wiry look to him, like he might have done some time in the military, but he didn't look like much of a fighter. "I'll help you carry her inside," she said. "You can help, too, Graham, if the doctor doesn't want to."

The boy moved slowly. Jolaine wondered if the reality of the situation was just beginning to settle on him— if he was just beginning to recognize the trouble they were in. His eyes had a look of hyperconcentration, as if examining a particularly difficult math problem. He responded to commands, but he seemed focused on a spot that only he could see.

Jolaine took Sarah's left arm while the doctor took

her right, and together they hefted her to a standing position and gave her a moment to settle herself.

"Can you do this?" Wilkerson asked. "Can you walk?"

Sarah nodded, but Jolaine questioned the sincerity. Pallor had given way to ashen gray, and her eyes seemed recessed into dark holes. Her body trembled with the effort of standing, and her skin felt cool and wet. These were the early signs of shock, and shock was a giant step toward death.

"We need to move," Wilkerson said. "While she's still conscious." He pointed with his forehead to the door he had just exited. He and Jolaine walked in step as they navigated the walkway, and then the two steps that led to the stoop, and the one step that led to the foyer. It wasn't until they reached the dim illumination of the porch light that Jolaine saw the blood trail. They were running out of time.

CHAPTER THREE

Washington, DC, was a city that wallowed in opposites. Everybody in this town had an opinion, and given twenty seconds and an ounce of alcohol, they'd be more than happy to share it with you. It was a town of blind ambition, flexible ethics, and no sense of either shame or loyalty. For all those reasons and more, Jonathan Grave hated the place.

Yet here he was at the John F. Kennedy Center for the Performing Arts, dressed like a penguin, paying a ridiculous price for a meal and a show, all in support of the Resurrection House Foundation. Founded anonymously by Jonathan via one of many cutout companies that he'd established for any number of reasons, Resurrection House was a residential school for the children of incarcerated parents. Officially run by Saint Katherine's Catholic Church in Fisherman's Cove, Virginia, the main building had begun life as Jonathan's childhood mansion. Thanks in no small part to the relentless marketing by Father Dom D'Angelo, pastor of St. Kate's and resident psychologist and headmaster, Rez House, as it was called by the locals, had become one of the "in" charities in Washington. The annual fund-raiser had become a place to see and be seen.

Among the four hundred people in attendance at the black-tie gala, Jonathan knew of only two who were aware of his involvement with the foundation, and they had been sworn to secrecy. In Jonathan's worldview, philanthropy that was broadcast through the media was a publicity stunt in disguise. He'd rather be an anonymous guy in the crowd.

If he really had his druthers, he wouldn't be here at all, but at home wearing shorts and a T-shirt, either reading a book or retooling his guns.

Ah, his guns. He missed the feel of the Colt 1911 .45 on his hip. This being the District of Columbia, where security was tight because of the dignitaries in attendance, and only bad guys enjoyed the privilege of being able to defend themselves, he had no choice but to join the ranks of bad-guy bait.

As ugly as the town was in its soul, he had to admit that it was home to a lot of beautiful places. Among them, he thought, was the Kennedy Center, but there were plenty of folks who would argue the opposite. The most common rap the place took was that it looked on the outside like a giant Whitman's Sampler candy box, and that the red-on-red-on-red interior made it look like a high-ceilinged whorehouse.

Clearly, the critics had never visited a real whorehouse.

Jonathan thought it was lovely and elegant. Presently, he was standing in line for the bar, where an overworked bartender struggled to keep up with the sissy drinks that were favored by most of the patrons. If Jonathan were king, the only ingredients that could be legally added to an alcoholic beverage would be olives and the occasional ice cube. Okay, and twists of certain citrus fruits. If good scotch were involved, even the ice cubes would be illegal.

His date for the night—because he wasn't currently in the market for a girlfriend—was Venice Alexander, the brains behind so much of what his company, Security Solutions, had been able to accomplish over the years. Pronounced Ven-EE-chay, the young lady who was currently charming the ambassador of Buttscratchistan over by the base of the stairs to the Opera House had been a friend of his for nearly as long as she'd been alive. The older he got, the less the eight-year age difference meant, but there were still more than a few people tonight who'd noticed that her skin was chocolate brown while his was Polish white. At one level, Jonathan lived for the moment when someone would have the balls to say something out loud.

Venice deserved a decent man in her life—God knew she'd endured her share of shitheads—and if a fancy-ass black-tie gala could help her find one, Jonathan was all over that. So long as love never trumped her loyalty to Security Solutions. No one on Earth matched her skills for making cyberspace dance to a prescribed melody.

When it was his turn, he ordered a neat Lagavulin for himself—one of the requirements for an open bar in his universe was to have decent liquor—and a Hendrick's with orange juice for Venice.

"Are you two-fisting your drinks this evening?" asked a sweet female voice from behind.

He turned to behold a pretty thirtysomething dressed in a clingy red gown and the ultimate in stiletto sandals. "Poison in one hand," Jonathan said, lifting the scotch, "and antidote in the other." He'd been sniffed at by too many bimbettes over the years to be drawn into her trap.

She smiled. "I'd offer to shake hands, but you don't seem to have one available. My name's Kit," she said. "That's what they call the offspring of a wolverine."

The words caused Jonathan to pause. Wolverine was the code name for a very senior official in the FBI. "Oh yeah?" he asked. "Do you know a lot about wolverines?"

"Only what I've been told on Ninth Street," she said.

Jonathan processed the words. The J. Edgar Hoover Building, FBI Headquarters, resided on Ninth Street, Northwest, in Washington, DC. Whoever this lady was, she had been dispatched by Irene Rivers, director of the Federal Bureau of Investigation. He raised the gin and orange juice, as if part of a toast. "I need to deliver a drink to my guest," he said.

"I'll be waiting right here," Kit said.

Jonathan peeled away and worked his way through the shoulder-crushing crowd to find Venice. She was in the sweet spot of her biennial crusade to lose weight, striking a stunning chord in her little black dress that had the power to stop traffic. "Excuse me," he said, interrupting her conversation with Ambassador What's-his-name. "This is for you."

Something in his tone caught her attention. As she reached for the proffered glass, she said, "Is there a problem?"

"Ask me again in a few minutes," Jonathan said. He turned and headed back toward the woman in the red dress.

Kit stood in front of the tall windows, purportedly staring out at the Potomac River, while in fact, he suspected, studying the reflections of the room. He approached from behind and took a spot next to her. "You got my attention," he said.

"My boss says that you've been hard to find for the last few weeks," she said.

"Apparently not," he replied. Not nearly enough time had passed since the last time he'd gotten pulled into the kind of political hot spot that threatened his life.

Kit turned to face him and offered her hand. "My real name is Maryanne Rhoades," she said.

Jonathan smiled. "Real enough for tonight, anyway," he said. "And to think that I could escape cloaks and daggers and spend an evening merely giving huge sums of money to charity."

"Being a billionaire must be a terrible burden," Maryanne said.

Her sarcasm made him like her less. He waited for her to make her point.

"We have an issue," Maryanne explained.

"Help me with 'we,' " Jonathan said.

"In this case, all freedom-loving people," Maryanne said.

Jonathan laughed before he could stop himself. "How long did you practice that line before you actually had to deliver it?"

Her smile evaporated. "Can we find a corner to talk?"

Jonathan looked at his watch. "Intermission is about to end," he said. "And I have a date."

"Your date is a coworker, and you don't like opera."

He wasn't going to argue with a stranger, but the fact was that he had recently found a place for opera in his life, thanks to the influence of a woman named Gail, who only recently joined a long line of women who ultimately couldn't live with the risks that defined his world. As for his date, she deserved better than to be stood up.

"Tell you what, Maryanne," he said. "Why don't you just hang out here till the end of the second act. I'll be back for the next intermission."

He turned and walked away. Irene Rivers would never have been so dismissive of Venice, and there were precious few crises in the world that couldn't cook for another hour or so. He considered it time well spent if it taught Kit-Maryanne a little humility and manners.

"Who's the lady in red?" Venice asked as he rejoined her in the line that was headed back into the Opera House.

"A friend of Wolverine," he said. "Lots of attitude. She can wait."

Venice turned and glared. "Digger! You can't do that."

He shrugged. "Sure I can. I don't work for them, and it's not right for a lady who's dressed as hot as you to sit by herself in a box seat."

Venice pulled to a stop. "Oh, my God," she gasped, feigning shock. "Did you just give me a compliment?"

Jonathan felt himself blush. "Oh, come on."

Venice grinned. "Go," she said. "Like it or not, important people have come to depend on you."

"But I want to see the end—" His phone buzzed with an incoming message. He reached into his inside jacket pocket and withdrew the electronic leash. The screen read *J. Edgar,* his little dig at Irene's professional heritage.

The text message was simple and to the point: "Don't be an asshole. She means well. We need you."

"Wolverine?" Venice asked with a knowing smile.

Jonathan sighed and took a healthy pull on his scotch. "Enjoy the show," he said.

The doctor's house looked much bigger on the inside than it did from the exterior—and far more opulent. A wide, round foyer led to a sweeping staircase to the second floor. The floor beneath Jolaine's feet appeared to be marble—some sort of white stone. Now in brighter light, Sarah's blood seemed even redder—not just where it flowed from her body, but where it smeared on every surface it touched.

The rooms that Jolaine could see screamed serious money. Overstuffed furniture atop Oriental carpets. From the masculinity of the décor and darkness of the color palette, Jolaine suspected that Wilkerson did not have a woman in his life. The place looked more like a country-club cigar room than a home.

She considered asking where they were taking Sarah, but didn't when she realized that she'd know soon enough. "Are you still with us, Graham?" she asked without looking back. When he didn't answer, she threw a glance over her shoulder. He seemed dazed by the crimson smears on the floor.

"Graham!" she shouted. It startled him. "Please come with us. Come help your mom."

"We should clean this," he said.

Jolaine felt a tug in her chest. The kid was losing it. Maybe she owed him a hug and a shoulder to cry on, but they didn't have the time, and the doctor wasn't slowing down.

"Later," she said. "I really need you to come with us. Please."

Wilkerson pulled on a giant picture on the wall that swung open to reveal a hidden panel, which in turn led to an elevator door. "There's only one way down," he said as they stepped into the elevator. "You're coming or you're staying, but I'm not waiting for either one of you."

"Graham!"

That seemed to break his spell. He looked up.

"Now. Please."

He started walking again.

Wilkerson reached past Jolaine to pull the door closed without them, and she pushed back. She didn't get why he needed to be such an asshole, but she'd kill him before she left Graham alone.

Five seconds later, Graham joined them, and Jolaine pulled the door closed herself. Wilkerson pushed the bottom of two buttons, and the car jerked. It wasn't till they were moving that Jolaine noticed the size of the elevator car. Like the house itself, it was bigger than she was expecting. Big enough to accommodate a stretcher.

The elevator jerked to a stop, and Wilkerson nodded

to the doorknob near Jolaine's hip. "Open it, please," he said.

The door opened onto a doctor's office—a surgical suite, really, complete with tile walls and floors, lights suspended from the ceiling, and an operating table.

"Wow," she said. An understatement.

"I have a very limited yet lucrative practice," Wilkerson said. "Uncle Sam likes to take care of his own." He led Sarah to the table, turned her, and then hoisted her faceup onto the stainless-steel surface.

She winced and yelled at the jostling. Jolaine thought it good news that she could respond to stimuli.

"Be careful!" Graham said. "You're hurting her." He rushed to the table to be near her head. "You're going to be okay, Mom."

Wilkerson pivoted to a nearby sink and turned on the water by nudging the knee-operated valve. "We're going to need you to say your good-byes and move away," he said. "I need to evaluate the wound."

"Are you working alone?" Jolaine asked.

"For the next few minutes, yes. I have a team on the way." He nodded to a pair of blunt-tipped scissors on the counter next to the sink. "Cut her shirt off for me, will you?"

Now Jolaine saw why he didn't want a kid around. To care for wounds, they needed to be exposed, and no boy needed to see his mother's naked torso. More than that, no child needed to see a parent's bullet wounds.

"Can you please stand over there?" Jolaine said to Graham as she returned with the scissors. "I need to take your mom's shirt off."

"No," he said. "I want to stay with her."

Sarah turned her head to face her son and smiled. "I'll be okay, sweetie," she said. "They just need to work on me a little. You don't want to see that. Besides, they'll be giving me something soon to help me sleep."

Graham's face turned red. "Are you going to die?"

"No, I'm going to be fine," she said. "The doctor is going to take good care of me."

"I don't like him," Graham said.

She smiled again. "Some doctors are just like that. It's late and he's tired." She ran a bloody hand through his hair, streaking it. "I love you."

Tears tracked his cheeks now. "I love you, too," he croaked.

Sarah lowered her hand. "Go on now," she said.

Graham looked up at Jolaine, who put a hand on his shoulder and pressed just a little in the direction of the plastic chair in the corner. He seemed smaller than he was before. Younger.

Jolaine jumped when Sarah's hand clamped her wrist. The grip was stronger than she'd expected.

"Bring him back," she said. "Never mind. Graham!" she shouted. "Come on back, baby."

He all but leaped back to his mother's side. "I'm here, Mom," he said. "Right here."

Sarah pulled a bloody piece of paper from her pocket—the very piece of paper, Jolaine realized in a flash of panic, that Gregory had given Bernard when he spilled into the front door.

"Take this," Sarah said to her son.

Jolaine reached out to intercept. "No," she said.

Graham shoved her. "Get out of my way," he said.

Jolaine didn't know what the paper was, but she knew that people had died for it, and that her most pressing job was to keep Graham from dying, too. "Really, Sarah?" she said. "He's your son."

Sarah made no indication that she'd heard. "Take this," she said to Graham.

"What is it?" He seemed to sense the danger, too.

"Please," Sarah said. "It's important."

"I'll take it," Jolaine said.

Graham and Sarah replied in unison, "No!"

Wilkerson stepped up to the table. "I told you to get her clothes off."

"Leave us alone for a moment, Doctor," Sarah said, grunting through a spasm of pain.

"You're going to die if we don't get that wound stabilized."

"It's my life to lose," Sarah snapped. "Two minutes." Without waiting for an answer, she rocked her head to readdress Graham, and she thrust the note closer. "Do you remember the protocol?"

Graham froze. Terror invaded his face. He said, "Um."

"You do, don't you?" Sarah said.

Jolaine asked, "What are you talking about? What protocol?"

Sarah stayed focused on her son. "You remember, don't you, Graham? You always remember."

Graham nodded.

"Sarah, I must insist," Jolaine said. "Whatever this *protocol* is, whatever the content of the note, if it endangers—"

"Shut up, Jolaine," Sarah snapped. "Take this, Graham." She thrust the note into his hand. "Look at it. Look at it *carefully.*"

"I don't want—"

"For crying out loud," Wilkerson said. "Look at the

damn thing. The quicker you do, the better chance I have of saving her life."

Graham took the note and opened it. When Jolaine tried to peek, he angled away so she couldn't see. The glimpse she did catch revealed a long string of numbers and letters. As far as she could tell, it wasn't an equation, and it spelled nothing.

As Graham studied the paper, trying to make sense out of it, she realized that Sarah had snared her son in a trap.

When Graham looked up from the paper, Sarah smiled. "You memorized it, didn't you?" She laughed and triggered another spasm. "You can't help it."

Jolaine knew it was true. Graham's version of photographic memory placed him in the one percentile of the one percentile. To read was to remember forever. He had no control over it.

"Give me the paper back now," Sarah said.

After looking at it one more time, Graham handed it back. Sarah stuffed it into her mouth and swallowed. "Execute the protocol," Sarah said. To Jolaine, she added, "Remember your mission, too."

"What is this, Sarah?" Jolaine demanded. "Why is all this happening? You owe me that much."

"The protocol," Sarah said again. "Graham knows the code and the protocol. Repeat it only in person, son. That's very important. In person, not over the phone."

"But the protocol *is* a phone call," Graham said. "That's all it ever was."

"You'll have to meet. The man on the other end will know what to do. Just follow his directions."

Jolaine stepped in again. "Sarah, he is not meeting

anyone unless I know what he's walking into. Is this code, as you call it, the reason why people are dying?"

"Follow the protocol," Sarah repeated. "Once the loop is closed, the killing should stop. There'll be no reason. Jolaine, protect Graham."

"Sarah, this isn't fair. I can't protect him if—"

Behind them, the mechanics of the elevator hummed. Jolaine's hand jerked to her holster, and one second later, her Glock was in her hand. She pushed Graham across the room and made herself as big as possible in the space between him and the door.

"That's my team arriving," Wilkerson said.

From a two-handed isosceles stance, she centered her sights on the middle of the door. "They need to pray that they don't have weapons in their hands," she said.

"For God's sake," Wilkerson said. "Take a breath. We don't need any more shooting."

Jolaine didn't bother to respond. She trusted her reserve and her resolve. She wouldn't shoot at anyone who didn't need shooting. Tonight, that bar was dropping lower by the minute.

The elevator hydraulics hissed, and then there was a soft thump. Two seconds later, the door opened. She moved her finger from the pistol's frame to its trigger. If it came to that, she could rain down ten rounds in a little under four seconds, every one of them drilling a hole within an inch of where she wanted it to drill.

The first man out of the elevator didn't look like a doctor. With gray hair and a jet-black beard that was a throwback to the Civil War, he looked like a sixties-era beatnik. "Show your hands or die where you stand!" Jolaine yelled.

The guy jumped. Had there not been three more men plugging the entrance behind him, he might have bolted back through the door. "Whoa, whoa, whoa!" he yelled. He held his hands out in front of him, his fingers splayed to ward off the attack. "I'm a doctor."

"Stop!" Wilkerson bellowed. "Jesus Christ, these are my colleagues. Put your gun away!"

Jolaine held her aim long enough to assess each of the faces coming off the elevator. Every one of them looked like they'd be more comfortable in front of a video game than engaging in a gunfight muzzle to muzzle.

Finally, she moved her finger outside the trigger guard and moved the weapon to low-ready—not aiming at anyone in particular, but still pointing at the floor in their general direction, just in case a target presented itself.

"Don't pay attention to her," Wilkerson said. "She's part of the Community, she's scared, and she's about to leave."

Behind her, Graham grabbed a fistful of the back of her shirt. She didn't know what it meant, but she knew that it was an appeal for help. Still not ready to re-holster, she lowered the Glock a little more.

"I think we're all right, Graham," she said. This would be over soon, one way or the other.

The arriving team moved to surround Sarah Mitchell. In seconds, it was as if Jolaine and Graham didn't even exist. It was actually the lack of attention that convinced her that it would be safe to holster her weapon. When it was secure, she turned her attention to Graham, looking him in the eye.

"How are you doing?" she asked.

He shrugged and made a jerky motion with his head. It might have been a nod, or it might have been just a twitch. His brain still wasn't processing it all.

"Here it is, Graham," she said. "We're going to have to leave. The doctors will care for your mom, but there's no place for us here. We need to move on."

The terror in the boy's face deepened and multiplied. "Where are we going?"

The truthful answer was *I don't have any idea.* Instead, Jolaine said, "We'll find a hotel room. We'll kind of hide for a while and see what happens."

"Who are we hiding from?"

Damn good question. "We don't know yet. What was on that piece of paper? What did it mean?"

Graham shook his head. "I don't know," he said. Tears balanced on his eyelids. "Mom said it was a code, so I guess it's a code. But I don't know what it means."

"Please don't lie to me, Graham. Not tonight."

"I'm not lying, Jolaine. I can tell you that it was a string of letters and numbers—I could even recite them for you—and according to Mom, they're some kind of code, but beyond that, I have no idea what they are."

"Why are they important?"

"I don't know that either."

She believed him. "It's time to go now."

"What about Mom?"

Jolaine ignored that question and looked to the crowd that had gathered around Sarah. "Doctor Wilkerson!" she said. "I'm going to need a car."

A voice from the clinical scrum said, "Find the kitchen upstairs. There are a set of keys on the hook by the door to the garage. Take whichever car you want."

Really? It was that easy? So much about this just didn't make sense.

"Let's go," Jolaine said. She put her hand back on Graham's arm.

"But what about *Mom?*"

"*Now,*" Jolaine said.

CHAPTER FOUR

Maryanne was waiting for him at the base of the JFK bust that to Jonathan's eye was the single ugly piece of artwork in the building. It looked like mud balls that had been crammed together. From a distance, it resembled the countenance of the thirty-fifth president of the United States, but up close it looked like an elementary school art project gone wrong.

"This really is important," she said as he approached within earshot.

Jonathan gestured toward the door that led to the terrace. It was a flawless night in Washington. The cherry blossoms had bloomed a few weeks ago, but the stifling humidity and heat that so defined the capital city still lay in the future. The terrace offered a spectacular view of the Potomac River.

He took another hit of his scotch. At this rate, it wasn't going to last long. "I'm all ears," he said. "What've you got?"

"First some background," Maryanne said. She looked soft for a Fibbie, too feminine. "You know that the Soviet Union collapsed back in the eighties."

"I believe I heard the rumor."

"Well, when it fell, it didn't fall softly. For years, the US has been running a network of informants in the former Soviet Republics—both the friendly ones, and the other ones."

"If that's supposed to surprise me, you've missed the mark," Jonathan said.

"Thing is," she continued, "the Russians are slouching back to their old ways. I'm sure you heard the news story a few months ago about the Russian sleeper cells that were operating here and in Canada. They brought down that airliner in Chicago before the Mounties took them out."

"I remember reading something about that," Jonathan said. It seemed inappropriate to mention that that had been his op. The fact that she didn't know told him that Wolverine had been appropriately circumspect in the information she shared.

"We have every reason to believe that nothing remains of the Movement, as they called themselves. But as cultural and religious tensions increase, the chatter has elevated immensely. We know that other cells exist, and for that reason, we continue to develop and run sources."

Jonathan checked his watch. So far nothing in this conversation trumped the Puccini he was missing. "You know that I don't work for Uncle Sam anymore, right? I'm out of the business of giving much of a shit about terrorist cells. I pay taxes for that stuff."

Maryanne took a breath. "One of our most prolific operators was killed tonight. Bernard Mitchell. He was a nuke expert."

Jonathan's neck hairs rose. If this pretty young thing

worked for Wolverine, then she knew better than to throw out details that weren't relevant. "A nuke expert for whom?" he asked. "Our side or theirs?"

She hesitated. "Both."

"Okay, which side did he love more?"

"Ours," she said. "We're almost positive of that."

In Jonathan's experience with government-speak, the difference between *almost positive* and *we don't have a freaking clue* was barely discernible.

"At this stage, we know very little that is concrete, but what we do know is disturbing. Bernard Mitchell is dead, and we received a panic code from their house, presumably when the attack was happening. Judging from the amount of damage done to the home, and the number of bullet holes and bloodstains, it was a hell of a fight, and more than just good guys were killed."

"Did Bernard live alone?" Jonathan asked. He felt himself being drawn in.

"No, and that's even more disturbing. We know nothing of the whereabouts of his wife, Sarah, their son, Graham, or an au pair named Jolaine. They have disappeared, and so has one of the Mitchells' cars. A BMW."

"Doesn't the smart money say they got away?"

"Under normal circumstances, yes," Maryanne said. "But there are protocols in place for events such as this, notifications to be made by survivors of a hit."

Jonathan considered where the conversation was going. "Let me guess. None of them were implemented."

"Exactly. They were to call a central number, and the person on the other end of the call would have given them specific instructions on what to do next."

"So you're saying that they disappeared."

"Essentially, yes," Maryanne said.

"Why are you telling me this instead of briefing a roomful of fire-breathing Fibbies?" As far as Jonathan could tell, there were only a couple of reasons for Uncle Sam to reach out to contractors, and more times than not, it had something to do with breaking the law.

"Because Wolverine asked me to?"

"Not enough this time," Jonathan said. "First of all, I don't see Wolverine. And second, I've got bullshit bells ringing in my head like it's Armistice Day. Let's start with the fact that these missing people—what are their names?"

"The Mitchells."

"Let's start with the fact that the Mitchells were first and foremost the responsibility of the federal government. It's not as if you folks are understaffed."

Maryanne seemed unmoved. "I revert to my original comment," she said. "Director Rivers asked me to ask you. She seemed to think that that would be enough incentive."

She had a point, and she seemed to know it. Jonathan shifted topics. "How were the Mitchells' covers blown?"

"We don't know."

"Aren't you a little worried?"

"We're a lot worried. We literally have no idea. All we know is what I've told you—Bernard is dead and the others are missing."

Jonathan considered the details. "The au pair," he said. "What do you know about her?"

"She's local talent, but recruited by us."

Jonathan laughed. "The feds are recruiting au pairs now? How about house cleaners? Do you recruit them, too?"

Maryanne smiled. Or maybe she had a gas pain. "Okay, she's more than your average au pair."

"More like a bodyguard, then?"

"Exactly."

"You're sure you can trust her?"

"You know my business, Mr. Grave. I don't trust anyone." Beyond Maryanne's left shoulder, a steady stream of taillights flowed across the Teddy Roosevelt bridge toward Virginia, while virtually no cars headed into the District.

"Yet you trust me," Jonathan said.

"Heavens no," she said. "I'll pretend to trust you because my boss trusts you." The smile turned menacing. "But if you cross me, I'll kill you."

The laugh escaped before Jonathan could stop it. He had Christmas tree ornaments bigger than she, but he admired her zeal.

"How old is the kid?"

"Fourteen. His name is Graham."

"Does he know about Mom and Dad's other life?"

"I don't know. If they followed the rules, no. But rule-following gets really murky when it comes to families."

"So what do you want from me?" Jonathan asked. This Maryanne chick had eyes that could melt the ice caps. Blue, wet, and beautiful.

Her face darkened. "I was hoping that would be obvious."

Jonathan smirked. "I've learned to live by hard requests. That old saw about assumptions making an ass of you and me applies in spades."

"We want you to rescue the mother and her son."

Jonathan crossed his arms and dug in for a second

swing at the details he wanted to know. "There's that first person plural again. Who's *we?*"

"Uncle Sam."

Jonathan cocked his head. This was the problem with young people. They said the lines without fully understanding the meaning. "How much of Uncle Sam?" he asked, not bothering to camouflage his smile. "All of him, or just certain parts?"

"I speak on behalf of Director Rivers," Maryanne said. "I can't speak for anyone beyond her."

Jonathan found himself liking this kid. She didn't show any of the know-it-all hyperbole that was so common to her generation. She stuck with the mission. Jonathan could count a dozen or more warriors he knew who had died at the hands of commanders who had violated that one sacred tenet of command—stick to the goddamn mission.

If Irene Rivers wanted him to march into harm's way, that was almost enough unto itself.

"Maryanne, I like your spunk and your approach. But I have a lot more experience at not trusting people than even you. If we're going to take another step together—Wolverine or no Wolverine—I want a straight answer to this. Why isn't my dear Uncle Sam making use of his enormous resources to take care of this rescue himself?"

She did something with her eyes, a casual glance away, a break in eye contact. It was a tell. "There are only so many routes for that kind of information to get out," she said.

There it was. "You're telling me that the Bureau continues to leak."

"Like a cheap diaper." She looked away, casting her glance upriver toward the Georgetown Harbor complex.

Leaks had been a burgeoning problem within the Bureau ever since Congress had gotten on its high horse and demanded that agents play by all the rules all the time, irrespective of criticality. Between the career advancement that was guaranteed for whistle-blowers, and the subterranean celebrity that was afforded to those who leaked information to the press, it had become harder and harder to keep a secret in this town.

"Tell me your worst fears regarding this case," Jonathan said.

"That the family will die."

"Bullshit. First of all, you answered too quickly, and second, saving families has never been a priority of the Bureau. Protecting careers first, catching bad guys second, and saving lives somewhere below that. This isn't my first trip to the races."

Jonathan let his words penetrate. He suspected that Maryanne was still young enough not to comprehend that difficult truth. All government agencies—not exclusively the FBI, but they were the worst offenders, in his experience—valued process over all. Careers were far more deeply jeopardized when a clerical error let a bad guy go than they were by the death of a citizen. More than anything else, that philosophy defined the chasm that separated the worldviews of elite law enforcement groups from those of elite military teams.

"We can't afford for them to be squeezed for information," Maryanne said.

"What do they know?"

"I can't tell you that."

"Okay," Jonathan said. "We're done, then. Have a good night." He turned and headed back inside.

"Really?" Maryanne said. Her voice sounded shocked. "That's all?"

Jonathan stopped, turned, and planted his fists on his hips. "What more would you have? I'm not a soldier anymore. I don't take orders. I make decisions whether a risk is worth its reward. There's never been a free agent freer than I. The rest is up to you. My team, my rules. Play by them, or pick a different field."

Not waiting for an answer, he turned and headed back to the opera. He figured that she'd come to her senses or she wouldn't. Personally, he didn't much care.

Jonathan was a little disappointed when he exited the Opera House and Maryanne wasn't there waiting for him. Now there was one more mystery in the world for which he would never know the resolution.

"What exactly did she want?' Venice asked as they turned the corner into the Hall of Nations, a vast corridor where the flags of dozens of countries hung from the sixty-foot ceiling—the flag of every country with which the United States had diplomatic relations, in alphabetical order. Jonathan had heard stories that after the fall of the Soviet Union, workers had to reorder everything to make room for twelve additional standards.

"A home was invaded in Indiana and the family was taken. They were spies for the good guys. She wanted our help getting them back."

"Isn't that what the FBI gets paid to do?"

"My thoughts exactly," Jonathan said. A set of doors led to the first of a series of escalators that would take them down to Jonathan's car.

"There must be some kind of internal problem within the Bureau," Venice said. "Why else turn to outside talent?"

Jonathan caught the drift that Venice's curiosity was piqued. "Again, you're channeling me. Too many outstanding questions to get any closer. History has proven that there's no upside to getting in the middle of a catfight between Uncle Sam's various children."

"Speaking of children," Venice said, "were any kids involved in the kidnapping?"

He held up his forefinger. "One," he said. "Fourteen. Plus a nanny-slash-bodyguard and maybe the mother. Dad was killed in the initial assault."

At the base of the first escalator, they turned and continued down. "This isn't like you. Don't you think—"

Jonathan touched her arm. "Perhaps this is a discussion to have in a smaller crowd." On the moving stairway, they were but two of hundreds who would soon be clogging the roads. Venice and he were speaking quietly enough not to stand out, so there was little chance of being overheard, but still. Also, Jonathan didn't want to talk about it anymore.

They made it to the second-level garage and Jonathan led the way to his BMW. As he unlocked Venice's door, Jonathan stopped her again with another gentle touch on her arm. She looked up, her brown eyes flashing a reflection of the harsh overhead lights. "You look stunning tonight," he said.

Her smile flashed brilliant white. "Why thank you, Mr. Grave. You clean up pretty good, too."

He wondered sometimes if the gap in their ages were less, would he have returned the crush she'd had on him as a teenager. While age differences meant less with every passing year, it had been an obscene and felonious gap back then, and even though they remained close, a slice of Jonathan's brain would always see her as the googly-eyed kid.

Jonathan was about to push the passenger-side door closed when he saw the business card that had been tucked under his windshield wiper. Even from a distance, he could see the emblem of the FBI shield.

"Uh-oh," he said.

"What is it?"

He pulled the card away from the rubber wiper and took a closer look. The name embossed on the front read *Irene Rivers, Director.* On the back were written the words, "This lvl, sect B row 2."

"Well, shit," Jonathan said. He handed the card to Venice.

She read it, and right away started to climb out of the car. Whatever it was, she was coming along.

"Before you get out," he said, "do me a favor and pull the black square out of the center console."

"The what?"

"You'll see it. And be careful when you handle it."

Venice looked and then rolled her eyes. "Oh, for God's sake."

Jonathan reached out his hand and wiggled his fingers. She handed him his Ruger LCP .380, already tucked into its pocket holster. He slid it into the front pocket of his tuxedo pants.

Jonathan craned his neck to get his bearings. The parking lot was massive, more typical of a shopping mall than an entertainment venue, and B2 was quite a hike from where they stood. With all the departing traffic, driving was not practical, so they decided to walk.

"Is that really Wolverine's handwriting?" Venice asked.

Jonathan shrugged. "I'm not sure I've ever seen her handwriting. It's always phone and e-mails."

Jonathan's relationship with Irene Rivers went way back, to the days when he was still in the Army, and she was a special agent working out of Alexandria, Virginia. He'd helped her with a problem, and that had started a history of off-the-record assignments that needed the special skills of a man with Jonathan's training, but could never carry Uncle Sam's finger-prints. When they first met, neither could have fore-seen her ascendancy to the big chair at headquarters. Then again, no one could have anticipated the events that launched her into Bureau superstardom.

"Did you notice that there's no space number?" Venice said. She kept studying the card, as if searching for a secret message.

"I did notice that," Jonathan said. Parking garages were inherently creepy places, which probably explained why they were so often featured in scary movies. The weight of the LCP in his pocket—all eleven ounces of it—reassured him. Far from his preferred weapon in a gunfight, it was better than being left with fingernails and fists if the shit hit the fan.

Fifteen seconds later, he realized that he wouldn't need to know the space. A standard government-issue heavy metal POS Chevy flashed its lights.

Jonathan stopped walking, and Venice pulled up short with him.

"What's wrong?"

"Never overcommit," Jonathan said. "Let them come to us. Anyone can use someone else's business card. It's not real until I see a face." He waited as a stream of departing patrons drove past them. After ten or fifteen seconds, the sedan's door opened, and Special Agent Maryanne Rhoades rose from the driver's seat to reveal herself.

It didn't take her long to get the point that he wasn't walking over to join her, so she came to him.

"Is Wolverine in the car?" Jonathan asked as she strolled his way.

Maryanne shook her head. "I left her card to reinforce the fact that I am here on her authorization."

"You misrepresented yourself," Venice said. "That's not a good way to start a relationship."

"Venice Alexander," Maryanne said. She pronounced the name correctly. "I've heard a lot about you. Director Rivers told me to tell you that the offer to join the Bureau is still open. We can always use skills like yours."

Venice more snarled than smiled. She shared Jonathan's distrust of federal agents, but she had a special distrust for those who looked beautiful in an evening gown.

"Ven's got a point," Jonathan said. "My cards are on the table. I know every detail or I don't play."

Maryanne made a point of looking over both shoulders to survey the garage. "Clearly this is not the place. Might I suggest that we pay Mr. Van de Muelebroeke a visit? I believe he lives close to here."

The man she referred to was Brian Van de Muelebroeke, Jonathan's friend and cohort from forever. Most people knew him as Boxers, and those who did generally knew better than to surprise him with a late-night visit. He wasn't always the most cheerful fellow, and at just south of seven feet tall and considerably north of three hundred pounds an angry Boxers could be ugly.

Jonathan grinned. "Sure," he said. "That should be fun. You know the address?"

"I found your car, didn't I?"

There was the Fibbie hubris that Jonathan had come to depend on, the self-aggrandizing nonanswer answer. "See you there in half an hour."

Graham pretended to sleep in the shotgun seat of the Mercedes sedan they'd taken from the doctor. It was every bit as comfortable as it was hot looking. Best of all, it was quiet.

So many numbers. Too many numbers. They swam in Graham's head like the schools of fish you see in documentaries, where great clouds of them swarmed and shifted directions and blocked out the view of anything else.

That's what life was like when you lived with a memory that recorded everything, all the time. He'd told his therapist once—Doctor Harper—that it was like eating a Thanksgiving feast every day, maybe twice a day. You get progressively more stuffed, but you keep cramming more in. That was an imperfect comparison, though, because you could always puke up a meal to make more room. His head just got progressively more full. Doctor Harper had assured him that his brain would not rupture from the pressure. He'd also promised that one day, Graham would learn to live with his ability—to *tame* it—and that he'd come to see it as more a gift than a curse.

But that's what parents and doctors always said. They marginalized everything with phrases like *one day* or *you're too young to understand* or *I'd give anything to be like you.* Somehow, they all forgot what it was like to be a freshman in high school, where all those other assholes lived *today* at *the age they were* in a world where being smart was punished by sack-taps in the hallway and bags of dog shit slipped into your backpack when you weren't looking. The fact that he'd be envied when he was thirty didn't mean a whole hell of a lot when he wasn't yet half that age.

He'd tried playing dumb, intentionally missing questions on tests, and spending five minutes figuring out math problems that he'd already solved at a glance, but that brought on a whole new breed of derision and animosity. Who knew that pretending to be stupid was insulting to people who really *were* stupid? Rather than waiting for him to *tame* what came naturally, how about somebody step up and tame the herd of assholes that swarmed the halls between classes?

Names and dates were one thing when they flooded his head. They got pushed into their own files, ready to be recalled when he needed them, but otherwise never to be thought of again. It was the number sequences that cost him sleep, that *obsessed* him. While words made sense in and of themselves—people arranged letters into words, and then words into sentences that had clear meanings—numbers were meaningless outside of a known pattern. Three digits plus three digits plus four digits was probably a phone number, but other less obvious number sequences appeared random, yet rarely were because someone had arranged them with a purpose. He could spend hours trying to decode such sequences. More often than not, he'd be able to add meaning, but he'd rarely know for sure if the solution he'd identified had any relation to the true intent of the sequence's author.

Graham liked to imagine that he had a kind of curator living inside his head—he even had a name. Linus never slept. Instead, he catalogued every phone number, address, locker combination, and historical fact that flowed through his brain. When Graham needed the information, whatever it was, Linus would produce the correct folder, and everyone would think that Graham was brilliant.

If sticking a coat hanger in his ear would kill Linus, Graham would have done it ages ago.

Right now, as Jolaine drove through the jet-black countryside, on their way north, the number sequence that bothered him most had nothing to do with the cipher on the bloody scrap of paper. At least not directly.

Follow the protocol.

The protocol was a telephone number. If anything bad ever happened to the family, or if he were ever threatened with harm, he was to call the number and follow instructions. Easy-peasy.

But there'd been no mention of codes. And there'd for sure been no mention of murder.

Even during the ridiculous evacuation drills that his dad had insisted on, where Dad would start yelling in the middle of the night and use a stopwatch to time how long it would take to get to the garage, there'd been no talk of codes or murder. There hadn't even been any guns.

The shit that was going down tonight was all brand new—and it had nothing to do with the *protocol*. That was just a trouble number to call when he was told to call it, a meaningless exercise that had never risen even to the level of 911 in the hierarchy of memorized phone numbers.

None of this was right. None of it made any freaking sense.

The smear of Mom's blood on his chest had begun to itch.

Why is this happening?

"We need to stop," Graham said without opening his eyes. "I need to make a phone call."

"Not tonight," Jolaine said. "It can wait till morning."

"But Mom said—"

"I know what she said. I was there. But not tonight. We're both exhausted and neither one of us is thinking straight."

"But the protocol—"

"It can wait," Jolaine snapped. "Look, Graham. The world is coming apart tonight. I have no idea what direction is up anymore. Until something makes sense— at least one thing—I don't want you calling anyone. I don't want you *talking* to anyone. Promise me."

She was glaring at him when she should have been watching the road. "But the protocol—"

"Promise me," she pressed.

Graham accepted that Jolaine was in charge. He didn't like it—he wasn't even sure he respected it—but he accepted it. She was right that nothing made sense, and there was no denying that bad people were gunning for them, literally and figuratively. Maybe a few hours really wouldn't make that much of a difference.

"Okay," he said. "I promise."

CHAPTER FIVE

Boxers lived on Swann Street, in a part of the city that had only recently begun to recover from the devastation of the 1968 riots. He'd bought his Federal-style townhouse—DC's answer to the New York City brownstone—ten years ago for a song, back when the street was a haven for drug dealers and muggers. Since then, gentrification had begun to take root, and in some stretches of the street, home values had more than quadrupled. Secretly, Jonathan had always wondered if the mere sight of Boxers entering and leaving his house hadn't convinced the miscreants on his block to take their business elsewhere.

No one wanted to mug Sasquatch.

"Are you going to call him first?" Venice asked.

Jonathan chuckled. "Not a chance. But I think it's probably important that mine be the first face he sees." He glanced at the dashboard clock. Twelve-fifteen. "Oh, yeah. I *definitely* need to be the first face he sees."

With the lateness of the hour came the challenge of finding street parking. Rather than rolling the dice on something closer, Jonathan took the first space he found, thus committing them to a four-block walk, three of them past places where gentrification had not yet begun. As they climbed out of the car, Venice said, "Clearly, you've never worn high heels."

"Only because you'd think less of me if I had," Jonathan replied.

Never much for the late-night party circuit himself, Jonathan was surprised by the number of revelers on the sidewalks up ahead. The fact that they were all headed *toward* the bars at the end of the street, as opposed to *away* from them, surprised him even more. From the way most of them walked, and the volume of their voices, he guessed that these bars were not the first ones they'd visited.

"Don't look so horrified," Venice teased. "There's a whole world outside of Fisherman's Cove."

"Oh, I know. I've blown up a lot of it, remember?" Jonathan got out of the car and walked around the Venice's side. He didn't want to let on, but his danger radar was pinging. He also didn't want to mention that they were still a block away from a house where a man had been murdered in his sleep, and whose killing remained unsolved. "Be careful on the brick sidewalks," he said as he opened her door and offered his hand to help her out.

As they walked away from the car, Venice's posture stiffened and she sidled closer to Jonathan. "This isn't a very safe neighborhood, is it?" she asked.

Jonathan didn't answer, though he wished he'd thought this through a little better. In Upper Northwest sections of the city, a hundred-thousand-dollar car drew a casual glance, but in this stretch, it was truly a traffic-stopper. It was bad-guy bait, too, and it wasn't until they'd begun their walk down the street that Jonathan noticed the scrawny predator tucked away into the alley just behind their parking spot. As they walked, the skinny fell in behind them.

Jonathan draped his right arm around Venice and pulled her closer still. "In a few seconds," he said, "I might ask you to take a step off to the side. If I do that, please don't ask for details."

"What's happening?"

"You're asking for details," he said. "Maybe nothing."

But when a second skinny stepped out from under the stairs two houses down, Jonathan knew that it was going to be something.

"Well, look at you two," said the skinny in front. "Aren't you pretty?"

Jonathan nudged Venice, and she retreated to the opening of a stairwell that led to what Jonathan believed was called an English Basement. Translation: a subterranean space for which the landlord could charge an obscene rent.

"I know that she's pretty," Jonathan said. "But I've always thought of myself as average." He test-drove a smile, but it didn't take. "Are we about to have a problem here?"

"Depends on how much money you've got in your wallet," Front Skinny said.

Jonathan heard the staccato beat of running footsteps behind him, and without looking, he knew that Back Skinny was charging him from behind. Jonathan whirled and smashed the heel of his hand into the space between the charging man's ear and his temple.

The guy's head spun nearly 180 degrees, and the rest of his body followed in a floppy horizontal pirouette that landed him faceup on the brick sidewalk. Jonathan thought he was still alive, but he didn't much care.

With the six o'clock threat neutralized, Jonathan faced off again with Front Skinny. "I'm sorry," he said. "We were in the middle of a conversation."

With quite the flourish, Front Skinny flopped open the locking blade of a tactical knife, the kind that is designed to cut deep and inflict mortal damage. "You're gonna die, white boy," he said.

Jonathan shook his head. "Actually, I'm not. And you don't have to, either, if you just walk away."

"Dig," Venice moaned from his right. It was a plaintive sound. It was one thing to hang around on the outskirts of violence, but it was something entirely different to be in the middle of it.

Jonathan ignored her. As of this instant, Skinny Front's future lay entirely in his own hands. "Think it through, son," he said. "There's still time to walk away."

"You hurt Jamal," he said.

"Only because he was trying to hurt me," Jonathan said. He took care to keep all emotion out of his voice. "And did you see how well I took care of him? He was unconscious before he knew he'd been hit. I gotta tell you, I'm pretty good at this beating-up-people shit." As he stated that last sentence, he realized it was a step too far. He'd forced Skinny Front's hand with a challenge. Maybe it was just as well.

The skinny made his move. He lunged at Jonathan, leading with the knife, coming in with an underhand slashing motion that worked in every action movie, but rarely worked in real life. Jonathan clenched the knife-hand wrist in his left fist, and fired a piston punch to the skinny's liver with his right, dropping him to his knees. Even as the kid sagged, Jonathan drove his right elbow into the kid's brachial plexus—the Mr. Spock place between the neck and the shoulder that served as the conduit for all the wiring to the skinny's arm. The kid yelled as he dropped his knife, and started to fall face-first. Jonathan stepped over the kid, never letting go of his wrist as he collapsed. Skinny Front had nearly faced-out on the brick walkway when Jonathan planted a foot between the kid's shoulder blades, pulling up as he twisted the wrist. A soft double pop—the sound of two twigs breaking in the woods—followed by a howl of pain told him than he'd snapped both of the bones in his attacker's forearm. The way it flopped to the sidewalk when he let go underscored the anatomical damage.

Having nearly broken a sweat, Jonathan turned back to Venice and offered his hand. "Sorry about that," he said. "I think it's safe now."

Venice didn't move. Her eyes were huge, her mouth slightly agape as she stared at him.

"It's really okay," he said.

"Oh, my God," Venice said.

For a second, Jonathan didn't get it. Then he threw a glance to the kids on the ground. One of them moaned for help, and one of them had no idea that he was of the Earth. "You're worried about them?" That was beyond his comprehension. "You know he was trying to kill me, right?"

It took her a moment to gather the words. "That was so . . . *easy.*"

Jonathan smiled. "A few years ago, it was easy," he said. "But trust me. I'll be sore tomorrow." He pointed up the street with the crown of his head. "We should get moving. On our way back, I'll bring the car to you, in case these guys have friends." They started walking.

"You should call the police," Venice said.

"Um, no. The situation is stable now."

"At least an ambulance."

"If they need help, they'll call for it. Not our problem." Jonathan's glance was drawn to Venice's stare. "Why are you looking at me like that?"

"I've never seen that before," she said. "I've always known what you do, but I've never actually seen it."

Jonathan scowled. "I can't tell if you're impressed or appalled."

"A little of both, I guess. Why would they come at us like that?"

"Easy money. They saw a guy in a penguin suit with a beautiful lady and they read us as weak."

Venice looked over her shoulder, back toward the spot of the scuffle.

"They won't follow," Jonathan said.

"I just hope they get home okay," Venice said.

Jonathan laughed. "Oh, good God."

By the time they got to Boxers' door, Maryanne's Chevy was already double-parked out front. One of the bennies of government plates was immunity from parking violations. In DC, where predatory parking enforcement was a major source of revenue, a parking pass was more valuable than gold.

Maryanne opened her door as they approached and met them at the curb. "Is he expecting us?" she asked.

"Yeah, sure," Jonathan said. He winked at Venice. "Follow me."

He opened the decorative wrought-iron gate and climbed up to the stoop. He pushed the doorbell. Over and over and over again. He heard Venice say, "Oh, my God, Digger," and then he heard movement from inside. He kept pressing the button.

"It had better be an emergency," Boxers roared from somewhere beyond the door, "or there's by God going to be a corpse on the sidewalk!" Not everyone who said stuff like that meant it literally. Boxers was an exception.

Jonathan saw Big Guy's shadow approaching from beyond the mottled glass and noted that he was moving . . . with purpose. Even as the door tore open to reveal Boxers' towering form, Jonathan continued to press the button.

"God*dammit!*" Big Guy roared. "This had better—" Recognition came immediately. "Dig? What the hell?" He looked past Jonathan's shoulder to see Venice and Maryanne. "Am I throwing a party I didn't know about?"

"Can we come in?"

Boxers hesitated. Uncharacteristically self-conscious, he looked down at himself. Clearly roused from bed, he wore a pair of—wait for it—boxers and a T-shirt.

"Don't worry," Jonathan said. "You're fine. We're the ones who are overdressed."

Big Guy pivoted out of the way to allow them to pass. Jonathan beckoned for the others, and thirty seconds later, they were inside and standing in the foyer.

"I didn't know you liked antiques," Venice said.

Because of his size and his penchant for violence,

many people underestimated Boxers' intellect and sensitivity. The artifacts in the room were more than mere antiques. Many of them were collectibles worthy of museums. To Jonathan, all of it was either a vase or a statue.

"I think I'll go put some pants on," Big Guy said. The ancient stairs creaked as he climbed to the second floor.

"I heard that he was a large man," Maryanne said. "But I don't think I understood the scale of it."

"Definitely better to have him on your side than the other," Jonathan said. "Let's have a seat." He led the way to the right of the foyer into the living room, which was dominated by a shallow fireplace. Typical of the nineteenth century, when fireplaces were a main source of heat, the lack of depth often made twenty-first-century citizens nervous about having a fire so close to their living space. Jonathan happened to know that Boxers had spent a small fortune getting that fireplace certified to modern fire codes, and that he routinely kept it stocked and burning during the winter months. The antique theme carried into the living room, but with a modern flair that allowed for comfortable, oversized cushions.

"Look at all the books," Venice said, taking in the floor-to-ceiling shelves that flanked the fireplace. "I had no idea."

"Box is an interesting guy," Jonathan said. He winked. "Don't let on to others that he knows how to read. It'll ruin everything."

Jonathan helped himself to the end of a love seat closest to the foyer, while Venice took the opposite end.

Maryanne shifted her gaze back and forth from the two leather chairs that flanked the fireplace. "Which one?" she asked.

Jonathan pointed to the one on the left. "That one has the bigger butt print," he said. "I'd take the one on the right."

She sat.

Boxers was back down in three minutes. "Okay, Dig. What gives, and who's this?" He pointed to Maryanne.

Jonathan brought him up to speed with what they knew so far. "Now, given Agent Rhoades's persistence, I'm guessing that we're about to hear the details that she previously didn't want to share." He looked at Maryanne. "Am I correct?"

Maryanne sat forward in her chair. "You can never repeat what I'm about to tell you."

Jonathan rolled his eyes. *Oh, please.*

Maryanne caught it. "Bear with me," she said. "Back in the late eighties, when people on our side of the Iron Curtain were drunk with our defeat of the Soviet Union, the apparatchiks on the other side were running for their lives, both literally and figuratively. Glasnost and Perestroika brought with them a world of insecurity for a lot of once-important and now irrelevant people.

"Power grabs became the way of their world, and there were a hell of a lot more groups to worry about. The Czech Republic, Georgia, the 'Stans, and God knows how many other former Soviet republics were all claiming their independence politically. That posed a huge problem in terms of strategic weapons."

"The nukes were spread all over the place," Jonathan said, jumping ahead in her story.

"Exactly. The Politburo, God love them, were the scaredest of the lot, presumably because they knew what disaster could be wrought by the loss of central command authority. They also knew that they couldn't account for every warhead. While that detail didn't become clear until later, the US had long suspected such."

Jonathan exchanged a look with Boxers but said nothing. Back in their Unit days, the two of them had crawled through the weeds in that part of the world to help determine that very fact.

Maryanne continued, "NATO forces initiated Operation Gardenia, funded mostly by our federal government, to locate and reconsolidate all the scattered nukes under central Russian control."

Venice reared back in her seat and raised her hand. "Wait a minute. You're telling me that we actually *helped* our scariest enemy reacquire nuclear warheads?"

Boxers laughed. "You look surprised. Do you have any idea how many times your boss and I have been shot at by weapons purchased by the same Uncle who sent us into battle against them?"

"Remember," Maryanne said, "after the fall, Russia was our new good friend. The powers that be were confident that they would never use the weapons against us."

"Unbelievable," Venice said.

"Moving on," Maryanne said. "We thought we got them all, but when you're dealing with those kinds of numbers, there was no way to be sure."

"Let me guess," Jonathan says. "We were wrong."

"Exactly. And by quite a lot. More than twenty, although that's really just a rounding error considering the thousands of warheads that were involved."

Boxers tossed his hands in the air and guffawed. "Well, then, if we're only talking twenty twenty-five-megaton warheads, what's the point of talking at all?"

"What does this have to do with the Mitchells?" Jonathan asked. "I know you told me he had nuclear engineering experience, but how does that come into play?"

"Here's where it gets a little complicated."

"Just use small words and I'll try to keep up," Jonathan said. He hoped his irony was transparent.

"Bernard and Sarah Mitchell are from Chechnya," Maryanne explained. "As you might know, that's not the most stable corner of the world."

"Never has been," Jonathan said. "Their terrorists make Hadji look like an amateur."

"So you already know," Maryanne said. "That's good. That's helpful. When he expatriated to the United States, he went to work for a company in Oak Ridge, Tennessee, called Applied Radiation Corporation, which managed the reclamation of radiologically contaminated military facilities."

"Uh-oh," Boxers said.

"It's not what you're thinking," Maryanne said. "Yes, he was involved in Operation Gardenia, but he was a good guy. A couple of years into it, he was approached by an old friend named Gregory, from Chechnya, who shared with him an ambitious plan to seek retribution for the years of Soviet brutality. He wanted Bernard to share information on the location of old nukes."

"Actually," Boxers said, "this is running pretty close to what I was thinking."

"Here's where it goes different," Maryanne assured. "This Gregory guy was a good friend, and there are few people in the world who hated the Soviet Union more than Bernard. But Bernard was also a family man, and he was proud of his then-recent American citizenship. He pushed Gregory away and told him to never contact him again."

"How do you know all of this?" Venice asked.

Maryanne continued as if she hadn't heard. "Gregory left, and he left angry. He called Bernard a traitor and he disappeared. Two weeks later, as Bernard was between the front door of his house and his car, on his way to work, an unknown man jumped from behind a bush and beat him with a baseball bat. Broke his right shin, his left forearm, and three ribs. Didn't say a word until after the beating was finished, but then told him that he would do as Gregory asked, or he'd find his wife blinded by acid and his son crippled with a baseball bat."

"Now *that* sounds like Chechen payback," Jonathan said. Chechen rebels had recently killed over three hundred schoolchildren in a terrorist raid in Russia. Nasty, nasty folks to get crosswise.

"This is where I come in," Maryanne explained. With a nod toward Venice, "And how I know all these details. Of course Bernard agreed to comply—it's always smart to agree with the guy who's trying to kill you—but he had no intention of doing so. He called the FBI, and I became his case agent."

"Case agent for what?"

"You doubled him, didn't you?" Jonathan guessed.

Maryanne nodded. "Historically, we've found that newly minted citizens are often the most patriotic. In Bernard Mitchell's case—"

"What's his *real* name?" Boxers interrupted.

"None of your business," she said. "And if that's a deal breaker, then we are done."

Jonathan didn't press the point. He'd seen this before. For whatever reason, aliases and birth names, once declared to be classified, tended to remain that way—to the point where confessed terrorists who had been put into witness protection in return for their testimony against their former jihad-buddies were able to disappear and recycle themselves in their old stomping grounds because nobody updated the no-fly lists with their new names. Jonathan saw no urgency in knowing Mitchell's real name.

"In Bernard Mitchell's case, he was furious at the threat to his family and ashamed of the actions of his friend. His was one of the best motivations in the world—revenge. I told him that the easiest way to protect him would be to put him to work for us. We would feed him with false information that was laced with just enough truth to make it seem reasonable. If we did our jobs right, as the Chechens followed the bread crumbs, we'd be able to see where they were going and what they were doing.

"Financially, it was a pretty sweet gig for the Mitchells. Bernard was on three payrolls simultaneously—the rebels were paying him for his espionage, we were paying him for playing along, and ARC was paying him for his real expertise."

"I don't quite follow what kind of useful, sustainable intel he could provide," Jonathan said. "I mean, you can dance for a while, but sooner or later, wouldn't he have to cough up a nuke?"

Maryanne smiled.

"You're shitting me," Boxers said. "You gave up nuclear warheads? Tell me they were dummies."

"They were *doctored,*" she said. "To set off a warhead requires a complex series of electronic impulses. To initiate the process requires a complex code. We changed the code."

"But there's still a nuclear warhead?" Venice asked.

"There had to be," Maryanne said. "There's a predictable amount of radiation leakage outside of the warhead casing. We needed to keep the radioactive material in place, or else the leakage wouldn't be there, and without the leakage, they'd know that they had a fake."

"I can't imagine a single thing that might go wrong with that plan," Boxers said, his voice heavy with sarcasm.

"Trust me," Maryanne said. "Without the codes, these things are just radioactive paperweights."

"You just used the plural," Jonathan said. "How many are we talking about?"

"A few."

"Can you put a little more meat on that number?"

"Five to eight."

Boxers' jaw dropped as he leaned in closer. "You don't even know the precise number?"

"It's complicated," Maryanne said, "but yes, we don't know the precise number."

"How big are they?" Venice asked.

Maryanne shook her head. "Not very. Full-up, with the casing, they're about six inches in diameter, a little over thirty inches long, and weigh under a hundred fifty pounds."

"So, they're not all that powerful," Venice concluded. She seemed relieved.

"Zero-point-seven-kiloton yield, give or take."

"Before you take solace in that number," Jonathan warned, "she's saying that the warheads are the equivalent of seven thousand *tons* of TNT."

"So, we're talking artillery rounds," Boxers said. "The equivalent of our W-forty-eights."

From the early sixties through the early nineties, the US, its allies, and the Soviets all developed nuclear warheads that could be fired from standard artillery pieces. They were rendered obsolete by more reliable delivery systems, but the Soviets apparently felt compelled to keep some of them around.

"Did the Russians know you were playing this game with their mortal enemies?" Jonathan asked.

"Of course not. In fact, Russian records showed that the very warheads we were tracking had in fact been destroyed."

"You're saying they lied?" Venice said.

"It's what they do," Maryanne said. "That in itself became an important data point. It was useful to know that our new allies would rather lie than be embarrassed."

"So what went wrong?" Jonathan asked.

"We're not sure. About a year ago, Bernard's Chechen friends started getting anxious, started making unreasonable demands. We got the sense that they were testing him to make sure he was really on their team."

Venice said, "That means someone tipped them off? That must have scared the Mitchells to death."

"It gets better," Maryanne said. "Not only do we suspect that someone tipped off the Chechens, we think someone tipped off the Russians, too. They found out that we were playing nuclear games with terrorists and they were not happy."

"This does not seem unreasonable to me," Boxers said.

"We were learning a lot about Chechen terrorist networks," Maryanne said. "So, now, all of a sudden, there's a back-channel diplomatic firestorm. CIA is pissed, and State is *furious*. The White House was blindsided, and your friend Wolverine has had some serious explaining to do. Overall, the last few weeks have been interesting."

"So," Jonathan said. "About the hit on the Mitchells."

Maryanne uncrossed her legs and recrossed them the other way. "Yeah, about that. We don't know exactly. As things got progressively hotter with the Chechens, Bernard fell out of touch with the Bureau. He started skipping our regular meetings, wouldn't return phone calls."

"Probably because he was frightened," Venice said.

"Undoubtedly. But that's not how it works. When you're on my payroll, you play by my rules."

"You started applying pressure," Jonathan guessed.

"I had to. I was worried that he might be considering going rogue and working for the other side. I needed to keep tabs, and he wasn't playing along."

Jonathan's eyes narrowed as a piece fell into place in his head. "I think I see where you're going," he said.

"You applied a little too much pressure. You drove him to the other side."

"I don't know that for a fact, but I suspect it, yes. And here's the *really* embarrassing part—we think he got the arming codes for the warheads."

Jonathan gasped.

Venice said, "I don't understand. I thought the codes were fakes. You said they were nuclear paperweights."

"They are. Except we left a back door in the coding software that would allow us to make them active again, just in case."

"In case of what?" Venice said.

"In case we don't have enough friggin' world crises," Boxers said. "You feds amaze me. If the world takes a step away from the abyss for just a few seconds, one of you steps in to push it closer again."

"Easy, Box," Jonathan said.

"Don't tell me to take it easy," Big Guy snapped. "Somewhere toward the end of this discussion, she's going to ask us to undo this mess, and you're going to say yes, because it's what you always do. I've earned the right to bitch about it, because that's what *I* always do." He turned back to Maryanne. "And how the hell did he get ahold of these codes?"

"We think the CIA gave them to him."

"Holy shit!" Boxers exclaimed.

"Why the hell would they do that?" Jonathan asked.

"I have no idea. I'm not even sure that's the case, but that's where the evidence points."

"Pretty incendiary guess."

Maryanne shifted her legs again. She wasn't going to expound, and Jonathan wasn't inclined to press too hard. Yet. "So, that's a lot of moving parts," he said. "If the Mitchells were going to hand over the codes, why would the Chechens hit them?"

"Who said it was the Chechens?" Maryanne asked. The speed of the delivery led Jonathan to believe that she'd been waiting for the opportunity. "For all we know, it could be the Russians in an effort to keep the codes out of the bad guys' hands. For that to be the case, though—"

"Somebody on our side of the pond would have had to tip them off," Jonathan said, completing her statement.

"Exactly. That could mean CIA, State, or even, I'm sorry to say, the Bureau."

"Which is why you're soliciting help from us instead of from the normal channels," Jonathan said. "You don't know who to trust."

Maryanne confirmed by arching her eyebrows.

"Ah, crap," Boxers said.

CHAPTER SIX

Jolaine didn't like the way the night clerk at the Hummingbird Inn looked at her as he entered her name into the computer. His name tag read *Hi, I'm Carl,* and she saw in his expression equal parts suspicion and anger, covered by a thin glaze of false pleasantness. "Just the one night?" he asked.

"I think so," Jolaine said. She'd presented herself as Marcia Bernard—the only name she could think of off the top of her head. "There's a chance we might extend, but I think it will be just the one night." She knew she was talking too much—always her habit when nervous.

Carl took forever to open the screen and type in her information. He'd asked for her identification, but she'd told him that she'd left it in the car and didn't want to go back out to get it. In a place like the Hummingbird Inn, she figured there were many guests who happened not to have identification, and she'd wager that most of them were named Smith or Doe.

"Is that a young boy I see out there in the car?" the clerk asked, straining to see past her shoulder.

"My brother," she said.

"And what's his name?"

Jolaine hesitated.

"I need it for the record," he clarified.

"Tommy," she said. *When in doubt, keep the lies simple.*

Carl's eyes narrowed. And he didn't type the name.

"Is there something wrong?" Jolaine asked. "You seem . . . bothered."

"No," he said, and he started typing. Then he stopped. "Actually, yes, and I don't know how to say this without insulting you. Still, it's got to be said."

Jolaine waited for it.

"I know it might not look like it, but I run a reputable place here. Always have. Time was, when my daddy started it, this motel was one of the premier inns on this whole strip of highway. Then the Interstates came through, and, well, you know that story. Every secondary road in the whole damn country knows that story."

"I don't think I understand—"

"The Hummingbird is not *that* kind of motel."

She still didn't get it. He nodded toward the car, and then she did. "Oh, my God," she exclaimed. "He's fourteen years old! And you're damn right it's insulting. He's my little brother!" There's a certain skill in pulling off righteous indignation and a bald-faced lie at the same time. She thought she'd done well.

Carl held up both hands in surrender. "Okay, okay. Like I said, I didn't mean to be insulting, but sometimes, you've just got to be sure."

Jolaine felt heat in her cheeks. All she needed was

to get some sleep, and for that, all she needed was a key.

Carl reached to the board behind him and plucked a key off a hook. It was the old-fashioned kind—a real key with a plastic fob dangling from it that displayed the logo of the Hummingbird Inn.

"Here you go," he said. "Room twenty-four. Last one down on the left."

As her hand touched the door to leave, Carl said, "Excuse me, miss, but what did you say your brother's name was again?"

Oh, shit. It was a trap, and it was well played. "Thank you, Carl."

Back in the car, Graham was awake now, though still unfocused.

"Where are we?" he asked.

"Napoleon, Ohio. We're going to stay here tonight."

"I need clothes."

"I know. We'll go shopping tomorrow." *You'd have clothes if you'd listened to me back at the house.*

Jolaine slipped the transmission into drive and eased the Mercedes down the line of rooms to the parking space in front of number 24. When she parked, Graham sat quietly, staring straight ahead, through the windshield, but at a point in space that was far beyond anything she could see.

"Time to go in and go to bed," she said.

He didn't move.

"Graham?"

He pulled the handle, opened the door, and stepped out. They met in front of the bumper and walked together to the assigned door.

The motel room bore the motif of classic roadside dump. The steel door hadn't been painted in many years, and the jamb had swollen to the point that she needed to give the door a shot with her hip to get it to open. The two double beds were separated by a night-stand whose lamp came to life when Jolaine hit the light switch just inside the door, on the wall with the big window to the parking lot.

"Not so bad," Jolaine said. "Not for one night, any-way." She stepped aside and let Graham pass.

He took two steps inside and stopped. She followed and closed the door. Now that it was just the two of them, and she could see him without the distraction of gunfire or a medical crisis, her heart sagged. He looked so young, so skinny and vulnerable. He needed a hug, but from someone else. He needed his parents.

From where he stood in front of the open bathroom door, he could see his reflection in the mirror, and then he looked down at himself as if to confirm what the image showed. Despite a fast and halfhearted effort to wash at the doctor's house, his arms and his chest were still smeared with his mother's blood.

"She's dead, isn't she?" he asked without eye con-tact. "They're both dead." He turned to look at Jolaine. "Aren't they?"

"I don't know," she replied. It was the truth and this was no time for conjecture. She took a step closer and put her hand on his shoulder. "You should take a shower. Clean up."

He jerked away and turned on her, his eyes red and angry. He shouted, "You were supposed to protect us!"

The outburst made her jump. "Keep your voice

down." She imagined that the paint on the walls was thicker than the walls themselves.

"If you'd done your job, none of this would have happened!"

"Graham, that's not true." As she spoke, she wondered if agreeing and shouldering the blame might have been the smarter move, might have defused things.

"This is *your* fault, Jolaine."

"You have to keep your voice down," she whispered. "We're in a lot of trouble here. You have to—"

"Don't tell me what I have to do! You *can't* tell me what I have to do. You work for *us,* remember? We tell *you* what to do. And right now, I'm telling you to go to hell!"

He stormed into the bathroom and slammed the door.

Jolaine made a move to stop him, to explain, but stopped herself. He had every right to be angry. He was scared. Everything he knew was coming unglued. The trauma and the loss were at a scale that was beyond his imagination. If the only way for him to process that was by lashing out at her, then what was the harm? She wasn't here to be liked, after all. She was here to do her job.

As the water came on in the shower, Jolaine moved to the nightstand and sat on the edge of the bed nearest the door. A call to the police might end this whole thing. Why did that seem so wrong?

Her mind replayed the events of the past hours—the past days. She remembered the building tension in the house, the quiet, intense conversations between Bernard and Sarah. The stifling sense of paranoia, particularly in the past five days.

Clearly, they knew that their family was in danger. If the solution were really as simple as a phone call, why hadn't Bernard or Sarah made it? And if the reason for all of the mayhem was the string of numbers Graham had swirling through his head, why in the world would Sarah have burdened him with them?

For now, she and Graham were safer than they'd otherwise be because no one knew where they were. A phone call would create a new trail that would lead directly back to them. That wasn't going to happen. Not tonight, anyway.

A seam of light painted the ceiling as a vehicle nosed into a parking space next to hers out front, and an alarm bell rang in her head. She rose from the bed and drew her weapon, but did not go to the window. This was probably nothing, but if it was indeed a threat, she didn't want to expose herself to an easy shot.

Across the room, on the other side of the bathroom door, the shower continued to run. She checked the knob and was not at all surprised to find that he'd locked the door. That hollow-core paneled door wouldn't stop a knife, let alone a bullet, but it was something.

Jolaine's concern deepened when the lights on the vehicle out front continued to shine. She could hear the engine running through the window.

The shower stopped three seconds before someone rapped on the door.

"Excuse me, Ms. Bernard?" a voice called from the other side of the door. The tone was all business, neither friendly nor aggressive. "This is the police. We need to talk with you."

Philip Baxter stood on the walkway alongside the Woodrow Wilson Bridge. He looked out over the Potomac River, Virginia on his left, Maryland on his right. The lights of Old Town Alexandria shimmered on the water. He wore his blue seersucker suit not so much to honor the formality of the moment, but rather to cover the 9 millimeter Walther P99 that he carried in a holster at the base of his spine. The amount of traffic at this hour—0130—surprised him. He expected the big trucks, but the number of passenger cars was more than he would have expected at this hour. Where did these people have to go?

This was his meeting, so the protocol demanded that he arrive first and wait in plain sight. Like that of the man he waited for, his was a paranoid profession. To ask a man to meet alone to discuss the kind of subject that lay ahead required a generous leap of faith. This spot in the center of the massive bridge span offered full visibility and made an ambush unlikely. A drive-by was always a possibility, but the presence of so many witnesses rendered that option impractical.

More to the point, the meeting spot was a mile away from any feasible sniper's nest, and the darkness, combined with the complexity of the air conditions over the river, made such a shot impossible for even the most talented shooters. Throw in the fact that traffic noise made it impossible to record a conversation from a distance, and this was the perfect place for a covert meeting.

Precisely at 01:30, his contact made himself visible at the Virginia end of the bridge. At this distance, he was only a silhouette, devoid of individual features, but there was no mistaking the awkward, limping gait that Philip knew was the result of a very close encounter with a 7.62 millimeter bullet fired a number of years ago by an American Special Forces operator. Because Philip had read the after-action report, he also knew that this man who approached had killed said operator with an amazing ninety-yard pistol shot before he slipped into unconsciousness.

As the man approached, Philip paid attention to the details. He knew the man was right-handed, and he noted that the right hand swung a little less easily than the left. That meant two things—first, he was armed, and second, the man was half-expecting to have to draw down. That kind of awareness translated to nervousness, which put a special burden on Philip to be benign and predictable. This was the most fragile moment of any meet. Any errant look or sudden movement could ignite a gunfight that no one wanted.

Philip continued to watch the river, his hands on the guardrail as he monitored the new man's approach.

Two minutes later, Anton Datsik was at Philip's left side, and together they looked at the vista before them.

"Good morning, Philip," Datsik said. His voice was leaden with an Eastern European accent.

"Hello, Anton. Thank you for agreeing to meet at such a ridiculous hour on such short notice."

"You're welcome. My instincts tell me that this is not to be a pleasant conversation. Even your chosen location speaks of violence."

Some time ago, a team of terrorists had wreaked

havoc at this spot during a frigid rush hour. The walls of the high-end Jersey barriers that separated them from the traffic still bore the scars of that shooting spree.

"You're overthinking," Philip assured. "I promise that there is no symbolism or implied threat in the locale."

Datsik nodded, seeming to accept Philip at his word. "I shall pretend not to know why you called me here," he said.

Philip got right to it. "A lot of people got killed last night in Indiana. Did you have anything to do with that?"

Anton pivoted to face Philip full-on. "We know each other long time, Philip. I don't trust you, you don't trust me. That is the one fact we both count on, and as a result, we form what you people like to call a bond. This is true, yes?"

It had long been Anton's way to thicken his accent and slow his speech when he was trying to make a controversial point. Now he sounded like Boris from the Rocky and Bullwinkle cartoons. "This is true, yes," Philip said.

"Over years, we have many conversations. Sometimes I speak to Philip Baxter, colleague—fellow spy—sometimes I speak to Philip Baxter, enemy to my country. Which one do I speak to tonight?"

It was a test question, of course, an invitation to lie. But even as the relations between the United States and the Russian Federation continued to deteriorate, Philip understood that the ability for people like him and Datsik to communicate honestly with each other could one day spell the difference between peace and Armageddon. He liked the guy, and he suspected that Datsik liked him back. The reality that either might one day get the order to terminate the other kept the relationship at arm's length.

"Today, I speak as a confused friend," Philip said. "And in this matter, I believe that our two countries have never been closer."

Datsik chuckled. "Is not a high bar, is it?"

Philip laughed with him. "No," he said. "Not a high bar at all. Please tell me what you can about last night."

A pair of tractor trailers passed in tandem, causing the bridge deck to vibrate, and drowning out all sound. As the roar dopplered away, Datsik continued. "First, let me emphasize what I think you already know. You never should have played your silly game with the Chechen dogs."

Philip shrugged. "As you might imagine, I don't make those decisions. But the effort was not a waste. We very nearly found out quite a lot about their terrorist networks."

"Very nearly worked," Anton scoffed, "is a bureaucrat's way of saying you failed."

"In large measure because your government overreacted," Philip countered. "Must we really have this conversation now? Neither one of us is a decision maker."

Datsik backed off. "True enough," he said. "As you Americans like to say, we are only pawns, yes?"

"Sometimes I feel more like the board the pawns play on."

Datsik chuckled, but his eyes showed no humor. He

looked out at the river, toward the lights of Old Town. "Things did not go well, as you know. We got our team in place on Morrow Road in Antwerp well in advance—"

"Were you there?"

Datsik paused, looked back at him. "I might have been."

From the tone and the sly smile, Philip took that to mean yes.

"That Chechen pig was already there, waiting in the blue pickup truck that we had been told he would drive."

"For the sake of clarity," Philip interrupted. "Which Chechen pig are we talking about? Adam Dudaev?"

"Yes. Our team was in place at least one half hour before Dudaev arrived, and once he did arrive, he waited in place for twelve minutes, lights on, engine running, until another car arrived. This was, we assumed, the contact who would pass along the codes."

"And who was that?" Philip said. Of all the intel to be gathered through this abortion of an op, that was the one bit of information that the United States needed most to know.

"I will get to that," Datsik said. Always a natural storyteller, Datsik liked to take his time to build the tension. "We were cautious," he continued. "We didn't want to, as you like to say, jump the gun. One day you must tell me where that expression comes from. The two vehicles faced in opposite directions, so that the drivers could speak without getting out. This posed a problem for us because we did not know what the other vehicle would look like. We thought it unlikely that this could be just a chance encounter, but given the stakes, we needed to be certain. We kept waiting for them to pass something," Datsik went on. "If they had done that, we'd have taken them both into custody, just as you asked."

That was the third reminder that the assault team had been acting on a direct request from Philip's bosses. Philip wondered if that was a hedge against some form of recording device—if, perhaps, Datsik was recording the conversation himself. "But . . . ?" Philip prompted.

"They never had the chance. Two carloads of men with guns swooped down out of nowhere and opened fire. They were too trigger-happy, shooting too early, hitting the vehicles but not the people. Our team engaged the other shooters, and things went crazy."

Philip felt a tug in his gut. No one else was supposed to know what was going down. This was another security breach of epic proportions. "Other *shooters?*"

"Other shooters. More Chechen pigs, we found out, after we searched their bodies."

"Why would they be shooting at their own? Weren't they getting what they wanted?"

Datsik gave a derisive chuckle. "Philip, my friend, perhaps you should spend more time trying to talk to dead men. It is an instructive exercise in frustration. In any event, those shooters lost, my shooters won. Is a good ending."

"But what of Dudaev and the codes?"

A deep sigh. "Alas, in all of the confusion, he got away. Unlike his contact, who took two bullets to the head. He had no identification on him, but our people are working to identify him."

"My boss will want the body," Philip said.

"My bosses will tell your boss to kiss their asses. Your boss started this. You don't get to write the rest of the script."

"This was an FBI screwup," Philip insisted. "My team had nothing to do with it."

"We don't care. One big government, one big screwup. The details don't matter."

Philip opened his mouth to pursue the issue, but decided that now was not the time. "So, Dudaev. What happened to him? Did he drive away with the codes?"

"We didn't know at the time, but later we found out that yes, he did."

"Did you follow him?"

Datsik cleared his throat. "In a manner of speaking, yes. We were not in a position to chase him—we were in positions away from our vehicles—but we knew where he would be going."

"To our friends the Mitchells?"

"*Your* friends the Mitchells," Datsik corrected.

The Russian had clearly missed the irony, and Philip chose not to correct him. As far as Philip's bosses in Langley were concerned, they could all die a fiery death.

Datsik continued, "At this point, our team decided to eliminate all of them. We get the code, we kill people who want the code, and everything will be all right."

A glimmer of hope grew in Philip's mind. "So, that's what you did?"

"Is what we *almost* did."

"Ah, Christ."

"Yes, was bad. Dudaev arrived at Mitchells' house already wounded, I think. When we got there, he is already on floor bleeding. Maybe Mitchell shoot him, but I don't think so. There is other shoot-out. Mitchell dies, Dudaev dies, but wife and boy get away along with their maid." Datsik scowled and shot a look to Philip. "Why would they have maid?"

Philip fell silent as he ran the facts through his head. This could still have a happy ending. "But the codes," he said. "You got the codes."

Another sigh, this one deepest of all. "No codes," he said. "We think maybe wife took them with her. What's her name?"

"Sarah."

"Yes, Sarah. We think she took codes with her. Sarah, maid, boy, codes, all gone. But she was shot and shot bad. Gut shot." He pointed to a place high on his own abdomen. "Maybe not live."

Philip's mind raced. That happy ending was feeling further and further away. "Wait here," he said.

Datsik recoiled. "Where are you going?"

Philip cupped the back of his own head with his hand and rubbed the lump that was a souvenir from a bar fight gone bad in his twenties. "I'm not going anywhere," he said. "I just need to think. I think better when I walk."

"If walking makes people smart, someone must have been sitting on his ass when they came up with this Chechen missile idea," Datsik teased.

Philip pretended not to hear.

Think this through, he told himself. *It can't be as dark as it seems. There has to be a way.* Because if there wasn't another way, the world—Philip's world in particular—was going to be in a very, very bad place.

Philip walked slowly, unaware, really, that he was

even walking. He thought through the logic. If this was an FBI operation, the logic had to be perfect, because Fibbies were that way, so buttoned-down and regulated that every one of them tied their shoes the same way.

Sarah, maid, boy, codes, all gone.

"Yeah, why would they have a maid?" he asked aloud, his words lost in the traffic rush. That was a significant point. Why would they even want a maid? The house they lived in wasn't that big to begin with. It would be tight enough with the three of them living there. A fourth person would just be in the way.

Perhaps she was just a housekeeper. You know, one who just comes in the daytime.

No. That wasn't it. The raid happened at night, and she was there. That meant she was live-in help, a conclusion that just circled him back around to his original question—Why was she there?

Then he got it. At least he thought he did. He turned and walked back to Anton. "You said the Mitchells got away with a maid," he said.

"Yes."

"Are you sure she was a maid?"

"Who else would she be?" Datsik asked. "You told me that they have only one child. A boy. Our intelligence confirmed. Who else would she be?"

Philip didn't want to jump to his conclusion. He had a tendency to do that. Once he had an idea in his head, his brain took ownership and then nothing else would make sense to him.

"You look like you're having a vision," Anton said. "You seeing God?"

"No," Philip said. "I think the girl you thought was a maid might be a security detail."

"Not much of a detail," Datsik scoffed. "One girl."

Philip rubbed his head again. "When you got to the Mitchells," he said, "what was their response?"

"They fought back," Anton said. "They were better fighters than the Chechens at the drop-off."

They were also expecting you, Philip didn't say. "That meant that they were prepared," he did say. "Which in turn means that they expected to have to defend themselves."

"That's what happens when you betray everyone all at once," Anton said. "Makes friends hard to find."

"The point," Philip pressed, "is that if they were expecting a possible attack, then they might want to have personal security."

"But only one person?"

"Probably for the boy," Philip thought aloud. "Was she young?"

Anton laughed. "To me, everybody is young. I guess under thirty, but not much."

Philip nodded. Yes, he'd seen this before. It was a trick used over in the Sandbox when defending important families. Young people are inherently resistant to personal protection, so to combat that, contractors would recruit younger operators for that purpose.

"You're smiling now," Anton said. "First vision from God and now something funny. What is funny about armed security guard?"

"It means they had a contingency plan," Philip said. "And plans have to make sense. To make sense, they have to follow a straight line."

"Straight line to where?"

He paused a beat. "I don't know yet."

"Is lots of help. You don't know."

It had been seven years since Philip was last directly involved in running field agents and field ops, so it took him a while to pull the standard protocols from memory. Of course, there was no guarantee that the Bureau would use the same protocols as the Agency, but the elements had to be pretty much the same. You had the routine components, such as never traveling predictable routes, and the tradecraft to recognize and elude tails. Then there were the elements that kicked in at the time when shots were fired—the specific actions to guard the protectees and get them out of harm's way. Those he knew for a fact were common not just to the two agencies involved in this mess, but also to Secret Service and State. Anybody who protected anyone.

Equally predictable, yet far more fluid, were the protocols to be followed if a protectee under assault was hit in the crossfire. Hospitals would be prequalified for their capabilities and preplanned as a function of the nature of the problem. Most any hospital could help a protectee with a gallbladder attack, but if a gunshot wound were involved, only a shock trauma center would suffice when such facilities were available. When the protectee was a senior government official, certain staffing requirements at the hospitals would need to be proved prior to the trip.

Coming into this meeting, Philip had known that people had been shot during last night's incident, but a check of hospital records had turned up nothing.

"Other than the mother, Sarah, were there any surviving wounded from either assault last night?" Philip asked.

"Yes," Datsik said. "But they were all on our team."

"And where did you take them?"

Datsik's expression turned dark, defensive. "We took them to what your government likes to call a secret, undisclosed location," he said. "That means none of your business."

Philip pointed at Datsik's nose. "Exactly."

"Exactly what?"

"Exactly the answer. When it is important to remain covert, hospitals are out of the question. At least standard hospitals are out of the question."

Anton smiled as he got the point. "You have secret hospitals, too."

Philip confirmed by making his eyebrows dance. "Won't it be really freaking weird if we both use the same doctors?"

"I doubt that to be the case."

The irony thing again. It was a strange part of Anton's personality. The guy had a biting sense of humor and he enjoyed a good laugh, but subtleties were often beyond him. Perhaps it was a language thing.

The question on the top of Philip's list was how to determine who that doctor might be. It was possible that the Agency and the Bureau used the same medical contractors, but extremely unlikely. Just as it would be awkward to run into Russian FSB operators, it would be equally awkward—maybe even more so—to run into a Bureau puke. The two groups did nearly as much warfare between each other as they did with the nation's enemies.

It was not uncommon for agents of the CIA to see agents of the FBI as the bad guys, and of course the reverse was equally true. The animosity came from different views of how the world operated, and what right and wrong looked like. Common to both agencies, however, was hatred of the State Department. All State wanted to do was surrender. Philip thought of it as serving the French model.

"I need to make a couple of phone calls," Philip said. "Private ones. I'm going to wander a few yards toward Maryland, but don't go anywhere. If you need to make some phone calls yourself to get your team back together, now would be a good time."

CHAPTER SEVEN

Jolaine put her Glock in the top drawer of the thin-walled faux-mahogany dresser.

The officer rapped again. "Ms. Bernard! Please!" His tone was harsher this time.

Jolaine looked at herself in the mirror. She saw nothing in the image that telegraphed the nightmare of the past few hours. All she saw was a young woman—an attractive one, she liked to think—who looked a little tired, but there was no tattoo on her forehead announcing that she'd killed people. Jolaine opened the door just as the cop was preparing to knock again. "Good lord, what is it?" she demanded as she pulled it open.

Outside, the officer who was doing the knocking stood off to the side. Another, with his hand resting casually on his sidearm, stood at a distance in the parking lot. Clearly, the agenda here was serious.

"Are you Marcia Bernard?" the cop asked.

With that question, she knew that the call had been placed by Hi-my-name-is-Carl, the only person in the world other that herself to know that she had an alias, let alone what it was.

"What's wrong?" she asked.

"May we come in?" the cop asked as his partner moved closer. The partner's hand never moved from his gun.

"I don't understand," Jolaine said. "Is there a problem?"

"I'd really prefer to talk inside," the cop said. "No sense waking the entire complex."

Jolaine's heart and head raced together to figure out a plan. She stepped back from the door and ushered them inside.

"I'm Officer Bonds," the first cop said. "This is Officer Medina. Is everything okay here?"

"Of course," Jolaine said. "Why wouldn't it be?" She played it as absurd, and hoped she hadn't oversold it.

"Are you here alone?" Bonds asked.

"No," she said. "I'm here with my little brother."

"And where is he?"

"In the bathroom. Excuse me, Officer, but I'm not comfortable—"

The bathroom door opened, releasing a cloud of steam, and revealing Graham with wild wet hair and a white towel wrapped around his waist. "Hey Jolaine, did we bring—" He saw the cops. "Holy shit."

"This is my brother, Tommy," Jolaine said, suddenly aware that she hadn't yet told Graham that he had an alias.

Graham said nothing, but his expression was an open confession to the Lincoln assassination.

"Who's Jolaine?" Officer Medina asked. He stood in the doorway to the parking lot, blocking the only route of escape. He asked the question to Graham, and the boy still couldn't find any words.

The cops' eyes shifted in unison to Jolaine. "I am," she said. She was winging it now.

Medina stayed focused on Graham. "And who are you? I mean *really?*"

"He's Tommy Bernard," Jolaine said. Her words clearly pissed off the cop, who was trying to get a rise out of the boy, but she had to get it out there if the kid was going to have a chance.

"I'm Tommy Bernard," Graham said.

"Uh-huh," Bonds said. "What's going on here?"

"My brother and I are on a trip," Jolaine said.

"Where to?" Medina asked.

"I don't see where that's any of your business," Jolaine said. They'd crossed the line where she felt her best defense—maybe her *only* defense—would be a little offense.

"Why did you lie about your name?" Bonds said.

"Is that a crime?"

"It could be. Let me see some identification."

As Jolaine fished through her pockets for the business-card folder she used to house her driver's license and credit card, Medina said to Graham, "How about you? Got any ID?"

Graham shook his head. Jolaine could tell that his own fear was giving away to annoyance. "No," he said.

"Why not?"

"Because I'm fourteen and I just got out of the shower."

"You got clothes in there?" Medina asked, craning his neck to see into the bathroom.

"Yeah."

"Then go put some pants on," Medina said. "But keep the door open."

Graham started to retreat back into the bathroom, but then stopped and gave Medina wicked glare. "Wait, you perv. I'm not going to take a towel off so you can watch me naked."

Medina's ears grew red as Graham stepped back to his original spot.

Jolaine's heart raced faster. She'd seen Graham after he'd crossed into high adolescent indignation, and it never made a situation better. Never. She pulled her driver's license out of its pocket and held it by the edges so Bonds could read it.

When he reached for it, she pulled it away. "Look but don't touch," she said.

"Excuse me?"

"This is my property. If I don't give it to you, you can't take it from me." Across the room, Graham seemed to like that.

Bonds gave a derisive, condescending chuckle. "I don't know what Internet law books you've been reading, but you have an obligation to provide identification to a sworn officer of the law."

"I am providing identification," she said. "I'm just not letting you have the card." Her fear was that if she gave him her license, he would have leverage over her, tacit permission to stick around until he was damn good and ready to give it back.

"You're a pretty smart-mouthed team, aren't you?" Medina asked. His color still had not recovered from the accusation of pedophilia. On one level, Jolaine thought he had it coming—that was, after all what Hi-my-name-is-Carl had thought of her, thus launching this confrontation in the first place.

"What we are," Jolaine said, "is a tired team. It's been a long day, and frankly, I'm feeling a little harassed right now. I know what the desk clerk was thinking when I checked in, and I know why you're here. And yes, frankly, it pisses me off."

"That so?" Bonds asked. "Why are we here?"

"Because you think Tommy and I are having sex with each other."

Graham's reaction was instant, and straight from the heart. "What? Eew. That's disgusting! Jesus, you *are* a perv."

Hearing it said out loud made it seem even more disgusting, and just like that, Bonds's discomfort became obvious.

"If you're not, then our friend Carl up front is," Jolaine said.

"How come you and your *brother* have different names?" Medina asked. From the way he leaned on the word, she could tell that he wasn't yet buying.

"Different fathers," she said. The explanation came so quickly that it made her proud.

"Where's your luggage?" Medina made a show of scanning the tiny room. "I don't see any suitcases."

"Okay," Graham said. "You got us. You want the truth? We were in this big shoot-out tonight where a lot of people were killed, and now international spies are chasing us and trying to kill us. That's why we're here. How's that?"

Jolaine nearly dashed over to shut him up. This was it, the end of everything.

"Man, you really do have an attitude problem, don't you?" Medina said. "I see punks like you every day when I put them in jail. What do you bet I'll see you one day, too?"

Holy shit, they don't believe the truth! Jolaine nearly laughed. "Come on, Officer," she said. "He's fourteen and he's tired, and you guys are riding pretty hard. Cut him a break." To Bonds, she said, "I don't know what to tell you, other than to say that so far as we know, we're not breaking any laws."

Bonds's eyes narrowed. "Are you two runaways?"

"I'm twenty-seven," Jolaine said. "Who would I be running away from?"

Bonds turned to address Graham. "Are you okay, son? If there's a problem, this is the time to tell me. No one can hurt you, I promise."

Graham rolled his eyes. "Jesus," he said, and he disappeared back into the bathroom, slamming the door behind him.

"I get to be with that for five days," Jolaine said. "Don't you wish you were me?"

Bonds regarded her for a while longer, then nodded. "Okay," he said. "You win. Sorry we bothered you."

After they were gone and the door was closed, Jolaine wasn't convinced they were really on their way. Finally, the cruiser backed out of its spot, and she could breathe again.

*   *   *

Morning came early.

All things considered, Jolaine decided it would be best if she left Graham in the room and shopped alone. It was just too damned hard to come up with an explanation for his near-nakedness. Having never bought clothes for an adolescent, she cursed herself for never having studied the labels in his clothes.

She had to guess on the sizes, but a clerk at the Walmart helped a lot. Turns out that at a certain age, all boys can fit into size medium T-shirts, and *no* boys would be caught in underwear that bore the word "briefs." She could verify that one, thanks to the laundry duties that came with her contract with the Mitchells. With no idea of appropriate shoe size, she bought one pair each of medium and large flip-flops. That was all Graham wore this time of year anyway, and it seemed to her that his feet were growing even faster than his disproportionately long arms and legs. It was no wonder that he suffered so from teasing at the hands of the other boys in his school. She suspected that the teasing came from the girls as well.

Forty dollars later, she was back in the car, ready to return to the Hummingbird. Sarah's last words haunted her.

Finish your mission.

Jolaine smacked the steering wheel. Goddammit, she hadn't signed up for this. She hadn't even applied for the job. The job had recruited her.

She'd just come back from her second tour as a civilian gunslinger in Afghanistan. The money was great, and the job was simple—until it wasn't. Her responsibilities mostly involved personal security for Afghan muckety-mucks who were important enough to require bodyguards, but not quite important enough to have the best. Not that she wasn't good at what she did—in fact, she considered herself to be damn good—but the outfit she worked for, Hydra Security, didn't have the clout to get big-money contracts. As a result, she'd been stuck with old-school M4 rifles and M9 sidearms while the big boys got the fancier MP7s and much lighter body armor.

Jolaine had been shot at plenty in her two tours in Afghanistan, but the intended targets had always been the people she was supposed to protect. Her response had been to lay down cover fire—a blanket of bullets that was more intended to keep bad guys' heads down than to kill identifiable targets—and to shove her protectees into their armored vehicles. The work was mentally engaging and exciting. And since she was still breathing—as were her clients—she liked to think of herself as pretty good at the job. When she was on her last break before her contract expired, she'd decided to sign on for another two years.

Then, three years ago, she was sitting in a Starbucks in Vienna, Virginia, enjoying a grande coffee and a blueberry muffin when a blond supermodel sat down at the table next to hers and made a point of staring at her. Jolaine tried to ignore her, but after ten minutes it became unbearable.

"Can I help you?" Jolaine asked. At the time, she'd assumed that it was a lesbian come-on, and she'd girded herself for the confrontation.

"You're Jolaine Cage, aren't you?" the lady asked.

Jolaine's protective shields shot up. "Who wants to know?"

The superhot blonde flashed a gold badge from the pocket of her slacks. "Can we take a walk?" she said.

Jolaine recognized the distinctive shape of the FBI shield. "Am I in trouble?"

The blonde smiled. "Not hardly. I just want to talk to you, and it's too crowded in here."

At the time—in the moment—Jolaine felt a surge of adrenaline. Within the community of freelance security folks, stories abounded of clandestine meetings in which operators were recruited to be Uncle Sam's muscle. "Sure," she said. Jolaine rose from her little table and started to walk away from her coffee.

"You're probably going to want that," the lady said, pointing to the paper cup.

Jolaine grabbed the cup by its insulating band and pulled it close to her body. "Where are we going?"

"Just out."

They stepped out into chilly October sunshine. Traffic on Maple Avenue was heavy more or less all day, thanks to traffic lights on every block. At this hour, about eleven in the morning, it was as light as it was going to get.

"Let's walk north," the lady said.

Jolaine noted that the left turn out of the Starbucks led them toward CIA headquarters, six miles down the road. "I won't get into a car," she said.

The lady laughed. "This isn't a rendition," she said. She extended her hand. "My name is Maryanne Rhoades. I'm with the FBI."

Jolaine shook her hand. "I got the FBI part in there. And you already know who I am."

"Yes, I do."

"*Why* do you know who I am?"

"We've been watching you."

A danger bell rang in Jolaine's head. She stopped walking.

It took Maryanne a few steps to realize that she was alone, and she turned. "You look unnerved," she said. "Don't be. This is all good."

"Then I think you should get to the good part," Jolaine said.

Maryanne smirked, as if hearing a joke that was audible only to her. "Do you like working at Hydra Security?"

A second bell rang in harmony with the first. "That's a question, not an answer," she said.

Maryanne cocked her head. "I'm getting the vibe that you don't trust me."

"If you know what you claim to know, then you should understand why. Over on the dark side of the world, you guys don't know what it means to play fair."

Maryanne shrugged. "War is hell."

"We're done," Jolaine said. She turned and started back toward the Starbucks. If this pinup bitch had been within a thousand miles of a shooting war, Jolaine would eat her own arm.

"Please stop," Maryanne said.

Jolaine stopped but she didn't turn.

"We want to hire you," Maryanne said.

Now that got her attention. "Hire me as what?"

"A contractor," Maryanne replied. "For personnel security."

Jolaine turned and regarded the other woman. "And why does the FBI, with four point three bajillion agents, want to hire me as a contractor?"

Maryanne shrugged. "I told you. We've been watching you. We like what we see."

They say that flattery will get you everywhere. While Jolaine was as vulnerable as the next girl, she also recognized the blowing of sunshine. "Not good enough," she said. "If you were watching me, then you were watching others. And if you were watching others, you'd know that there are tons of people out there whose work is exemplary."

The smirk didn't fade. "Your attributes are special," she said. When Jolaine didn't rise to the bait, she clarified, "You're a woman. This job is specifically for a woman."

Jolaine's imagination went right to a mission to sleep with the enemy, and she rejected it out of hand. "No," she said. She started walking again.

"Dammit, Jolaine, will you quit doing that?"

She stopped and turned. "You've got two sentences to show your hand," she declared.

"It's a bodyguard gig," Maryanne said. "For a young boy. The parents want the bodyguard to be a woman."

And just like that, she was intrigued. She took a few steps closer. "Are we talking witness protection?"

Maryanne's head bobbled noncommittally on her shoulders. "Not exactly, but that's close."

"What's closer?"

Maryanne smiled. "For that, we have to keep walking."

Jolaine approached, and then together they continued north. "Why is walking important?"

"Motion makes eavesdropping more difficult."

They stopped for the light at Center Street.

"Who would be listening in?"

"In this town, anybody," Maryanne said with a chuckle. With its proximity to CIA headquarters, sleepy little Vienna, Virginia, was one of the spookiest towns in the world. "In our case, it could be one of several parties. Unfortunately, at this juncture, I'm not at liberty to share that information with you."

The light turned and they continued walking northward. "Makes it kind of hard to evaluate your offer."

"I'm sure it does," Maryanne confirmed, "but I'm also sure you can see the chicken-and-egg problem. Unless and until you're on board, we can't afford to share details. You know how this business works. Sometimes you say yes to the unknown and just hope that you're not signing on for a suicide mission."

Jolaine felt a chill. "I don't do suicide missions. Let's establish that up front."

"Duly noted."

"How much danger is this kid in?"

"I really don't know," Maryanne said. "His mother and father feel threatened. This is their demand—that the boy have protection."

"So they're working for you," Jolaine said. "Why else would you be concerned?"

Maryanne said nothing.

Jolaine nearly apologized for wandering into territory that had already been declared off-limits. "Would the family be my responsibility, too? Would I be part of a larger team?"

They stopped on the sidewalk to allow three cars to

exit the driveway for the Maple Inn, while two others entered the same lot. There were no better chili dogs in the world than those from the Maple Inn.

"No team," Maryanne said. "Just you. You'll be the body man for the boy—sorry, body girl. You'll go where he goes, and take him to and from wherever that is. During the day, the mom and dad will fend for themselves however they intend to do that. We've paid for a good alarm system at the house, so at night, once the boy is tucked in, you'll be more or less off-duty."

"More or less?"

They started walking again. "You go where the kid goes. As long as he's in motion, you'll be in motion, too."

"That's a lot for one person," Jolaine said. "When I pulled gigs like that over in Afghanistan, we had four-to six-person teams for 'round-the-clock coverage."

"That's interesting," Maryanne said in a tone that made it clear how little she was interested. "You're free to say no. Remember, though, you're not going to have to worry about IEDs, and I'm predicting that the sniper risk is virtually nil. You won't have to do advance work, and, frankly, there's a whole world of honest local law enforcement to keep the technicals off the street."

Jolaine recognized a "technical" as a rust-bucket pickup truck fitted with a machine gun and laughed in spite of herself. Point made and taken. Perhaps it was a waste to attempt to compare the two missions.

"How old is this boy?"

"Eleven."

"Oh, God."

"What's wrong with eleven?" Maryanne asked. "There's no butt-wiping involved."

Jolaine said, "Eleven is all whiny insecurity and drama. I'm not sure I want to sign on for drama."

Maryanne laughed, amused by whatever she saw in Jolaine's face. "You won't be his mother. You'll be his protector."

"Why on earth would the mother and father want a woman to be in charge of a developing hormone factory? I'd think they'd want a stronger hand."

Maryanne stopped in the middle of the sidewalk, just in front of the town's new war memorial. "I've met this kid. I've met the whole family. He's . . . less than respectful of authority. I believe their thinking is that a male bodyguard would just not work."

"So, I *would* be his mother."

"Only if you let that happen. Like I said, I know this family. They're not bad people. Mom and Dad don't have a real strong hand on the parenting tiller, but Graham is basically a good kid." She blinked as she let his name slip.

Jolaine felt a rush as she heard the mistake, but right away wondered if Maryanne had let it slip on purpose to make Jolaine feel a victory. This was precisely the kind of second-guessing and mistrust that made Jolaine hate so much of the security industry.

Maryanne sensed that something was wrong, and gestured to the benches in the sun on the far side of the memorial. "Let's take a seat," she said. She led the way past the granite disk that praised "those who served our country" and past the poles that flew the flags of the United States, the Commonwealth of Virginia, and the Town of Vienna. This was a slice of tranquility in the midst of commuter chaos.

Maryanne sat on the north end of the bench and waited for Jolaine to help herself to the other seat. Jolaine sat sideways, her left calf tucked under her right thigh.

"Talk to me," Maryanne said. "Tell me what you're thinking."

Jolaine steeled herself. Should she open up and tell the truth, or should she play the same game she suspected that Maryanne was playing?

"I'm thinking that this is coming out of nowhere," Jolaine said. "I'm thinking that I don't know you from Adam, and that this is a bizarre assignment. I think that you're holding out important details, and that those details define the reason why you're coming to me when the FBI is fat with salaried, career agents. Then, when thinking about those assets that you're choosing not to use, I begin to think you're here because I'm considered expendable."

Maryanne gave her a long, hard look. "How old are you?"

"You already know that," Jolaine said. "I suspect that you know just about everything about me. And the fact that you just asked that question does nothing to make me feel better."

"The question was more rhetorical than real," Maryanne said. "I'm just amazed that you can be burdened with so much cynicism when you're only twenty-four years old."

"Cynicism is born of experience," Jolaine said. "As you so eloquently said, war is hell. Remember, I've done two tours soldiering as a non-soldier. I've seen what happens to careers and futures after contractors have done their jobs exactly as they'd been instructed, only to have official Washington shove a knife in their backs as soon as something goes a little wrong. I don't want to be one of those people."

"You're in the United States now, not in Afghanistan. The rules are different here."

Jolaine waited for more.

"Okay, here's the deal," Maryanne said. "In broad strokes. Do you know what a double agent is?"

"A spy."

"A very special kind of spy. In this case, a man whose foreign bosses think he's spying on us when in fact he's providing information to us about the other guy."

"I assume we're talking about the father now?" Jolaine asked.

"Exactly."

"And one of his rules for helping you is that his son be protected from retaliation."

"Correct."

Jolaine wasn't buying. It didn't all add up yet. "This circles back to my previous question," she said. "Why just the boy? Why not the whole family?"

"Because the boy—Graham—is the best leverage point. The family and the FBI both agree that if the bad guys discover that they've been betrayed, they'll just kill Mom and Dad outright. There'd be no reason to do otherwise. But if the bad guys only *suspect* that they've been betrayed . . ."

Jolaine finished the thought for her: "They could kidnap the boy and use him as leverage to make sure."

"Yes."

"And my job is to make sure that they can't get close enough to make that happen."

"Right."

"By myself. How the hell am I supposed to do that?"

Maryanne pressed her lips together. "There are a couple of moving parts here," she said. "The first is what we just discussed. The second is the fact that Graham doesn't know about any of his parents' behavior. They don't want him to know—another condition of moving forward."

Jolaine scowled. "Then how are you going to explain the lady with the gun going to school with him?"

"We'll create a cover story. The nature of his father's work is sensitive—that's true, by the way. That's why we're working with him and why the bad guys want information from him. We'll tell Graham that the extra security is just an abundance of caution."

It still sounded like a lonesome loser of an assignment to Jolaine. She waited for more.

"Which brings me to the final set of moving parts," Maryanne said. "I believe that this whole exercise truly is one of abundant caution. Overkill caution. I think the danger involved is miniscule."

"That's abundantly dismissive," Jolaine observed. "Especially from the vantage point of one who will not be in the crosshairs if things go bad."

Maryanne shrugged. "What can I say? That's the nature of the job. We'll make sure you're well armed and well trained. There will be communications protocols in place. In addition to your salary, we'll also pay for you to finish your degree."

Jolaine laughed. That last part came out of nowhere.

"My degree? When would I have time to pursue that while working twenty-four seven?"

"You'll be staying at the house," Maryanne said, the very essence of reason. "You can take online courses during the nighttime hours."

Jolaine couldn't see that working out, but she supposed it was a nice benefit to offer. She fell quiet.

"Look," Maryanne said. "We know what you did for the Azizi family while you were working protection for them."

Jolaine felt something stir in her belly. Was it possible that she was about to be arrested after all? "I don't know—"

"It's okay," Maryanne assured. "You're not in trouble for that. You just did your job."

Toward the end of her most recent tour, Jolaine and her team had been escorting Behnam Azizi and his two children, eleven-year-old Afshoon and her nine-year-old brother, Fahran, from their armored SUV into a local coffee shop when a car erupted in an enormous fireball less than a hundred feet away, launching shrapnel like hundreds of bullets toward every compass point. Knocked down by the pressure wave, Jolaine rolled back to her feet, scooped the Azizi children into her arms, and ran. She'd assumed—correctly—that the bomb was an attempt to assassinate Behnam Azizi, and she wanted the children as far away from any ensuing gunfight as possible.

When it was all over, Behnam Azizi and three Taliban gunmen were dead—along with eight civilians who just happened to be on the street when the bomb detonated. Some of the locals who'd seen Jolaine running away with the panicked children had assumed that she was kidnapping them. Her teammates had assumed that she'd turned cowardly and fled the gunfight. Both assumptions led to her being prematurely rotated out of Afghanistan.

"Your instinct was to save the children," Maryanne said. "The instinct of the penis possessors on your team was to stand and fight. Your approach is more compatible with the job we need done."

And so, after some negotiation on pay, Jolaine accepted the offer.

Reflecting back on that conversation, and the training that followed, Jolaine remained stunned by the degree to which everything that could have gone wrong did.

If the Mitchells were so damned important, why didn't they have a security detail of their own? And what could they possibly know that could justify this kind of carnage?

Once she started down this road of inquiry, the questions wouldn't stop. If Maryanne—Jolaine's only lifeline in all of this—was so securely on top of all that was happening, where was her warning to the family when everything was going to hell? Where was her phone call, or her FBI SWAT team? Why did the FBI seem to care so little about things alleged to be so important?

Who was the wounded little man who stumbled through the front door in the opening moments of this nightmare? Clearly, that goddamn code was something that the good guys wanted and the bad guys wanted them not to have. Those numbers were the key to everything. And now that Graham had seen it, it was imprinted forever. Sarah had deliberately pulled her son into the kill circle. Why would she do that?

Jolaine had to get back to Graham. It was entirely possible—maybe even likely—that he was awake by now. Despite the note she'd left him and his boisterous declarations of independence, it wouldn't take long for him to feel abandoned. Nothing good could follow from that.

CHAPTER EIGHT

Ten feet under the parking lot that separated Jonathan's firehouse home from the basement of St. Katherine's Catholic Church, Jonathan and Boxers worked together in the twenty-five- by twenty-five-foot armory, selecting the weapons and tools they might reasonably need to meet the requirements of the upcoming 0300 mission. Built of reinforced concrete, and accessed by an enormous steel door that was originally designed for a bank vault, the armory was a place of solitude for Jonathan. Something about the combined smells of Hoppe's solvent, gun oil, and the hints of isocyanates from the explosives brought him comfort.

The room was lit as brightly as a surgical suite. Heavy fireproof cabinets lined the walls, and two wooden workbenches with additional lighting took up the space in the middle, their tops covered in a carbon-rich conductive plastic that was connected by braided copper cables to the grounded floors. On the occasions when Jonathan or Boxers would manipulate primary explosives, say in the creation of specialized initiators, they would wear conductive shoes and electrically bond themselves to the workstations via conductive bracelets. Explosives knew few enemies more dangerous than static electricity.

"Wish we had better intel," Boxers said. Anticipating the need for quick action, Big Guy had followed Jonathan home and spent what was left of the night in the guest room on the firehouse's first floor. "We're packing for every contingency."

No argument from Jonathan. He took a sip of his coffee. Not knowing where they were going, or what they were going to find when they got there, they had to plan for both mechanical entry and explosive entry. Not knowing what kind of reconnaissance they would be able to perform, they had to plan for multiple contingencies there, too. And so it went with every element of the upcoming operation.

"These are all clean, right, Boss?" Boxers stood at the gun locker.

"Affirm," Jonathan said. After every operation where shots were fired, the weapons involved needed to be retooled so that they could not be traced to past or future uses. Because of their spooky pasts, both men were so far off the grid as to have no official, truthful pasts or identities, but the additional attention to details improved their already stacked odds of never getting caught.

Jonathan heard footsteps approaching from the tunnel beyond the door, and recognized Venice's quick stride. "Don't shoot," she said as she closed the distance. It was an unnecessary step, but an understandable one under the circumstances.

"Come on in," Jonathan said. When Venice appeared in the doorway, he noted the laptop and notebook in her arms, and he pulled the elements of his deconstructed Colt 1911 closer to make room for her. "Help yourself to some coffee. You're up early."

Venice set her stuff down. "No, *you're* up early. I see seven in the morning every day."

"And I see it as rarely as possible," Jonathan confessed. "What brings you all the way down here?"

Venice took him up on the offer for coffee and headed for the pot. "I've been scouring the Internet and other sources looking for some mention of the grand shoot-out that allegedly happened last night."

"Allegedly?" Jonathan asked.

Venice looked into the coffee pot and winced. "When did you make this?" She poured some into a cup—one that bore the logo of the Central Intelligence Agency— and added enough cream and sugar to turn it into a dessert drink. "I say allegedly because I find no mention of the assault anywhere. Not even on ICIS, and if past is precedent, a shoot-out is exactly the kind of event that would have ICIS buzzing like a beehive."

Jonathan recognized ICIS (pronounced EYE-sis) as a post-9/11 program that documented ongoing police investigations in real time so that other law enforcement agencies could be aware of what was going on, in case they wanted to weigh in and recognize similarities in their own jurisdictions. "What are you thinking?" he asked.

"I'm just making an observation," she said. "If it was as big as we've been led to believe, that would be a lot of people not showing up to work or the breakfast table. You'd think somebody would make a report."

Boxers laid a pile of empty thirty-round magazines for his HK417 onto his bench next to the open ammo box filled with loose 7.62 millimeter bullets. "Uncle's suppressing the news," he said as began pressing bullets into the first mag. "That's what I would do if I had a big secret to keep and unlimited resources to keep it with."

"Still no word from the nanny bodyguard?" Jonathan asked as he concentrated on applying a drop of oil onto the pistol's slide rails.

"She's still lying low," Venice said.

"That's the smart play," Jonathan said. He used a one-by-one-inch fabric patch to wipe away the excess oil. "With the world coming apart around you, it's easy to feel expendable. I'd hide, too, at least until I knew it was safe to be visible."

"Maryanne said that it might even be our guys who are chasing them," Boxers recalled. "I hope she's well armed."

"If she knows that the government might be on the other team, she can't even call the police," Jonathan said. With the oil distributed, he reinserted the pistol's barrel and guide rod. "You brought your computer, Ven. Do you have info on Jolaine and Graham?"

"Some," Venice said. She carried her computer over to the coffee station and hooked it to the USB cable that dangled from the wall-mounted television. Because of explosion-proofing issues, the screen itself was contained within a clear Lexan box. A few seconds later, the television had converted to a computer screen.

"I wasn't able to find many pictures of her," Venice explained. The screen displayed an institutional image of a surly-looking young lady with thin lips and utterly average features. Devoid of makeup, she stared into the camera. Her hair was so tightly pulled back that it was impossible to tell what color it was.

"This is the picture I lifted from her security badge from when she was a contractor with Hydra Security."

"Looks like she's under arrest," Boxers said.

"Probably felt like it, too," Jonathan said. He was familiar with Hydra, and he was not impressed. "Hydra came late to the game and gave bottom-feeders a bad name." In the post-9/11 rush to staff private security contractors, it became impossible to keep standards high. Not all of the Hydra guys were pukes, but too many of them were.

"Here's a nicer picture," Venice said. She clicked, and the screen revealed a younger version of the same face, this one vibrant. Her broad smile revealed a row of white, uneven teeth that to Jonathan looked more attractive than the engineered perfection that passed for pretty these days. "This one is from six years ago, before she got into the war-fighting business."

Jonathan looked back to the pistol to concentrate on reinserting the slide stop. "Are those the only two images?"

"She's got a Facebook photo, too, but that looks even older." Venice clicked and the screen filled with what appeared to be a smiling college student, framed in the familiar setting of a Facebook profile. Jonathan glanced long enough to see that it appeared to be a professionally composed portrait shot, and then looked back at the pistol.

"She's got only a hundred and twenty-four Facebook friends," Venice said.

"Only?" Boxers interrupted. "That's a lot of people." With the current mag filled, he tapped the back edge against the table to seat the rounds, and then picked up another empty.

"Not in the world of social media," Venice corrected, "and especially not for someone her age. I haven't been able to turn up much on her earlier years, except for the fact that she appears to be some sort of orphan."

Jonathan looked up. "How many sorts of orphans are there?"

Venice's jaw dropped. "You fund an entire school for sort-of orphans."

"Ah." He slid the recoil spring into place and reached for the plug that would hold it in place.

"Jolaine Cage grew up in a series of foster homes, starting, from what I can tell, at a very young age. I'm talking four or five. I haven't yet tracked down whether her parents are dead or were druggies or criminals."

"Are we talking good foster homes or bad foster homes?" Jonathan asked. He twisted the barrel bushing back into place and cycled the 1911's action a couple of times. The pistol was whole again.

Venice said, "If you're in enough orphanages, I imagine you live the whole spectrum. She didn't excel in school, but she did slog her way through a history major at the University of Florida."

"What about the kid?" Jonathan asked. "Graham, right?"

"Nothing," Venice said. "He's fourteen and in school and otherwise unremarkable."

"Don't forget scared shitless," Boxers said. "I bet he's that."

Jonathan holstered his Colt and pulled his shirt over

to conceal it. "What else do you have?" He walked to the gun locker and helped himself to his own pile of thirty-round mags and a box of 5.56 millimeter ammo.

"Since the Antwerp shoot-out flew below the radar, I thought I'd do a little extra digging on ICIS," Venice explained. "Turns out that shots fired were reported just a few hours ago in Defiance, Ohio, a short drive from Antwerp."

Jonathan placed the ammo and mags onto his workbench and started loading. "Close enough to maybe be the same incident but with different labels?"

"I don't think so," Venice said. "The times are too far off. The strange thing with the Defiance incident is the lack of follow-up by police."

"I'm not sure what you mean."

"There's a report on ICIS of a call being placed about a shots being fired, but then there's no follow-up. No report filed, not even a report of a unit being dispatched."

"Maybe the cops thought it was bogus," Boxers said.

"Possible," Venice said. "It's just an interesting confluence of events, especially with the boss's views on coincidences."

"They don't exist," Jonathan said. "I know this is all the result of a lot of work, Ven, but it's not much to go on."

"There's more," Venice said. "And this is probably the most important of the lot. Arrest warrants have been issued for Jolaine Cage and Graham Mitchell."

Jonathan paused with his hand hovering over the ammo box. "What's the charge?"

"Interstate flight to avoid prosecution."

"That's a federal rap," Boxers said.

"To avoid prosecution of what?" Jonathan asked.

Venice pulled from her coffee. "The warrant doesn't say. Or if it does, no one put it up on ICIS, which would be very unusual."

Boxers asked, "Does ICIS say which agency is looking for them?"

"DHS."

Jonathan chuckled. "Does DHS actually issue warrants under their own name?" Following a series of reorganizations in the months after 9/11, the Department of Homeland Security was created as a new repository for federal agencies, among them the Secret Service, and the Coast Guard. Jonathan never liked the idea. "Homeland" sounded too much like Fatherland or Motherland, European constructs that had resulted in far too many wars.

"Aren't warrants issued by the constituent agencies?"

"I don't remember ever seeing it before," Venice said. "Maybe it's just a smoke screen."

Jonathan put the mag on the table. "Why hire us to bring these folks to safety and then swear out warrants for their arrest?"

Venice said, "Maybe the FBI wants to bring them in, while the CIA wants to put them in jail."

Jonathan shook his head. "The CIA can't do that. Not on American soil."

Venice rolled her eyes. "Okay, then the Secret Service. Or maybe the CIA drags them out of the country and renditions them. Work with me. Since we're only guessing, there could be a thousand possible scenarios."

Jonathan turned his attention back to loading. "Let's

go through it again," he said. "What did the police reports say about the shooting in Ohio?"

"Nothing," Venice said. "That's my point. A call was made and a complaint was filed. After that, there's nothing. It's as if nothing happened."

Jonathan looked over to Boxers. "In context with the other non-shoot-out and the warrants, that's very strange," he said.

"Maybe the arrest warrant is really a protective custody thing," Boxers offered. "You know, bring them to safety long enough for the FBI to shelter them from people who would hurt them."

Jonathan dismissed the idea. "Why spin up every police department in the Lower Forty-eight to be looking for felons when the real point is to give them an administrative hug?"

"What's your theory, then?"

"I don't have one," Jonathan said. "What I have are fears. If one arm of the federal government is fighting against another arm, we're in the middle of a fight that we can't possibly win."

"Who do *you* think the two arms are?"

Jonathan had no idea. "I think the smart money says the FBI is one of them. After that, I would guess CIA, but only because they've been such a pain in the ass over the years. But if that's so, why aren't the warrants issued by them?"

Venice fell silent for long enough to pull Jonathan's attention back to her. "You're troubled," he said.

"You mentioned context," she said. "Well, let's go to an even bigger context. This Maryanne Rhoades chick makes my skin crawl. Just the way she comes on. First, there was the familiarity, and then there was the aggressiveness. I learned a long time ago to trust my instincts, and she makes my instincts uncomfortable."

"You suspect she's lying?"

Venice gave him *that look.* "I think everyone's lying, thanks to you," she said. "Hanging with you is to take a master class in mistrust."

"You're welcome," Jonathan said with a smile. In Washington, DC, mistrust was a survival skill, particularly when it came to senior political appointees. It wasn't that they were unpatriotic—in fact, they were so friggin' patriotic that they believed their zeal to be better than the words in the dusty old Constitution. They scared Jonathan more than the crooks. Crooks did what they did for personal gain. Jonathan might not agree with their logic or their approach, but at least he understood it. The ones who purported to speak for the public's own good gave him the willies. Paging Adolf Hitler . . .

"Why would Maryanne lie?" he asked.

"I have no idea. I've only just begun my investigation into her."

"Give me a theory," Jonathan pressed. "Why would Maryanne, handpicked by Wolverine, want to work both ends against the middle?"

Venice counted off on her fingers. "Okay, there's money, sex, secrets—"

"In other words, you don't have a theory," Jonathan interrupted. He went back to his bullets.

Venice explained, "Last night at the gala, Maryanne approached you at what, ten-thirty, eleven o'clock?"

Jonathan hitched his shoulders. "Sounds about right."

"And that was maybe an hour after what happened in Indiana, right? If that?"

Jonathan saw it. "How did she know so many details so quickly?"

"Pretty well dressed at the spur of the moment, too," Boxers added.

Venice touched her nose. *Bingo.* "More than that, how come she knew all that she knew, yet didn't know anything else?"

Jonathan laid the magazine on its side on the table. He was fully engaged now. "Advance knowledge? It would have to be. This is really beginning to smell bad."

Venice's computer dinged, drawing her attention. She scowled as she jiggled her mouse and leaned in closer to her computer screen to take in whatever information was being delivered. "Huh," she said.

Jonathan and Boxers exchanged looks. It was best to let Venice process information at her own pace. She'd share when she was ready.

"Now this is interesting," she said. "I got a hit on a filter I set up through ICIS. There was an interesting incident last night on the outskirts of Napoleon, Ohio. Same general area as all the rest."

"Another shoot-out?"

"No, more interesting than that. There was a potential statutory rape call." She leaned into the screen again. "The Hummingbird Motel. Sounds like a place where you'd rent rooms by the hour."

"And why is this interesting?" Boxers asked.

"Because it's within a reasonable drive of Antwerp, Indiana, *and* Defiance, Ohio," she said.

"I think Big Guy meant, why is a statutory rape call interesting?" Jonathan said. Venice's mind was wired differently than other people's. Asked to solve the arithmetic problem for the sum of two plus two, she was apt to investigate the origin of the word "two" and the reason why it has a silent *w*, and in the process still come up with the answer more quickly than a math major sitting next to her.

Her expression said, *Duh*. "Because it was all about a young woman and a teenage boy. I thought that might be our PCs."

"Of course you did. And?"

She sighed. "And nothing. The police investigated, and their report says it was a sister and brother traveling together."

"I recognize that look in your eye," Jonathan said. "There's more."

"Maybe," she said. She returned her gaze to the screen and started reading aloud, skimming and compressing information as she spoke. "The call was placed by the front-desk manager—he said he didn't like the way she was acting, like she was trying to hide the fact that she had someone else with her. The ICIS file contains a security-camera image."

"Jolaine?"

"Really close," Venice confirmed. She tapped a few keys, and the image transferred from her screen to the larger one on the wall. "You know how the angles are on those cameras—always just a little bit wrong. But if you ask me, I think it's her."

Jonathan agreed. "Let's finish up and pack, Big Guy. We're deploying to Napoleon, Ohio." He stood.

"I think that's a mistake," Venice said. And then she

disappeared into her head and her keyboard while she attacked the keys. "Sit back down and give me a minute," she said without looking up. "Please."

Ninety seconds later, she fist-pumped the air. "Yes!" When she made eye contact again, she was beaming. "The chances of them still being in the motel aren't very high, I don't think. They'd want to stay moving, right?"

"But I don't want to lose time hanging around in Virginia while the PCs are somewhere in the Midwest," Jonathan said. "Particularly not with cops looking for them. What do the police have to go on, by the way? What are they looking for?"

"Just descriptions," Venice said. "And pictures. They're the same ones we looked at."

"Do they have a license number for a car?" he asked. "Or a make and model?"

"Not that I know of," she said, then she gave a triumphant whoop. "But I think *I* do. The Humingbird Motel uses ProtecTall Security for their alarms and video."

Jonathan felt a rush. ProtecTall was a premier low-end physical security company, with contracts for roughly half of the free world, and Venice had conquered their computer backstops ages ago.

"There were only a few cars in the parking lot last night," she said. "One of them was a black Mercedes that happens to be registered to a Douglas Wilkerson from—wait for it—Defiance, Ohio." An image of the car materialized on the screen.

"The shoot-out town," Boxers said.

"Bingo."

"And who is Douglas Wilkerson?" Jonathan asked.

"Give me a second." Venice started typing again. Over the course of three minutes—enough time to load four mags—Venice's face ran the full gamut from confusion to discovery and back to confusion. "I have no idea who Douglas Wilkerson is," she announced. "Ask me why."

Jonathan sensed that he already knew, but he played along. "Why?"

"Because he doesn't exist." They said it together.

"Yet there's an auto registration," Jonathan said.

"With a real physical address," Venice said. "When you're dealing with a motor vehicle bureau, real addresses are important. I did a search of the address and learned that the same fake citizen, Doug Wilkerson, is listed as the resident."

Jonathan looked to Boxers.

"What the hell?" Big Guy said. "How bad can a place be when it's named Defiance?"

CHAPTER NINE

Graham peeked out of the curtains again. *Where the hell is she?*

Jolaine was gone, and she'd taken the car and the guns with her. The note said that she'd gone shopping, but how long could it take to snag a T-shirt and a pair of shoes at Walmart?

Graham had been awake for nearly two hours now. It was going on ten o'clock, and according to the sign on the back of the door, checkout time was eleven. What was he supposed to do if it got to be 11:01 and Jolaine wasn't back yet? What kind of coward must she be to disappear on him like this? She was supposed to be protecting him, for God's sake!

He deeply wanted to take Jolaine at her word—take her note at its word—but after a while, when everyone you've known or loved is being shot at, faith is hard to come by.

Daylight made everything more real, and he hated that. Thinking back to the events of the past twelve hours made him dizzy. It was hard to differentiate reality from nightmare. If he were to believe the evidence, his father was dead, his mother was grievously wounded, and some undefined, anonymous entity was trying to make him dead, too.

It couldn't all be true, could it? There had to be some semblance of his life left as it used to be. Otherwise, what had he done to deserve all of this? What had his parents done? The harder he thought about it, the less he could identify the holes in the fabric of his living nightmare.

Graham Mitchell was a nobody among nobodies. His parents went to work every day, doing whatever it was that parents did when they went to work every day. Then they came home and were boring. What could they have done to make the kind of enemies that would bring so much violence? Some of the awfulness had to have been imagined. He *had* to believe that.

His imagination couldn't explain away the blood, though. Or the dying man in the foyer of his house, or the stream of men with guns, or the blood that he'd had to wash off his chest and hands and legs last night. He had the towels on the floor of the bathroom to prove the reality of that.

There was the reality of the hole in his mother's stomach. The reality of the weird, twitchy doctor.

"Oh, my God," he said aloud, bringing a hand to his mouth to stifle a sob that rose from nowhere. *I'm an orphan.*

That thought shut down all others.

Tears streamed down his face, but he wasn't aware of them until one of them tickled his nose. He wiped it away and tried to clear his eyes, but it didn't work.

Dad is definitely dead. He had to be, and for evidence, he needed only to remember that Dad had never left the house, and that when Graham had asked Mom about him, she had dodged his question.

Jolaine.

The mere fact of her presence in his life was testament to the fact that he'd been living in real danger for three years. Why hadn't he put that together in his head before? Mom and Dad had told him that Jolaine was merely a security precaution, that he shouldn't worry about anything. Hell, Jolaine had told him that herself. Had people been hunting them for all this time, and he'd just never known it? Was last night just a realization of the inevitable? Had the last peaceful months actually been the accident, and the shoot-out preordained?

He swiped again at his eyes. He couldn't let Jolaine see him crying like a little boy. She had little enough respect for him as it was.

He needed to think of something else. Anything else.

The television in this dump of a motel room sucked, both the machine itself and the programming it showed. At this hour, the broadcast networks were all about shows that attracted consumers of erectile dysfunction medicine, and there were no cable programs to speak of—unless you wanted to listen to a bunch of screaming newsreaders, or watch people cook or fix houses.

He pressed the power button and killed the set.

The silence brought demons.

Graham was tired of depending on everybody else for his survival. He was supposed to trust Jolaine, but where the hell was she?

"You made a promise," he said aloud. Hearing the words made it real.

Follow the protocol.

How many times had Mom said it in the last hour that they were together? She was his *mother,* for crying out loud. And Jolaine was only a . . . whatever the hell Jolaine was. A nanny with a gun. If Mom hadn't thought that that number was important, she wouldn't have made him memorize it. And if it wasn't important for him to deliver it, she wouldn't have made him *promise* to do just that. No way did Jolaine outrank that.

Graham turned his head to look at the phone on the nightstand. He knew without searching that Jolaine had taken her cell phone with her. Just as well, because cell phones were traceable. He'd seen on television that as long as you didn't stay on a landline for more than a few minutes, calls made from them couldn't be traced.

Jolaine's words rang in his ears. *Everything but doing nothing is a risk.* Did she know things that he didn't know? Was she a better judge of what was the right thing to do? Maybe better than him, but not better than Mom.

Follow the protocol.

Until today, he didn't even know what that word meant—he still didn't, if he really thought about it. All he knew was it had to do with something his parents had been planning for a long time. Follow the protocol meant follow the plan.

Graham sat back down on the bed and he picked up the phone. He hesitated. Then he dialed.

"Two nine four one," the voice said through the phone.

Graham opened his mouth to speak, but found that his vocal cords were hesitant. He had no idea what he'd been expecting when he called the number, but it had been more than that.

He heard the tentativeness in his own voice when he said, "Um, hello?"

"Two nine four one." There had been urgency in the man's tone before. Now it was joined by annoyance.

The protocol.

Mom had made him practice this part. If ever there was an emergency, he was to find a phone and follow the protocol. She'd made him recite the phrase. Now all Graham had to do was remember what the hell it was. "Um, Billy Bob Seven Nine," he said. They were the correct words, but he had no idea what they meant, or what weight they might carry.

"I copy Billy Bob Seven Nine," the voice said. "What is your status?"

Graham hesitated. He didn't know what to say.

"Billy Bob Seven Nine, what is your status?"

There might have been an accent. While Graham had never been to Chechnya himself, he thought he recognized that in the man's voice, the same accent as his father's. "I don't know what you want me to say." When all else fails, he thought, go for honesty.

The annoyance in the man's voice magnified. "What is your status? Are you hurt?"

"No," Graham said. "I'm fine."

"And others?"

"I don't know."

A pause. "You are calling a panic number," the man said. "Why?"

"My mother told me to," Graham said. "If anything bad ever happened, this was the number I was supposed to call."

"Are you alone?"

"I am now."

The man on the other end of the phone sighed deeply. "Try to think past the words and listen to the message. Were you alone five hours ago, and will you be alone five hours from now?"

He got it. The guy was really asking if Jolaine was with him. "I have Jolaine," he said.

"And your parents?"

Just like that, Graham found himself without enough air to speak. "No," he said. It was the best he could do.

"I need details," the man said.

What could he say? How could he describe the awfulness of what had happened? "They attacked our house," he said. "Men with guns. My mom was shot. I think my dad was . . ." He couldn't complete the sentence.

"Killed?"

Graham didn't answer.

"What is your location?" the voice asked. "And where is . . . your friend?" He seemed hesitant to say Jolaine's name.

"I think she's out shopping," he said. "She wrote that in a note."

"A note? Where are you?"

Graham felt a flash of uneasiness. This whole conversation had been far too one-sided. "Where are *you?*"

"Right where I'm supposed to be," the man said. "You, however, seem to be in trouble. How long do you want to continue playing games?"

"This isn't a game," Graham said. "This is my life. This is our lives. Why are people trying to kill me?"

"That's complicated," the man said.

"I want it to stop," Graham said. "Can you make it stop?"

The man on the other end paused. "Do you have information for me?"

Warning bell. "What kind of information?" He was hedging, seeing how much the guy on the other end already knew.

"I think you know," the man said. "How about a string of numbers and letters?"

So he knew.

"What do they mean?" Graham asked.

There was a smile in the man's voice when he said, "So, you do have them."

Graham felt a flash of anger. He wasn't ready to give that away yet.

"Your mother did well. I need you to give me that code."

"So it *is* a code," Graham said. It felt like a victory to turn it back on the man. "What's it for?"

"You don't want to anger me, young man. Graham, isn't it?"

Graham didn't respond.

"You want me as a friend, Graham. More important, you don't want me as an enemy. Your mother asked you to do her a favor, didn't she? She asked you to make this phone call. You've been a good son. Now why don't you continue being a good son and tell me that code."

His mind raced, trying to find a way out. He knew he should just hang up, but he couldn't make himself do that. He didn't know why. He understood now what

Jolaine had been trying to tell him. This man was not his friend. If anything, he was the enemy.

"I don't have it anymore," Graham said. "I lost it."

The man laughed. "Now you're lying to me, Graham."

"No, really, I'm not." He didn't like the way this asshole kept using his name. It was creepy. "I had it, but I lost it."

"Then why are you calling me?"

"To tell you that." Graham was proud that he manufactured that lie so quickly. "My mom told me to call and she gave me this piece of paper. But in all the stuff that happened last night, I lost the piece of paper."

"Liars go to hell, Graham. You have what they call a photographic memory. Less than one percent of the population of the world can do what you do. Your mother brags about that a lot."

A glimmer of hope. "You know my parents?"

"Of course I do. How would I know so much about you if I didn't know them?"

Now who was lying? It was something in the man's voice, like he was making fun of him. *Sure, I'll tell you anything if it'll get me what I want.*

Graham's eyes shot to the clock radio. How long had he been talking? Was it long enough for them to trace the call?

Goddammit, why hadn't he looked at the clock before dialing?

Shit!

He dropped the receiver back onto the cradle and brought his hands to the sides of his head. What had he done?

"Shit, shit, shit." He said it aloud with brittle emphasis. "Ah, shit." When he brought his hands down they were shaking.

A noise beyond the draped window pulled his attention to the left. The noise sounded like a car, and it sounded very close. Very, *very* close.

Graham jumped to his feet. Christ, how could they be so fast? They must have been waiting for him. His pounding heart was the loudest sound in the room. He glanced down at his chest—past the downy patch of dark hair that had begun to decorate his breastbone— and he could see his flesh pulsating with each stroke.

This was it. He fought the urge to rush to the window and look out, because he knew with certainty that a man with a gun stood on the other side, waiting for him to do that very thing. It would be a man with murder in his eyes, and he'd be committed to inflicting upon Graham the same fate that he'd inflicted on his parents.

God*damn* that Jolaine! Why hadn't she left him with a gun? Or a knife or a frigging brick—anything that he could use to defend himself? He'd shot a gun before, after all. At Boy Scout camp, he'd shot .22 rifles and he was damn good at it. Why had she taken all the guns with her? Why had she left him defenseless? Even if he didn't know how to shoot and he totally screwed it up, so what? Dying in a fight beat the shit out of dying with your hands in the air in a crappy motel begging for mercy.

Graham braced for a fight, a physical fight to the death that he knew he was destined to lose. He weighed a hundred thirty-five pounds after a big meal, and he'd never actually been in a fight—not a real one, like the ones on television. He had no idea what he'd do if a guy with a gun actually did kick open the door, but he was for sure going to do *something*.

Just please, God, let it be something other than dying a painful death.

The engine shut down. If something was about to happen, it was going to happen soon. And probably fast. In sixty seconds, Graham Mitchell would know if checkout time would see him dead or alive.

As terrifying as that thought was, he found it invigorating.

He braced himself.

Someone knocked on the door.

CHAPTER TEN

Jolaine paused as she approached the motel room. If Graham was awake, he had to be frightened. If she walked right up to the door and slipped the key into the lock, he might panic. Knocking seemed like the better way to go. She rapped with a single knuckle. Light and friendly. She hoped that Graham would hear the knock, look through the peephole, recognize her, and all would be right.

None of that happened.

After waiting fifteen or twenty seconds, she knocked again and said, "Graham, it's me. It's Jolaine. I'm coming in."

As she slipped her key into the slot, she was struck with the possibility that things might not be normal on the other side of the door. As remote a possibility as it might be, she supposed that the bad guys might have found Graham while she was gone. She'd struggled with the decision whether to leave the M4 in the room as a hedge against a door-crashing invader, but as far as she knew, Graham didn't know which end of the gun the bullet came out of. Any mistake made at 2,300 feet per second was as bad a mistake as could be made.

She laid her bags on the walkway to clear her hands, and poised her right hand on the grip of the pistol strapped to her chest. If it came to that, she could draw and fire in less than two seconds.

The lock turned and Jolaine paused before shoving the door open about 50 percent too hard. She'd intended it to float inward, when in fact it exploded open and bounced off the perpendicular wall.

In a single glance, she eliminated the possibility of a bad guy, but she sensed danger—from Graham. He stood between the beds, poised in a comical Bruce Lee–wannabe pose, his feet wide set, his fists clenched.

"Relax, Graham," she said. "It's me."

He didn't move.

"Graham?"

"Where have you been?" He looked younger than she'd last seen him—more vulnerable.

"Didn't you find my note?" she asked.

"You left me."

"You were asleep," she said. "And I couldn't exactly take you along half-naked." If it were a normal day, she would have reminded him of her warning back in the house to get dressed.

"I thought you were gone," he said. His chin muscles trembled.

"I'm sorry I worried you," Jolaine said. "I thought I left it all in my note. I'm here now. I didn't leave you. More importantly, I *wouldn't* leave you. You have to believe that. You have to trust me."

As Jolaine spoke, she removed the key from the

lock and pocketed it. Keeping her right hand free, she picked up the bags and stepped inside. She pushed the door shut.

Graham's eyes reddened. "Are my parents dead?"

"I don't know." Jolaine launched the words to get them out before she could show that she didn't believe them. "But I think they may be. Hand to God, I don't know anything more than you do. But what we both know leads mostly to bad conclusions. I'm sorry."

Graham stared at her as he processed the words. He seemed to have found a neutral place in his mind, neither calm nor stressed. It reminded Jolaine of the mental space she sought when she was about to step into harm's way. It was the spot you went to when you realized that tomorrow may never come, yet you were too old to cry.

"What's happening, Jolaine?" Graham half sat, half fell back onto the bed.

Jolaine had learned a long time ago that hyperstressed situations required hyper-fidelity to the truth. "I don't know," she said. "We're under attack, and as far as I can tell, we can't trust anyone."

Graham's eyes darkened.

"What?" Jolaine asked.

"How do I know I can trust *you*?"

Jolaine placed the shopping bags onto her bed, the one closest to the door. With both hands clear, she pointed to her eyes with both forefingers. "Look at me," she said.

Graham rolled his eyes, dismissing the overkill.

"No, I'm serious," Jolaine said. She'd modulated her voice to be serious and then some. "Look in my eyes."

Graham's entire face morphed into a scowl. But his eyes met hers.

"Think of the person that you trust more than anyone else in the world," she said. "You can trust me fifty points more than that."

Graham's scowl deepened. "Why? You're not even part of our family. If people are trying to kill Mitchells, why wouldn't you just hand me over and go home safe?"

Jolaine wished that she had something lofty to say. Again, she defaulted to the rawest form of the truth. "Because that's what I signed on for," she said. "Keeping you safe is my job."

Graham seemed unsatisfied. "Is that all of it?"

She knew what he was trolling for. He wanted to believe that her interest was personal—that she was motivated to protect him because she *cared*. With all that had transpired, she knew that he was in a dark place, that he needed affirmation that he wasn't alone in the world. Believing that her mission was to protect Graham-the-individual as opposed to Graham-the-obligation would put him in a better place emotionally.

But preservation of his emotions was not on Jolaine's priority list. Her focus was exclusive to his physical body. When the dust settled on all of this madness, she could claim victory if the boy still had a heartbeat.

"That's most of it," Jolaine confessed. Reading his eyes and the sagging of his shoulders, she added, "But that doesn't mean I don't care for you. This personal protection stuff is complicated."

Graham took his time forming his next question.

"Bottom line. Are you supposed to give up your life for mine?"

Emotion stirred in Jolaine's gut. "My job is to see that you're still breathing at the end of every day," she said. "I have no intention of dying in the process."

"Good," Graham said. "I don't think I could live with the thought that someone had gotten killed protecting me."

Jolaine was thunderstruck. She'd never heard a selfless word from him before.

He gestured toward the bags on the bed. "So, what did you buy me?"

The Defiance County Memorial Airport offered precious little in the way of creature comforts, but it had a long, flat runway that was more than capable of handling the little Lear that a client named Mannix had made available for Security Solutions' short-notice call. It was a nice thank-you present to acknowledge Jonathan's safe return of Mannix's daughter from a very unpleasant place.

Boxers flew the plane, as he always did—there were few machines with wings, wheels, or rotors that Boxers couldn't pilot with the best—and Jonathan sat up in the cockpit with him. In the back, in the area where Mannix no doubt entertained his hotshot friends and clients while in flight, Jonathan and Boxers had stacked duffels filled with the tools of their trade. That translated to long guns, pistols, body armor, a few explosives, surveillance toys, and enough ammunition to launch an invasion.

Once on the ground, they needed a car, but they needed one without the traceability of a rental. Here's where Venice's command of the Internet came into play. While the guys were airborne, she'd worked the online ads and found an SUV for sale that would fit the bill. She'd contacted the owner and negotiated a figure that was ten percent above his asking price, on the condition that he have the vehicle at the airport in time to meet Jonathan's flight.

You'd think that the spectacle of two men carrying a couple hundred pounds of equipment divided into four duffel bags would attract attention in an airport, but therein lay an important benefit of using the civil aviation terminals. People minded their own business. After parking the Lear in its assigned slot and locking it up, they just walked straight through the Spartan departure lounge and back out into the sunlight.

Boxers pointed to a ten-year-old blue Ford Expedition that was parked at the curb. "Is that it?" he asked.

As if to answer the question, the driver's door opened and out stepped a guy in his sixties. Tall and trim, he wore all the accoutrements of a cowboy, from the jeans to the boots to the hat and the plate-size belt buckle. The man approached readily, yet warily. This was a guy who'd been around the block a few times, and from the lines etched into his face, Jonathan sensed that he'd seen as many bad times as good. Not a man to jerk around. He wore a sleeveless denim jacket covering a T-shirt, leading Jonathan to wonder if he, too, was concealing a firearm on his hip.

"Howdy," the man said as he approached. He offered his hand. "Name's Wortham. Are you Mr. Smith?" he asked Jonathan.

Actually, Jonathan had no idea what name Venice had given the guy. He chose to say nothing and just shook the man's hand. "Good afternoon," he said. "Are you the car guy?"

"I am," Wortham said. "I knew you was the two I was supposed to meet when I saw this big fella here." He offered his hand to Boxers as well. "The nice lady on the phone told me to look for him and I'd find you. That was your wife, was it? The lady, I mean."

"A colleague," Jonathan said. "That truck's in good working order, right?" He started walking that direction. The longer they stood in one spot, the more likely a security camera would pick them up. Not that they were doing anything particularly camera-worthy, but he didn't like to dawdle.

"I'd say it works pretty good, yeah," Wortham said. "I'm the only owner, got all the scheduled maintenance done on time, and never missed an oil change. I got the receipts in the glove box if you want to see them."

"Your word is good enough for me," Jonathan said.

"Me, too," Boxers growled in his deepest, scariest tone. Translation: *You don't want us to find out you sold us a lemon.*

"It's just exactly as I say," Wortham said. He darted around them to get to the back lift gate. "I'll open this up for you," he said. "All that stuff will fit in there with room to spare."

They laid the bags on the bed and proved him to be right.

"Now I believe I owe you some money," Jonathan said. In addition to duffels with weaponry, Jonathan also carried a soft briefcase with cash. Hundred-dollar bills were often even more persuasive than a firearm.

For convenience, the bills were banded in stacks of $1,000, and Jonathan pulled out first four packs, and then another four. "There you go," Jonathan said. "Eight thousand dollars."

Wortham's eyes flashed. As he accepted the cash, he said, "You know, I've been on this earth for quite a few years, but I don't know that I've ever seen eighty hundred-dollar bills all at one time. But I got to tell you, the actual price was only seventy-eight hundred." He thumbed through a stack, isolated two bills, then peeled them off and handed them back.

Jonathan reminded himself where he was. In this part of the world, honest people took their honesty very seriously. Venice had told him that the negotiated price was exactly what Wortham said it was, but for Jonathan, that was a rounding error. To present it as such to a man who made his living the hard way could have been a huge insult.

"Thank you," Jonathan said, accepting the two Franklins.

"Don't you want the title?" Wortham asked.

Actually, he didn't. Just as he didn't want a receipt, a bill of sale, or any other paperwork. Still, he understood that some states took the transfer of personal property more seriously than others. "Sure," he said. "I was just getting to that. Do you have it with you?"

Wortham pulled it out of an inside pocket of his jacket, and as he did, Jonathan caught a glimpse of the pistol he'd suspected was on the man's hip. In Ohio, this was not necessarily a source of concern. "You just fill out your name and address right here," he explained, pointing to the appropriate blocks on the title.

Jonathan made stuff up to fill in the blanks, random

numbers and names for the street, but concluded with the real city, Coronado, California, 92118. The only way he was able to pull that zip code out of his ass was because of a Navy SEAL buddy who lived there. He listed his name as John Smith and signed accordingly.

As Jonathan handed the title back to Wortham, the other man hesitated. "I don't believe you're who you say you are," the old guy said.

Jonathan felt a tug of something uncomfortable. "Is that so? Who do you think I am?"

"I think you're a man who doesn't ask nearly enough questions before handing over this kind of money."

Jonathan shrugged. "What can I say? You look like a trustworthy guy."

"Bullshit," Wortham said. He looked at the title. "John Smith? Really? You don't even have more imagination than that?"

Jonathan felt Boxers shifting behind him, growing uncomfortable. "Maybe you need to count that money again, Mr. Wortham. Those bills are all real. It's more than anyone else will pay you, and I've filled out the form. You've done everything that the law requires. I think we should leave it at that."

Wortham hesitated. "I don't like this," he said. "I think you two are heading for trouble. That doesn't bother me so much, but if you get in trouble, that might pull me into trouble. I don't need none of that."

"You know what, Mr. Wortham?" Jonathan said. "I haven't been navigating the planet for as long as you have, but I'll share one of my big lessons with you. Sometimes, the best information comes from the questions that go unasked."

Wortham thought about that.

Jonathan continued, "At this point, everything is completely legal. You've done what you need to do, and I've done what I need to do. If, hypothetically, I have lied in my paperwork, then that is my problem, not yours. Are you catching my drift?"

Wortham took a long time answering. "Where did you two serve?" he said, at length.

"Excuse me?" Jonathan asked. It was mostly a stall for time.

"You both have a military bearing about you," Wortham said. "An awareness and a look in your eye. I know that sounds like romantic bullshit, but there you go. I trust romantic bullshit. Where did you serve?"

Jonathan cast a look back at Big Guy. How much dared they share?

"I only ask because I'm a vet myself," Wortham continued. "Back-to-back gunship tours in Vietnam. Got the shrapnel to prove it."

"Thank you for your service," Jonathan said, and he cringed at his own words. "Jesus, that sounds clichéd and simple, but I really mean it. Thank you."

Wortham smiled. "You're welcome, Mr. John Smith of Coronado, California. Those are nice words. But you still haven't answered my question. Where did you serve?"

Before he could say anything, Jonathan heard Boxers make a growling sound again. It was Big Guy's way of warning him not to engage. Wortham could be the nicest guy in the world, but he still had no need to know.

"Let me put it this way," Jonathan hedged. "You had the military part right. Now, think about every hot spot in the last thirty years or so, and there's a really good chance that we were there."

"Are you guys Special Forces or something?" Wortham asked. The facial reactions he saw confirmed it. "Ah. Okay." Wortham rubbed the back of his head for a few seconds, and then when he looked back up at them, his face was frozen in a place between pain and curiosity. "One thing," he said. "Just promise me that if I knew what you were doing, I'd be proud to tell people that I'd sold you my car."

Jonathan smiled. He held out his hand, as if to seal a bet. "That's a deal, so long as you promise never to tell your friends anything like what you just said you'd be proud to tell them."

Wortham shook on it. "I miss it, you know," he said. "It's terrible to be a man my age and think back and realize that my life was most exciting when I was twenty-two years old."

Something tugged at Jonathan's gut when he heard that. It was the secret that civilians could never grasp: As hellish and bloody and deadly and overall awful as war was, nothing outside the battlefield could come within 10 percent of the adrenaline rush.

"Either way," Jonathan said. "I promise on a stack of Bibles that my friend and I are on the side of the angels."

Wortham slapped Jonathan's shoulder. "In that case, I wish a quick trip to Hell for whoever's on Satan's side." With that, he started walking back toward the terminal.

Jonathan felt a flash of guilt. He had the old guy's car, which meant that the old guy had no wheels. "Hey!" he called. "Mr. Wortham!"

The older man turned.

"Can we drop you somewhere?"

He flashed two rows of perfectly aligned teeth. If they were natural, they were an anomaly for his generation. "Are you shittin' me? I'm at an airport and I got a pocket full of money. I figure the world is mine, at least for the next month or so. Plus, I won't have to answer phone calls about where my truck might have ended up. Whatever you're doin', good luck to you."

The old guy disappeared into the executive terminal as Jonathan grabbed the cash bag and brought it up front with him. The Expedition was an Eddie Bauer model, complete with beige leather and beige everything else on the interior. "Nice guy," Jonathan said.

"Don't you ever just grunt and ignore people?" Boxers asked. "I mean, Jesus. You flash money like it's friggin' manure, and then you tell him we were part of the Unit. Christ, why don't you just give him a business card with a lipstick print? I wanted to put a friggin' sock in your mouth."

Jonathan granted bragging rights to Boxers as the man who'd saved his ass more times than anyone else on earth, and as such granted a huge margin for stepping out of line. This was an unusual break.

"I sense you have a problem," he said.

Boxers laughed. "How very intuitive of you," he said. "It's not a big deal, Dig, but you just need to start taking OpSec more seriously. You're getting chatty in your old age."

That was a double shot—old age and flouting security—and Jonathan opted to ignore both of them. They had stuff to do, and they didn't need the pall of an argument.

Jonathan pulled two radios out of the cash duffel. He handed one to Big Guy and kept the other for himself. Not much bigger than a pack of cigarettes, the radio represented the best in satellite and encryption technology. He hooked it onto his belt at the small of his back and slipped a wireless transceiver into his right ear. He pressed the tiny transmit button on the earpiece and said, "Mother Hen, Scorpion. You there?"

It took a few seconds before Venice's voice crackled, "Right here. You're loud and clear."

"Just so you know, we're on the ground and on our way," Jonathan said over the air. "I'll reestablish contact when we're close."

"Got it," Venice said. "I'll be standing by."

CHAPTER ELEVEN

I made the phone call," Graham said. He'd changed into the new clothes and everything fit. He thought she needed to know.

Her face turned pale. "Tell me you're kidding. Are you talking about the panic call?"

Graham nodded. He knew she was pissed. No, she was beyond pissed.

"Why would you do that?" she shouted. In all the months they'd been together, he'd never heard her raise her voice before.

"Because I promised my mom," he said. His voice caught in his throat as he spoke, and tears burned his eyes. "You said yourself that she's probably dead. How could I not?"

"But you didn't know—" Jolaine stopped herself. She held her hands in front of her, palms out, as if to tell someone to stop. Or maybe to tell the anger to stop. "Okay," she said. He wasn't sure to whom. "Okay, what's done is done. Tell me about it. Tell me what happened."

"I really didn't mean any harm," Graham said. He

didn't think he could handle anyone being angry with him right now. He needed friends. He had enough enemies.

"Please just tell me what happened on the phone call."

Graham told her about the conversation with the mysterious man on the phone. He tried to be as complete in the details as possible, and he didn't intentionally leave anything out. The deeper he got into the story, the darker Jolaine's expression became.

"So, did you or did you not give him the code?"

"I did not." Not only was that the truth, but he also sensed that it was the right answer. That made him feel less shitty.

Jolaine fell quiet as she thought through the details. Something passed through her brain that made her eyes light up. "Wait a minute," she said. "What phone did you use?"

Graham pointed to the phone on the nightstand. "That one."

Jolaine shot to her feet. "Oh, shit. Oh, Christ, now they know where we are."

"I don't think I talked long enough for them to trace the call," Graham said.

"Really? I mean, *really?* This is the twenty-first century, Graham. This is the age of caller I.D. and instant recognition. They knew where you were the instant they answered the phone." She looked around, clearly on the edge of panic. She was scanning the room for something. She darted into the bathroom and looked there, too.

Graham felt a surge of panic in his gut. "What?" he said. "What is it? What's wrong? Why are—"

"Do you have anything important in here?" Jolaine asked. She reappeared from the bathroom with the toothbrush she'd bought for him. She tossed it and the toothpaste into one of the shopping bags.

"No, I don't think so."

"Then get to the car," she said. "We have to get out of here."

"Where are we going?"

"Anywhere," she said. "We can't stay here. They're coming for us."

"Who?"

"I don't know!" she shouted. "The same people who came for us last night, Graham. The same people I told you not to call, but you decided to call anyway." She slapped the lamp that sat atop the dresser and sent it to the end of its electrical cord tether. From there, it crashed to the floor.

"Jesus, Jolaine." Graham retreated between the beds. He'd never seen her like this.

"You don't get it, do you?" she shouted, taking a step closer. "I mean, you really, truly, deep in your heart of hearts don't get it. We are at war, Graham. And we don't know who the hell the enemy is! People are trying to kill us."

She spun and moved to the door, the shopping bag dangling from her hand. "Come on," she said. "Right now. We're out of here." She beckoned him with a vast, circular motion of her entire arm.

"What is it?" Graham moved as he spoke. "You're scared."

"Damn right I'm scared," she said. "The bad guys are close. We didn't drive that far last night. Maybe, what, an hour? Hour and a half max? When did you make your phone call?"

Graham glanced at the clock. It was past checkout time. "I hung up about twenty minutes ago."

"Shit." Her beckoning motion grew even larger. "Now. We're gone."

Casting a final glance around the tiny space to make sure that he hadn't left anything—how could he when he hadn't brought anything?—he darted over to join Jolaine at the door.

She hesitated before opening it. Almost as an after-thought, it seemed, she looked through the peephole.

"Anybody out there?" Graham asked.

"No," she said. She pressed the button on the car key fob to unlock the doors, then spun around. She planted her back against the door, and reached out to place both her hands on his shoulders. She squeezed tightly enough to hurt. "You have to listen to me, Gra-ham. And you have to do exactly what I say or I swear to God I'll shoot you myself and be done with this shit. Do you understand me?"

Even after the pep talk of a few minutes ago, he halfway believed that she really would shoot him. "Yes," he said. "I promise."

"We're going to go straight to the car," Jolaine explained. The intensity in her eyes could have lit a fire. "We're not going to run, but we're going to walk with purpose. I will have my hand on your back, and you will not fight me. We are both going to get in on the driver's side, and you are going to crawl across to the passenger side, then we're going to get out of here. If anything happens—I mean, if *anything* happens—if there's shooting or God knows what else, I want you on the floor and I want you to stay there. I know what I'm doing, and you don't. Are we clear?"

Under any other circumstance, Graham would have launched to the stratosphere if anyone had spoken to him like that—especially if that someone was Jolaine. As it was, he knew he'd screwed up, and now he'd agree to anything. "We're clear," he said.

"All right," Jolaine said. "Let's do this." She moved him to the side of the door, but kept one hand on his shoulder. She drew her pistol with her other hand. "When I tell you to open the door, I want you to open it all the way. Just leave it open, and we'll head to the car."

Graham pointed to the shopping bags. "What about our stuff?"

"I'll buy you another goddamn toothbrush, okay?"

It was a stupid question.

She nodded. Just once, a single twitch of her head. "Open the door."

Just as she'd told him, he pulled on the door, but it stuck. After three tries, it pulled away from the jamb and opened all the way. The door hadn't even stopped moving before Jolaine was pushing him out the door and into the parking lot.

He heard the SUVs turning the corner into the lot before he saw them. There were two of them and they screamed past the little front office building where the clerk had decided that Jolaine was a pedophile and headed right for them, moving fast enough that Graham didn't think they'd be able to stop before ramming them.

Graham didn't have a chance to react before Jolaine bent him at the waist and pushed him to the far side of the vehicle—the passenger side. Just seconds into this, and already they were breaking the rules.

The SUVs screeched to a halt and the doors flew open. The first man Graham saw was the driver of the first vehicle. He stepped out with a rifle in his hands and even before his feet hit the ground, Jolaine fired her pistol twice. Blood flew from the guy's forehead and he dropped in a heap.

"Get in the car!" Jolaine commanded, opening the door for him. She fired twice more, but he couldn't see the result.

The world erupted in more gunfire. Bullets tore into their Mercedes, launching puffs of glass, and making the entire chassis vibrate with the individual impacts. Graham cowered on the ground as Jolaine returned fire.

"Where's your machine gun?" he yelled.

"In the trunk!" She fired again. Again, again, and again.

Graham rose to his knees to peer through the shattered windows to see what was going on. What he saw both surprised and terrified him. Three men lay on the ground near the first vehicle. Two of them lay still, and the third was writhing on the pavement, screaming for help. Others hid behind open doors, firing blindly, exposing only their rifles. Their bullets raked the front of the motel and probably the sky, but precious few impacted the car.

Jolaine, on the other hand, stood tall, allowing the body of the car to serve as a shield as she fired two-

and three-shot combinations at the attackers. Graham was watching when the slide on the top of her pistol locked open.

Oh, shit, she's out of bullets.

Not yet, she wasn't. With her eyes never leaving the people she was shooting at, she dropped the clip—he thought that's what it was called—out of the bottom of her gun, and then she produced another one from somewhere under her shirt and slapped it into place. She started firing again.

"How many more of those do you have?" he asked.

She didn't answer, and he interpreted the silence as the worst kind of news. He didn't know how many bullets she had left, but it didn't take a genius to know that once they were gone, both he and Jolaine would be dead unless she somehow killed them all first.

"I'm getting the machine gun," he said.

"The hell you are!"

"The hell I'm not!" Graham was tired of hiding, and he was tired of being a victim. Like before, when all this shooting shit was just a thought in his head, he was not going to die hiding. Only cowards died hiding. His dad died shooting, and his mom, if she had in fact been killed, died shooting. He was going to be part of the family tradition.

Graham dropped back down onto the ground to get behind the steel, and he moved to the rear door.

"Graham!" Jolaine yelled.

"I'm getting in the friggin' car!" he yelled. "What do you want from me?"

He pulled the door open and slid like a snake along the floor. He lost a flip-flop in the process, but he'd worry about that later. Or, he wouldn't. Right now, it didn't matter. His legs were still hanging out the door when he reached up and pulled down the armrest in the middle of the backseat. He was working a hunch, and it proved to be correct. There was a hatch behind the armrest that opened up to the trunk. If some asshole hadn't locked it—

He pulled and it opened.

Yes!

There weren't many advantages to being short and skinny when you're fourteen years old—in fact, before today, he wouldn't have been able to name one—but it turned out that being able to slither into a tiny space to retrieve a machine gun was one of them.

He entered like Superman, his arms outstretched over his head, and when his shoulders were clear, he started feeling around. This space defined darkness. But for the tiny streams of light that penetrated through the bullet holes, the blackness would have been perfect, absolute. That dim light, however, provided only shadows, no definition. As the world continued to explode outside, his hands found what he thought might have been a lug wrench, and also something that felt squishy that he didn't like touching at all.

There it was! His hand landed on the tip of the barrel first—the muzzle and the sight—and he grabbed it. As he backed out of the hole, it occurred to him that the muzzle was pointed directly at his forehead—his Scout Camp counselor had pounded them on the importance of never allowing a gun to point at anything you weren't willing to destroy—but now was not the time.

His shoulder cleared the hole, and two seconds later, he had the rifle in his hands.

He tumbled back out onto the parking lot just as Jolaine's gun locked open again. She looked at it with anger, as if it had betrayed her.

"Jolaine!" he yelled.

Her eyes darted first to him, and then to the rifle he held. She smiled and ducked below the level of the fender just long enough to grab the carbine. "Good for you," she said, and she rumpled his hair. "Now go back in there and get the rest of the ammunition. I've got a bunch of extra magazines in pouches. Hurry!"

Graham was a total shit for not obeying her orders, but when this was over, she was going to have to give him a hug. Jolaine didn't know what she'd been thinking when she locked her only decent weapon into the trunk of her car, but as the Glock ejected her last shell casing, the appearance of the M4 felt like a gift from God—like a sign that they were destined to survive this round.

Whoever their attackers were, they were not experienced warriors. They fought as if they were afraid of being shot. Of course, everyone in a firefight was afraid of getting shot, but those who were experienced understood that the best way to avoid catching a bullet was to aim your shots and make sure they counted. As a mentor of hers had once said, the secret is to shoot first, shoot fast, and shoot well. As an added bonus, it never hurt to shoot dirty, too.

That first kill—dropping the driver of the first vehicle—had rattled the attackers, and despite their larger numbers, that rattling had given her the advantage. At least for as long as her ammunition held out.

Now that she was armed with thirty rounds of 5.56 millimeter devastation, the other team was going to learn just how bad a mistake they'd made.

Because she was the last person to handle the M4, she knew that a round was already chambered. She used her thumb to change the selector switch from safe to single-shot and she rose again. With the weapon pressed against her shoulder, she moved from behind the Mercedes and advanced on the SUVs and their cowering occupants.

Way back when she'd first loaded the magazines for her carbine, the anticipated threat had been vehicle-borne kidnapping, and as a result she'd loaded them with armor-piercing ammunition. As she stepped out, she scanned for targets. Where she saw legs on the ground, she zeroed in on a spot about three feet north of the legs and fired through the steel panels that obscured the torsos. The titanium-tipped bullets hit with enough energy, concentrated at an infinitesimally small surface area, to liquefy the steel at the point of contact, only to pass through, intact, to pierce whatever—who-ever—lay behind the shield.

Two attackers hit, two attackers killed, for a total of five dead, so far.

There had to be at least one more, maybe several. Not only had she thought she'd seen them when they drove up, but it made no sense to have two vehicles with only five people. In a perfect world, the smart move would be to wait them out, let them make the first move, and then pick them off when they did. But this much gunfire and this many bodies were going to attract a lot of attention, and that attention was going to come with badges and guns. She didn't want any of

that. They couldn't afford any of that. There was no
way to explain the inexplicable.

"Graham," she said. She never took her eyes off the
real estate in front of her.

"Right here."

"Are you hurt?"

"No, I'm fine. I have the extra bullets."

"Okay, good. Now, get out, stay behind cover and
look on the ground near the front of the car. Do you see
the keys? I dropped them and they should be down
there."

She heard him moving.

"Got them."

"Have you ever driven a car?" she asked.

"I don't have my license."

"Different question. Have you ever—" She stopped
the question because the answer was irrelevant. "You're
about to drive the car," she said. "Get behind the wheel
and start it up."

"But there's broken glass—"

"Graham!"

"Okay, okay."

Jolaine saw movement behind the SUV that was farthest from her. A crouched bad guy was duckwalking
to get position behind the engine block for better cover.
She didn't see the man as much as she saw the gun barrel. He held it a little too high.

Jolaine switched the selector from semi- to full-auto
and fired a three-round burst into the engine block.
Even the armor-piercing rounds wouldn't penetrate the
thickness of the engine, but they would burrow deeply
enough to disable the motor and to give the guy a religious experience. Just for good measure, she fired an-

other three-round burst through the other SUV. There would likely be survivors among the attackers, and she didn't want them to have a way out.

She had just begun to wonder what Graham was doing when the Mercedes engine turned over and then revved as Graham gave it way too much gas. "Get in!" he yelled. "We're ready."

"Hold on a second," Jolaine replied. That guy behind the fender, and whatever other friends he had left, were a problem. She dared not turn her back on—

There were two of them side by side and they popped up together, their weapons at the ready. They opened fire, on full-auto. They emerged from precisely the spot where Jolaine had been watching, one of them standing into the red dot of her gun sight. She dropped him with a bullet to his chin.

His friend reacted with impressive speed, diving back for cover while the head mist still hung in the air. Jolaine swung her aim and got off a shot, but it wasn't a clean hit. She thought she saw an impact on his shoulder as he fell, but she couldn't be certain. She needed to be certain.

With her M4 at the ready, pressed in tightly and her finger outside the trigger guard, she advanced on the spot where he fell. Behind her, she heard Graham plead for her to get back into the car, his voice squeaky with panic. But their only route out of the parking lot was through these guys, and that would mean driving through the kill zone of an ambush. Unacceptable.

Jolaine had lost track of time since the shoot-out began, but she was confident that it was still under two minutes. The other cars in the parking lot meant that other guests were either watching through windows—a foolish choice—or cowering in corners. Either way, lots of phone calls were being made to 911, and that meant she and Graham were in a hurry.

Impossibly red blood traced rivulets in the uneven pavement of the lot, almost all of it from the ruined head of the first shooter to pop up from behind the second SUV.

"Jolaine, please don't!" Graham cried.

She ignored him. There'd be time to explain later. Now she needed to concentrate on the potential threats. She heard the Mercedes transmission slip into gear and she knew without looking that Graham was backing out of the parking spot to be prepared to drive off. She was fine with that so long as he did not try to pass her.

Or panic and leave me behind. That thought made her regret that she'd crippled the other vehicles.

As she carefully turned the corner around the front bumper of the target SUV, her mind filtered out the hideous sight of the dead man with the exposed brain and instead scanned for signs of the living. She led with her carbine as she whipped around the corner to encounter whatever threat lay beyond.

The second man she'd hit sat against the rear wheel of the vehicle, his legs outstretched, his face gray and twisted in agony. His right arm and the right side of his shirt glistened with blood. She'd hit him harder than she'd thought. His rifle—she saw now that it was an MP5—lay on the ground next to him, and he made no effort to reach for it.

Keeping low, Jolaine kicked the weapon away and turned her attention to the rest of the parking lot, searching for additional targets. Movement close to her rear caused her to whirl, but she broke her aim when she saw that it was Graham with the Mercedes.

She held up her hand to tell him to stop, and said, "Don't move any closer, Graham, and don't get out of the car." Her eyes never stopped scanning all compass points. "Keep an eye out for other people and tell me anything you see."

"We need to go, Jolaine," Graham said. "Please, let's just go."

"Ten seconds," she said. She turned her attention to the wounded man. "Who are you? Why are you attacking us?"

The man moved slowly, as if lifting his head consumed all of his energy. "Not you," he said with a heavy accent that sounded nearly identical to that of Bernard Mitchell. "The boy. The boy will get you killed. We do not care about you."

"Why him? What did he do?"

"He has something that belongs to us," the man said. Bloody froth bubbled at the corners of his mouth, and Jolaine realized that she'd hit his lung. "He has codes."

"What codes?"

The man coughed, launching a pink spray that somehow missed Jolaine. "Don't be a fool. He needs to follow protocol, then this all ends."

"What is going on?" Jolaine said. She heard an edge of desperation in her own voice.

"Follow protocol. Otherwise, everyone else wants to kill him. To kill you, too."

"Everyone," Jolaine repeated. "Who is everyone?"

"Without protocol, everyone is everyone. Russians, Americans, Israelis, Chinese. Everyone."

"But why?"

Sirens grew louder in the distance.

"Please tell me why."

The man managed a laugh that triggered a gout of blood from his mouth. He spat but made no effort to wipe it away. "First you kill me and then you ask for favor," he said. "You have balls. Protocol is your only way to live," he said.

"I don't know what you're talking about."

"Boy knows. Ask him. Go. Go now and run. Live quickly because I think you will die soon."

"Jolaine!" Graham yelled. "They're coming! Don't you hear the sirens?"

She watched the wounded man's smile, his contentment obvious. He'd said all he intended to say, and would be dead in minutes.

Jolaine stood and walked around to the driver's door of the Mercedes. "Out," she said. "I'm driving."

"Thank God," Graham said. He ran to the other side.

His ass had barely touched the seat before she hit the gas and they were on their way.

Protocol is your only way to live.

CHAPTER TWELVE

At one level, Jonathan thought that Venice had the hardest job of all of them. While she didn't get shot at—well, except for that one time—she had the burden of waiting and listening until someone chimed in with a sitrep. Jonathan didn't think he'd be able to do it.

It was nearly four in the afternoon now, and the sun hung high and hot over the gently rolling terrain.

"According to Venice's satellite downloads, this isn't going to be an easy house to find," Jonathan said. He knew they were close, but the unrelenting woods were loath to give up driveways. "What's that up there?" A medical caduceus had been nailed to an otherwise un-remarkable tree.

"I see a cross and tangled snakes," Boxers said. "Doctor shit."

They turned into the drive, through the heavy woods to another turn at another caduceus, and up to the front of the house. A nice place, bigger than he was expect-ing, but nothing remarkable in its two-story design.

"Ready for things to get interesting?" Big Guy asked.

"Soon enough," Jonathan said. "Go to Vox." From this point on, everything they said would be live on the radio, without having to push a transmit button. "Mother Hen, Scorpion," he said.

Ten seconds passed. "Go ahead, Scorpion," Venice said. "I'm here. Nice to hear from you. It's been a while."

"Big Guy and I are home now," Jonathan said, knowing that she'd understand them to be at the target house. "How are your eyes?"

"Still blind," she answered.

Jonathan had been hoping for satellite support from SkysEye, a satellite imagery service established by his now fabulously wealthy former Unit compatriot named Lee Burns. Built with private funds under the auspices of assisting in petroleum exploration, the SkysEye network had proven to be extraordinarily helpful to Jonathan over the course of his freelance years—well worth the staggering price tag—providing nearly military-quality imagery of fine details from a couple hundred miles in the sky.

Given their past relationship, and the nature of the missions upon which Jonathan embarked, Lee Burns typically moved heaven and earth to accommodate his needs. Sometimes, though, the timing just didn't work out. Lee had a business to run, after all, and Jonathan imagined that sometimes it would be hard to tell the representatives of Mega-rich Oil Company that their multimillion-dollar contract would have to wait while the system was repurposed to support an illegal operation.

"Big Guy and I are both on VOX," Jonathan said. "The security plan is hot now." The security plan mandated situation reports—sitreps—every seven minutes, or more frequently if the situation warranted. Translated, that meant that the risks of getting hurt had just multiplied.

"Speak up, Big Guy," Venice said.

"Right here," Boxers replied, thus completing the radio check.

"I'll take the front," Jonathan said, "and you take the back. When we're both in position, I'll knock. If someone answers, we'll play it by ear. If they don't, we'll crash the door."

As an afterthought, Jonathan added, "Mother Hen, before we make a mess here, you are one hundred percent sure that this is the house where the car is registered, right?"

"One thousand percent," Venice replied.

Jonathan looked to Boxers, and Big Guy nodded. "All right, then. Report when you're in place."

As Boxers disappeared toward the black side of the building, Jonathan headed toward the white side. Jonathan estimated the age of the place at around thirty years—old enough to need new fascia board but not so old for the need to be urgent. Having traveled the world several times over, mostly focused on the dirty bits that normal people tried to avoid, he'd seen all different terrains, from the vertical to the flat. It occurred to him as he looked back the way they'd come that this place was just boring.

Jonathan hated approaching a building that he only *suspected* concealed a bad guy. If he knew for a fact that an enemy was in place, he could approach with guns blazing. When less than certain, the mere presence of a firearm could turn a benign situation violent, converting otherwise good guys into bad when they reacted with legitimate fear at the sight of the weapons.

Jonathan walked warily down the weed-infested brick sidewalk with his Colt holstered and concealed by his denim jacket. If needed, he could draw the weapon and have shots downrange in two seconds, but that brought him little comfort. Not many gunfights lasted as long as two seconds.

As he closed the last few feet to the front door, he stopped short as his attention was drawn to the doorjamb. The wood near the dead bolt was splintered, hunks of wood avulsed from the rabbet. The effect was to leave a giant scar of raw, unpainted wood.

It was time to draw down. As he reached for the .45, his earbud popped. "Scorpion, Big Guy," Boxers said. "I've got signs of forced entry back here."

Just like that, everything changed. "Me, too. Are you prepared to crash the door?" Jonathan asked over the air.

"Oh, yeah." It was like asking a kid if he was ready for Christmas.

"On my count," Jonathan said. He gripped the Colt with both hands, thumbed the safety off, and poised it close to his chest, the grip an inch from his breastbone.

"Three . . . two . . . one."

They needed a new car. The Mercedes was still drivable but it had been shot to shit—not suitable for being seen in public.

"Here's what we're going to do," Jolaine said.

"You killed those people," Graham said. His eyes were huge. His hands trembled.

"I'm sorry you had to see that," Jolaine said. "But we've—"

"Don't apologize." He seemed appalled that she would even think such a thing. "You were friggin' amazing. I mean, Christ, they were going to kill us, and you just mowed them down."

Jolaine appreciated the enthusiasm, despite knowing that after the adrenaline wore off, Graham would suffer from the reality of those images.

Grateful that the streets were relatively empty, but fully aware that she and Graham were far from invisible, she whipped the Mercedes into an alley between two buildings that looked underutilized, if not abandoned. The windows had been soaped, and grass grew through cracks in the pavement. It was exactly the kind of industrial neighborhood that one would expect to be served by the Hummingbird Motel. She created her own parking space next to a bulging Dumpster.

"We need to get out," she said. "This car is too obvious." As she spoke, she opened the door. "We need to walk."

"To where?"

"Anywhere but here." She placed the empty Glock back into its holster and covered it with her shirt. "This vehicle is a magnet for cops. We need to buy some time."

Graham pushed his door open as well and stood. "Time to do what?"

"To live a little longer," she said.

"What about the rifle?"

"Leave it. We can't go walking around town with a rifle."

"But your pistol is out of bullets."

Jolaine made a circulating motion with her arm, encouraging Graham to move faster. "Maybe we can find some more. Meanwhile, we've got to get away from here."

He joined her, looking over this shoulder, back at the car. In the distance, the sirens continued. "Shouldn't we wipe it down for fingerprints?"

"It won't matter," Jolaine said. "Our fingerprints are all over everything—the car, the rifle, the motel room. When they find it, they'll know that the car belonged to the people who rented the room. What we hope they won't know is who we really are."

They walked behind a long line of industrial lowrises. The only business that seemed busy was an auto mechanic shop whose employees seemed to avoid eye contact. Jolaine wondered how many of them would scatter if the police came by. The whir of impact wrenches and the pounding of hammers on metal drowned out the sound of sirens. Jolaine considered that a good thing.

"Where are we going?" Graham asked. He kept throwing nervous looks over his shoulder, and in general acting jumpy as hell.

"I need you to walk as if nothing is wrong. The more nervous you look, the more attention you'll draw to yourself. To us."

"That's kind of hard when you know people are trying to kill you."

"Graham, everything is going to be kind of hard until this is settled. You need to trust me."

"I do trust you," he said. Then, with a wry chuckle: "Not that I have a whole lot of choice."

The alley behind the low rises dead-ended at a street without a sign. Jolaine estimated that it ran roughly north-south. She turned right to head north, away from the main drag. Ahead, there was a patch of woods that would provide additional cover. She headed that way.

"Do you know where we're going?" Graham asked.

"Toward the woods. We'll be less readily seen there."

"Is that really a good idea? I mean, I'm not saying I won't go, but aren't they going to dispatch dogs or something pretty soon? If we're just hanging in the woods we'll get caught right away."

He had a very good point, Jolaine thought. She stopped and turned, colliding with Graham.

"Whoa," he said. "What are you doing now?"

"You're right," she said. "We need a car. Come this way." She started back toward the main drag.

Graham trotted to catch up. "And where are we going to get a car?"

She led the way to her answer. The easiest cars to steal—to hotwire and drive away—were of an older vintage, the older the better. It was damn near impossible to hotwire anything made in the past ten years or so—certainly that was beyond Jolaine's limited ability. As luck would have it (it was about time for some *good* luck for a change), the ideal candidate sat parked along the curb outside a low-rent apartment building. It was an old Honda Civic that appeared to have the original paint job, which was to say very little paint at all. Call it red. Maybe brown.

As she approached, Jolaine drew her Leatherman tool from its pouch on her belt and opened it up. In a second stroke of good luck, the driver's door opened when she lifted the handle. That was often the case, she'd been told, when people parked their cars in poorer, crime-ridden areas. It was better to leave the car unlocked and let thieves find out for themselves that there was nothing worth stealing, than to make them break a window to discover the same result.

Once inside, she wondered if the owner actually *hoped* that someone would steal these wheels. The gray cloth seats were worn nearly transparent in the spots where they weren't torn, and the headliner drooped like old cobwebs from the ceiling.

Graham climbed in the opposite door. "Do we really have to be in *this* much of a hurry?"

She ignored him. She folded out the flat-head screwdriver, jammed it into the keyway, and twisted. The engine jumped to life. That done, she stuck the blade into the gap between the steering wheel and the steering column to find the tab that would release the steering wheel lock. That was always the toughest part of this operation. It took a good twenty seconds, but when she found it, she pressed down and the wheel was free.

"There," she said, more to herself than to Graham.

He gaped. "How do you know this shit?"

"I used to hang around with tough people," she said. In reality, she used to hang around with a former SEAL named Darrell, whose youth had introduced him to all levels of thievery. She'd held him in her arms until he bled out and died in some rocky village near J-Bad in Afghanistan whose name she'd forgotten.

She pulled the transmission into drive, and they were on their way. She still didn't know where they were heading, but north seemed right, so she swung a U-turn and headed wherever the road would take them. Canada, maybe, if she could figure out a way to get them some passports.

"Who were those people?" Graham asked. "And why were they shooting at us?"

"You tell me," Jolaine said. She made sure her tone was leaden, devoid of humor.

In her peripheral vision, she saw Graham's head whip around. "What?"

"You heard me," she said. "You tell me why people are trying to kill us."

"How am I supposed to know?"

She cast him a glance, then returned her eyes to the road as she navigated out into the country. Buildings were already becoming sparser. "How do you think?"

"I don't know," he said. "What the hell is wrong with you? How did you become my enemy all of a sudden?"

"The last thing I am is your enemy," Jolaine said. "Tell me about the phone call you made this morning."

"I already told you about that."

"I have it on good authority that you left out some good parts," Jolaine countered. "What did you say?"

"I talked to a creepy guy and I hung up on him."

"But why?"

"I talked to him because my mom asked me to. I hung up on him because he was creepy. What aren't you understanding?"

Jolaine settled herself. Getting frustrated or getting angry would only be counterproductive. "Please try not to be obtuse," she said. "You talked with the creepy guy, you said something, and then all of a sudden the world is trying to shoot us. Last night, they were shooting at your parents. I don't think it's a coincidence that your mother filled your head with some secret thing and a phone number, and now our lives are in jeopardy." She paused and glared through his head. "What do you have, Graham? What justifies all of this?"

"I don't know."

"Bullshit. You know I'm risking my life for you, right? I could drop you off on the side of the road and let you fend for yourself. No one wants to hurt *me* because of what I know. They only want to hurt me because of my association with *you*." It felt good to utter the truth, even though she took no pleasure in hurting him.

"Let me off, then," he said. She'd triggered his defiant streak, always a mistake.

"That's not the point, Graham, and it's not going to happen. You know that. My job is to protect you. And yes, it's to protect me, too. But you owe me what you know."

"I promised my mom not to tell anybody but the guy on the phone."

"And how's that working for you?"

"I wasn't supposed to tell him over the phone. It could only be in person."

Jolaine slapped the steering wheel. "Goddammit, Graham, whatever she told you is the reason we're running for our lives."

"You don't know that. Mom told me that the only way to escape alive was to follow the protocol."

"What protocol?"

"I don't know!" he shouted. "Okay? I don't know what any of this is about."

"But you do know something," Jolaine insisted. "The man on the ground outside his car—"

He shouted, "3155AX475598CVRLLPAHQ449833 D0Z."

Jolaine reared back in her seat. "What?"

"You asked me and I just told you," Graham said. "That's what's on the piece of paper. That's what Mom told me. Do you want to know the phone number, too?"

No, she didn't. What kind of code—

"It's completely random," Graham said. "I don't see any pattern, the repeats are insignificant. There's no dictionary code that I can find, and while I was alone in the motel, I tried to find some kind of Bible code, but couldn't. Did you know they have a free Bible in the nightstand?"

Jolaine wasn't interested in nibbling at the Gideon bait. "Say the code again," she said.

"Why? Would you know if I missed something?"

There was the petulance that she'd come to know so well over the years. But he also raised a good point. "You mean, you really can remember all of that."

He repeated the code. "Ask me in three hours or five days, and it'll still be the same."

"How?"

"The shrinks at school say it's my *gift*." The way he leaned on that word told her that he considered it to be anything but. "I just remember every friggin' thing. Numbers are easiest and names are hardest."

Jolaine processed all of that. At least, she tried to

process it. "So, it's numbers and letters," she said. "What do they mean?"

"I don't know!" His voice squeaked with frustration. "And I swear to God I'm telling the truth. I asked her, and she told me not to worry about it. She said I didn't need to know what it meant. I only needed to remember it. So, now I've got this shit in my head, and a *protocol* to follow—whatever that means—and people are trying to kill me. Are we having fun yet?"

Something about his delivery made her believe him. He seemed genuinely bewildered by it all.

"What did the wounded guy say to you?" Graham asked.

Jolaine sensed the turnaround was an honesty check, and she wondered if the boy had done it on purpose.

"He said if you follow the protocol, all of this will end."

Graham shrank in his seat. "So, I should have just talked with him. But you told me—"

"Don't draw the wrong conclusion," Jolaine said. "I'm not sure you did the wrong thing, and I'm *really* not sure that sharing that code—whatever it means— would do anything to take us off whatever hit lists we're on."

"What are you saying?"

Jolaine sighed again as she weighed the propriety of going where this conversation was leading them. *Screw it. In for a dime . . .*

"I don't want you to panic about what I'm going to say—"

"Oh, crap."

"—or even overly stress. But think about it. Those

numbers and letters—that code—are what the people attacking us want. If it's worth killing for, then it's worth killing to protect after it's revealed."

"I don't understand."

"*Think*," she said. "You possess a code that people *really* want to have. That's motivation to keep you alive. But once you reveal the code to the people who want it, that motivation goes away." She pulled up at a stop sign, came to a full halt, and then moved on. Little towns were famous for speed traps and overzealous cops.

Graham shook his head. "No, that can't be right. Those people in the parking lot a few minutes ago weren't trying to save me. They were trying to kill me."

"I'm not sure that's true," Jolaine said. "I think they may have been there to kidnap you. I think we surprised them by shooting back. In fact, I'm convinced of it."

"So, what does that mean?" Graham asked. "To us, that is."

Jolaine considered the question. "It means that we can't trust anyone about anything." She wasn't sure that she could connect the dots verbally, but she gave it a try. "Whatever the code does—I assume it unlocks something secret and important, else why have a code in the first place?—it makes sense to me that it was as important to your parents to have it as it was for the shooters to guarantee that they didn't get it."

"Or maybe the shooters wanted it for themselves," Graham offered.

That was good. He was on the same page as she. "Extrapolating out, then," Jolaine continued, "whichever side wins in the struggle, the other side is going to want to destroy the code."

Graham leaned his head back into the headrest and closed his eyes. "And the code lives in my head," he said. He lolled his head over to look at Jolaine. "This is really, really bad, isn't it?"

CHAPTER THIRTEEN

At this point in monitoring an operation, not much could pull Venice's attention from her team's radio traffic. The alert bell on her computer was one of them. The bell meant that based on the parameters she had established to track the actions of Jolaine Cage and Graham Mitchell, ICIS had found something worth reporting. She pulled up the screen, and her heart skipped. The police had been dispatched to a shoot-out in the parking lot of the Hummingbird Motel in Napoleon, Ohio. Multiple reports to the emergency operations center of machine gun fire with people dead in the street. Police were on their way.

This was not the time to interrupt Jonathan with such a new development—if ever there was a time for uninterrupted concentration, it was when he was about to crash a door—but she needed more details.

Generally speaking, ICIS ran five to ten minutes behind real time. It was a great way to dial in to fairly obscure events, but when something was this high profile, local television news was often the fastest route to a thorough overview. Reporters might not get the nuances correct in the early moments, but these days every station with more than ten kilowatts of power had its own fleet of helicopters, and they would shoot each other out of the sky to air the first live feed of a crime scene.

A CBS affiliate had a bird near the scene. Other networks had franchises in the area, but she'd long ago hacked the code to access the live feeds for CBS—their video was transmitted in real time, in unedited form—so whenever possible, she went there first.

At any given moment, dozens of live feeds flooded news networks from all over the world. They didn't just beam from their own camera operations, either. Newsrooms monitored the feeds from every competitor, as well as those from Al Jazeera and BBC, and God only knew how many other news organizations. That required a fair amount of sifting, but she'd done this enough times before that she made fairly quick work of it.

ICIS dinged again. Police units were on the scene, and they confirmed six dead, with several of the motel guests unaccounted for. Officers were in the process of interviewing witnesses.

The no-coincidences rule lived on. Venice already knew who was on the other side of that gunfight, and because the original reports made no mention of a wounded child—always the headline, even for cops—she knew that at a minimum, Graham was well enough to not to have died on the spot.

The video feed she'd selected showed images from too far away as the news chopper approached the scene and the cameraman sharpened his focus.

Venice wondered if the police had connected the same dots that she had, that the suspected child abuse call from the previous night was linked to this incident.

If so, it hadn't gone up on ICIS yet. She assumed that she was ahead of the police, at least for now. The thought brought her comfort, if only for the bragging rights.

In her ear, she heard Jonathan's voice say, "The security plan is hot now." Without looking, she tapped the button on the top of the digital timer that would count down seven minutes.

She keyed the mike on her radio. "Speak up, Big Guy."

"Right here."

She turned back to her computer screens while Digger and Boxers discussed the logistics of their entry plan. First, she pulled up the police report from the suspected pedophile incident to verify the room number where it occurred. She wasn't sure yet what to do with that tidbit of information, but she'd learned over the years that information collected one tidbit at a time eventually combined to be a chunk of useful stuff.

The news feed on her other screen had settled down to something viewable. She saw two SUVs arranged in a kind of haphazard formation in the middle of the motel's parking lot. Their doors were all open, and bodies lay on the ground next to the vehicles. As was frequently the case with the early moments of video news collection, the camera operator zoomed in as tightly as he could on the faces of the victims and their wounds. These were the more prurient details that the general public would never see, and she wondered if newsroom personnel secretly grooved on the gore.

Venice had hoped that the location of the victims relative to the PCs' motel room would provide some insight, but that turned out to be a disappointment. The layout of the place was such that about half of the rooms were all more or less equidistant from any one spot in the parking lot.

So, she thought, what could she do with the room number before the police could? What would they want to check? Obviously, they'd do all the physical forensics stuff—fingerprints, DNA, et cetera—but that had to be done on-site. What could she do from—

"The phone." She said it aloud and grinned. She could check the phone records! Okay, it was a long shot because they'd be out of their minds to use a hotel phone. But in the years she'd worked with Jonathan, she'd lost track of the number of forehead-smack dumb things people had done. There was always a chance.

Accessing said records could be a challenge, but what was life without the occasional challenge?

Jonathan didn't even bother with the knob. He knew at a glance that the lock was demolished, that the door was held in place only by inertia. With his weapon poised, he gently shouldered the door open and let it drift in of its own momentum. Elsewhere in the house, presumably from somewhere in the back, he heard a giant crash and knew that Boxers had taken a less subtle approach.

"I'm in," Big Guy said in Jonathan's ear.

"Me, too," Jonathan said. "Report everything you see."

"How about what I smell?" Boxers said. "I don't see any flies yet, but they can't be too far behind."

Jonathan smelled it, too, and it was a stench unique to death. Sweet in the most awful, perverted form of the term—like rotten meat, but with hints of shit and piss. To the uninitiated, it was a smell that triggered a gag reflex. Sadly, Jonathan thought, he'd smelled it often enough that it was no more offensive than charred wood, gun oil, or any of the dozens of other pungent smells that were part of his professional world.

Dead was dead. If no one touched a corpse, it would eventually turn to dust right where it lay, never posing another threat to anyone. What *was* a threat, however, was whatever person or thing had caused the dead person to die.

Jonathan knew that the bad guy was already gone in this case. The strength of the death smell made it certain that the killings had occurred hours ago. Still, he refused to lower his guard. In his experience, complacent operators died younger than paranoid ones.

The house showed no sign of violence, at least not yet. The owner of the place was clearly of significant means, though the interior was far more impressive than the exterior. Somehow, what appeared to be maybe twenty-five hundred square feet from the outside felt more like five thousand once he was in. Maybe it was all the marble and polished wood. Certainly, this was not the home of a man who wished to fly under the radar. In Jonathan's world, plain vanilla equated to survivability.

"The foyer is clear," Jonathan said as he swept the area with his pistol. Without looking, he used his foot to push the front door closed again. Behind closed curtains, the lights were on, so the main floor remained brightly lit. Did that mean that the violence here happened at night?

"I'm stepping into the main hall," Boxers said. Jonathan heard it simultaneously over the radio and through reverb against the walls. That was Big Guy's way of making sure Jonathan didn't shoot him.

"I'm checking the front rooms," Jonathan said. The first room to the left off the marble circle was the dining room. Keeping his weapon in play, he stepped in and pivoted like a gun turret, his .45 poised and ready to shoot. No targets showed themselves. "Dining room's clear," he said.

Beyond the dining room lay a butler's pantry and beyond that, he assumed, a kitchen. He heard Boxers moving around in there, so Jonathan stayed to the front and crossed the foyer to what he imagined they called a living room. Maybe a parlor in this part of the world. A sofa and two chairs flanked a very traditional fireplace. It, too, was clear, and he announced it as such right after Boxers declared the kitchen to be clear of bad guys.

Jonathan returned to the central hallway to head deeper into the house. "I'm coming your way, Big Guy," he said.

The death stench skyrocketed as he passed the massive stairway to the second floor, causing him to pause and look around more. Where the hell was it coming from? He saw no blood on the floor, no signs of a struggle.

He moved on. Past the stairway, the foyer gave way to a cross hall, where Jonathan and Boxers joined together to clear a warren of rooms that showed no signs of people or violence. As time went on, Jonathan felt progressively safer. He didn't reholster the .45, but he eased his stance to low-ready.

"I believe this is what we call a McMansion," Big

Guy said. "Or what you would have called the servants' quarters growing up."

They found a back stairway to the second floor, climbed it, and explored the bedrooms.

Up here, things turned ugly. There were no signs of struggle in the master bedroom, but the other two bedrooms were wrecks. Both bore the standard décor and detritus of mid-grade children, one a boy and one a girl. Covers were strewn across the floor, as if their occupants had been dragged out of bed. In the boy's room, the entire contents of the top of the dresser—a lamp, a television, a bunch of action figures—had been pulled to the floor. In Jonathan's mind, he could see a kid trying to grab hold of the dresser and being pulled along anyway.

Boxers made a growling sound.

"Yeah," Jonathan agreed.

Beyond the signs of violence, and a couple of spots that might have been blood on the walls and the carpet, the second floor was empty. They holstered their weapons more or less in unison and headed back to the first floor via the main stairs. Here, the putrid smell was at its worst.

Jonathan stopped. "Where's the basement?" he asked. "I never saw steps to the basement."

"Maybe there isn't one," Boxers said, though clearly he didn't believe that to be true.

"Gotta be," Jonathan said. "I walked on those floors down there. Those hardwoods are not on a slab."

"Scorpion, Mother Hen," Venice's voice said in his ear. Scared the shit out of him. "There is definitely a basement."

The two men exchanged smiles and continued to the

first floor. "Found the building plans, did you?" he said, stealing her thunder.

"I did," she said. "According to the drawings, there's a door to the basement in the wall under the curved part of the main staircase."

"And to think we missed something so obvious," Boxers said.

"That was sarcasm, wasn't it?" Venice said.

"Yeah, just a little bit."

On the main level again, Boxers and Jonathan stood together at the spot where the door should be, but a decorative bench sat crosswise at the spot, under a huge painting of red flowers against a black background. The painting was maybe five feet wide by eight feet tall, and now that he looked at it—really *looked* at it, as opposed to noticing it through his peripheral vision—Jonathan thought that it looked out of place.

"Damn, that's a big painting," he said.

"Almost big enough to be a door, isn't it?"

Together, they dragged the bench out of the way to gain better access, and saw why the bench was there in the first place. It disguised the bottom two feet of what was most definitely a door.

Jonathan ran his fingers down the back side of the left edge frame, expecting to find some kind of latch, but when none was there, he pulled. He felt some give, so he pulled harder. On the third tug, he heard a *thunk,* and the picture floated away from the wall, suspended by a recessed hinge on the right-hand edge.

"Look what you did," Boxers said.

"The door is masked by a painting," Jonathan said for Venice's benefit.

That door led to a second door immediately behind it, but the second door was locked.

"Step away," Boxers said. "I can open that." He took a preparatory step back, prepared for a kick.

"Stop!" Jonathan said, raising his hand. "Look." He'd found the buttons for the elevator, recessed into the jamb. This was definitely a custom-built job, much larger than most household elevators.

Boxers looked disappointed that he didn't get to kick anything. They both drew their pistols again.

The instant Jonathan pushed the button, the elevator began to hum, and the floor vibrated. Together, through shared instinct, the two men flanked the door. It never made sense to stand in front of a closed door.

"We're going off VOX," Jonathan said, and he flipped the appropriate switch on his radio. This was a time of high concentration. He didn't need the distraction of knowing that he was broadcasting live.

Jonathan could tell from the hissing of the mechanism that the elevator operated on hydraulics, and that the basement was either very deep, or the elevator moved very slowly. A bump announced the car's arrival on the first floor.

"How do you want to handle it?" Boxers asked.

"You pull and I'll shoot," Jonathan said.

Since Boxers was on the hinge side of the door, it made sense that he would nab the knob and pull it toward himself while Jonathan took a position in front of the expanding opening. Jonathan prayed that all he'd see was empty elevator car.

His prayers were answered. But the stench of decay, driven by the breeze of the opening door, hit him like a wall. Blood smears painted the floor of the car. And when he looked behind him, back into the foyer, he could see evidence that someone had cleaned blood from the floor out there.

Boxers recoiled from it. "Ah, shit. I'm gonna have nothing but nightmares, aren't I?"

With a growing sense of dread, Jonathan led the way into the elevator car, closed the door, and pressed the down button, triggering another bump and another hum. Jonathan found himself breathing through his mouth as they descended.

"I don't expect to find any threat," Jonathan said. "But—"

"We've got to be prepared," Boxers said, finishing his sentence for him. "We've danced this number a few times, you know." His Beretta M9 hung by his thigh.

When the elevator settled on the basement floor, Jonathan steeled himself with a deep breath—through his mouth—and reached for the doorknob. "You ready?"

"No."

Jonathan understood that to mean yes. "All right, here we go." With his pistol held high, nearly under his chin, Jonathan dropped to his right knee and pushed open the door. "Ah, shit." Even without looking, he knew that this was the kill room.

He stepped out of the elevator into a modern medical suite, complete with blinding lights and stainless-steel everything. He recognized it right away as a clandestine hospital, a place where government agencies sent patients for treatment that never officially happened. The suite explained the opulence of the house, as well. Uncle Sam did a shitload of things wrong, but when it came to taking care of his damaged covert operators, no expense was spared, no corner cut. Jonathan himself had had a foot or two of colon removed in one such place not all that long ago.

"This is not what I expected," Boxers said, taking in the details.

Coming off the elevator, there was only one direction to turn, and that was to the right. Jonathan led the way, as he always did because of his relative size. Ahead and to the right lay a brightly lit operatory, its curtains pulled wide open. The blood-smear motif continued on the floors, though less concentrated than in the elevator.

Jonathan approached cautiously, with Big Guy half a step behind him.

There was no way he could have prepared himself for what he saw as he button-hooked the corner.

CHAPTER FOURTEEN

Venice fist-pumped the air. The fugitives had in fact made a phone call from their motel room. She didn't know the content, of course, but she did have the number they called and the duration of the conversation. It was a Michigan number, from the greater Detroit metropolitan area, and the conversation lasted for just a little over six minutes.

"Why would they do that?" she asked aloud. "Why would Jolaine allow that to happen?" She was supposed to be smart about such things.

The fact that the call went to Detroit rang a big warning bell. Michigan sported a greater concentration of Muslims per square foot than anywhere else in the country, and as much as Venice knew in her heart and in her brain that the vast majority of Muslims were wonderful, peace-loving people, she was enough of a realist to embrace the fact that the religion also fielded the lion's share of the world's terrorists.

"Stop it," she said. "Let the facts drive the conclusions." It was one of the most important lessons she'd learned from her boss: always sideline presumptions until such time as they can be supported by facts.

Right now, the only fact she knew was that a phone call had been made, and that wasn't necessarily a causal link to anything. At least not yet.

The link materialized about thirty seconds later, when she cross-referenced the time of the call to Detroit with the time of the first calls to 911 to report the shooting. Less than thirty minutes' difference. That raised the coincidence to the level of undeniability. The call triggered the shoot-out.

How?

"By tipping their hand to their location." Venice often talked her way through difficult problems. Somehow, when she heard her voice say the words, her thoughts fell into place more easily.

"And that makes the person on the other end of the phone a bad guy!" She supposed it was obvious from the beginning, but it felt like a real *ta-da* moment.

"Okay, Mr. Bad Guy," she said. "Who are you?"

The number traced to a physical address in Highland Park, Michigan—another surprise, because if Venice were going to be a bad guy, she'd use only disposable cell phones. The fact that he didn't could mean any number of things, but in this case, she assumed that he was a rookie at this terrorism thing. There was a lot of that going on around the world now.

The address in Highland Park was an apartment rented to Muhammad Kontig, who, according to the databases that Venice could access most quickly, was something of a nobody. Certainly, he was not on any of the publicly accessible terror watch lists, and he didn't have a known criminal record.

Not that that meant anything. It just reinforced her first thought that the guy was a rookie. He owned a car, though, and the car had a license plate number that traced to a two-year-old Chevy Impala. Beyond that, she had nothing.

It was time to bring Jonathan into the loop.

The room in the farthest corner of the basement hospital suite was a slaughterhouse. All but the deepest pools of blood on the floor had coagulated. Great fans of blood reached high on the walls, with even a few spatters on the ceiling.

"Jesus Christ," Boxers said. He sounded like he had a bad cold. Like Jonathan, he had developed a knack for using his soft palate to shut off his smeller. It was a skill that had saved Jonathan from a lot of puking.

At first glance, the bodies were unrecognizable, just lumps amid the gore. Upon closer examination, though, Jonathan noticed that the body that sat tied into the hard-backed chair—he guessed it was stolen from a dining room and brought down—was that of a naked female, and that the body trussed to the cylindrical steel ceiling support was that of a middle-aged man. Three other men lay dead of bullet wounds to the head.

It was the sight of the children that turned his stomach. A preteen boy and a younger preteen girl sagged against the wall opposite the man, each of them bound and mutilated. This wasn't so much the scene of torture as it was the scene of ritual murder.

Jonathan had seen too many horrible sights to even catalog them, let alone rate them in order of awfulness, but this one was beyond the pale.

"Whoever did this wanted information that came too slowly," Boxers said. "Looks to me like they tortured the kids in front of the parents."

"I bet one parent," Jonathan said. "I think the lady is Sarah Mitchell. This is a covert hospital. She came here to be treated, but the bad guys caught up to her."

"And who, exactly, *are* the bad guys?" Boxers asked.

"I don't know," Jonathan said. "But I have every intention of finding out."

"So long as I get to pull the trigger," Boxers said. Big Guy had a thing for kids in jeopardy. Jonathan had never asked the questions to pursue it further, but there had to be something in Boxers' past that made him particularly homicidal when it came to protecting kids. All things considered, it was hard to think of that as anything but a strength.

"Are you okay?" Jonathan asked.

Big Guy puffed out a little. "I'm fine," he said. Lest anyone doubt, Big Guy was far too tough to be affected by something so simple as a couple of gutted kids. "Like I said, I get dibs on pulling the trigger on whoever did this."

Jonathan said nothing for long enough to draw Boxers' gaze.

"I got this, Dig."

Jonathan acknowledged his friend with a quick nod. "You say you've got it, you've got it." Part of the job was to accept reality for what it was, free of the demonstrative emotion that defined humanity. For Jonathan and Boxers, the job required an ability to project false normalcy.

Jonathan keyed the mike on his radio. "Mother Hen, I think we've found Sarah Mitchell and Doctor Wilkerson," he said on the air. Boxers had already pulled a camera from his pocket to take pictures of the bodies. "We'll have images coming to you in a few seconds. Prepare yourself. They're pretty awful."

"They've definitely been tortured," Boxers said. "Look at this. The lady's had her skin peeled away, and the guy on the floor looks like his legs and arms are broken."

Jonathan walked out of the room. He'd take Big Guy's word for it. "Take care not to leave any trace," he said. Sooner or later, these bodies were going to be found by law enforcement personnel, and the last thing they needed was to leave evidence that could be traced back to either of them.

Thanks to the work they'd done in their previous lives for Uncle Sam, no record existed of either Jonathan or Boxers. No fingerprints, no DNA, no hair samples, no pictures, no anything. Jonathan harbored no fear of being identified through forensics. He did, however, worry about someone connecting the dots of various "crime scenes"—every hostage rescue done in the private sector technically violated the law—and creating a road map of sorts for curious reporters or prosecutors. If that happened, and the various pieces of the puzzle were tracked around the world, the emerging profile would threaten everything.

Even when the chances of getting caught were infinitesimal, it paid to take precautions.

"I don't know where we're going," Jolaine said. "East for now. We're putting distance between us and last night."

"Do you think those cops last night know who we are?" Graham sat in the front passenger seat with both legs drawn up beneath his butt.

"I think if they did, we would have been stopped by now," Jolaine explained. "I think we got a bye."

"At the motel," he said. "Did they really think we were . . . lovers?" He snorted out a laugh, but Jolaine knew that he secretly lusted after her. In all fairness, though, fourteen-year-olds lusted after any girl with a heartbeat.

"Actually, no," she said. "I think they suspected prostitution." As soon as she said it, she knew she'd made a mistake.

He laughed. "Ha! They thought you were a hooker!"

Jolaine smirked and let his laughter peak before she said, "Feel better?"

"A little bit, yeah."

"Well consider this," she said, shooting him a glance over the console. "You were the one without any clothes on. I think they thought *you* were the hooker."

"*What?*" The look of horror was everything she'd hoped for.

"Sure," she said. "There are boy whores just like there are girl whores."

Graham laughed again. "Paid to have sex. Huh. I might have found my career plan."

She laughed in spite of herself. "I don't think it's the carnal carnival that you think it would be," she said.

"I'd get *paid*," he reiterated. "To have *sex*. How could it get better than that?"

How should she put this? "You watch cop shows," she said. "Do you know what the police call prostitutes' customers?"

It took him a few seconds. "Johns, right?"

She tilted her head and waited for him to get it.

"Oh," he said. "You mean dudes?"

"I mean dudes," she said. Beyond the windows, farmland continued to expand. Inside, the stink of mildew from the upholstery was beginning to irritate her eyes. "And not to be unkind, I'm not sure what a boy your age would have to offer to a more . . . experienced woman."

"Like you, you mean."

Okay, this conversation just crossed the line into weirdness. She started to answer, but didn't know what to say.

Graham sensed the hesitation and went for the gold. "First of all, you obviously haven't peeked at me in the shower."

"Oh, good God."

"No, I mean seriously," he said. "We're talking eight or nine inches." He held out his hands marking the appropriate separation.

She'd opened the door for bullshit guy banter, and she knew from her years with Sandbox boys barely older than Graham that the banter quickly became self-perpetuating.

"Plus, I'm young," he went on. "I have stamina."

"Is that what you call it?" she countered, rising to the bait. "Is stamina the reason why your right arm is so much bigger than your left?"

Graham laughed hard, loving this. "Jolaine!" he mocked. "You're talking dirty to me." He made a muscle. "Wow, it *is* big, isn't it? My arm, I mean."

Jolaine made a chopping motion in the air. "Okay," she said. "That's it. We're done with this topic."

Graham fell silent, but pantomimed two-handed masturbation of something the girth of a two-liter soda bottle.

"Graham!" she snapped through her laughter.

"Oh. Oh. Oh, almost there."

She smacked his arm. "Stop!"

He retreated against the door. "Oh, yeah, baby. Beat me. Make it hurt."

She repeated the chopping motion. "Okay, you win," she said. "Just please make it stop."

Graham still seemed spun up for more, but he controlled himself. All that was left was the residual laughter. Somewhere inside all the adolescent swagger and attitude, there resided a pretty decent kid, she thought. A handsome kid beyond the gangliness, with dark hair, bright brown eyes, and a quick smile when he deigned to employ it.

The silence after the laughter didn't last long, but it brought a palpable drop in the mood.

"How will you know when we've gone far enough?" Graham asked.

"I don't know," she said. Again, it was tough not to sugarcoat things for him. "I hope that—oh, shit." A flash of blue and red drew her attention to her rearview mirror. A jolt of adrenaline lit her up like a horse kick.

A cop car was on her tail, demanding that she pull over. As she eased to the shoulder, she tossed her pistol onto the floor of the backseat. She pulled to a stop.

Graham looked horrified. "Jesus, Jolaine, what's happening?"

Jolaine didn't look at him as she said, "Do whatever they tell you to do. It's going to be scary. They're going to have their guns drawn."

In one fast eruption of panic, Graham thumbed the seat belt and flung it away. He rose to his knees and peered out the back window.

"No!" Jolaine yelled, but it was too late.

Graham understood the instant he saw the two cops react to his movement. They flung open both cruiser doors and ducked behind them for cover. They had their guns in their hands, and they looked ready to shoot.

"Shit!" Graham shouted, and he ducked for cover.

"No," Jolaine said. She continued to sit tall in her seat, her hands poised at ten and two on the steering wheel, as if mocking a bitchy driver's ed teacher. "Sit up," she said. "Keep your back to them and sit so they can see you."

"The hell I will. They've got guns!"

"Graham, do what I tell you. Of course they have guns. They're cops."

Graham pressed himself harder against the floor. "I'm not going to get myself shot."

"Please listen to me, Graham," Jolaine said. "What you're doing is what's going to get us shot. The police don't like sudden movement, and they sure as hell don't like people ducking out of sight after they've been seen."

As if to confirm the point, a booming voice, propelled by a loudspeaker, said from behind, "In the car. Sit up and be seen. Keep your hands visible."

"We need to run, Jolaine," Graham said. "This is about the killings. We can't just give up. You said yourself that we can't trust—"

"I also told you that you *had* to trust *me*. You said that you would." She glanced back into the mirror. "We can't outrun a radio. Running will just make it harder on us."

"How do we even know that they're real cops?"

Jolaine hesitated. She hadn't thought of that.

Graham drove his point home: "Aren't we just making it easier for them to kill us?" He rose from the floor to the cushion of the shotgun seat, but he slumped way down, careful not to expose himself.

Was he right? she wondered. Was this really the end if they surrendered?

"Come on," he said. "Give us a chance."

"Respond to my orders," the cop's voice boomed. "Do not make this worse for yourselves. Do not escalate this to a level where you don't want it to go."

Jolaine's shoulders fell. The cop was right.

Graham made his last pitch. "I thought your job was to protect me," he said. "So now you're just going to give up and get me killed?"

"Here's what I need you to do," Jolaine said, "and

listen carefully because we don't have much time before they're on us. When they come, do everything they say. Follow every order, and do not resist. They're probably going to hurt you when they put the handcuffs on, but that will just be to get a rise out of you, an excuse to charge you for resisting. It's a favorite trick when arresting kids your age. Do not give them the satisfaction. Just let them do what they're going to do."

Graham felt his breathing taking off like a steam engine. "But Jolaine—"

"Listen. To. Me. They're going to ask you questions. I don't have any idea what they're going to be, but they're going to ask them. Don't lie, but don't confirm or deny anything. I mean *nothing,* understand?"

Shit no, he didn't understand. He didn't have a goddamn clue about a single goddamn thing that was going on.

Jolaine didn't wait for an answer. "I cannot emphasize that point enough. Everything that has happened since last night—everything at your house, and in the car and in the doctor's place and at the motel—represents the key to everything."

"Do they know that I know about the code?"

"I don't think so," Jolaine said. "These are local police. I don't think that local police would know about that. The code would be more of a concern for the feds."

Graham's stomach flipped again. "Then it has to be about the shooting in the parking lot."

"Maybe, maybe not. Say nothing about that."

"I get it!" Graham shouted. "Don't say anything about any—"

"We are not telling you again," the cop boomed over the loudspeaker. "You in the passenger seat. Sit up straight and let me see your hands."

"Look," Jolaine said. The rhythm of her words had increased, almost to the point where they were indecipherable, like the guy who reads the disclaimers at the end of car commercials. "There are different groups of information. There's what the police don't know, what they do know, what they think they know, and what they want to know. You won't be able to tell from them which is which. So your best bet is to say nothing."

He found himself trembling. "Can I tell them my name?"

"Do you have identification on you?"

"No."

"Then if they don't have it, I wouldn't give it to them."

"So I just sit there and say nothing."

"If you can get away with it, yes."

"Isn't that going to piss them off?"

She nailed him with her eyes. "First, you wanted me to start a high-speed chase, and now you're worried about pissing them off with silence?"

He started to answer, then stopped. "I hope you know what you're doing," he said, and he sat up.

"I assure you that I do not," Jolaine said.

"Hands in the air!" the cop yelled.

Graham did as he was told, pressing his palms into the roof liner. "What are you going to do about the gun?" he asked.

Her eyes softened. "Not touch it," she said. "Oddly

enough, in this part of the world, having the gun is one element of the law that we haven't broken."

Jolaine's eyes darkened, and he could see that she was focusing on a spot beyond him. "Here they come. Good luck, Graham. Do your best."

"At what?"

Graham's peripheral vision caught sight of a uniformed cop just beyond his window, his gun drawn and pointed at Graham's right ear.

The same voice as before boomed over the loudspeaker, "You are surrounded. We do not want to kill you, but we will not hesitate to do so. Do exactly as we say."

Graham saw movement on his left now as another uniformed cop revealed himself. This one had a rifle pressed against his shoulder, with the muzzle leveled at Jolaine.

"Driver, do not move!" the voice of God commanded from behind. "Keep your hands where they are."

Graham's sense of fairness was offended by the fact that she got to rest her hands on the steering wheel while he had to hold his in the air.

"In the passenger seat, keep your right hand in the air, and reach with your left hand to open the door."

It took Graham a few seconds to process the stage directions. "Okay," he said aloud, "I can do this." Keeping his right hand held aloft, he leaned to the left, across Jolaine, and reached for the driver's door handle, which was at least five inches beyond his reach.

Jolaine pushed him away. "What are you doing?"

"Freeze!" He heard the command as a unison chorus from three different sides. "Sit up, asshole!" one of them yelled. "Sit up, or I swear to God I'll shoot you in the head!"

Graham froze. What did they want him to do, freeze or sit up? Why were they yelling in the first place, when he was doing exactly what they'd told him to do?

"Good God, Graham," Jolaine said.

"What? I'm doing—"

The passenger door opened, and a talon of a hand closed around Graham's ankle. They pulled him feet-first across the seat. The effect was to force him to fall back across the gearshift. As he felt himself sliding along on his side, he realized that very soon, his shoulders would be free of any support, and that gravity was quickly destined to become his enemy. He flopped over onto his back, figuring that having the back of his head flop down onto the concrete was a better option than going face-first. He'd spent too many years in braces to smash out all his teeth.

The impact to the back of his head wasn't as bad as he'd feared, but it was hard enough to ignite stars behind his eyes. On his back now, on the ground—it felt like the street, actually—he held his hands up and splayed his fingers. "Dude, look," he said. "I'm not fighting."

"Gun!"

Someone must have seen the pistol on the floor. It was important enough for a kick into Graham's ribs, propelling the air out of his lungs and launching a lightning bolt of pain from his pelvis to his jaw. He yelled.

"Shut up," someone said as they rolled him onto his face and pulled his hands behind his back just a few clicks further than his shoulders were designed to accommodate. "You ain't felt nothing yet."

Something cold and hard impacted the sweet spot between his thumb and his wrist bone, the nerve that apparently connected his thumbnail to his elbow, because that was the path the lightning bolt took. He heard the ratcheting sound of the handcuffs, and he understood that Jolaine had been right on the money. Then he wondered how she could know such things. Had she been arrested before?

The process of shackling his left hand hurt less than his right, and fifteen seconds later, Graham Mitchell was completely immobilized. Despite his efforts to keep his head arched up away from the black pavement, he was certain that there'd be road rash on his cheeks, chin, and lips.

"On your feet, kid," someone said, and his arms were pulled tight behind him. The pulling continued until he was leveraged up to his knees. From there, they gave him five seconds or so to find his balance and stand.

On the other side of the car, Jolaine lay pressed face-down over the hood, her arms behind her and cuffed. One of the beefier cops kept her pressed against the metal hood with the pressure of a horseshoe grip around the base of her skull. To his right, at the head of the vehicle, a cop—good God, where did they all come from?—displayed Jolaine's pistol like a friggin' Stanley Cup trophy, holding it aloft so that everyone could see it.

Graham heard light applause from somewhere, but

he had no idea who it was or where it was coming from. All he knew was they were happy, and he was terrified.

When Jolaine looked up and made eye contact, she was crying.

CHAPTER FIFTEEN

"**S**corpion, Mother Hen." Venice's voice in his ear startled him.

"Go ahead."

"We have a problem," she said.

"Of course we do," Jonathan quipped. Murphy—of Murphy's Law—was a prophet. Whatever could go wrong would in fact go wrong at precisely the worst possible moment. "What is it?"

"I just got a hit on ICIS that Jolaine Cage has been arrested in Lambertville, Michigan."

Jonathan's stomach fell. The day had just become vastly more complicated. "What about the boy? About Graham?"

"Also in custody," Venice said. "He's at a police station, but that might only be until he can be transferred to a foster home."

"That *might* be the case, or it *is* the case?"

"As of now, all we know is that he's in custody at the police station."

Jonathan was interested in dealing only with facts.

Conjecture was the same thing as wild-ass guess, and soothsaying had never been his long suit. "What was the arresting agency?" Jonathan asked.

"Local police. No charges have been filed."

"Stand by," Jonathan said. He stepped into the elevator. The corpses would be just as dead three hours from now as they were right now. The arrests, on the other hand, were a dynamic, developing situation that needed immediate attention.

Plus, he could talk on the phone outside the doctor's house, and avoid the stink.

"I don't understand," Jonathan said as he stepped into the foyer. "How can she be arrested but not charged?"

Venice explained, "At least no charge has been entered into the public record. Maybe because it was a federal warrant. Interstate flight to avoid prosecution."

"Do we know yet what prosecution they're allegedly avoiding?"

"No."

Jonathan considered the moving parts. Since he wasn't a cop, he didn't have intimate knowledge of the procedures used for taking people into custody, but he knew when something didn't feel right. In the context of people trying to kill other people, it was a feeling that often spelled tragedy.

"I don't like this," Jonathan said. "Download the coordinates of both locations to my GPS. We're going to—where is it?"

"Lambertville, Michigan," Venice said. "What are you going to do when you get there?"

"I have no idea," he confessed. "But being closer is better than being farther away." He leaned back into the elevator and yelled, "Yo, Big Guy! Finish up. We gotta go." Back on the air, he said, "When you get the photos Big Guy is sending you, I'll need you to process them quickly."

"Is one of them Sarah Mitchell?"

"That's what the smart money says, but I need you to verify and get the info back to me. And to Kit."

Venice's silence reiterated her displeasure at trusting Maryanne. She asked, "When you leave, do you want me to call the police to clean up the bodies?"

"Negative. If we can verify that one of our targets is among the dead, pass that along to Wolverine. She'll want to use her own cleaners." Corpses posed a difficult problem in the covert world. You couldn't just let them fester and rot, but you also didn't want to get local authorities spun up with a lot of difficult questions. Among the cadre of specialists who took care of things in that world were people who specialized in the removal and disposition of bodies.

"And just so you're prepared," Jonathan said, "some kids are involved."

Anton Datsik stood at the corner of Wisconsin and M Streets in Georgetown and considered his options. A turn to the left would take him uphill toward the residential sections, and a right would take him downhill to the Potomac River. When the light changed, he decided to continue east—straight ahead—past the restaurants and chain stores that had ruined the most prime real estate in Washington, DC. This part of the city had evolved into a college town, pandering to the shallow tastes of trust-fund adolescents. He was old enough to remember the days of the Cellar Door and the Crazy Horse, trendy nightclubs that featured the most cutting-edge performers in an environment that was at once sleazy and trendy. Now, it had all turned to plastic.

His job this afternoon was to remain invisible as the events in Indiana and Ohio played themselves out. Any day that could be spent away from his office in the embassy of the Russian Federation was a good day.

Datsik had always admired the United States and its people. Compulsively friendly, they also seemed willfully naïve, a combination that resolved to charming. Unlike his bosses, he'd never wished them harm, but he was certain that harm was inevitable. Once fierce and self-reliant, they had evolved into a passive culture that valued politeness over victory. Such cultures always collapsed under the oppression of aggressors who valued power over peace.

The light turned, and he headed toward Thirty-first Street, Northwest.

Datsik considered himself a professional—not political—and he believed that it was not possible to be both. Professionals stayed focused on things that were important—what Americans liked to call the Big Picture.

Being of a certain age, Datsik had witnessed personally the speed with which political priorities can change. He'd witnessed the implosion of security services in his Motherland as the Soviet Union collapsed into disarray. He'd watched as the void of leadership seeded the grounds where the *Bratva* and the *Organi-*

zatsiya flourished with a brutality that exceeded anything meted out in Russia after the reign of Yuri Andropov.

After Gorbachev and that fat drunk Yeltsin rolled over and gave a big blow job to successive American presidents, these so-called Russian mafia organizations grew fat and powerful skimming their shares off the billions of dollars the United States pumped into the new Russian Federation. Datsik never ceased to be amazed by the naïveté—the intentional myopia, it seemed—of the American public. Surely they did not believe that the great democratic experiment they were able to launch in 1776 was somehow relevant to the modern world.

Those US dollars created monsters of unspeakable cruelty, and those monsters were able to buy and sell politicians like the commodities they were. To do what the oligarchs wanted was to become wealthy beyond imagination. To cross them was to find oneself and one's extended family tortured to death.

Those had been Datsik's formative years. He'd been an officer in the KGB for five years when the KGB ceased to exist. He was not senior enough to know how the transition actually happened in the historical sense, but to him, it happened literally overnight. He went home one night as an officer, and then when he reported to work the next morning, he discovered that work no longer existed.

Throughout the former Communist states, every agency that once was responsible for keeping order either disappeared or dissolved into some weak imitation of its former self. For more than a few men and women less fortunate than he, the transition meant death at the hands of the angry mobs who stormed headquarters buildings and dragged the occupants out into the street. He'd witnessed no such violence himself, but he'd heard stories from multiple sources. It was all far too reminiscent of Benito Mussolini.

Being nonpolitical didn't mean he couldn't work a roomful of politicians. He sensed early on that those who lost power would soon grow hungry for that power to return, and he aligned himself with as many of them as he could. Hungriest of all, it turned out, were those who were ousted from the security services. Theirs was a special kind of power that was rooted less in money—although there was plenty of that—than it was in information. The kind of information that could make a man or ruin him.

The current leader of the Russian Federation came from that very group, and Datsik was pleased to find himself on the president's good side when the dust settled and the flow of blood slowed.

The KGB became the FSB, the oligarchs who spouted democratic thoughts were ripped from power and stuffed in prison, and even the organized crime syndicates were finding it easier to operate elsewhere. Like all criminals, they thrived here in the United States and in the United Kingdom, where the fear of offending trumped the strict rule of law.

In the middle of the block that separated Thirtieth Street from Twenty-ninth Street, an overweight couple in their sixties made eye contact with him and the husband pulled a map from his back pocket. "Excuse me," the man said. "Are you a local?"

Datsik smiled. It was the structure of the question that amused him. He in fact knew this city as well, if not better than, most locals, but the instant he opened his mouth to speak, they would hear the accent, and that might trigger questions he had no desire to discuss.

He said nothing, and kept walking.

Among the problems that remained in his Motherland were the Georgians and the Ukrainians. Among the former Soviet states that sought their independence, the Chechens in particular had focused on brutality as the best means to an end.

The hatred between Chechnya and Russia spanned generations, a mutual loathing so innate that it might have been genetic. Animals that they were, Chechen terrorists didn't care who died in their attacks that were designed to slaughter by the hundreds or the thousands.

Now those animals were *this close* to having access to nuclear warheads, all because of a scheme devised by academicians in the hierarchy of American security to eliminate terrorists by arming them.

As a professional, it was his job to keep that from happening. And he was getting ever closer to his goal. Two of the Mitchells were dead, and the third would soon be found. Given the resources that Philip Baxter had promised to dedicate to the task, no one could remain invisible for long.

Mitchell. Did they really think that they could pull off such a quintessentially Middle American name? So desperate were the desires of Daud and Lalita Kadyrov to assimilate into American society that they studied the language and the customs, and, with some help from the United States government, they thought they could just shed the bonds of their past.

With Chechen pigs, that level of change was impossible. Their fellow separatists embedded here in the United States would never have allowed that to happen. Their plan was doomed from the beginning.

And now here was Datsik, cleaning up yet another mess—doing that at which he was best.

When his cell phone rang, he checked the number, and he knew that the final stage had begun. "Yes?" he said.

A female voice said, "I'm afraid there's been a major complication." She didn't bother to identify herself because that would have been a waste of time for everyone. "It seems that our enemies got to the targets first."

Datsik spat out a curse. "You told me that you didn't know where they were. You told me that no one knew where they were because they were impossible to find." This was devastating news.

"It's not as bad as it might have been," she said. "There was a gun battle, but the Mitchell boy seems to have gotten away."

This made no sense to Datsik. "A gun battle? How is that possible? The pigs want the boy alive. He's useless to them dead."

"I can only assume that it was a kidnap attempt," the woman said. "No other motivation would make sense."

"How big a team did they send? And what kind of amateurs could lose—"

"Datsik, I keep telling you not to underestimate the abilities of Jolaine Cage. You insist on referring to her as a maid or as a nanny, and I've told you from the very beginning that that was a mistake. Now you understand why."

Though anger boiled in his gut, Datsik nonetheless felt admiration for the young lady he'd never met but about whom he'd heard so much. The Chechens fielded professionals for missions such as this. He could only imagine that they, too, had underestimated their opponent. "What was the damage done to the assault team?"

"Six dead. I don't know if any got away."

"And how were they able to find them when you and the entire United States government could not?"

"What's done is done," she said. "What difference does that make now?"

"It makes a great deal of difference," Datsik said. "It comes down to an issue of competence, doesn't it? An issue of trust. Wasn't *trust* what this was all about in the first place? Isn't that what you told us?"

"I don't know what went wrong," the woman said. "I think it's clear that the Chechens had access to information that we did not."

"I think more than that is clear," Datsik said. "I think that you must find a way to become more intelligent, and that that needs to happen quickly. I have people working on this as well, you know. If we find the boy first, there will be no need for you. As we have discussed before, you do not want to become irrelevant. Irrelevance shortens lives."

He clicked off without waiting for a reply. In situations like this, it was always best to keep the other party on edge. People achieved remarkable feats when they understood that the alternative was death.

He'd spoken too long as it was. Whenever on a cell phone or on any broadcast device, he made it a point to speak in single syllables whenever possible, and always as short a time as possible. While his phone was untraceable, he had no doubt that the American security services were listening in, cued by a voiceprint that was buried in the database.

He needed that boy, and he preferred to have him alive. It was troubling that young Graham knew what he knew, but that was a problem to be solved with a single bullet. More troubling was the fact *that* he knew anything in the first place. Datsik and his superiors needed to understand the flow of that information. They needed to know at least as much as the Americans knew, and that could take time. Taking custody of the boy would cure the problem of the codes—if, in fact, he even had them, as Datsik's sources had alleged—but extracting additional information could take both time and patience. And quite a lot of discomfort.

Datsik wished that he disliked such things, but the truth was quite the opposite. One could not excel in a skill if one did not enjoy the practice of it. He found hurting children to be distasteful, but sometimes it had to be done.

Besides, the Mitchell boy was, what, fourteen, fifteen years old? For generations, that was the age of soldiers. They and those even younger were heroes of the Motherland during the Great War.

Graham Mitchell was an adult in soldier years.

Bringing him into custody was the single hurdle. From there, the diplomatic channels had already been greased, as the Americans liked to say, for the boy to be whisked to Russia, where the real work would begin.

*   *   *

The lady on the other side of the table had a nice smile, but hard eyes. Graham didn't trust her. In fact, as he sat there, sipping his Coke and eating his Twix bar, he realized that he didn't trust anyone anymore. They sat in a yellow-brown concrete block room, where the only furnishings were a beat-up steel table and two chairs that were both bolted to the floor.

After being beaten up by the cops who arrested him, he'd been put in a car and driven to this building that he assumed was a jail. For a long time, he'd just sat here by himself. They'd taken the cuffs off his wrists, and they hadn't said anything about walking around, but there was nowhere to walk, nothing to do.

It was sort of a relief to have another person in the room. At least she was willing to talk—more than he could say about every cop in the building, who pretended that he wasn't even there. She wasn't particularly friendly—in fact, she seemed intent on being the opposite of friendly—but at least she was another heartbeat in the room.

"I asked you if you know why you're here." The lady said her name was Peggy, but Graham didn't believe her.

"Because the police brought me here," he said. It was a violation of the say-nothing rule that Jolaine had sworn him to, but he'd learned the hard way that saying nothing pissed people off way more than saying something that sounded like an answer, but really was not.

"And why do you think that happened?" Peggy asked.

"I don't know."

"Take a guess."

Graham hesitated, worried what the reaction might be, then decided to roll the dice. "Because they had nothing better to do tonight?"

Peggy's cold eyes hardened even more. "Do you think this is a funny time?"

"No," Graham said. Finally, a chance to be 100 percent truthful. "I think this is a scary time, and I think you are a scary lady."

She seemed to enjoy that. "Really." She said the word as a statement, not as a question. "Why do you think I'm scary?"

Graham hesitated. Then he said nothing.

"Come on, Graham. You can answer. What makes you think that I am scary?"

He hesitated again. He sensed that Peggy was trying to trap him into saying the wrong thing, and that the wrong thing would get somebody hurt. At this point, silence was his most loyal ally.

Twenty seconds passed. "Graham, you realize you're in custody, right? You realize that I control your future. That Twix bar could be the last bit of food you get for the next two weeks."

"There," he said. "You just threatened to starve me. That's what makes you scary. I think you want something from me, and I think you want that something more than you care whether I'm dead or alive."

He'd intended that to be startling, but Peggy took it in stride. In fact, she might have looked pleased. "Tell me what has happened over the past couple of days."

"You go first," Graham said. "Tell me what you think has happened."

Peggy's face morphed into something ugly. She

probably thought it was a smile, but it looked more like pain laced with raw hatred. "So something *did* happen," she said. "I wasn't sure, but you just confirmed that for me. That's how it works here. If you don't tell me the truth, I'm going to find it out anyway. You don't want to screw around with me, kid."

This bitch wanted him to cry, or panic, but he wasn't going to give her the satisfaction. Jolaine's words raced through his mind—don't say anything to anyone, don't reveal any details—but Jolaine wasn't here to help him. She wasn't anywhere, in fact. For all he knew, she was dead, or she was saying things that would get him into trouble.

His mind raced for words that would create the *feel* of sharing information without actually sharing it. Were the cops even allowed to talk to kids without some other adult around? Didn't he read a book or watch a movie or maybe a *Law & Order* episode where everything turned on the presence—or in the case of the program, the *absence*—of an adult during questioning?

"I want a lawyer," he said. In the show, that had been the line of dialogue that changed everything. Once you asked for a lawyer, all the questioning had to stop.

Peggy laughed. "Gonna lawyer up, are you?" she mocked. "That's cute. You think you're in charge. That's extra cute. Here's the deal, Graham, and I need you to wrap your head all the way around it. You are not in control. You don't even have a control to reach for. I control everything that happens to you from this point forward. You need to understand that. You also need to understand that pissing me off is a bad platform to start from. Now, I'm going to ask you again, but I'm only going to ask you once. What happened last night?"

"Probably something a lot like what you think it was," Graham said. While he had no clue what was happening, he had the sense that Peggy was more bluster than action. How much could she do, after all, in a place that was teeming with cops? That was another thing: He didn't believe that she was a cop. He didn't know what she was, but she didn't have the swagger of a cop.

Whether that was good news or bad news was a different discussion.

Peggy glared. Graham saw real anger behind her eyes. He glanced up at the camera in the corner near the ceiling. He pointed to it. "People are watching," he said. "You gonna hit me?"

Peggy seemed to grow larger, as if there were a big balloon inside of her that someone had pumped with air.

"I need you to tell me what happened last night," she repeated.

"Why?" he asked. "Why do you think that anything at all happened?"

Peggy turned red.

"Want to know what I think?" Graham taunted. "I think you think that you already know, and you just want me to confirm."

"There was shooting," Peggy said. "At your house. People were killed."

Graham said nothing. He realized what Jolaine had been trying to tell him in the moments before they'd been taken into custody. People don't really know anything until someone confirms it for them.

"Your parents were involved in the shootings," Peggy went on. "Your father was killed."

Those words landed hard, like a slap. He understood that she'd said it to knock him off balance, and as much as he wanted it not to be so, he realized that she'd succeeded. He felt tears press from behind his eyes. "Does this make you feel big?" he asked.

"Excuse me?"

"Does it make you feel big to bully a kid who can't defend himself? Does it make you feel all-powerful and shit to tell me that my father was killed? What kind of father did you have if you could talk to me that way?"

"Watch your mouth, Graham."

Graham heard movement on the far side of the door, and then the distinctive sound of a key sliding into the lock. It turned, and the door opened, revealing the brown-uniformed cop who had earlier taken him to the bathroom.

"That's it," the cop said. "This interview is over."

Peggy looked at him like he was a cockroach. "No, it's not," she said.

"Yes, it is," the cop said. "As of right now."

"Who the hell are you?" Peggy demanded.

"I am Deputy Milford Price," the cop said. Unremarkable in every regard except for the mole under his right eye, his face was redder than the last time Graham had seen it. "And you are Peggy Darnell, who happens to have no profile in any record I accessed."

"That fact alone should tell you something," Peggy said. "Don't interfere with what I'm doing."

Deputy Price crossed the threshold and walked to Graham's side of the table. "He had it right, you know," he said. "You're a bully and you prey on kids. It doesn't get a lot lower than that."

"I have business to attend to, Deputy." She said the word *deputy* as if it smelled bad.

Price smiled. He beckoned Graham with two fingers. "Come with me, son."

Graham stood. He wasn't sure what was going down, but he sensed that he was destined to come out on the positive end of it. He felt a sense of peace when Deputy Price placed a hand on his shoulder.

"I'm sure yours is a complicated job," Price said. "That's the impression I got from the word that came down not to interfere with you."

"It's a good idea to follow orders," Peggy said.

"Except for the immoral ones," Price countered. "That was a hard-learned lesson for my father, and he made sure that I learned it, too. He was in the Army, back during Vietnam, when all the lines got blurry. Back when I was a boy—"

"Oh, for Christ's sake, must we really—"

"Yes, we must really," Price said. "He was never right after that war. He was never able to justify the choices he was forced to make, and he never even confided in me what those choices were. But I knew for damn sure what the lessons were. He drove them into me just as surely as a nail is driven into wood."

"Oh, good God, I cannot wait to hear." Backed into a corner, Peggy became 100 percent bitch.

"When my daddy found out that I was going into law enforcement, he told me to pay attention to one thing above all others. And that one thing was the morality of what I was doing. Not all laws are just, he told me, and not all criminals are bad. Sometimes, people do bad things for good reasons. As an officer of the law, my job is to know the difference."

"This is truly moving," Peggy mocked. "I'm sure there's a point here somewhere."

"I'm sure there is, too," Price said. "Just as all criminals are not bad, not all folks with badges are good. In fact, some folks should never be given badges in a million years because they don't respect the power that comes with it."

Graham watched the discussion like a tennis match, his head pivoting from point to point.

"And you think I'm one of those people," Peggy said. Her body language said that she was bored and angry.

"I *know* that you're one of those people," Deputy Price said. "What kind of monster does an adult have to be to speak to a child the way you were speaking to this young man?"

"I believe I made it clear to your superiors that I am here on a matter of national security."

"That's no excuse for the way you've been speaking to Graham."

"And how do you know what I've been saying to Graham?" Peggy said. She stood. "I left specific orders that this discussion was to be off the record."

Deputy Price gave the kind of mocking smile that told Graham that he was definitely on his side. "Well, you know how it goes sometimes. Word doesn't always leak down."

Peggy glared.

"This isn't your station house, Agent Whatever-your-real-name-is. This is *my* station house, and we're in the United States of America, not in some secret CIA prison. The boy asks for a lawyer, you stop asking questions. You start taunting him about the loss of a parent, and I step in. You're done."

"You have no idea what you're messing with," Peggy said.

"You have no idea how little I care," Deputy Price replied. "I sleep well at night, and when my journey on this spaceship is over, I expect to have a pleasant eternity in Heaven." He paused for effect. "I have every confidence that we won't run into each other there."

Using gentle pressure on the base of Graham's neck, he urged the boy toward the door. "Come on," Price said. "We'll get you settled down someplace more comfortable."

This time, there were no handcuffs.

The walls of the hallway were made of the same yellow-brown brick as the interior of the meeting room. The floor tiles were the same brown-flecked white, too, only out here, the floors had a sparkle. Graham suspected that had something to do with people caring enough to clean them from time to time.

"Where are you taking me now?"

"We're going to get you a warm bed in a house with nice people."

Graham stopped, took a step backward. "I don't know anybody here," he said.

Deputy Price smiled. "I know plenty of nice people," he said. "Trust me."

Graham felt a flash of panic. *Trust me.* He couldn't

imagine anything that he could less afford to do. He couldn't trust anyone. Everything about the past two days had proven beyond any doubt that no one was worthy of his trust.

He sensed movement behind him, and he turned to see that Peggy had stepped out into the hallway. Whatever about her had pretended to be nice before was all gone. All he saw on her face was anger as she glared past Graham and through Deputy Price.

"Listen to me, Barney Fife," she said. "I think it's time to place a call to your chief. You are way, way over your head right now."

"Been there before," Price said.

Graham made his decision. No matter what the other options were, all of them had to be better than sticking with Peggy.

"Think of the boy," Peggy said. "You're just going to make it all more difficult for him."

Graham saw something flash behind Deputy Price's eyes. She'd just pissed him off. "Just what are you suggesting?" he asked. "Are you *threatening* this young man?"

Graham took a step closer to the deputy.

Peggy walked toward them. A stroll, really—unhurried and deliberate. Graham pivoted around Deputy Price, keeping the man's body between him and the dragon lady.

She stopped when she was just a foot away from the deputy and she glared. Graham could feel the reflected heat of it, but Deputy Price seemed unbothered.

After a few seconds, Peggy walked on down the hall and disappeared out the door on the far end.

Graham's heart raced, and he found himself trembling. "Who *is* she?"

Deputy Price patted him between his shoulder blades. "She's nobody," he said. "Just a lady who thinks she's way more important than she really is." He gave Graham a nudge. "Come on," he said. "Let's get you that comfortable bed I promised you."

CHAPTER SIXTEEN

"**S**corpion, Mother Hen."

Jonathan keyed the mike on his portable radio. "Go ahead." They were only two hours into their three-hour drive. He sat in the shotgun seat as always, and he turned the volume up so that Boxers could listen in.

"ICIS is beginning to light up about our friends," she said. "Graham is going to be transferred to a foster home in the next half hour, forty-five minutes."

"Do you have specifics?" Jonathan asked. If they could get a name and an address, they could lie in wait and grab the boy as he arrived at the foster home. Typically, that was the simplest kind of snatch, when the parties thought they were beyond any danger.

Venice relayed the name of the foster family—Markham, in Lambertville—and the address.

Jonathan wrote it down on the pad that always resided in the pouch pocket on his right thigh. "And the girl? Jolaine?"

"That's a little more interesting," Venice said. "She's scheduled to be transferred from her current location in the adult detention center in Lambertville to a federal facility in Chicago."

Jonathan exchanged confused glances with Boxers. "Any word yet on the specifics of the charges?"

"That's a negative," Venice said. "But it gets better. On a whim, I decided to call the federal facility in Chicago. They don't know anything about the transfer."

Jonathan scowled. "You just called them?" he asked. "An inquiry out of the blue is going to get a don't-know response nine times out of ten."

"I told them I was calling on behalf of Andrew Barron, an AUSA from Chicago."

Jonathan recognized the acronym for an assistant United States attorney, a federal prosecutor. "And you think they bought it?"

Venice did not respond to the question. Of course they bought it. Venice had a telephone voice that was unlike any other that Jonathan had ever heard. It pissed her off when he called it her phone-sex voice. Fact was, she could talk anyone into believing anything over the phone.

"Okay," Jonathan said, breaking the silence. "What should we conclude from them not knowing about the transfer?"

"I think we have to assume that the transfer isn't real," she said. "I think we have to assume that the bad guys are going to take her when she's in the car."

Jonathan recoiled in his seat. That was a hell of a leap.

"I have a hard time connecting those dots," Boxers

said. Because Jonathan hadn't yet pressed the mike button, his comment did not go out over the air, but Scorpion could not have agreed more.

"Help me with logic," Jonathan said on the encrypted channel.

"I assume we're hunting for ducks," Venice said.

Jonathan laughed. In that one sentence, she'd spoken paragraphs. If a creature looked like a duck and walked like a duck and quacked like a duck, it was unreasonable to conclude that it was a penguin in disguise.

He got her point. Someone was after Jolaine with the intention of doing her harm. She was in custody on a nonspecific charge that now involved a transfer that no one know about.

"I got it," Jonathan said. "When does the transfer happen?"

"That's unclear," Venice said. "The best I can estimate is when they get their stuff in order enough to make it happen."

"Tell you what," Jonathan said. "Get your new buddy Maryanne on the phone and patch her into this conversation. Let's get her take on this."

Hesitation. "You know I object, right?" Venice said.

"Duly noted. The way I look at it, there's no harm talking. Surely she's as dialed into ICIS as you are."

"You know that begs a different question," Venice said. "It's counterproductive for anybody on her side of the equation to know that we are even aware that ICIS exists, let alone that we have access to it." Access to ICIS was among Venice's early victories as a brilliant tickler of electrons.

"Then we won't mention it," Jonathan said. "Get

back to us when you have the patch ready." He didn't want to discuss this anymore.

"We've got ourselves a dilemma, Boss," Boxers said. "It's entirely possible we're going to have two transfer events happening at the same time."

Actually, it was close to a certainty, Jonathan thought. The question was, on which event should they focus their intervention?

"The kid is the one with the information," Boxers said, reading his mind.

Jonathan nodded. Graham was for sure the primary target in terms of national security. He was the one with the photographic memory, and, presumably, the arming codes that so many people were willing to kill to obtain.

"Jolaine's the one who'll be most under guard," Jonathan said. "And the guards will likely be cops. We're not in the business of endangering cops."

"But apparently the kid is stable," Boxers said. "At least he's being taken to a place of safety."

"Unless he's not," Jonathan said. "If the enemy—whoever they are—is coming at Jolaine, doesn't it make sense that they'll come at the boy, too? Why go for her and not for him?"

"Agreed," Boxers said. "But we need to choose, and our single best opportunity to get Jolaine back will be while she's in a vehicle being transported between points A and B. Once she's ensconced in another secure facility, we won't have many options. You worry about tangling with law enforcement personnel, well, that would be one hell of a fight."

On the other end of the easiness factor from snatching people from a home where they least expected it was snatching people from a facility designed specifically to prevent snatchings.

"It would help to know where they intend to take her," Boxers said.

"It would help to know who intends to take her there," Jonathan countered.

The radio popped to life. "Scorpion, Mother Hen."

"That was fast," Jonathan said. "Maybe we're about to find out." He keyed his mike. "Go ahead."

Venice said, "Kit, you are on with Scorpion and Big Guy. I am Mother Hen. Scorpion, I have filled Kit in on what little we know."

Jonathan got right down to it. "So, what are your thoughts, Kit?"

"That's us," Maryanne said. "We're taking her to safety. It's over."

Jonathan looked to Boxers. "What do you mean, it's over?"

"It means mission accomplished," Maryanne said. "Uncle Sam thanks you for your service, and wishes you a good day."

"This feels way too easy," Boxers said off the air.

Jonathan agreed. "When did you intend to tell us?" he asked.

"I'm surprised you knew," Maryanne said. "I didn't even know until a few minutes ago. I won't ask how you pulled that off because Wolverine cautioned me about asking too many questions about how you do what you do."

Jonathan found himself silently cursing the doubt that Venice had planted in his head about Maryanne. This should be good news, but he found himself not trusting it. The fact that she was blowing sunshine up his ass didn't help at all.

Jonathan keyed the mike. "Was it you guys who swore out the warrant for interstate flight to avoid a noncrime?"

"Say again?"

Jonathan said, "The PCs were pulled over and taken into custody— but not arrested—on a charge of interstate flight to avoid prosecution. Was that you guys?"

"How do you know about all of this?"

In his head, he could see Venice getting mad. "Remember what Wolverine told you," Jonathan said.

"I don't get the sudden change in attitude," Maryanne said.

"You know you're not answering my question, right?"

"At what point in what parallel universe did the FBI start owing answers to its contractors?" Maryanne said. Clearly, Jonathan had thumped a sensitive button.

"Was that a yes or a no?" Jonathan pressed.

"We're done," Maryanne said, and there was a click.

"What the heck was that all about?" Venice asked. "Why dial her in and then piss her off?"

"Yeah," Boxers said, "I was kind of wondering that myself."

This wasn't a discussion for the airwaves. "Mother Hen, I'll be back to you in a while." To Boxers, he said, "This just doesn't feel right. It was a simple enough question. Did they cut the warrant? Why wouldn't she answer it? I think she got pissed when she found out what we knew. But why wouldn't she want us to know? If we're all on the same team—and that's what she promised from the very beginning—why is she trying to shut us out?"

"Maybe because she's with the FBI and that's what they do. They compartmentalize."

"I keep coming back to Venice's question," Jonathan said. "How did Maryanne know so quickly about what happened to the Mitchell family? If you think about it, the gunsmoke must still have been hanging in the air when she reached out to Venice and me at the concert. How could she know so fast?"

"Well, it could have been a telephone call," Boxers said, "but I don't think that's where you're going. You're thinking that the pretty hot thing is in on this somehow."

"I certainly think it's worth looking into. In fact, Venice's looking into it as we speak."

Boxers rumbled out a laugh. "And I bet she's having a ball doing it, too. Full cavity search?"

"She's looking for anything that looks like motivation."

"What about Wolverine? What does she have to say about this?"

Jonathan groaned. "I haven't spoken to her. I don't imagine she'd take too well to having one of her trusted lieutenants accused of betrayal. I've got to be one hundred percent sure before I launch that balloon."

"Ah," Boxers said. "That whole loyalty thing. You know, you'd think after Aldrich Ames and Robert Hanssen and Edward Snowden, the three-letter groups would start looking at themselves a little more closely."

Jonathan sensed the birth of a political rant, so he retook control. "Here's where I see it. Kit says our work is done and that we're off the case, and Wolverine hasn't been dialed in. That means we're alone if we keep going."

Boxers grinned. "We're not backing off, are we?"

Jonathan shook his head. "No, we're not. At least not for a while."

"Fine by me," Big Guy said. "But I always like messing with people. Why are you staying in? What's in it for you? For us?"

"Start with the stakes," Jonathan explained. "We've dealt with Chechens before. I know they've got solid grievances with the Russians, but their methods are ten clicks too brutal even for the Hadji. The thought of them with a nuclear capability is just too much. That can't be allowed to happen."

"Okay." Boxers drew out the last syllable, clearly waiting for more. "So you think that Maryanne and the FBI are going to hand the PCs over to the Chechens so that they can blow up Mother Russia? Why would they do that?"

Jonathan realized that he was thinking faster than his mouth could move. "No," he said. "I'm not convinced that the people running the pickup are FBI. That's the significance of Venice's discovery that the field office or whatever it is in Chicago doesn't know that the PC is on her way."

"So, you think it's a snatch," Boxers clarified. His expression said that he wasn't yet completely on board with that.

"No," Jonathan said. "I don't think that it *is* a snatch. But I think it *could* be a snatch."

"One that's being organized by Wolverine's girl Friday." Boxers didn't seem to like the taste of the words. "I just want to make sure I got this right."

"It all comes back to the stakes," Jonathan said. "I keep running the outcomes through my head. If Maryanne is in fact a good guy and is in fact telling the truth, then the FBI gets their hands on our PC first, and presumably, there's no harm, no foul. We'll just have wasted a lot of time."

"And if the Chechens snatch them, a lot of Russia will go boom," Boxers said. "And Wolverine's girl Friday would have started that ball rolling. That's the part I'm having trouble with, Dig. I mean, God knows my cynicism has no limits, but even I have—"

"I might be wrong," Jonathan said. "Let's stipulate that I probably am. What are the consequences if I'm not? That's a lot of dead people. And then there's the retaliatory strike. How do you think President Darmond and his team will handle a crisis like that?"

"Jeez, Dig. That is so desperately not my problem. If I start thinking in those terms, the world gets pretty dark."

"There's a third possibility, too," Jonathan went on. "The Russians by far have the most to gain by getting their hands on the PC. They kill him and the codes die with him."

"Doesn't that solve everything?" Boxers asked. "I mean, that would suck for him, but that might be the perfect thing for the rest of us here on the planet."

"He's a kid, Box," Jonathan said. "Nothing good comes from killing a kid, I don't care who he is. But more than that, you're missing the point." He felt his impatience growing. "Or maybe I'm not stating it well. These PCs—Jolaine Cage and Graham Mitchell—are just trying to survive. He's a kid, and she's a young vet doing her job. The Mitchells hired Jolaine to protect the kid, and then all hell broke loose. Now they're in danger, and in one of our three outcomes, Graham is killed by Chechens after he gives them what they want, and in a second, he's killed by Russians to keep him quiet. From the bad guys' point of view, there's no other option."

"And in the third scenario?"

"The third scenario is to deliver the PCs to Wolverine's FBI, the one that really does care if good wins out over bad."

"Isn't Wolfie part of the problem? At least maybe?"

"For now, no," Jonathan said. "I think she's in the dark. But you know Wolfie. Presented with the evidence, she'll come around to our side."

Being processed into jail was every bit as humiliating as Jolaine imagined it would be, right down to the oft-rumored cavity search. To their credit, the staff of the jail remained courteous and professional through the whole thing.

Taking her own advice, she said nothing. She answered questions regarding her identity and her physical state—she had no known diseases or allergies, she was in excellent physical health, had not had any recent surgeries, blah, blah, blah—but otherwise offered nothing. She didn't even ask where they had taken Graham.

She'd never seen such a look of terror as she saw on Graham's face, and that included young grunts who found themselves in a war zone for the first time. At least in combat, there was an element of empowerment, a way to affect the outcome of your own life. There on the street, on his belly, with his hands ratcheted into handcuffs, there was only misery. She had no idea what the next chapter in his life was going to be, and she didn't ask because she was confident that no one would tell her.

She sat alone in a holding cell that looked more like the pictures she'd seen of supermax prisons than what she'd envisioned a county jail to look like. Assuming the tiles on the floor were one foot square, her rectangular corner of the world measured roughly five by seven. A heavy steel door occupied the narrow dimension at the front of the cell, with a tiny wire-reinforced glass window that looked out into the hallway—or would look out into the hallway if the sliding panel on the far side were open. She imagined that the other panel in the door, this one about waist high and made of metal, was a hinged flap that would allow the guard staff to pass food to her without opening the door. It looked just big enough to accommodate a cafeteria tray.

Her cot was actually a concrete half wall that ran the length of the long dimension of the cell, and it was topped with a thin mattress that had been rolled up around her pillow and nudged up against the back wall. Hospital-green sheets and a blanket sat folded in front of the bedroll. The most prominent feature in the left-center of the space was a squatty, mushroom-shaped stainless-steel bar stool that served as the chair for the stainless-steel desk that folded up to reveal the stainless-steel toilet. Efficiency at its most hideous.

Aware of the fisheye camera in the corner of the ceiling nearest the door—enclosed, of course, by what appeared to be bulletproof glass—she wondered what bizarre pleasure some of the guards must have gotten from watching prisoners take care of bodily functions. It wouldn't surprise her to learn that there was a porn channel devoted to just that.

As she placed the sheets onto the desk and began to unroll the mattress, she took inventory of where she was and how she'd gotten here. As far as she could recall, the arresting officers had never told her what she she'd been arrested for, and she hadn't asked because (a) it would violate her rule of saying nothing, and (b) it would all be revealed sooner or later.

Imprisonment was a first for her. There'd been a close call back in her teen years where a kindhearted magistrate had overridden the desires of a county cop following a DUI charge, but to date, she'd never spent a moment in jail. She surprised herself with her own calm. Sure, it was scary, but she'd scored a single room where she didn't have to deal with the politics and violence of other prisoners, and the entire ordeal was only a few hours old.

Give it a few more, she thought. Once nighttime came, and the boredom of her own company began to crush her, she imagined that there'd be plenty of panic to deal with.

For the time being, she committed herself to treating this mess as an adventure. If nothing else, she was experiencing an adrenaline rush of a magnitude she hadn't felt since the Sandbox.

Jolaine's sole experience with the rigors and processes of the criminal justice system was limited to what she'd seen on television. As she spread the nearly see-through thin green sheet across the mattress, she thought through the events of the past couple of hours, and she tried to reconcile the facts of her situation to the fiction that she'd seen so often.

They never read me my rights, she thought. The realization startled her. Wasn't that a requirement whenever someone was arrested? Yes, she was certain of it.

Come to think of it, they'd never actually said that she was under arrest. That thought brought her bed-making to a halt. She stood there, with the top of the sheet tucked in and the bottom of the sheet suspended like a flag as she tried to figure out what that might mean.

I'm in jail, but I haven't been arrested.

The thought paralyzed her. She dropped the sheet and sat heavily on the bed. She felt the blood draining from her head, but she forced herself to sit upright anyway so as not to give whoever was watching her camera feed any indication of fear. She didn't know why that was important, but it was.

Jolaine told herself to calm down and to think through exactly what she did and didn't *know.* What she thought and what she feared were irrelevant. It was too easy to shoot out to the worst-case scenario, and to extrapolate from there that all roads and all options led to tragedy. Panic was the only result of bad assumptions, and panic always resulted in tragedy. She needed to think it all through.

Fact: Her arrest violated all of the rules she was aware of regarding arrest procedures.

Counterfact: She wasn't a lawyer, and not everything you saw on television was true. Hell, depending on what channel you watched, only half of what you saw on the news was true.

Fact: Graham was the sole possessor of some kind

of code that a lot of people thought was worth killing for.

Fact: If her observations about her nonarrest were true, then someone was asleep at the switch because—again, if television lawyers knew what they were doing—any case against her would be fatally flawed and the government would be guaranteed to lose.

Unless they don't care about losing.

But why would that be? This couldn't all be some scare tactic, could it? Could that possibly be legal? Wouldn't there be consequences to pointing guns and pulling people out of their cars just to make a point?

No, she thought, it was more than that. Just as she had seen the terror in Graham's eyes, she had also seen genuine fear in the eyes of those cops who took them down. They'd been expecting bad things from Jolaine, and that expectation had driven all of the rough handling that had followed. Even down to manhandling a fourteen-year-old boy.

Where did such fear come from?

Clearly, the police had been alerted to be on the lookout for them. That in turn meant that someone had told them what and who to look for. But who? Who would even know what car she was driving?

Fact: No one had asked her any questions. They hadn't even fingerprinted her.

After all of the drama and all of the violence and near-violence, why would there be such silence? It was almost as though they'd been instructed not to say anything.

That's it. She didn't know why, exactly, but in that moment of clarity, she knew beyond all doubt that the jail staff had in fact been instructed not to speak with her. Just the basics, to make sure that she didn't pose an unreasonable threat, and then nothing else. All the praise she'd awarded herself for holding her tongue had in fact been a gift delivered by others. She hadn't needed to speak because no one wanted to speak with her in the first place.

So, who was doing this? Why was she here? Who had she pissed off so badly?

Whoever it was, they were important and they were powerful—powerful enough to mobilize a law enforcement agency. FBI, maybe? CIA? She imagined that a conspiracy this complex had to be run by some kind of alphabet agency.

What's their next move? she wondered. Why take her to jail and then just let her sit? That didn't make sense.

Then she got it. As the realization bloomed, her heart rate doubled. This was only the beginning of her journey. This was a holding place—a place to be only for as long as it took for whoever was in charge to move her someplace else.

And she knew with certainty that when that transfer happened, she would come face-to-face with the agency that was pulling the strings. And then what?

That answer was obvious, wasn't it? They'd take her away and squeeze her for information that she didn't have.

Jolaine stood again and paced her cell. To hell with what the camera watchers thought. She needed a plan, and she needed it before people arrived with keys and took her away. Just as certainly as she believed she'd landed on the reality of her nonarrest, she knew that after she left this place—after the bad guys, whoever they were, came to take her away—the fuse on her life would burn down to nothing. Once these people got from her what they wanted, they would stuff her into a shallow grave and never look back.

The damn stool in the middle of the cell made it impossible even to pace. She needed to pace. She needed to scream. What the hell was she going to do?

She hated the Mitchells for putting her in this spot. What had they been up to?

She wanted to think that the Mitchells were patriots, and as such would never try to pass along a secret that could harm her country.

But to learn otherwise would not surprise her. She knew that there were some foreign affiliations, and that not all of them were friendly. When Bernard and Sarah argued, it was always in their native language—someplace in Eastern Europe—and consequently, Jolaine never knew the true substance of what they were saying. But she'd sensed growing tension over the past weeks, and she'd sensed that it had something to do with the visitors who'd been coming by with greater frequency. They gathered with the Mitchells for meetings in the same foreign tongue that she could not understand. Voices were often raised, however, and the visitors rarely departed happier than when they'd arrived.

It was possible, she supposed, that the substance of those meetings was to conspire against the United States, but how could she know? And if that were indeed the case, that would mean that the Mitchells had willingly and willfully recruited her as a coconspirator. Would they really do such a thing after all she'd done for Graham and for the family?

How could she know?

Jolaine sat on the shiny stool. The fact of the matter was that she couldn't know, not with any certainty. By extension, then, she had no choice but to assume the worst and act accordingly.

So, now what? She asked herself that question as if she had choices. Locked in a concrete room, her options were limited to one: Wait. For what, she had no clue, but the wait was a guarantee.

Sooner or later, that door would open, and when it did, options would arrive. She suspected that they would all be terrible ones, but at least they'd be options. She could not allow herself to be taken into the next stage. If a transfer lay in her future—and now she was certain that it did—she needed to make sure that the transfer would never be completed successfully.

If it came to that, she'd die trying, because the one thing she knew beyond all doubt was that she intended to survive.

CHAPTER SEVENTEEN

Deputy Price led Graham down the hallway and through a locked door into a part of the building the boy hadn't seen before.

"Is this a jail? Graham asked.

"Technically, no," the deputy said. "This is just a police station. We have some holding cells and some interrogation rooms—you know all about one of those—but the jail itself is down the road a bit."

"Why am I here?"

The far side of the locked door opened up on a much larger area that looked like a hospital waiting room—or at least what Graham imagined that a hospital waiting room would look like. Molded plastic chairs, blue and orange, littered the area in what looked to his eye to be a random order, as if people moved them throughout the day to form their own conversation groups and then never put them back where they belonged. The yellow and brown theme continued out here, but the floors and walls seemed dirtier. Most of the chairs were empty now, and the occupants of the ones that were taken had all pulled theirs away from the others. No conversation groups were currently in session.

"Not sure how to answer your question," Deputy Price said.

"You could just tell the truth," Graham said. He'd meant it to be a flippant remark and it hit its target squarely.

Price got a little taller. "I'm cutting you a break, kid. Don't make me regret it. Have a seat."

Graham felt a gentle pressure on his shoulder—there was no way to call it a push—and he helped himself to a blue chair. Deputy Price pulled over an orange one and he sat sideways in it, with his legs crossed and his left arm slung casually over the back. Now that they were sitting, the difference in height was almost nothing.

"Graham, I'm going to be honest with you. I have no idea why you're here. We got orders to stop the car you were in and to take the occupants of that car into custody."

"Why?" Something about the way Deputy Price handled himself put Graham at ease. As long as they were just talking like this, he felt safe.

"I don't have an answer for that," Price said. "Sometimes that happens. We get an order to pull someone over and bring them in, and sometimes we don't find out what the reason is. Doesn't happen often, but sometimes. This was one of those times."

"So, am I under arrest?" None of what was happening fit into any of the *Law & Order* episodes he'd watched with Jolaine.

"No. You're in custody, but you're not under arrest."

"So I can leave?"

"Do you have someplace to go?"

The question hit Graham like a smack. Something sagged in his chest. On top of everything else that had turned shitty, he was homeless. Homeless, and maybe an orphan. He felt a rush of sadness that made him gasp. Words wouldn't come.

Deputy Price leaned in closer. Close enough to touch, but he didn't touch. "Talk to me, Graham. I want to help you. Have you and your friend Jolaine been up to no good?"

Graham wanted to answer. He wanted to tell this cop with the friendly eyes all about the people who invaded his house and shot up his family. He wanted to tell about the doctor in the middle of nowhere, and about how terribly pale his mother looked the last time he saw her. He wanted to tell the cop about everything, and then he wanted to be free from it all.

Graham wanted a do-over. He wanted a time machine where you just climb in, turn a few dials, and flip a few switches, and suddenly nothing is what it was. He wanted to do anything that would take away that horrible feeling in the pit of his stomach, the fear—no, the *certainty*—that something terrible was going to happen to him.

Yet as much as he wanted it—as much as he would have sold his soul to attain it—he knew that none of it was possible. He knew that telling Deputy Price anything would pose more problems than it would solutions, just as Jolaine had said. They'd listened to the radio in the car, and they'd watched television in the motel room, yet there'd been no mention of all those terrible things. How was that possible?

With no police reports to back him up, no one would

believe his story anyway. And even if they did, and they drove all the way out to Antwerp to investigate, they'd find a lot of bullet holes and dead bodies, and then they'd start asking why he and Jolaine were on the run instead of calling the police in the first place.

And that would be a hell of a good question, Graham thought. Last night, it didn't make sense to him why they didn't call the police, and it didn't make any more sense right now. They didn't call because Jolaine said that it would be a mistake to call. That was the only reason, and what kind of reason was that?

Reason enough for her to risk her life to save me and Mom.

"I don't know what you're talking about," he said.

Price's shoulders sagged. "Son, I can't help you unless you talk to me."

Something about the deputy's delivery rubbed Graham the wrong way, and his filters kicked in again. Maybe it was use of the word "son." He already had a father, he didn't need another one. "Let me ask you a question," he said.

The deputy shrugged. "I'm all ears."

"That ugly lady. Peggy. She said she wanted to help me, too. She told me that the best thing I could do was to tell her everything. Now you're saying I should do the same thing. Why should I believe anything you say?"

Price took his time answering. "You can't honestly tell me that you don't trust me more than you trusted her."

"That just makes you the good cop."

"Excuse me?"

"The good cop. You know what I mean. It's in every

friggin' cop show. She was the bad cop, and you're the good cop. You work in a team so that she pisses me off, and then you butter me up."

Price's eyes narrowed to the point of squinting. "It's not like that, Graham. I promise you."

Graham wanted to believe him. He thought he did believe him, but trust was just too big a risk. "That's exactly what you would say if I was right," he said.

Deputy Price took a breath to reply, but then he let it go and smiled. "I got nothin' to say to that," he said. "You're right. That's exactly what I would say if I were trying to trick you. That's not where I'm coming from, but I understand where you're coming from. I got no answer that you can dare believe."

Silence fell between them, and it lasted probably two minutes before a door on the far end of the room opened up and a young man and woman entered from the outside and walked to the front desk—a window thing with thick glass and a microphone. The couple didn't look much older than Jolaine.

"I believe those are your foster parents for the next day or three," Price said.

Graham felt a jolt of panic. "You mean I have to leave?"

"I promised you a comfortable bed. We don't have any of those here. You'll be fine. They're the Markhams, and they're very nice people. You'll be safe with them."

"But I was beginning to feel safe here."

"This is a police station, Graham. It's not a place for fourteen-year-olds. You'll be better off there."

Graham watched them at the little window as they talked to the lady in the uniform. They turned in unison and looked straight at him. The wife waved at him with the tips of her fingers. It reminded him of a cat scratching at a screen.

"I don't like them," he said.

"I'm telling you they're good people," Price said. He leaned over to the side to gain access to his back pocket and he pulled out a little black leather wallet. Inside was a stack of business cards. He slid one out and handed it to Graham. "This is me. My numbers are on it. If you have any problems or concerns, if you get scared, or if you just want to talk, you give me a call anytime—day, night, or early morning."

Graham held the card in both hands. Why was this guy being so nice? What did he want?

Price pointed with his head to the Markhams. They were approaching, and he held up a hand to tell them to stay back for a bit. They stopped and moved to some chairs on the other side of the waiting room.

"Look at me, Graham," Price said.

Graham looked. He saw a mask of concern on the deputy's face.

"I know some bad things have happened. I don't know what they are, but just in watching the emotion in your face and in your body language, I know that something really bad is going on. I know that you feel as though you can't trust anyone."

He paused, as if waiting for Graham to confirm or deny. He did neither.

"I'm going to tell you something important," Price continued. "Whatever your secrets are, they're yours to keep, from whoever you want to keep them. Now listen to me. If you're not willing to tell me—and that's fine that you're not, I respect that—I don't want you to tell anyone, understand? Whatever your secrets are, people are trying to hurt you to get them. That's not right. That scares me, and it should scare you. You keep your secrets secret, understand?"

Graham's sense of fear deepened. Price was serious, and he looked genuinely worried for him.

"Am I going to be okay?" Graham asked.

Deputy Price looked away. "I don't know, Graham," he said. "I just don't know. That's not the answer you wanted to hear, and I apologize for that. But it's the only answer I know how to give."

Price leaned forward and put out two hands in a clamshell gesture. "I pray to God that this is all just nothing," he said. "But if the shit hits the fan—pardon my French—you give me a call and I'll be there for you. Please trust me that much. If you find yourself without any other options, I'm worth a roll of the dice."

Graham found tears tracking his cheeks before he knew that he was crying.

Price sat up straight. He shot a glance over to the Markhams. "No tears, Graham," he said. "That's no way to start with the new family. I hate to put it to you this way, but now's the time to suck it up and roll with what's coming. Don't show weakness, know what I mean?"

Graham in fact did not know what he meant, but he knew that nodding yes was the right thing to do.

Price smacked the side of Graham's knee twice. "Good," he said. "I know this is all very scary, but try to think of it as an adventure."

With that, the deputy stood and beckoned for the Markhams to come over and join them. They rose in unison and walked nearly in step. They stopped when they were six feet away and they smiled.

"Anita and Peter," Price said, "this is Graham Mitchell. Graham, this is Anita and Peter Markham."

Anita smiled wider and Peter extended his hand. "Hi, Graham," he said. "I'm sorry that you're going through tough times. I'd consider it an honor to have you join us at our home."

The words sounded at once sincere and rehearsed. Graham wasn't sure how they pulled it off, but it didn't feel threatening. He accepted the hand and they shook. Peter treated him like a girl, accepting only Graham's fingers in the handshake. That felt strange.

"Hi," Graham said.

Anita's hand shot out next. "I'm Anita," she said. "This is Peter."

Graham made a smile face and shook her hand, too. "I got that," he said. He stood.

"Are you ready to go?" Peter asked.

Graham improved his posture and settled his shoulders. "Sure," he said.

And it was done. The three of them headed toward the front together. As they reached the door, Graham shot a look back to Deputy Price, but he'd already moved on to other matters.

The lock turned and Jolaine's cell door opened. She stood from her concrete cot.

A guard—an *officer* (they didn't like being called guards)—said, "Are you Jolaine Cage?"

"Yes." Who the hell else would she be? They'd put her here, for God's sake.

"It's time to go."

She instinctively took a step backward, away from the door. "Go where?"

"There's a team here to transfer you to Chicago."

"Why?" Jolaine asked.

The guard half smirked, and assumed a weird, asymmetrical stance with one hand notched over the nightstick that resided where a firearm would be if he were a real cop. "I know I look like I run the place," he said, "but you'd be surprised the shit they don't tell me."

Jolaine sensed that she was supposed to laugh at that, but she was disinclined.

"Yeah, okay," the officer said. "I need you to turn around so I can cuff your hands."

Jolaine didn't move.

The officer rolled his eyes. "Oh, come on, don't do this to me. It's almost the end of my shift. Don't make me call the crisis team."

He said that as if she had any idea what a crisis team was. "I don't understand," she said. While mostly a statement of truth, it was also a delaying tactic, buying time for one of those options she'd been waiting for to materialize.

The officer said, "What's to understand? You turn around and I cuff you."

"But I don't want to go anywhere," Jolaine said. "What's in Chicago? That's a long way from here."

"Great food and a pretty city," the guard said. "Though I don't think you're scheduled for a lot of sightseeing." That joke fell flatter than the first one. "Look, I don't know, okay? I have orders to deliver you out front. For me, that's the beginning and the end. And please believe me when I tell you that I have every intention of following my orders."

Jolaine remained in place.

"Your call," the officer said, "is whether it all happens easily or if you end up bloody in the process."

"But I haven't been charged with anything," Jolaine protested.

The guard shrugged with his whole body. Handcuffs dangled from one of his outstretched hands. "That's yet another thing that lies outside my give-a-shit zone," he said. "I've told you what my orders are. Now, you have to decide whether or not you're going to follow them."

"Don't you see that this is wrong?"

The guard said nothing. He just stood there, the handcuffs dangling from one fingertip.

Jolaine tried to think of an alternative, but no option seemed available. She could refuse to leave, but then the crisis team would storm in—she imagined burly guards in riot gear with nightsticks and pepper spray. The result would be blood and bruises and she'd still end up in the car where she didn't want to be.

Or, she could fight this guy. Same result.

She had no option but to comply. She turned her back and surrendered.

Venice Alexander entered the final bit of code into her keyboard and bingo! Her screen jumped to life with a checkerboard of color images from the local jail in Lambertville, Michigan. That one had been a difficult hack—far more difficult than the security feed from the police station down the street where Graham Mitchell was being held. Once in, she now had to cope with an embarrassment of riches. In the case of the police station, she was faced with a matrix of sixty camera images. For the jail, it was at least twice that many. Choosing which images to concentrate on was a dizzying challenge.

After only a minute or two of watching both banks of images among four screens, Venice opted to ignore the police feed and concentrate on the jail instead. As the mother of a young teen herself, her heart belonged to Graham, but the boy had one big thing working against him. The most recent picture she had of the kid was nearly three years old. Kid years and dog years shared the common element of vast physical changes in very short periods of time. Even if she found the image of someone who likely was Graham, there'd be no way for her to be sure.

With a few clicks of her mouse, Venice reduced the police station to blackness and then split the jail feed among the four screens. As was often the case with jails, every cell had its own camera with its own video feed, but the voyeuristic element of it made her exceedingly uncomfortable, especially when it came to the cells of young men, who, she'd decided, were incapable of keeping their hands off their private parts for more than a few minutes at a time.

It was that thought, in fact, that awarded her first big break in the challenge to locate Jolaine Cage within the jail. While she hadn't had a chance to figure out the logic in the order of the camera feeds—assuming that there even was such a thing—she knew that wherever she found a male prisoner, she no longer had to worry about finding Jolaine.

In the end, it turned out that fewer women committed crimes in Michigan than men, and by a large margin. By the time she narrowed the images down to the ladies' cells, it was a simple matter to locate Jolaine. She looked exactly like her photo.

If she wanted to, Venice could have manipulated the camera from her desktop, but she opted not to because of the risk. Somewhere in that jail, a guard (or ten) was watching exactly the same images she was, and if something started to pan or zoom without affirmative input from them, the result would likely be unhappy. Like Peeping Toms (Tomasinas?) everywhere, she needed to be grateful for the view she had, even if it wasn't as good as it could be.

As she watched, Jolaine was in the middle of a conversation with someone who was just outside the edge of her camera's view, and it was not a happy exchange. From the way Jolaine moved, Venice imagined that she was trying to put space between herself and whoever was speaking with her.

Since the cells only held one prisoner apiece, that meant that the other party had to be outside the cell, which by definition meant that the other party had to be in a hallway.

Splitting the images yet again onto different screens, she was able to increase the size of the thumbnails, and increase their clarity. Venice scanned the dozens of squares looking for the image of someone in the mirror image of Jolaine, facing the edge of a frame while engaging in a heated discussion. She did this while glancing back to Jolaine's frame every couple of seconds just to keep track.

"There," she said. The sound of her own voice startled her, and she pointed at the screen, as if to display her discovery to someone else. A man in a uniform stood in the middle of a long hallway, dangling what appeared to be handcuffs from his fingers. Details were difficult because it was a fairly long angle. Venice imagined that the camera had been placed at the end of the hallway to capture all of the doorways in a single frame.

She dragged that frame over to the screen that displayed the interior of Jolaine's cell and she watched. It wouldn't be beyond the technical capacity of the security system to capture sound as well, but Venice had not had the time to untangle that part of the knot. She'd have to settle for just the video.

Venice keyed her microphone. It was a gooseneck that rose from the table and allowed her to multitask while minding Jonathan's business and keeping him out of trouble. "Scorpion, Mother Hen," she said.

Jonathan's voice told her to go ahead.

"I've tapped into the video feed from the jail where they're keeping PC Two. I have eyes on her right now."

"I copy," Jonathan said. "We're still ten to twelve miles out. What's the situation?"

Venice keyed the mike and then released it as she watched Jolaine turn and offer her hands to the guard behind her. "Stand by," Venice said. "I need to pay attention to the keyboard and screens for a few minutes."

Multitasking was one thing, but she sensed that what was coming was going to require intense concentration, and she was right. As Jolaine moved her hands behind her on the left-hand side of the screen, the man in the uniform applied handcuffs to someone on the right. The actions were too perfectly choreographed to be anything but two angles on the same action.

"I think they're moving her right now," Venice said into the microphone. "I see them applying handcuffs. Yes, they're moving. Stand by."

Venice watched the hallway feed as the guard ushered Jolaine out. With Jolaine's cell now empty, Venice
killed that image from her screen, and watched as the
PC was led directly toward the camera. She understood
that it was a mistake to ever look in a PC's eyes, even
through a television screen. They eyes were a person's
window to emotion—their window to personhood—
and Jonathan had told her a thousand times to keep the
emotion out of 0300 missions, rescue missions. Until
they were safe, PCs were merely objectives—pawns
worth dying to protect—and as such, it was a mistake
to get involved in the emotions or the injustice of their
situation. Jonathan's theory maintained that sympathy
got in the way of sound decision making.

Still, Venice saw the terror in Jolaine's eyes, and her
stomach tensed. They disappeared as they crossed
under the camera, and Venice jerked her head to the
thumbnails on her other screen, scanning for the movement that would match the images she'd just seen.

This time, she saw them twice, in adjacent thumbnails from the front and the rear. They appeared to be
approaching an interior guard station of some sort. The
man in the uniform kept his hand on Jolaine's arm, just
above her elbow, and Jolaine moved with a mechanical
stride, her head cast downward. She seemed to be
dreading what lay ahead.

The uniform had a brief discussion with whoever
was in the booth, and then they started moving again,
disappearing from view.

Venice felt as if she was getting the hang of this
now. Her eye caught the movement in the next frame
right away as Jolaine and her escort headed down yet
another hallway that was remarkable only for the fact

that it was so unremarkable—no doors, no other people, no anything. When they turned the next corner to the left, Venice picked them up in a screen that looked like a waiting room. It was too Spartan for the public, but it certainly was not intended for the incarcerated. The chairs looked too comfortable.

From those too-comfortable chair arose a matching pair of men who had to be affiliated with a federal law enforcement agency. Venice had no personal frame of reference, but she'd seen enough of these guys over the years to assume that they slept and showered in their suits, and somehow ended up always looking pressed and neat. There was a brief discussion between the guy in the uniform and the men in the suits, and then the suits took custody of Jolaine.

Venice clicked a freeze-frame—essentially a photograph, courtesy of the security feed—to capture the moment, and then watched them leave with Jolaine sandwiched between them.

"Two men in suits have just taken custody of Jolaine," Venice said into the radio. As she spoke, she clicked a freeze-frame that nabbed all of the faces.

"Any idea where they're going?" Jonathan asked.

"Give me a minute," Venice said. At her core, Venice was a law-and-order gal—the kind of person who would stand ten minutes in a grocery line because her basket had sixteen items instead of the fifteen that limited access to the express lanes—but this business of breaking into computer systems and seeing things that she wasn't supposed to see was the thing that made her life worthwhile.

As the threesome approached the limits of the picture frame, Venice scanned ahead on the other thumbnails. She expected that the next element would be to step out into the night, so she concentrated on those images.

And there they were.

Venice keyed her mike. "Scorpion, they're exiting the jail now. They'll be on the road in a minute or two. What's your position?"

"We have no chance," Jonathan said.

Venice heard the frustration in his voice, and she shared it.

The feds—whoever they were—had parked close to the jail building, in the turnaround apron in front of the main entry. They led Jolaine to a standard nondescript Ford sedan—it looked black, but at this hour, any car might look black. Venice watched as one of the suits put his hand on the back of her head and pressed her into the backseat and then moved to the shotgun seat up front.

They sat there for maybe ten seconds, and then they started moving. They'd be out of frame in just a couple of seconds, and if that happened, Venice feared that they'd be lost. How do you find a nondescript Ford when that's the only identifier you have?

Her eyes scanned the other thumbnails. There had to be another image. She only needed one more—

"Yes!" she shouted, and she clicked the freeze-frame.

"Good news," Venice said into the radio. "We got a license plate number."

CHAPTER EIGHTEEN

The Markhams put Graham on edge. They were too . . . nice. They were so intent on being cheerful that they never asked a question about him, not even how he was doing, the gold standard for meaningless questions.

After Deputy Price handed him off, all the Markhams talked about was how safe he was, and how happy they were to have him as part of their family. He didn't bother to tell them that he had no desire to be part of their family. He didn't want to be part of their neighborhood or their tribe, or even their thoughts. He wanted life to be what it was thirty hours ago, and the fact that that was not possible didn't do anything to change the reality of the wish.

"Let us know if you need anything," Peter Markham said. "I know this is a tough time, and we want to make it as easy for you as possible."

"I hope you like dogs," Anita Markham said. "We have a poodle who loves people."

Graham considered lying telling them that he was deathly allergic to dogs just to mess with their heads, but decided not to. They meant well, and while his Stranger Danger Spidey-senses were going crazy, they seemed like nice enough people and they were trying their best to help him.

But he was scared—more scared than he'd ever been of anything at any time in his life—and he knew that it was a mistake to trust anyone.

Except, sooner or later, you had to, right? He was only fourteen years old. He knew he was smart and he knew that he could be tough when he had to be, but there was a whole lot of the world that remained out of reach for someone his age. He couldn't drive and he couldn't earn a living. Where would he live—*how* would he live—if he didn't ultimately trust someone? He'd have no choice. The question would be deciding who that trustworthy person would be. So far, all he knew for certain was that he wasn't allowed to trust any of the people that everyone else was supposed to depend on. According to Jolaine, the police were his enemy, and so was the FBI. Who else? And if those people were the enemy, how was he supposed to decide who were his friends?

Was it safe to assume, just because the Markhams had picked him up, that they were automatically on the trustworthy list?

For the time being, it didn't matter. He was in their backseat and the car was moving. Unless he wanted to take a header out the door onto the road, he was pretty much stuck with one option, and that was to enjoy the ride.

The three of them drove in silence through the darkness. From the backseat, all Graham saw were trees. They passed quickly in the wash of the headlights.

"How far do we have to go?" Graham asked. It felt like they'd been on the road for over an hour.

"So you *do* have a voice," Peter said with a laugh. "For a while there, we were wondering. Nice to meet you."

It was a teasing attempt at being friendly, of striking up a conversation, but Graham wondered if they had any idea how many bullets had been fired at him in the past day. If they did, maybe they'd understand that his sense of humor wasn't everything it used to be.

"It's not that far," Anita said. "Maybe twenty minutes. Are you okay? Do you need to stop?"

"I'm okay," he said.

Peter shot him a look over his shoulder. "We're really sorry you're having to go through all this," he said. "I don't know the details of your particular case—and I don't need to unless you want to talk about it—but if it makes you feel any better at all, we deal with a lot of kids who are in the same position as you, and this night—the first night—is almost always the very worst. Things get better from here."

More nice words from a man who clearly had no freaking clue what he was talking about. His father was almost certainly dead, his mother had been badly wounded, and the people who did it to them were now trying to hunt down the survivors. For all Graham knew, one of those survivors—himself—had been successfully hunted down and now was being taken to a place he didn't know to endure whatever was coming. Where in all of that was any possibility that the worst was over?

When you can't say something nice . . . Graham opted to say nothing.

A few seconds later, the car slowed. Then it slowed some more.

"What's wrong?" Anita asked.

"This guy behind me," Peter replied. "He's been on my tail for the last five miles. I'm giving him a chance to pass."

Graham looked out the back window into the headlights of the vehicle behind them. They were too bright for him to tell whether they belonged to a car or a truck, but they were very close. They made no effort to pass. Graham's heart rate doubled.

"Go faster," he said.

"Oh, no," Peter said. "I'm not getting caught up in road—"

"They're going to try to take me," Graham said. Hearing the edge in his own voice raised his anxiety levels even higher.

"What?" Anita said.

Peter laughed. "Whoa, Graham—"

"Whoa yourself, Peter," Graham snapped. He didn't know how he was as certain as he was, but there was zero doubt in his mind that he was correct. This was the hit team. "We're out in the middle of nowhere. This is exactly the right place."

"Perhaps a few too many FPS games there, young man," Peter said.

Graham recognized FPS as first-person shooter games, and he hated them. "Did they tell you that people tried to murder my whole family?" Graham asked. "Did they tell you that my mom is in some secret hospital, and that my friggin' au pair is really a bodyguard and she's being hunted down, too?" Graham knew damn well that no one had told them that because until right now, Graham hadn't told anyone either.

"You're making that up," Anita said. But he heard the doubt in her voice. The fear.

"No, I'm not," Graham said. "Why would I—" He cut himself off. He wanted to live, not argue. "If you don't believe me, speed up."

"Why?"

"If they speed up, too, then we'll know I'm right."

"I don't want to know you're right," Anita said. Fear had hijacked her voice and transformed it into a squeak.

"Okay, then," Graham negotiated. "If they don't, then we'll know I'm wrong."

Peter said nothing, but the engine noise grew as their car accelerated. Graham saw the concern in Peter's eyes as his gaze darted between the road and the rearview mirror. Graham undid his seat belt so he could turn around in the seat. "They're not falling behind," he announced.

"So I noticed," Peter said. He picked up more speed, but the distance between the two cars actually decreased.

"My God, Peter," Anita said. "Slow down. You'll kill us all."

"No!" Graham shouted. "Better him killing us all than them killing us all."

"Peter, come on," Anita coaxed. "Be reasonable. This can't be true. We don't even know this boy."

"You don't need to know me. I don't know you, either. Just don't stop!"

Peter fixed him with his eyes in the mirror, then

glanced beyond him into the lights of their pursuer. He backed off the accelerator.

"What are you doing?" Graham shouted. "We've got to go faster."

"No, we don't," Peter said. "We've established that they're trying to follow us. It's not important to outrun them. As long as we keep moving, nothing changes. We'll drive to a public place—a restaurant parking lot or maybe a firehouse or police station. Whatever needs to be settled can be settled there."

"I'm calling the police," Anita said. She dug in her purse for her cell phone.

Graham started to object out of reflex, then realized that that was a pretty good idea.

Anita stared at her phone.

"What's wrong?" Peter asked.

"No signal," she said.

He sighed. "Yeah, this is a real dead zone in here."

Dead zone. Did he really just say dead zone?

"Turn around and buckle in, Graham," Peter said. "You staring out the window doesn't help anyone. We're going to be—"

Anita yelled, "Look out!"

Graham was still turning when Peter slammed on the brakes, and before he had a chance to register anything that was going on, he found himself rebounding off the back of Anita's seat on his way to land on the floor of the backseat.

"Oh, my God!" she screamed. "It's a trap! They set up a roadblock!"

Graham hadn't seen it yet, but he didn't have to. Didn't want to. His ribs landed hard on the hump on the floor, and something sharp jabbed his leg—he thought maybe it was an ice scraper left over from last winter.

"Run!" he shouted, and he scrabbled along the floor to find the door handle.

He still hadn't looked when he pulled the latch and pushed the back door open on Anita's side. He expected gunfire at any second, so he kept his head down as he spilled onto the road. He hit first on his back, lighting up the pain in his ribs, but then he rolled to his hands and knees, found his feet, and took off at a run.

"There!" someone yelled. It was a man's voice and it was heavily accented. "He is running away!" That extra bit allowed Graham to recognize that accent as Chechen. Friends of his parents, perhaps? Were they here to help? Were they among the people it was safe for him to trust?

No. Trust no one. He ran.

"Graham!" The man yelled. "Do not run! We are here to help."

Bullshit.

Graham lowered his head and concentrated on the wall of leaves and branches that lay ahead of him. They were going to hurt when he ran into them at this speed, but the fact that they were dense and it was dark meant that they would be able to provide him with shelter. He'd just have to duck in far enough to be covered, and then he could hunker down—

"Your mother sent me!" the man yelled. He panted through the words, which seemed to be coming from less far away.

Graham didn't dare look behind. He didn't dare do anything that might slow him down. He wished now that Jolaine had bought him running shoes instead of—

A heavy hand landed between his shoulder blades, a shove that sent him face-first into the ground. He got his hands out in time to catch himself, and they slid through rocks and sticks, tearing the hide from the heels of his hands, and also from his knees. He reflexively clenched his teeth to keep his jaws from snapping together and maybe biting his tongue.

Once splayed out and stabilized, he struggled to find his feet again, but it was too late. The man was on him. The collar of Graham's T-shirt went tight as the guy pulled on it, and then he felt another hand on his arm as he was lifted to his feet.

Graham struggled against the man's strength, wriggling like a grounded fish to break his hold. He got his arm free, and used the momentum to spin and try to back out of his shirt. He heard the fabric tear, and he felt the constriction release a little, but then the man punched him. Graham didn't see it, but it felt like a closed fist and it landed hard on the exact spot where the center hump had nailed him when they screeched to a stop.

The blow triggered a cough and Graham tasted blood. His knees sagged.

"I am sorry, Graham," the man said. "I do not mean to hurt you. You leave me no choice. I hope I hurt not too bad."

"Leave me alone!" Graham yelled, but it was a weak sound. He took a step to run again, but knew it would be a wasted effort. Whatever the guy had hit had ruined the wiring of his chest. It didn't hurt so much as it didn't work anymore. He couldn't take a full breath.

"The pain will pass soon," the man said. "I am sorry. You must come with me now."

Through his gasps for air, Graham managed to ask, "Who are you?" Looking up at the man, he saw no features. Perhaps it was the darkness of the night, but perhaps he was wearing a mask. Graham thought that to be more likely the case.

"If you promise to walk with me, I will promise not to hurt you anymore. Do we have a deal?"

Graham nodded. "Yes," he said. Even as the words left his lips, he knew that it was a deal that he wouldn't hesitate to break.

"Good," the man said. "Let us walk back to the cars."

As they made the walk back, Graham saw for the first time what the Markhams had seen before they slammed on the brakes. Two pickup trucks had blocked the entire road. If they had continued to speed, as Graham had wanted them to do, God only knows what might have happened. They'd probably all be dead. There was absolutely zero room for them to have sneaked by.

"Who are you?" Graham asked again.

"That doesn't really matter," the man said. There was a dismissiveness—a finality—to his tone that told Graham that it would be useless to ask that question again.

He'd run farther than he'd thought, probably a hundred yards. It took a long time to negotiate the walk back, and the trip was made longer still by the fact that somewhere in the encounter, Graham had run out of one of the replacement flip-flops they'd issued to him at the police station. It was annoying enough walking on one that he paused in the stroll back to pull the other one off and walk barefoot.

"I have him," his escort said to the crowd that had gathered around the Markhams' car. Peter and Anita had been pulled out, and were standing on the passenger side—the side closest to Graham—with their hands on their heads. They both looked terrified.

"What is going on?" Peter demanded. "Why are you doing this? We've done nothing wrong."

Graham thought he might have been hearing his own words from a few hours ago being recited back to him. "I'm sorry," he said to Anita as he passed within speaking distance. "I tried to warn you."

He felt a hand on his shoulder, pulling him to a stop. "What did you tell them?" The malevolence in the man's tone told him that he'd accidentally crossed some kind of line.

"Nothing," Graham said, but he knew that the word had come out too quickly. "Nothing that they probably didn't already know." He tried to make eye contact with the man he was speaking to and saw that he was in fact wearing a mask—the kind you would wear in the middle of winter to prevent frostbite on your nose, but made of a lighter material.

"I see," the man said. He looked over at Anita, who stood maybe ten feet away, and at Peter, who stood three feet farther.

From somewhere under his shirt, the masked man produced a pistol. He pointed it at Anita and fired a single bullet through her forehead. She dropped straight down, as if her body had been unplugged.

Graham didn't know if the voice he heard yelling was his own or if it was Peter's. Two seconds later, he knew it was Peter's voice because it fell silent as the gunman's second bullet caught the man in the mouth and killed him instantly.

"There," the gunman said. "Now it doesn't matter what you told them."

CHAPTER NINETEEN

Venice pressed the transmit button. "Scorpion, Mother Hen."

"Go ahead."

"PC Two was just picked up at the jail by a team claiming to be federal agents. I don't have access to their names, but the car they're driving is registered to Emin Zakaev of Detroit, Michigan. That happens to be the same person who lives at the address called from the Hummingbird Motel just minutes before the shoot-out in the parking lot."

In the pause that followed, Venice imagined Jonathan and Boxers discussing the importance of the disclosure. After fifteen seconds, Scorpion's voice came back, "What do we know about the owner?"

"Really, not very much. Not yet, anyway." As she spoke, she continued to plow through whatever data she could pull up. Sometimes, it was difficult to decide which was the better move when delivering news to her boss. Should she deliver the headline by itself, or should she wait until she had the whole story? In this case she went with the headline simply because of the speed with which everything was changing.

"Roger," Jonathan said. "Get back to me when you know something."

Venice owed an answer, and she was going to find it. Every person on the planet had some kind of past, and for every past, a record existed somewhere in cyberspace. Maybe it was an application to a zoning board to put an addition on their house, or maybe it was as simple as a driver's license. Each of those documents—and thousands of variations of tens of thousands of different possibilities—opened a door to other information, and if one were talented enough in the business of wrangling ones and zeroes, most of those doors could be opened. She often thought of herself as a digital burglar. Armed with a unique set of lock picks, she could enter spaces where she was not welcome and peek into the most private parts of people's lives.

She assumed that Emin Zakaev was a pseudonym of some sort. In the short term, that meant that she wouldn't be able to dig up much about his past that would be relevant to her right now. Tracing aliases was not especially difficult, but it was outrageously time consuming, and time was the commodity of which she had the least.

She decided to treat the name as if it were real, thus ignoring his past and concentrating on the present. If he used the same pseudonym to register his car and pay his phone bills, there were likely a lot of other things he did with the same name. People rarely thought about the width and depth of the footprints they left every day simply by going through the motions of life. The e-mail address you use to read the *New York Times* is the same one you use to order toys off the Internet. The credit card you use for cable television is the same one you use to eat at restaurants. Once Venice was able to break into one usage of a credit card, and was able to learn the password, a person's entire life lay right there, spread out for her to explore.

As was often the case, the phone company records proved easiest to breach. Armed with Emin Zakaev's MasterCard and his password, she was able to gain access to every expense he had charged over the past three years. Most of it was useless to her—at this stage, she didn't care what food he preferred or what books he read, though that could prove important later.

For the time being, she just wanted *something*. More often than not she didn't even know what the *something* was until she stumbled upon it. In a perfect world, the something would somehow lead her to—

"Oh, my God!" she exclaimed. It came out half as a shout and half as a laugh. "SecureTrace!"

It was her first real break, and it was a *giant* one. SecureTrace was a GPS-based subscription tracking service that automatically called the police if the car's airbag deployed. Operators responded to calls for directions, or, in the most advanced and expensive versions of the program, would provide a kind of valet service to help lost drivers find their way to a particular location.

As with ProtecTall Security, SecureTrace was the most common service of its kind, and as such, Venice had penetrated their firewall ages ago, in support of a different case. Since then, she'd been careful to leave no traces of her occasional visits. As long as a company had no idea that their security had been violated, they had no reason to make substantial changes. Fewer changes, in turn, meant continued easy access, and that, boys and girls, was the Holy Grail of hacking.

SecureTrace was even kind enough to put customers' account numbers on their credit card invoices. They used that same account number internally. Once inside their system, all Venice had to do was type in the account number, and she'd be able to find the precise location of the enrolled vehicle, written in longitude and latitude. A simple conversion from there would give her a satellite view of the location. The view wouldn't be real time, of course—in fact the satellite photos could be years old—but at least she could find it on the map and relay directions if needed.

In this case, Emin Zakaev was on Route 474 headed north toward Detroit.

"I got you," she said with a grin.

Jonathan never had much respect for the law enforcement community. He thought that too many cops put their careers ahead of matters of right and wrong—a trait that was trumped three times over by the prosecutors who saw every indictment as a political statement, the next rung in the ladder of their electoral aspirations. During his days as a hired gun for Uncle Sam, he'd run into a few such careerists in the Army, but precious few of them within the Unit.

Disdain for the profession notwithstanding, he had to respect their ability to pull stakeout duty. Boxers and he had been sitting in the car watching for Peter and

Anita Markham for over an hour. It was a pleasant little street in a pleasant little neighborhood, which roughly translated to being a boring as hell spot in the middle of the American nightmare called suburbia.

"How do we know when we've waited long enough?" Big Guy asked.

"When they get here, I guess. How long can it take?"

Boxers started to answer, but stopped and dipped his forehead toward a spot ahead of them. "Looks like we might have friends," he said.

A copper-colored van with tinted side windows approached headlong from the opposite end of the street and took up a position on the other side, about equidistant from the Markham residence. In the dark, he couldn't make out any other details.

"They're not even subtle," Boxers agreed. "How do you want to handle it?"

Jonathan shrugged. "There's nothing to handle yet. They're just a couple of guys out for a drive. Just like us."

"It's that just-like-us part that I worry about," Boxers said.

The driver of the other car killed his lights. No one opened a door.

Jonathan brought binoculars to his eyes. "Copy down this license number." He read off the Michigan plate number.

"Got it," Boxers said. He'd written it on a page of the notebook he'd pulled from a pocket on his thigh.

Jonathan was reaching for the transmit button when his radio broke squelch and Venice said, "Scorpion, Mother Hen."

He looked over at Big Guy. "Okay, that was scary." He keyed the mike. "Go ahead, Mother Hen."

"I have virtual eyeballs on Emin Zakaev," she said.

Jonathan sighed. "I'm tired, Mother Hen. What do virtual eyeballs look like?"

She explained about SecureTrace and revealed the physical location of the vehicle. "That's only about a thirty-minute head start from you," she concluded.

"Zakaev has PC Two," Jonathan said, referring to Jolaine. "She's substantially less important to us than PC One. What do we have on the boy?"

A pause. When Venice's voice returned, it was heavy with concern. "Nothing that I haven't already told you. Has he not shown up already?"

"Negative," Jonathan said. "But we have some friends who have. Tell me when you're ready to copy a license plate number."

Tracing plates barely qualified for Venice 101. "Ready when you are," she said.

Jonathan read the number that Boxers held up.

Seconds later, Venice announced, "That number traces to a Kathryn Kennison out of Muncie, Indiana. It's a Prius."

Boxers chuckled. "Did you know that Prius means 'little penis' in Latin?"

Jonathan laughed. He had no idea what Prius meant, but he was nearly certain it wasn't that. "That's not the vehicle I'm looking at," he said over the radio. "I'm assuming there's no report of the Prius being stolen."

"That's almost always the headline of motor vehicle reports," Venice said. "I don't see anything like that."

"Stand by," Jonathan said. He looked to Boxers. "Any thoughts?"

"I defer to the brains of the outfit," Big Guy said. "I just drive and break things. You think all the lofty thoughts."

Jonathan smiled. Reading through the bullshit, he understood that Big Guy had no better idea of the next step than he did.

"I'll tell you something that bugs me," Big Guy said. "As far as I know, this dance has only two sides, the bad guys and us. Those guys in the other car are bad guys by default. The Markhams are way late getting here, and that's not good. If 'not good' happens to the good guys, it has to be at the hands of the bad guys. So, how come the bad guys are watching the same house we are?"

Jonathan was impressed. It was a very good point. "You know what?" he said. "I think we should go out and have a little chat with—"

"Break, break, break," Venice said. There was a new edge to her voice, something close to panic. "Emergency traffic. Scorpion, are you there?"

Jonathan punched the transmit button. "Go ahead," he said.

"This is bad," Venice said. "I just got an urgent update from ICIS. There's been a multiple shooting on the road between the police station and your location. Two people shot, a man and a woman. The notice uses the phrase 'execution style.' "

Something twisted in Jonathan's gut. "Is it the Markhams?"

"No names yet," Venice said. "The investigation is just beginning. All I know is that the victims are young, and they were driving a car that matches the description of the Markhams' car."

Jonathan closed his eyes. This was bad. "Any mention of a teenager?"

"Negative."

Jonathan slammed the dashboard with his hand. He looked to Boxers and keyed the mike at the same time. "You know this means they got him, right?" he said.

"That means they've got both of them," Boxers said.

"And they're split up," Jonathan noted. "I don't know that they knew what they were doing, but that's a smart move. We have to choose our targets."

"We're choosing the kid, right?" Boxers asked.

"In a perfect world we would," Jonathan said. "But we don't know his whereabouts. We do know where the girl is."

"She's not the primary target."

"That's why we have secondary targets," Jonathan explained. "When the primary is unavailable, you go for second best."

Boxers shook his head. "No," he said. "We're not choosing a trained professional over a helpless kid."

"We're not *choosing* anything," Jonathan corrected. "We're playing the only hand we were dealt. In Column A we know something—it's not much, but it's a GPS tracking point. In Column B we know zip. It makes no sense—"

"Then let's learn something," Boxers said. He opened his door and stepped out into the night.

"What the hell—" Then Jonathan got it. Big Guy was going to confront the men in the other car. "Box, no!"

Too late. Big Guy was already striding toward the van.

"Shit," Jonathan spat. He opened his own door and stepped out to cover his friend. "If you've got a plan, this would be a good time to clue your boss in on it."

"Just gonna chat," Boxers said. He moved with surprising grace and speed. For the Big Guy, chatting and head-breaking were often synonymous.

To their credit, the guys in the van read the situation for what it was. They pulled away from the curb and drove off. In a hurry. At first, they seemed to be heading directly toward Boxers, but when Big Guy didn't dodge out of the way, they swerved around him.

"Do not draw down on them!" Jonathan commanded. Boxers hadn't made a move for his Beretta, but Jonathan knew the man well enough to anticipate.

"Cowards," Boxers grumbled.

"What the hell was that?"

"They're bad guys," Boxers said. "They know where Graham Mitchell is." He glared after the van as it disappeared down the residential street and turned the corner.

"No, they don't," Jonathan countered. "We just discussed this. If they were scoping the place out, then they didn't know that the Markham vehicle was hit."

Boxers shifted his eyes and looked down at Jonathan. Realization dawned. "Well, shit," he said. He started walking back toward their vehicle. It was as close to an admission of a mistake as Boxers was capable of making.

Jonathan pressed the transmit button on his radio. "Mother Hen, Scorpion. I need you to send me the co-ordinates for PC Two's location, and a probable intercept point."

In all the years Jonathan had been plying his trade, he had never lost a precious cargo. He wasn't starting now.

CHAPTER TWENTY

Graham's world had no meaning. After shooting the Markhams, his captors had descended upon him. It was five against one, maybe more. He couldn't resist as they shoved some kind of cloth into his mouth and sealed it in with a long strip of what looked and felt like duct tape. They passed three loops around his head, and then he was silent. He'd tried screaming, but the sound went nowhere. Next, they pinioned his arms behind his back. They wrapped something—rope, maybe, but it felt wider than that—around his wrists, and then they wrapped more of it around his elbows.

With his mouth and arms taken care of, they'd pressed lumps of what felt like moist clay against his eyes and wrapped them in place. Then they did the same thing with his ears. The final step was to bind his knees together, and then his ankles. He was blind, deaf, and dumb. As time passed, and his limbs fell asleep, he was also paralyzed.

He'd lost all track of time. Someone could have told him he'd been wherever he was for hours or for days, and he wouldn't be able to argue. All he knew was that he was in a vehicle of some sort, and he only knew that because of the constant bouncing movement. He also smelled the faint aroma of gasoline. Nothing strong or nauseating, but definitely there.

There was also the stink of his own sweat and his own fear. He didn't think he'd pissed himself, but the smell was definitely there.

God, it was hot. He was soaked through with sweat. He'd hoped for a while that the sweat on his face would loosen the tape around his mouth, but he'd had no such luck. Not yet, anyway.

His nose was clogging up, and he was terrified of suffocating. He kept blowing out hard and then trying to inhale easily. God only knew how much snot he'd blasted all over himself and his surroundings.

These people wanted him dead.

Or did they? Killing him would have been the easiest thing in the world to do. They didn't hesitate for even a second before killing the Markhams. How difficult would have been to shoot him in the head just as they'd shot Peter and Anita?

The Markhams, he thought. *I killed them. If it hadn't been for me, they'd still be alive.* Even as the thought formed in his head he knew that it wasn't true—not completely, anyway—but it was true enough not to be false.

How many more people had to die because of this ridiculous code? What could possibly be so important, so vital, that a stupid, random string of numbers and letters was worth killing for? And what had the Markhams done to deserve being shot and left in the grass to be found by animals?

Out of nowhere, images of wolves and buzzards appeared in his head, tearing and picking away at the Markhams' dead bodies. He tried to will the images away, but they wouldn't go. He knew that wolves didn't even live in this part of the country, but that didn't stop the horror-movie footage from playing in his brain. They rooted deeply into Peter Markham's gut, pulling out intestines and—

The car hit a huge bump, big enough to make him bounce, and it seemed to be slowing. In fact, there were a lot of bumps, making him wonder if they'd gone off-road.

Oh, shit. No one will ever find my body!

Graham shook his head and thumped it against the floor. He had to quit thinking things like that. He needed to become more like Jolaine, more logical. Not everything was a huge crisis. Not everything spelled his imminent death.

"Settle the hell down," he said, though the words came out as a muffled, jumbled mess. He remembered Jolaine's words: Always think, and wait for an opportunity to take action.

But what action could he take when he couldn't even move?

That couldn't last forever, could it? Sooner or later, they were going to have to at least free his mouth. They wanted information from him, after all. If he couldn't speak, there wasn't a hell of a lot for him to say, was there?

He decided that the first and only thing that he would say was that he wouldn't say anything until they untied him. He'd heard that arms and legs could get gangrene or some such thing if they didn't get enough circulation, and gangrene meant getting the arms and legs cut off. Well, that for damn sure wasn't going to happen to him.

The motion stopped.

Graham didn't know whether he'd felt the vehicle stop, or if he'd just noticed the stillness for the first time. He sensed movement, and then hands were on him and he was being lifted. Unable to kick his feet, he tried an inchworm motion that seemed to loosen their grip, but only for a second before someone got a good hold on his bound knees. From there, he was destined to go wherever they decided to take him.

After a minute or two of manhandling, they rested him on a hard surface. It felt cold against his sweat-soaked T-shirt. The chill was a relief at first, but then not so much. It was a little *too* cold. They laid him faceup so that his bound hands pressed into the small of his back, hurting his thumbs and stretching his spine backward past the extent it was supposed to go.

Graham knew that people were talking around him, but there were no discernible words, only muffled rumbles that had the rhythm of speech. He jumped as someone touched the bare flesh of his knees, and jumped again when they touched his ankles. When hands fumbled at his head as well, he understood that they were in the process of untying him. That in itself was a relief until he realized that the serious business of why he was here was about to begin. For the time being, they needed him alive. That gave him a few more minutes, anyway.

They freed his ears first. He felt the pressure of the bindings releasing from around his head, and then there was a soft *pop* as the clay stuff was pulled away.

The tape didn't come off easily from around his

mouth. The effort jerked his head first to the side, and then off whatever surface he was lying on. When the final loop came free from around his mouth, it hurt like hell. He wondered if they'd torn skin off with it.

"Ow!" he said through the gauze in his mouth.

"You can spit that out," the man with the accent said.

Graham tried, but his mouth was so dry that the edges of the material stuck to his lips. Ultimately, he had to force it out with his tongue.

"I would help you," the familiar voice said, "but I fear that you would bite me. Then I would have no choice but to pull all of your teeth out with a pliers. I wouldn't want that. I don't think you would want that, either." The man spoke the horrible words with such an easy tone that Graham didn't doubt one bit that he would do exactly as he said.

"Now, sit up, Graham," the man said. "Let's give your arms and shoulders some relief."

They helped him roll to his side, and as he did, he jumped as his feet and legs fell.

"You are on a table," his captor explained. "Do not be afraid. We will not let you fall."

Graham relaxed a little, and then realized how stupid that was. They could just as easily push him down on his face as live up to their promise.

Only they didn't push him down on his face. Hands gently leaned him forward as they worked first on his elbows and then his wrists.

"There will be some discomfort in your arms," the man said. "They will feel stiff, and your hands are swollen from being tied. Do not worry about that. The discomfort will not last for long."

After his hands were freed, Graham tried to flex his

fingers, but they wouldn't work. It was as if they were frozen open.

"That is the swelling," the man said.

The compresses were lifted from Graham's eyes, and his first instinct was to look at the swelling. His fingers were the size of sausage links, and they were purple. His heart skipped.

Gangrene.

"Do not look so frightened," the man said through a heavy accent. Graham realized now that he was the same guy who had chased him down in the woods. The same man who had killed the Markhams. "You might have guessed that I have done these things many, many times. The swelling is really perfectly normal."

The smile on his face matched the smile in his voice. *Relax, kid, I'm a professional torturer. You have nothing to worry about. I'll only hurt you as much as I need to, and not a bit more.*

Graham squinted against the yellow light of the room. The table he sat on was made of metal, and it seemed to be in far better, cleaner shape than anything else in here. The room itself was maybe twelve by twelve feet, and except for the other men in the room— all of whom wore beards and burned hatred in their eyes—the table was the only furniture. Dozens of sharp, menacing hooks hung from the ceiling. They looked like fishhooks for a whale, only without the barbs. It took him a while, but Graham recognized them as meat hooks.

He shot a look toward the man who'd taken him.

"This is a meatpacking plant," the man explained. "Or, it was at one time. Now it is merely a playground for people who do my kind of work." He cast a glance over his shoulder at the array of hooks. "Frightening things, aren't they? I imagine that they would hurt wherever I put one of those, but I can think of a few places where they would hurt particularly bad."

The man shifted his eyes to Graham. "I bet you can think of some of those places, too. Yes?"

Graham felt a chill, and he started to tremble. "W-who are you?"

"I am nobody," the man said. "I am just a soldier in an army you've never heard of." He seemed amused by his words, broadening his smile. "But I understand that names are important. Call me Teddy, then. As in a big cuddly teddy bear. Do you like the name Teddy?"

Graham had no idea how to answer the question. He worked his mouth, but the resultant squeaking sound embarrassed him.

"I understand that you are frightened," Teddy said. "And for good reason. Here you are, away from home, away from your parents, and away from your nanny. You're in this frightening place with so many sharp hooks. They used to hang cow carcasses from those back when the factory was still in business."

Moving with the speed of a striking snake, Teddy grabbed the nape of Graham's neck and enclosed it in a viselike grip, squeezing hard enough to make the fibers of the muscles in Graham's neck feel as if they were being pried apart. With his other hand, Teddy poked his forefinger under the boy's jaw, in the soft spot just behind the point of the chin.

"This is my favorite spot to put the hook on people who do not cooperate with me." He pressed hard with the finger. "The point goes into the flesh and out again under the tongue. People can hang that way for longer than you probably think."

Graham found himself crying. He feared he might throw up.

Teddy let go and Graham coughed.

The torturer smiled again. "I know that the table is not very soft, but try to make yourself comfortable. Sit back. Relax."

Graham didn't move. He didn't know if the man's words were a trap, or if he really wanted him to do something. In the end, it seemed not to matter.

"You know, Graham Mitchell, we are very nearly friends. Did you know that?"

Graham shook his head.

"Sooner or later, you will need to speak words," Teddy said. "Now is as good a time to start as any."

Graham cleared his throat. "No," he said. "I didn't know that we are friends. I don't remember ever meeting you before."

"I overstate by saying *friends,*" he clarified. "You spoke with a colleague of mine this morning. You called him with a message, and then you hung up without giving him the information that you were supposed to give. Do you know what I'm talking about?"

Graham nodded. "Y-yes. But like I told him, I forgot what the number was."

Teddy landed him with an openhanded slap that felt more like a closed-fist punch. Graham saw stars and smelled blood. He damn near fell off the table.

"Now, you see, young man, I believe that was a lie you just told. Lying is a sin, and I cannot abide liars. You disappoint me."

Teddy glared at Graham for what felt like thirty seconds, and then he changed. Tension seemed to leave his shoulders. He looked to the four other men in the room. "Come," he said. "We should give young Mister Mitchell time to think about his options."

As one, the men all moved toward the heavy metal door that led out into what appeared to be a concrete hallway. Teddy was last to leave. As he got to the door, he paused and looked back at Graham, who hadn't moved from his spot on the table. "Try to stay warm," he said. "This is, after all, a freezer."

Teddy stepped out into the hallway and closed the door behind him.

A heavy lock slid shut on the other side of the door. Graham was trapped.

Somewhere behind the walls—maybe from up in the ceiling—a motor started. Within seconds he felt a breeze of frigid air pouring out of three huge vents that hung too high to reach.

To avoid the direct blast of air, Graham lowered himself from the metal table onto the tiled floor. He pulled his legs up, Indian style, and he pulled both arms out of the stretched-out sleeves of his T-shirt and he hugged himself. He'd stay as warm as he could for as long as he could.

This is, after all, a freezer.

CHAPTER TWENTY-ONE

It took the better part of an hour for Boxers to pilot the Expedition to the coordinates Venice had dictated over the radio, only to find that the coordinates were approximate, at best. They took them to the right neighborhood, but from there, the search went manual and old-fashioned.

"I don't often think we're under-gunned," Boxers grumbled as he approached the turn from Gratiot Avenue onto Maple Ridge Street. "But tonight, I'm worried."

To say this was a bad neighborhood was to give bad neighborhoods a bad name. This was the worst of Detroit's urban blight. North of Grosse Point Park, they were square in the middle of zip code 48205, the deadliest real estate in one of the deadliest cities in the Western Hemisphere.

Jonathan took in the scenery. Despite the darkness of the night, which got very little help from the streetlights that were mostly burned out, the Expedition's headlights washed over the facades of buildings on Gratiot Avenue that clearly had once been thriving businesses. This was a well-built downtown area—lots of brick and stout construction—but as many of the buildings were boarded up or burned out as they were still alive. Those that still seemed to be in business sported bars and barricades that were every bit as intimidating and secure as anything he saw in the war zones where he'd served.

"Not exactly Mayberry, is it?" Jonathan asked.

"Only in a world where Barney Fife is played by John Malkovich," Boxers said.

Jonathan laughed. The image tickled him. "And Christopher Walken as Andy," he said.

That elicited a big, genuine laugh from Boxers. "That's a whole different show, isn't it?"

Now that they'd turned the corner onto Maple Ridge Street, the boarded-up businesses had become boarded-up houses. Again, it was sad. You could see the middle-class roots in the homes. Most of them were one story to one and a half. Jonathan imagined that they had been built post–World War II, and at one time they were occupied by families whose futures were bright. They couldn't have foreseen the strife and the riots and the neglect that came to define what was once one of the greatest cities in America.

And now was simply a mess.

Jonathan keyed his mike. "The license plate we're looking for is—" He recited the number from his notes.

"That's it," Mother Hen confirmed. "It will be on a black sedan. A Lincoln. The make and model are not clear from the video, but from what I can see, the size and the shape of the car are consistent with a Lincoln. Not the big one, but an intermediate one."

How many could there be? Certainly, a new vehicle—

anything younger than ten years old—should stand out like a beacon against the primer-coated wrecks that lined the streets.

Most of the houses were surrounded by chain-link fences whose height spoke more to keeping dogs in than keeping intruders out—though the two goals often intersected. Jonathan had donned his NVGs—night-vision goggles—in an effort to make out the terrain and the license numbers, but even in the intensified green light that mimicked a weird lunar form of daylight, the cars along the street all looked similar—and precious few of them had license plates.

As they cruised the neighborhood, the spacing between the houses opened up. Before long, they were in the middle of an abandoned industrial area. Dormant, diseased factories rose up against the urban backdrop, black stains against a black night. Jonathan noted one smokestack in particular that rose from the middle of a long, wide, flat-topped building, as if to flip off the community for the terrible fate that had befallen its inhabitants.

"Kill your lights," Jonathan said. "Go to NVGs." He was worried that the slow-moving headlights would attract the attention of whatever street gangs controlled this part of the city. And he bore no doubt that the neighborhood was controlled by a gang. In cities like this, where only one out of five ambulances was operational, and the average response times for police approached two hours—God knew they couldn't come with less than a platoon of cops and an arsenal of weapons—citizens depended on gangs to keep them safe. Hell, they had to depend on *somebody*.

Jonathan imagined that Boxers appreciated the opportunity to drive with NVGs instead of headlights. They'd replaced the two-tube NVG arrays that they'd gotten used to in the service with the more current, higher tech four-tube arrays, which solved the age-old problem of tunnel vision. Now, when they viewed the world through their NVGs, they had nearly a panoramic view. Jonathan's only problem with them were that they looked funny. Every upside came with a downside, he told himself.

"What do you think about this factory?" Boxers asked.

"By the nature of the question, I think you have a concern you're not sharing with me," Jonathan replied.

"Well, we've got these big fences," Big Guy said. "They present a perimeter of, what, a hundred, two hundred yards?"

"Something like that."

Boxers shrugged. "I'm just saying you can hide a lot of rolling stock back there and we'd never see it."

It was a very good point, Jonathan thought. They were big buildings that sat far from the road. How difficult would it be to drive into the middle of the compound and then just park your vehicle—hell, it could be the size of an eighteen-wheeler—behind a wall and out of sight?

"I'm switching to thermal," Jonathan said.

When you paid as much for a set of night vision devices as he paid for these, you got options that the hunting public never experienced. By flipping a switch on his NVGs, the device switched from image enhancement—essentially reflecting infrared beams that were shot out to the target object—to true infrared reading, which captured the heat signatures that were emitted by target objects.

His vision flashed. After a day as bright as this one, every surface emitted heat, so he needed to dial down the gain.

Once the images were stabilized, he would be able to read the relative heat signatures of the various buildings and vehicles. A car that had recently been driven, for example, would paint as hotter than one that had not been driven in a while, even though both may have been in the hot sun all day. It worked the same way with buildings. Those that were occupied should show up as warmer than those that were not.

Boxers drove slowly as Jonathan scanned the horizon. Nothing jumped out as significant.

Jonathan pressed his transmit button. "Mother Hen, can you give us anything more specific on the location?"

"Of course," she said, but there was an edge to her tone. "I could give the actual address and close-up pictures if I wanted to, but as usual, I've decided to let you wander aimlessly."

"Ooh," Boxers said. "The lioness is cranky."

"I'll take that to mean a negative," Jonathan said. He made no effort to keep the irritation out of his voice. "I'll take whatever you can give me, up to and including a reliable gut hunch."

"So, what's *your* gut hunch, Boss?" Boxers asked. "I figure you've always got one."

"I'm thinking that if we find Jolaine Cage, we're also going to find Graham Mitchell."

Boxers made a groaning sound. "Congratulations,

then. Because you're a hell of a lot more optimistic than me."

"Everybody's more optimistic than you."

"Har, har. I'm just sayin' that I don't think there's a chance in hell that either of them are still alive."

"The kid has to be alive," Jonathan said. "He's got the information they want."

"Unless the Ruskies got to him first. He's got the information they want to keep quiet. And as for the Chechens, the second the kid opens his mouth and gives them what they want, he's toast."

Jonathan waved him off. "No, now that's not true, either. Not right away, anyway. They'll want to buy some time to make sure that what he gave them is actually the code."

Boxers laughed. "Oh, good. Even better. So terrorists will wait to confirm that they have nuclear capability and *then* kill our PC. Yeah, good. Now I feel better. So tell me this: Why keep the girl alive?"

Jonathan sighed. "That's a tougher one," he said. "I'll only give even money on her. Maybe not even that much. Whatever it is, they drove her all the way out here for a reason. Maybe it's just to get rid of the body, but it's a reason. There's also a reason why Graham wasn't killed with those others. That tells me that his snatchers are of the Chechen variety, not the Russian variety."

"Well, there you go," Boxers said. "Case solved."

They cruised for another two hundred feet. The first factory, first of several in a row, showed no signs of life. As they approached the next, Boxers pointed at a spot beyond the windshield. "Hey, Boss," he said. "Trouble at twelve o'clock level."

Jonathan pivoted his head to the right to see a clutch of young men approaching them in the dark. They were all black, and they all walked with attitude. He cursed himself for being so involved with his survey of the area that he missed the obvious.

"I see weapons," Jonathan said. The young toughs were not even making an effort to conceal their fire-power. Among the six of them, Jonathan recognized two MAC-10s and at least four pistols.

Next to him, Boxers drew his M9 and cocked the hammer. "I'm ready," he said. "I'll take the three on the left."

"Not yet," Jonathan said. "Only if they fire first."

"Shit," Boxers spat. "You know, if they fire first, they might just hit something, right?"

"This isn't the fight we want," Jonathan said. "I am *not* dying at the hands of some untrained gangbanger. I've lived through too much shit to die that way."

Over the years, Jonathan had listened to Boxers describe countless venues in which he intended not to die. On balance, that was a good thing. "You know, if you took up less space you'd be a smaller target," he said.

"Then you've got no chance of ever bein' hit, little man. No wonder you feel cocky."

Jonathan flipped him off. "I'm going to meet them halfway," he said. "You stay put. If they shoot me, take out the MAC-10s first."

"Machine guns first," Boxers parroted. "Really? Wow, I never would have thought of that. I normally aim for the guy with the slingshot first, but if—"

Jonathan tuned him out and opened his door. He

drew his Colt, but he kept it dangling by his thigh. If any of them so much as twitched, he could drop three of them before his first ejected shell casing hit the ground, but that would still leave three, and those odds sucked.

"Good evening, gentlemen," Jonathan said. He modulated his voice to be just loud enough to be heard, but not so loud as to draw attention from anyone who might live in the neighborhood. He rocked his NVGs up out of the way, but kept them on his head in hopes of looking different enough to give the young men pause before doing something stupid.

The young people Jonathan had dealt with in any detail were all athletic, they all had short haircuts, and they all wore the same clothes. He knew that he was ill-prepared to deal with a bunch of teenage gangstas whose pants hung halfway down their asses.

"Who the hell are you?" one of the young men asked. He walked in the lead, so Jonathan assumed him to be the leader.

"I'm just a guy who wants no trouble from you," Jonathan said.

"Then you shouldn't be driving in my 'hood without lights on."

All things considered, it was a good point.

One of the kids behind the leader and off to the left made a move to lift his pistol to a shooting position. Jonathan reached out with his free hand in a stopping gesture. "Please keep your firearm pointed at the ground," he said. The urgency in his voice drove his volume to a higher level than he wanted.

His comment prompted the leader to turn back to his crew. "Georgie," he said. "Be cool."

Georgie went cool, but he took his own time doing it, finally shifting the muzzle of his pistol to a neutral position pointing to the ground.

"Thank you," Jonathan said. He shifted his own weapon around his back to his left hand, extended his right hand toward the leader and approached. Cautiously. "My name's Scorpion," he said. "What's yours?"

"Screw you," the leader said.

"Nice to meet you, Screw You," Jonathan said without dropping a beat. "Is that Chinese?"

Jonathan waited for the line to land. When they laughed, his hand remained extended. "Don't leave me hanging here," Jonathan said. "I mean no disrespect."

The leader modified the handshake to a knuckle-knock, and Jonathan complied.

"The hell kind of name is Scorpion?"

Jonathan smiled. "It's a kind of street name."

"You tryin' to be all scary and shit, right?" The kid laughed. "And what's that shit on your head?"

"I'm still waiting on a name," Jonathan said.

"And I'm still waiting for you to get the hell outta my 'hood."

This was a tough point in their negotiation. The kid needed to save face in front of his pals, and at one level, Jonathan did owe him an explanation. He was, after all, in the kids' 'hood, just as they said.

Jonathan made a point of holstering his Colt, but he kept the safety off, just in case. "That's not going to happen," he said. "My friend and I have business to conduct here." Without looking back, he called, "Hey, Big Guy."

The driver's door of the Expedition opened, and Boxers unfolded himself. "Right here, Boss." Maybe just for show, but probably for effect, he brandished an HK417 rifle, muzzle pointed to the sky. Chambered in 7.62 millimeter, the rifle looked every bit as badass as it was. If it came to a firefight, these guys would be dead before their fingers touched their triggers.

"Holy shit," the leader said. Several of his friends took an instinctive step backward. "He's one tall drink of water."

Jonathan laughed. He hadn't heard that phrase in years. "Yes, he is," he said.

"So, what are you? Cops or something?"

To bluff or not to bluff? "Well, we're something," Jonathan said. "But we're definitely not cops."

"You look like cops," the kid said.

"They look like the Army," another kid said. "What's with the commando clothes?"

Jonathan and Boxers both wore black on black on black. "I'm still waiting on a name," Jonathan said. "There's no need for us to be adversaries."

"There's no need for us to be adversaries," the leader repeated in a pretty spot-on impersonation of Jonathan's voice. "Shit, man, you're like a robot. So which is it, army or cops?"

"We have no desire to get into your business so long as you stay out of ours."

Georgie said, "Far as I'm concerned, you got no business here for us to stay out of. This is our turf, not yours."

Jonathan was tiring of the banter. They had work to do, and these guys were a problem. They jeopardized the overall security of the mission—whatever the hell that turned out to be—and they posed an overt threat through their firearms and their attitudes. Under different circumstances—say, they were on foreign ground—the smart move would be to eliminate the lot of them just to keep them from posing a threat to Jonathan's six o'clock once they started moving.

But this wasn't foreign ground, and different rules applied. From the kids' point of view, Jonathan was the invader, and they were defending—

"LeBron," the leader said. "My name's LeBron." He pointed to the factory beyond the fence. "What are those dudes doin' in there? Are they, like, terrorists or something?"

Jonathan's heart skipped. LeBron knew something, and the something he knew could be of great value. "They could be, yes," he said.

"Don't bullshit with us," another kid in the crowd said. "Either they are or they ain't."

"It's not that simple," Jonathan said. "If they're the people we think they are, then yes."

"I knew it," Georgie said. "Rag-head douche bags. I told you—"

"Not that kind of terrorist," Jonathan said. He looked back to Boxers, who just seemed bored. Or ready to shoot someone. Sometimes it was hard to tell the difference in the dark. "Can you tell us what you know?" Jonathan asked.

"What kind of gat is that?" LeBron asked, nodding to the rifle in Boxers' hands.

Boxers raised his rifle a little higher to get it in a better position in case it was needed, yet without pointing it directly at anyone. Jonathan took a half step to the right to make sure he had a clear firing lane in case LeBron was planning to do something stupid. "That's a Heckler and Koch Model 417 assault rifle," he said.

"Like an M16?" LeBron asked. "Kinda looks like an M16."

"Think M16 on steroids," Jonathan said. He didn't bother to clarify the difference in calibers and the dozens of other factors that made the 417 and its little brother the 416 (christened the M27 by the US Marine Corps) head and shoulders better weapons than the old M16.

"Machine gun?" LeBron asked. "Fully automatic?"

"It can be," Jonathan said. "I gotta tell you I'm not comfortable with the direction this chat is taking."

"I'm just tryin' to figure out why a non-army non-cop has fancy guns and a big truck, and they're watchin' a place I been worried about for a long time."

"Sounds like we might be on the same side," Jonathan said. "If they're who I think they are, we can help you get rid of them."

"What'd they do?"

Jonathan shook his head. "Nope. You first. Tell me what you know."

LeBron shifted his posture as he considered his options. Even in the dark, Jonathan could see his eyes sharpen. Everything about the kid's demeanor screamed intelligence. Everything, that is, except the wardrobe.

"Not out here," LeBron said. "I got a crib around the corner. We'll talk there. Just you, though. Gigantor will scare my babies."

"We're a team," Jonathan said. "We stay together."

LeBron considered some more. "Why don't we just

shoot you all down and be done with it? It's what, six against one."

"Not nearly good enough odds," Boxers said. His words rumbled the sidewalk. His delivery dared someone to question the veracity. "Where he goes, I go."

More thought. "All right, then," LeBron said. "Follow me."

"Just give me an address," Jonathan said. "I'll drive to it and meet you there."

"I'm serious, man," LeBron said. "It's just around the corner, not two hundred feet from here."

"Let's get going, then," Jonathan said. "We've spent too much time parked at the curb as it is."

CHAPTER TWENTY-TWO

Graham had never been so cold. It was winter-cold inside this little room with its metal table and its forest of hooks hanging from the ceiling. He was wearing so little that the cold seemed to wrap around him like some kind of cooling blanket. He couldn't stop trembling, but he suspected that a lot of the trembling was due to fear instead of cold.

He'd rather it be from the cold. *Show no weakness,* Deputy Price had said.

Jolaine's words resonated even louder. All he needed was time and opportunity. With those things, he stood a chance of getting out of here. With just those things.

But he'd need strength, too, and with all the shivering, he could feel energy draining out of him. He couldn't remember the last time he'd eaten, and that thought triggered a rush of hunger that consumed his gut, cramping his stomach and making him feel nauseous.

Jolaine.

Another wall of emotion broke over him. Jolaine

was all he had left. She was the last one who gave a shit about him at all. Now it was just Graham and these terrible people.

3155AX475598CVRLLPAHQ449833D0Z.

The thought came from nowhere, still intact, still ready to go. The code that was more important than so many lives. How was that even possible? What could it mean?

Well, that was easy, wasn't it? It meant the difference between life and death for Graham, and maybe for Jolaine as well. As long as he kept it to himself, they would have to keep him alive.

Another terrifying thought bloomed: Maybe that was the plan. This shit with the freezer and the cold air was a form of torture, right? Sure it was. He'd seen it on TV. It was the kind of thing that happened to the Iraqi prisoners in that prison he'd read about in the history books. The books called it torture.

Well, what was the point of torture?

In this case, it was to get him to talk. They'd made that very clear. They'd make him suffer until he gave them what they wanted. And then what?

Well, Jolaine said that if he gave up the information, they'd kill him. So, his choice was to suffer or to die.

That wasn't a choice at all. That was—

The lock on the other side of the door moved. It made a loud sliding sound followed by a solid *thunk* when it reached the end of its travel. He waited for what was coming next. Under the table as he was, occupying the same spot for all this time—a spot that had therefore become at least a little warmer—he hoped that he wouldn't be seen.

Should he be ready to lunge at whoever opened the

door? Was this the opportunity that Jolaine had told him to be ready for? How could he know?

The door opened quickly. That was a surprise, because in his mind, the opening would have been a long, drawn-out event, complete with creaking noises and a demonic laugh. He couldn't see the door because it was blocked by the vertical rectangle that served as one of the legs for the stainless-steel table, and for long seconds, nothing happened. No one entered as far as he could tell, and he didn't move. The heavy thrumming of his heart was the loudest sound he could hear.

"Come on out, Graham," said a heavily accented voice. It wasn't Teddy, but it might have been his brother. The same accent, but a lot thicker. "I know you are here because there is nowhere else for you to be."

Graham didn't move, as if by remaining still he could become invisible.

"So you want to play seek and hide," the man said from the door. "Sure. Fine. We can do that."

The hiding strategy suddenly seemed like a bad idea. What was the sense of pissing them off? It would be different if he'd set a trap, or if he had some kind of ambush plan. As it was, all hiding could do was make all of this more difficult, more uncomfortable for him.

"I'm here," Graham said. It came out a little too loud, but that probably didn't matter. He scooched his butt along the floor the point where he was clear of the table, and then he stood. He didn't realize he'd raised his hands until he saw that he'd done it, and the realization embarrassed him. When he was standing at his full height, he lowered his hands to his sides.

The man had only advanced a few feet into the doorway, but he stood funny, as if one side of his body were heavier than the other.

"What's wrong?" Graham asked, reading the expression on the man's face as one of anger. "I'm right here."

"I knew where you were," the man said. He showed an odd smile, an unnerving smile. Then he shifted his weight to point something at Graham.

At first, it registered to Graham as a gun. He started to dive for cover, but before he could hit the floor, a spray of high-pressure water was on the way. The sheer volume of the flow told Graham that it was from a fire hose. When the solid pillar of water hit him in his chest, it threw him backward and down onto the floor.

The stream pummeled him with bruising force, knocking the air from his lungs. When the man redirected the stream to his face, Graham brought his hands up to protect his eyes. Even with his face covered, the water got into his nose and mouth and choked him. The act of coughing brought in more water, and he thought he was drowning.

The pillar of water shifted in an instant, and then it started tearing up his belly and his legs. Again, he tried to cover up, but then the stream returned to his face. As soon as he covered it, the stream went back to his balls. This asshole in the doorway was having a great time.

Graham rolled on the floor to turn his back to his attacker. The force of the stream pushed him across the floor until he was pressed up against the far wall.

Still the hydraulic beating continued, raking the length of his body, from the soles of his feet to the crown of his head. This went on for at least two minutes. There'd be brief respites of five, ten, maybe fifteen seconds when the water stream wasn't being driven directly into his body, but the flow continued.

And then it stopped, a smash cut from full on to full off.

The attacker didn't say a word before he left. Graham heard the door close and the lock slide back into place. Then all he heard were the sounds of water dripping and draining and puddling. It was a sound that was worse than silence.

When he was sure he was alone again, he rolled away from the wall and onto his back, and from there to a sitting position. Water ran from everywhere. Where it wasn't running off a surface, it dripped in a rapid, staccato rhythm that might as well have been a stream. He sat in a puddle that was at least an inch deep, maybe deeper. He could not have been more soaked, not if he had jumped into the deep end of a swimming pool. Every surface of the room was soaked, in fact. Not a dry square inch to be found anywhere.

As he rose to his feet, he noted that the water was deep enough to cover his toes. When he walked, his feet created tiny bow waves that rippled across the width of the room.

When the coolers kicked on again, he understood what they were doing.

They were going to freeze him to death.

Anton Datsik sat at his desk in the study of his modest home in Arlington, Virginia, playing solitaire on his computer as he waited for the phone call that had to come soon if it were to be of any use. When it arrived, he answered on the first ring. "Tell me you have news I want to hear," he said.

"I do," the woman said. "We know where the boy is. He's in the custody of the Chechens as we speak. There's an old meatpacking plant in Detroit." She gave him the address.

"How do you know this?" Datsik asked.

"I just know," she said.

"Who else knows?"

"I can't answer that."

"Does your boss know?"

"Absolutely not," she said. "Or if she does, I don't know how. My sources and hers are entirely different. And mine are much more reliable."

Datsik typed the address into his computer to check out the location. It was both urban and accessible. He checked the clock. "How long has he been there?"

"I don't know. Maybe one hour. Not much more, I don't believe."

"Are you there on the scene?"

"I am not."

"They cannot be allowed to leave," Datsik said.

"I believe that is what the Agency hired you for." There was defiance in her voice this time that hadn't been there before. He didn't like it. "I have done my part," she said. "I have delivered him to you. Now be sure to tell—"

Datsik clicked off. He knew what she was going to ask and didn't need for that to be out in space for the NSA to listen to. Besides, he had more pressing matters to attend to.

Using a different phone—an encrypted satellite phone that was dedicated to a single purpose—he dialed a number and waited.

Philip Baxter answered on the second ring. "Yes," he said.

"The clock is ticking," Datsik said. "I need a plane, eight parachutes, and a pilot who has no memory."

Baker paused. In the background, Datsik could hear the sound of a television. Sounded like a romance. "Do you know what time it is? How am I—"

"I can end this tonight," Datsik said. "But I have to work quickly. Telling you the truth, it might already be too late. In two or three more hours, this will either be over, or the world will have nuclear-capable terrorists. All of that, my friend, is on your shoulders."

He deliberately used the most provocative words he could conjure.

"Your team is ready?"

"It is."

Another pause. "I'll get back to you in ten minutes," Baxter said.

LeBron hadn't exaggerated. His crib was indeed just a few hundred feet away, the first house on the corner. It took LeBron and his crew less time to walk the distance than it took Boxers to drive. Big Guy parked the Expedition in the alley behind the house and locked the doors.

"Somebody steals this car, they're gonna get quite a stash," Boxers said.

It was a hell of point, but they didn't have a lot of choice. Jonathan was betting on the fact that within the neighborhood, stealing from LeBron was understood to be a bad decision.

"Maybe I should stay out here and guard it," Boxers offered.

"I'd rather you be inside," Jonathan said. "It's only the two of us this time around, and we're on a really tight clock. I want your opinions."

Boxers laughed. "Are you really going to plan an 0300 op off the word of a bunch of gangbangers?"

Jonathan scowled. "It's local intel. We do it all the time. These guys know more about their neighborhood than we do."

"We don't even know if the guys they don't like inside that factory are the same guys we don't like."

"That's what we're here to find out." This wasn't like Big Guy. "Why's there a bug up your ass on this?"

Boxers started to speak, then changed his mind.

"Talk to me, Box."

"You know we're gonna get screwed in this thing, right?" Boxers said. "We've got government agencies fighting each other for a piece of this pie, and we're the ones in the middle who don't officially give a shit about the outcome so long as we extract the PC from the bad guys."

Jonathan shrugged. "That's what we do," he said. "We're mission oriented, not politically oriented."

"Big words," Boxers said. "Where are you going to be when we're in the middle of a crossfire between FBI and CIA?"

Jonathan recognized that his answer would seem obtuse, but he didn't mean it that way. "We're going to save the PC," he said. Really, it was the most obvious thing in the world. "The alternative is to let the PC die. That won't happen. Not on my watch."

"And what do we do about the bodies that bear government credentials?"

"We say that they shouldn't have tried to kill a child." Even in the most cynical corners of the most corrupt governments on the planet—of which, unfortunately, the United States was numbered, thanks to the Darmond administration—it was understood that children were not to be harmed in political operations.

Boxers held Jonathan's gaze, then defaulted to his dismissive chuckle. "Yeah, okay. Fine. I say we wear body armor."

Now, there was a point where Jonathan could not argue. Before moving ahead, each of them donned their ballistic vests, which were preloaded with three hundred rounds of ammunition for their preferred long guns— the M27 for Jonathan and the HK417 for Boxers.

"As long as we've got the ammo . . ." Boxers said.

"Yeah, we'll take the weapons, too." Jonathan didn't believe in his heart that they were walking into an ambush at LeBron's house, but there was no way to know for sure. Bottom line: No one in the history of mankind had ever offered up a curse to all things holy for being too well armed or having too much ammunition.

"Let's kit up all the way," Jonathan said. A full-on, high-end show of firepower couldn't possibly work against them. Plus, the more they carried on their persons, the less they risked losing in the event that the Expedition was stolen.

When they were done, Jonathan's M27 dangled like an exclamation point down the center of his body. His left thigh bore a 4.6 millimeter HKMP7, and the ubiquitous .45 Colt 1911 rode on his right thigh.

He saw that Boxers was similarly outfitted, but with the 417 where Jonathan's M27 hung, and a Beretta M9 instead of his Colt. "What the hell," Jonathan said. "Let's take the rucks, too."

With the rucksacks on their backs—Jonathan's weighed in at around seventy pounds, Boxers' at just north of one hundred—they had nearly everything they needed to invade anyplace that needed invading. Certainly, they had LeBron's living room covered.

"That covers the theft issue," Boxers said with a smile. "Sure am glad I brought it up."

With his tiny wireless transceiver inserted in his right ear, Jonathan connected his portable radio to the transmit button in the center of his chest and he pressed it. "Mother Hen, Scorpion."

"Loud and clear," Venice's voice responded.

"I have a research project for you," Jonathan said. He read off the address of the factory. "I need you to find out everything you can about the inside of that building. Anything and everything."

"Okay," she said. For reasons known only to her, Venice avoided military speak such as "roger" for okay, or even the civilian version, ten-four. "How long do I have?"

"An hour ago," Jonathan said.

"Are you preparing to go hot?"

"Sooner than later," Jonathan said. "We're still determining if that's the right place. But we think it is. If so, then we go hot right after."

"Okey-doke," Venice said. "I'll let you know when I have something worth sharing."

Jonathan looked to Boxers, who'd been listening to the same radio traffic. "Anything else to add, Big Guy?"

"I'm just anxious to get moving."

As Jonathan led the way toward the back door, it opened to reveal LeBron standing expectantly in the opening. "Jesus," LeBron said, eyeing the weaponry. "You know they're not here, right?"

Jonathan waited till he had climbed the steps to say, "If the gear is with me, I know it won't be anywhere else."

LeBron recoiled from the words. "What, you think my boys are gonna steal from you?"

"A couple of minutes ago, your boys were gonna shoot me," Boxers said. "Where I come from, stealing isn't as bad as shooting."

"Well, you're in Detroit now," LeBron said. "Stealing and shooting are different things, but one almost always leads to the other. Your shit would have been safe back there."

"We mean no offense," Jonathan said. "May we come in?"

LeBron stepped aside. "Just don't make a lot of noise. The babies are asleep."

One day, Jonathan was going to learn to tame his prejudices and preconceptions about people. This neighborhood was a shit hole, and he'd expected the same of LeBron's house. In fact, the place was spotless. The furnishings weren't much—he imagined that many of them came from charity thrift stores—but everything was thoroughly dusted and neatly arranged.

They entered through the kitchen, which had all of the necessary comforts, though twenty years out of date.

The Formica of the countertops matched the Formica of the metal-legged table. The appliances were old-school almond, and the floors were flowered linoleum, but overall, the place had a well-loved look. The house exuded pride.

LeBron led the way through a doorway that was slightly smaller than Boxers into the living room, where a sofa and three chairs were all arranged for easy viewing of a nineties-vintage twenty-six-inch television set that was turned off. Dozens of books, if not hundreds of them, lined the short wall from floor to ceiling on the far end. LeBron's posse had dwindled to one—Georgie, whom he introduced as his little brother.

"This is my wife, Dawn," LeBron said, nodding to an attractive woman dressed in sweats. She smiled back at Jonathan, though her eyes showed confusion. She looked as though she might have been sleeping.

"Good evening," Jonathan said. "I'm sorry to intrude."

"What is this about, Lebby?" Dawn asked. She kept her tone light, but Jonathan was sure he heard an undertone of anger.

"This is Scorpion," LeBron said. "And his friend, Big Guy. They're—"

"Why are all of those guns in my house?" Dawn said.

Jonathan moved to explain. "Ma'am, I promise you that we're not here to do any harm."

"And they're not police, either," LeBron added. "They're here about the men across the street in the Excalibur Foods plant."

"Those men are trouble," Dawn said. "I don't want to know nothing more about them."

"Where's the rest of your team?" Jonathan asked. There was no issue more critical than the location of unaccounted-for firepower.

"I sent them on their way," LeBron said. "Dawn doesn't like guns."

"Including yours," Dawn said.

"I apologize," Jonathan said. "But as LeBron told you, those guys in the factory are big trouble."

"What did they do?" Dawn asked.

"They kidnapped a young boy," Jonathan said. Off to his side, he more sensed than saw Boxers stiffening. Big Guy hated it when Jonathan shared anything with anyone.

"Oh, my God," Dawn said, bringing her hand to her mouth. "Why would they do such a thing?"

Jonathan eyed the chairs that were as-yet unoccupied. "May we sit down?"

Dawn seemed hesitant.

"We'll take these off," Jonathan said, shrugging out of his ruck and laying it on the floor. Boxers followed suit. Both kept their body armor on, and their weapons either holstered or slung. When he sat, Jonathan took care not to snag the fabric with any of the festooned weapons.

When Boxers sat, he looked like an adult sitting at a little girl's tea set. Only slightly less comfortable.

"Excuse the gear," Jonathan said. "We're sort of obsessive about being prepared."

"So, who are you really?" LeBron asked. "You never gave me a straight answer."

"I'm in the business of not giving straight answers," Jonathan said. He tried to sell it with a smile. "I'm sorry, but that's just the case."

"So, you're with the government," Georgie said.

A lie would have been so easy here. Given that his client was the FBI, it wouldn't be that big a stretch just to say yes, but he sensed that that would not necessarily be the right answer in this crowd. "How about I tell you this," he said, hoping to find a compromise. "We used to work for the government. In fact, we worked for him for a long time."

"Are you assassins?" Dawn asked.

Jonathan was tempted ask her if that would be a problem. "No, ma'am. While I can't tell you exactly who or what we are, I can tell you with absolute certainty that we're the good guys. We're on the side of the angels."

"Then how come you don't have cops with you?" Georgie asked.

Boxers took that one. "Because they're not always on the same side as us."

The conversation was meandering, and Jonathan wanted to bring it back on track. "Tell me about your concerns with the Excalibur plant across the street."

LeBron and Dawn exchanged glances, and Dawn nodded. "That plant's been empty for almost three years," LeBron said. "Tore this place up when they left. Took two hundred jobs away because the politicians were too busy putting money in their own damn pockets to pay any attention to the little guy. I used to work there. So did Dawn. Terrible, terrible thing when it closed."

Jonathan heard Boxers stir and prayed that he would keep his mouth shut. So far, nothing LeBron had said was relevant to anything they wanted to know, but it was a mistake to push people who had just started talk-ing.

"So, it just sat there, you know what I'm sayin'? Just sat there like it was mocking us. They put up that big fence with the warning signs, and then it just sat there."

"Until about two months ago," Dawn said. "We started to see all kinds of traffic coming in and out, but none of it looked official."

"Bunch of damn Arabs, I think," Georgie said. "Lots of Muslim hats and shit."

"We called the anonymous FBI hotline, but they didn't do nothin'," LeBron said. "Asshole on the phone tried to make me the crazy one. Even called me para-noid."

"What do you think they're doing in there?" Jonathan asked.

"I don't have any idea, but I know it ain't right. I never thought about kidnapping, but why not? They could be making crystal meth for all I know."

"And that would be a problem?" Boxers said with too much of a smile in his voice.

"Yeah, Hagrid, that would be a problem," LeBron said.

Boxers swelled in his seat. He did not like being teased about his size.

LeBron wasn't done. "Just because I'm black and just because I live in a damn slum don't mean that I'm stoned out on drugs. I grew up here, asshole. This is my home. You think I want some outsider coming in here and stealing the minds out of all the neighborhood babies?"

"Look," Jonathan said. "I'm sure Big Guy didn't—"

"You shut up," LeBron snapped. "Don't make excuses for him. He want to make excuses, let him make his own damn excuses."

"I'm sorry," Boxers said.

Jonathan almost fell to the floor. He wasn't sure he'd ever heard Big Guy say those words before.

"I was wrong and I'm sorry."

LeBron seemed surprised, too. Sort of deflated.

Boxers pointed a forefinger at Jonathan. "And like he said, you shut up."

"So, the bottom line," Jonathan said, "is that those folks have been squatting where they don't belong."

"Tell 'em about the guns," Georgie said.

Jonathan arched his eyebrows. Guns were always a relevant topic.

"Those guys don't bother nobody," LeBron said. "I got to be honest with you about that. I mean they don't get in my grill, and I leave them alone, too."

Jonathan waited for the rest.

"But I watch them," LeBron went on. "I mean there's a lot of bad shit goin' down in this neighborhood, so I watch a lot."

"Like you were watching us," Jonathan said.

"Right. Exactly like that."

"Except you use binoculars for them," Dawn prompted.

LeBron seemed embarrassed. "Well, yeah. 'Cept I use binoculars to watch them."

"And you've seen guns?" Jonathan asked.

"*Lots* of guns. Rifles, missile launchers, all kinds of crap like that."

Boxers leaned forward in his seat. "What did the FBI say when you told them about those?"

"To hell with the FBI. They don't want to talk with

me, they don't want to talk with me. I ain't callin' back to beg."

Jonathan understood the feeling, and at one level, he admired it. It never ceased to amaze him how shocked bureaucrats became when the public at large spontaneously developed ways to work around their bullshit.

"What do they do with the guns?" Boxers asked.

LeBron looked to Georgie and got a shrug. "Nothing, really. I mean they don't come to the road or anything. But when they're down there at their space, they've always got guns."

"You said they had missile launchers," Jonathan said. "What makes you think they're missile launchers?"

"Because I watch the Military Channel," LeBron said. He seemed insulted at such an elementary question.

Jonathan looked to Boxers. "What do you think?"

Big Guy shrugged. "He watches the Military Channel. Not a lot else looks like a missile launcher."

Jonathan didn't bother to ask for a hypothesis of why they would want that kind of weapon. While not all portable weapons systems were created equal, they all shared the common purpose of blowing shit up. They were equally useful as offensive or defensive weapons, provided the operators had adequate training. And what else did they have to do while sitting around an abandoned meatpacking plant but train?

This was all bad news, though none of it particularly surprising. In a perfect world, 0300 missions were executed against sleeping unarmed hostage takers. Alas, it so rarely turned out that way.

"How many of them do you think there are?" Jonathan asked.

"What do think, Georgie? Fifteen? Twenty?"

"I'd say at least twenty," Georgie said. "It's hard to tell because they come and go all the time. Sometimes new faces, sometimes old ones. Always dudes, by the way. I haven't seen a single woman go in there."

"But the rag heads are like that, right?" LeBron asked. "They don't let women do nothin'."

Jonathan determined in two seconds that nothing good could come from a discussion launched by that statement. He figured it was the way of the world that everybody needed to call names at someone else.

"So, let's call it twenty-five people," Jonathan said.

"We've faced worse odds," Boxers said. His face showed not the slightest trace of concern.

"Only with better intel," Jonathan said. "I think we should launch the Raven."

At the mention of the word, Boxers' eyes darted to the others in the room. He hated sharing operational details.

"It's declassified now, I promise," Jonathan said. "It's public domain."

Big Guy hesitated for just long enough to demonstrate his displeasure, then he stood and walked back out to the Expedition.

As Boxers exited, Jonathan addressed the others in the room. "I'd like to ask you a favor," he said. "I'd like to use your lovely home as a kind of command post. Just for a little while. I promise we'll be careful with your stuff."

"No," Dawn said. "The babies are upstairs."

"I swear to you that we will not draw fire to this location. We just need a spot—"

"Will not *draw fire?*" Dawn said. "Who talks like that?"

"I think they're like the Army," LeBron said.

"You should see the shit they've got in their truck," Georgie said. "It's like a fort or—"

Dawn turned on LeBron next. "Is that why you're doing this? Is this about your dream to be a soldier?"

"Excuse me," Jonathan said to defuse what sounded like it could devolve into a long-standing, oft-repeated argument. "Remember what's at stake here tonight. We believe that the men you describe have kidnapped a young boy after murdering his parents. There's a young lady involved, too. We don't know if she is dead or alive."

Dawn looked horrified. "Who would do that?" she asked. "How do I know that you're telling the truth?"

"You *do* know that I'm telling the truth," Jonathan said. "I can see it in your eyes. And I can't get into details."

"So, you *are* the government," LeBron said.

Jonathan surrendered. "Yes," he said. "Well, not exactly, but essentially, yes. It's complicated. But I can tell you this: If we don't help that boy, the consequences will be awful. Not just for him, but for thousands of people." He paused as the words sank in.

"That's a really shitty deal, I know," Jonathan continued. Then, to Dawn, "Forgive my language. Some words are hardwired, but I promise I'll try." To the group: "I know I'm asking you to take a leap of faith, but I'm telling you exactly the way it is."

Sensing a crack in Dawn's barriers, Jonathan rose, pivoted, and walked three steps to his ruck and pulled out the money satchel. "I have something for you here," he said. With his back turned to the others, he counted off two banded stacks of hundred-dollar bills.

He turned back to the room. "Here's two thousand dollars for your troubles," he said. "Again, you have my word that no harm will come to your house or your children. Consider this payment for your inconvenience."

Jonathan walked past LeBron and headed for Dawn. "Here you go, ma'am," he said. "Thank you for your assistance. In advance."

Dawn's eyes shifted from the money to Jonathan's eyes and back again. "Who are you really?" she asked.

"Honestly," Jonathan said. "If I could tell you, I would. For now, I'll just have to be Scorpion." He'd been told by countless others that when he smiled, his eyes flashed in heart-melting ways. He wasn't sure what that meant, but he'd learned to use the expression to get his way.

Dawn reached out for the cash. "I'm trusting you," she said. "And I don't trust nobody." Her eyes turned steely. "Don't you dare let me down."

Jonathan crossed his heart. "Thank you," he said.

A loud noise drew their attention to the back door in unison.

"Holy shit," LeBron said. He was the only one in position to see what was going on.

CHAPTER TWENTY-THREE

Graham thought he remembered hearing in health class that once hypothermia sets in, the last thing that preceded death was that you stopped shivering. If that was true, then he had a lot of life left in him.

He was beyond shivering. The trembling was near convulsive. He lay on his left side on the floor, back under his table and curled into a fetal ball, his knees drawn up and clutched against his chest. But for his constant, spastic movements, his shirt and his pants would have become part of the ice slick that was the floor.

He couldn't begin to imagine what the temperature was inside the locker, but he figured it had to be below zero. The cold had turned his skin cherry red. His fingers and toes burned. The nail beds on both looked pure white.

"I'm sorry," he said softly. "I'm so, so sorry." Though he had no idea what he was sorry for. Maybe for living. Maybe for dying.

If he could just die, it would all end. The pain would

go away. The fear would go away. He could be back together with—

The locker door opened with a *whoosh* that created a warm breeze. Graham was dimly aware that he hadn't heard the lock slide open this time. Did that mean he'd fallen asleep? Maybe he had in fact died.

No, he prayed silently. *Don't let me be dead.* If he was dead, then this was definitely Hell.

He heard words, but he couldn't comprehend them. He was aware that the words were in a language he couldn't understand, but that didn't fully explain his lack of comprehension. There were no consonants and vowels. He perceived no real words at all, not even foreign ones. The voices existed as part of a fog, like sounds heard from underwater.

Someone placed hands on him, but he didn't know who. He thought he might have seen a face, but like the noise, the faces appeared through a kind of mental gauze. He was floating now, and the cold was falling away.

Time passed. Minutes perhaps, but certainly seconds. Maybe hours. He was flying and he was getting warmer, and he didn't care.

Warm became warmer. Warmth rushed up and surrounded him like a hot bath—the same hot bath he'd prayed to God to feel again when he was in the throes of his frigid muscle spasms.

Did an answered prayer mean that he was dead after all? It was all so confusing.

He heard water. More specifically, he heard splashing—but he heard it in the same way he'd heard the voices. All mushy and far away.

There. He heard it again. Definitely water. Definitely warm water, definitely a bath. But was it his—

"Graham, wake up."

That time, the voice was clear. Couldn't have been clearer, in fact.

"Wake up now, son."

Dad? Was that his father's voice? Was that possible? He might have recognized the voice, but his head was so full of stuff—snot? Cotton? Concrete?—that he couldn't be sure.

No, that wasn't possible because his dad was—

"Graham!" The voice was loud this time. Angry. Frightening.

A hand landed on his shoulder. It squeezed him and shook him. Hard.

"What?" That time Graham recognized the voice as his own, and his tone was even louder than that of the man who'd shouted at him. As his eyes opened and consciousness returned, he saw that his fantasy was true. He sat fully clothed in a tub of hot water. It came up nearly to his chin. When he moved, a wave broke over his lower lip.

"Welcome back."

And he *was* back. Back in the awful place with the awful people. Graham recognized the voice before he recognized the face it belonged to.

"Life is such a capricious thing, is it not?" Teddy said. "This is among my favorite words, capricious. We have no equivalent in my language. Capricious. One moment we suffer terrible agony, the next we are bathed in comfort and warmth."

It all came back to Graham in a rush. The cold, the

pain. The pleasure Teddy took from inflicting it. With the memories came the fear.

"Please don't hurt me anymore," Graham said.

Teddy smiled. "There we go," he said with a big smile. His teeth were yellow. "Finally, the boy comes to his senses."

Graham's tub was not a bathtub, not really. It was a stainless-steel container that was three times the size of an average bathtub. He didn't want to know what its real use was. Five people stared down on him, all of them armed with rifles, and all of them looking very pissed.

"Why are you doing this?" Graham asked.

"Please do not waste our time by asking questions to which you already know the answers," Teddy said. "That makes everything so much more difficult. More difficult for me, and much, much more difficult for you."

Graham started to speak, but then stopped himself. He'd already told them lies, right? At least he thought he had. Before he said anything more, he needed to remember what the previous lies were. He needed to be consistent. He tried to stall.

"I told you I don't remember anything," he said.

Graham hadn't realized that Teddy was squatting to be face-to-face until the man stood up. Teddy folded his arms across his abundant chest, creating a set of man-boobs. "This is why I love my favorite word so much," he said. "We make choices, we live with the results."

Panic started to bloom. "But I—"

Teddy held up a hand to command silence. "You

need to choose your words carefully now, Graham. I don't want to hurt you more than I have to."

Graham's mind screamed. *No more pain. Please, please no more pain.* "Can I ask you a question?" he said.

Teddy smiled. "A question." He looked to the other men who stood nearby. "Certainly. Ask your question."

Graham took a deep, settling breath. "If you were right—you're not, but if you were—and I really did remember the code thing that you think I know, why wouldn't you kill me after I gave it to you?"

The question seemed to intrigue Teddy. Maybe even entertain him. "Ah," he said. "The hypothetical question. If A is so, what must be the result of B?" He laughed. "All right, I will play your game in kind. Let us say that I believe that you are lying about not remembering the code, and let us say that I would do everything and anything to get that information from you. Are you with me so far?"

Graham nodded as his stomach churned more.

"Very well," Teddy said. "Because that is indeed the case. Rather than asking if I would want to kill you after you gave me what I seek, you should ask yourself what would be your desire to live in terrible pain?"

Graham's heart hammered.

Teddy continued, "So far, you have merely been uncomfortable. You have been cold. But your fingers and toes have not yet been broken. Your knees have not yet been shattered and your testicles have not yet been crushed. Hot wires have not yet been inserted into your eyes. I have done all those things to others, and there is no reason why I would not do the same to you. *If* you give me what I want, and *if* I kill you after, I give you my word that it will be quick." He looked to his gang and they all laughed.

Graham stared. Whatever they saw in his face made them laugh harder.

"You are frightened," Teddy said. "It's good for you to be frightened. I will make a deal with you. Stay here for a while in the warm tub. You think about what I say, and about what you want. We will walk away for a little while—not long, but for a while. We give you time to decide which you like more, comfort or pain. Is fair, no?"

Graham nodded because it was the only thing he could think to do.

"Good," Teddy said, and he clapped Graham on the shoulder. "You give me your answer when I come back. Then life becomes capricious again."

Jonathan walked to the kitchen archway to see if Boxers needed help with Security Solutions's latest toy. The long gray box that looked like it might contain a set of golf clubs in fact contained an RQ-11 Raven UAV—unmanned aerial vehicle, a drone. The man-portable aircraft, when assembled, had a fifty-five-inch wingspan and weighed a little over four pounds. Propelled by an electric motor, the Raven could stay airborne for over an hour at a cruising altitude of five hundred feet at a distance from the controller of six miles and change. It was the most expensive model airplane that Jonathan had ever bought.

The container in Boxers' other hand was a bit smaller, but much heavier. It contained the electronics, the antennas, and the various support equipment that were necessary to control the aircraft. Once it was over the target, Raven would transmit high-definition images back to the command post from its tiny but amazing camera.

"You okay there, Big Guy?" Jonathan asked.

"I'm fine," he said. "I've got it."

"What is all that crap that you're bringing into my house?" Dawn asked. While the money had opened her home, her heart apparently remained disengaged.

"Some very cool technology," Jonathan said.

His earbud popped as it broke squelch. "Scorpion, Mother Hen."

Jonathan pressed the transmit button on his vest. "Go ahead."

"Who are you talking to?" Dawn demanded.

LeBron reached out and touched his wife's arm. "Dawn," he said.

Jonathan ignored her and focused on the voice in his ear. "I've been able to pull up some details on the building in question. Are you in a position to receive?"

"Not yet," he said. "Give me five minutes."

"Who are you talking to?" Dawn demanded again. "And what happens in five minutes?"

"I'm talking to the folks back at home." Jonathan moved to his ruck as he responded, and ripped open the Velcro on the main pouch. He lifted out his heavy-duty laptop computer and a collapsed satellite antenna.

"And where is home?"

"You have no need to know," Jonathan said. He had neither the time nor the desire to engage in small talk. His hands working from muscle memory, Jonathan unfolded the tiny antenna and placed it on top of the television set, pointed out the front window.

"What's that for?" Georgie asked.

"A signal for my computer," Jonathan replied. He hooked up the cable and began the boot-up process.

"We have wireless Internet," Georgie said.

Jonathan shook his head and smiled. "Not for this, you don't." He wasn't going to attempt to explain the complex encryptions or other tech speak because, quite frankly, he didn't understand it very well himself.

When he was booted up and ready to go, he pressed his transmit button. "Okay Mother Hen, we're set."

LeBron laughed. "Mother Hen? Really?"

"She doesn't like it much, either," Jonathan said.

The screen on Jonathan's laptop flickered once, and then it was filled with a daytime image of a rectangular industrial building and its immediate surroundings. "This comes from a commercial mapping company," Venice said in his ear. *Commercial mapping company* translated to *illegal tap into our friends at Fort Meade.* "Before we go any further, is this the facility you're talking about?"

"Hey, look!" Georgie said, pointing to the screen. "That's our house."

Jonathan pressed Transmit. "Affirmative. That's the location."

"Is that Google Maps?" LeBron asked.

"Like that," Jonathan said off the air. "Look, I'm going to need a little space, okay? If you want to watch, watch, but try to keep the talking down." He didn't bother to look back at Boxers. If it were left to Big Guy, the family would be gagged and locked in the closet where they couldn't see anything. Jonathan understood his point—the only way to maintain operational security is to reveal the least amount of information to the fewest people—but sometimes the nature of the operation required including others. Jonathan was confident that their lack of official identity would provide them with adequate backstop against any details of this evening that LeBron and his family might leak to their friends.

Jonathan's screen changed to reveal a highly detailed street view of the same property, which now clearly was a factory. The sign over the door read Excalibur Meatpacking Enterprises, Inc.

"That's amazing," LeBron said. "You can count the bricks in the wall. How can you get that kind of detail?"

"Was 'try to keep the talking down' really that complicated an instruction?" Boxers asked.

"Don't you get bossy in my house!" Dawn snapped.

Boxers said, "Yes, ma'am."

Jonathan smiled at that exchange. Deep down inside, Boxers had always been moderately terrified of women. It wasn't something they talked about, but Jonathan had long suspected that Boxers had grown through an odd childhood.

Using a tiny button of a joystick, Jonathan was able to manipulate the image for a 360-degree walk-around tour of the entire plant. "Come take a look, Big Guy," he said. Two seconds later, a shadow loomed behind him. Over the course of the next five minutes, they noted the main routes of ingress and egress, the location of the loading dock, and other details that might be important, such as the height of windows and the nature and locations of structures on the roof.

Jonathan pressed the transmit button. "Okay, we got that."

The computer display shifted to a blue background

with white lines and words, clearly a digital rendering of an old-style blueprint. "I got this from the Department of Public Works," Venice explained. "The graphics aren't optimal, but it's the best I could do in the limited time window."

"What's the date on this document?" Jonathan asked. The labels appeared to be handwritten, which he hadn't seen since the advent of computer-aided design rendered traditional draftsmen irrelevant in the late 1980s.

"Nineteen thirty-two," Venice said.

Boxers gave a low whistle. "What do you bet they moved a few walls since then?"

"He can hear, too?" Georgie said. "That's not fair. Why can't we hear?"

"Shut up, Georgie," LeBron said.

"Be nice to your brother," Dawn said.

Venice explained, "The basic bones of the place should be the same. I did a quick but thorough search of building permits in the last twenty years, and nothing showed up."

Jonathan transmitted, "Of course that assumes that they would necessarily file for permits instead of just building stuff out themselves."

"I think that's a good assumption," Venice said. "Hoping to find a trail to something more recent, I also scoured the fire inspection records, and saw no mention of structural changes."

Jonathan looked to Boxers, who shook his head. "I don't know how the hell she thinks of this shit," Big Guy said. Then he shot a glance at Dawn. "Pardon my language."

"Page four gives you the best overview of the floor plan," Venice said.

Jonathan clicked his way to page four, which revealed a plan view for a manufacturing facility that looked like every other manufacturing facility. The offices lined the front part, while the much larger processing area featured labels that included an offal room, a bleeding pit, and a head washing station. These in addition to storage rooms, a pre-cooler, a cooler, and a freezer.

"That's disgusting," Boxers said. "Almost makes you want to be a vegetarian." For Big Guy, *almost* was the key word there. The amount of red meat he could consume at one sitting made him legend among his fellow Unit operators back in the day.

"I just hope they cleaned it up before they abandoned it," Jonathan said. "After a few years in a freezer without electricity, I bet that can get pretty ripe."

"They have electricity," LeBron said.

Jonathan's and Boxers' heads turned in unison. "Excuse me?" they said.

The unison chorus made LeBron laugh. "Yeah, they've had it for a while."

Jonathan keyed his mike and passed that detail along to Venice.

"That doesn't sound right," she said. "Stand by one."

Jonathan turned to LeBron. "How long have they had electricity back?"

The kid turned to his wife and brother. "What, three months?"

"About that," Georgie said.

"Less," Dawn said. "About ten weeks."

Ten weeks it was. It didn't matter all that much, and Jonathan was not going to challenge Dawn. Truth be told, he was a little afraid of some women, too.

"Scorpion, Mother Hen," Venice's voice said. "I'm sorry. I checked the electric bill by the company name, not by the address. They're right. The electricity is on at the facility. It has been for about the last ten weeks."

Jonathan smiled and winked at Dawn. She had no idea what it was for, but it made her smile anyway.

Jonathan checked his watch. It was time to shift from general plans to specific plans. "Mother Hen, I have a mission for you. Please find the locations of the external electrical shutoffs and download them to my GPS. I'll also need you to monitor local police and fire frequencies and keep us from getting in deeper than we can handle."

"I've already sent the electrical shutoffs," Venice said. "I'm also downloading the locations of the nearest public trauma center and the nearest clandestine facility. Just so you know, if it comes to that, I'd shoot for the clandestine shop. Their record is better and they're only three miles farther away."

Jonathan didn't acknowledge that transmission because it was inappropriate traffic to begin with, and he didn't want the surrounding civilians to know that there'd been more conversation.

He looked up at Boxers. "Do you have anything more for Mother Hen?"

Big Guy shook his head. "Not for now," he said.

Jonathan keyed the mike. "You're off the hook for a while, Mother Hen. We'll let you know when we're ready to go hot."

Jonathan closed the laptop and stood. "Okay, Big Guy," he said. "Time to play with our new toy."

CHAPTER TWENTY-FOUR

As the water cooled, Graham stood in the tub and climbed out. Teddy and his posse had been gone for a while. Until a few minutes ago, Graham had been in a blind panic. They were going to kill him, one way or another. That's what Teddy had said—not in so many words, but that was what the words he did say actually meant. The question he had to deal with was a Faustian deal of the highest order. (Yes, he'd read *Faust*.) He could declare defeat and give them what they wanted, and the reward would be to die immediately, or he could hold out longer and preserve his life.

That wasn't really a choice at all, now that his heart had calmed a little and he could think clearly. More time on the planet was better than less time. Plus, deep in his heart, he didn't believe the part about breaking bones and crushing his balls. If it came to that, then he would fight until he had nothing left to fight with.

When it was all done, if he'd lost the fight and the breaking and the crushing got to be too much, he could always break then.

Graham was shocked that his panic had subsided.

He was still frightened and sad, but he felt as if those emotions had somehow made him stronger—not physically, but mentally. Thirty-six hours ago, more or less, his life had been normal—pretending to study for a math test he could have done with his eyes closed, hoping against hope that Avery Hessington and the rest of the high school royalty would let him walk the halls unmolested.

Thirty-six hours ago, it mattered what names people called him—freak, geek, gay, pussy, queer (he'd lived with them all for as long as he could remember). It mattered who would dare to sit with him in the cafeteria, and it mattered that he lived in fear of being called on because he always knew the right answer.

That all seemed so distant now, so irrelevant—though as the memories rejuvenated in his head, they triggered vivid resentment. Who the hell was Avery Hessington to put him through that kind of hell? And how could Graham have taken it so seriously? If he ever got out of this, he was going to tell Avery what an asshole he was.

The first step was to climb out of the tub. He stepped over the lip and onto the concrete floor.

Graham's fingers and toes had turned pruny and white from the water. As he explored this massive room, the water draining from his matted clothes left a slick on the floor. He walked to the far wall, where windows lined its entire width. Through the thick layer of grime, he could see the wire reinforcement in the glass. He felt a flutter of hope in his belly. Could escape really be so easy? As he approached, he had to climb over all kinds of abandoned . . . *stuff*. Much of it was shiny, and while much of it was heavy, nothing he saw was either pointy or sharp. Nothing that would make a good weapon.

But maybe something would make a good glass breaker.

He lifted a heavy T-shaped object, maybe ten inches long, that looked like it might have been a mallet in a parallel universe. He tested the weight of it in his hand and then looked up at the window. Tall and narrow, the windows opened by rocking in, like the windows in his old school, but the lock and the handle were eight or nine feet off the ground, way too high for him to reach. The bottom sill of the window started at chest level and rose from there nearly all the way to the ceiling.

He needed to work quickly. Teddy said he'd be back soon. Graham lifted the hammer to crash it through the glass, but paused. Remembering that nothing had gone his way since this ordeal had started, he decided to check first to see what was on the other side. He squeezed his soaked T-shirt to wet his hand, and then used the hand to swirl a viewport through the filthy windowpane. He saw nothing. Literally, nothing—just his own reflection staring back at him.

Screw it. I'm out of here.

He took a step back, closed his eyes, and delivered a full overhead blow to the left side of the pane. When he looked to check his damage, he saw that he'd left a wide, circular spiderweb fracture in the glass. It wasn't a hole yet, but it was an indentation. And Jesus, was it loud! But at this point, loud didn't matter. Getting caught didn't matter. All that mattered was getting out of this hell house.

He swung the hammer again, aiming for the same

spot. And again and again. Again. Each hammer blow to the glass reverberated through his arms and his shoulders. *Bam! Bam! Bam!*

Liquid spattered the glass and the concrete walls, whether from his soaked clothes or from his own sweat he didn't know and he didn't care. Finally, the head of his makeshift hammer broke all the way through. He had a hole!

It wasn't yet big enough to climb through, but it was a goddamn hole!

He picked a new spot on the window adjacent to the first and he started pounding there. After God only knew how many strokes, there was another hole, and by pounding the spot, the two holes joined into one big one, but together they were only twelve or thirteen inches in diameter.

Pausing to throw a glance over his shoulder to see if they were coming for him yet, he turned and hammered some more. His arms were growing heavier with every additional blow, but what difference did that make? He had to keep going. He *had* to. To stop now was to guarantee his death. Teddy was not going to be happy when he found out that Graham had beaten up his torture chamber.

The word *torture* brought back a stab of the panic as it passed through his head. It meant everything that was awful, everything that hurt. It meant the end of hope.

Now that he could see the faint outlines of hope on the horizon, he realized that that was all he had left. He'd get out on his own or he would die at the hands of others. If he could just make a hole big enough—

A third hole appeared, and with a final blow, that one joined with the other two to form a kind of three-circle Venn diagram where the intersection of the sub-sets formed a hole.

One more and he should be good to go. For this one, he swung lower than the others so that it would be eas-ier for him to access the opening when he was done. How stupid would he be—how worthy of the Darwin Award—if he made his escape hatch too high off the ground to reach?

Graham had no idea how many times he smashed away at the glass. Fifty? A hundred?

I won't stop. Not till I'm outside and free.

The fourth collection of spiderwebs became a fourth hole, and with five more swings—the heaviest thing he'd ever wielded, as his shoulder and his neck screamed for relief—the connecting web broke through, and the resulting hole was worth trying. It reached nearly down to the sill. He finished it off by pounding out the space at the very bottom, where he'd be dragging his body as he made his way outside.

Graham didn't know he was bleeding until he placed his hammer on the floor. He'd already placed it gently on the concrete—his effort not to make noise—when he realized how ridiculous a notion that was. He just wasn't thinking right. And while he wasn't bleeding badly, he was bleeding from about a million places on his hands and arms, no doubt from the shattering glass that he'd never felt cutting his flesh.

While that, too, didn't matter, the cuts reminded him that he was surrounded by shards of glass and bits of wire, and that he was barefoot and that his clothes were so wet that everything would stick to them.

Picking up his hammer again, he used it as a broom to sweep off the sill to remove the big pieces. After two passes, he decided that he'd spent enough time being neat and careful and now it was time to climb. Using his forearms as leverage against the sill, he hoisted himself up until he was high enough to support his weight with his knee.

Headfirst or feetfirst?

If only because of the height, he decided to back out of the space feetfirst. There were lots of things that could go wrong with that plan—not the least of which involved dropping out onto a lot of broken glass—but all of the scenarios he could think of were better applied to his feet than his head. He didn't have time to second-guess.

He took care when maneuvering on the narrow ledge not to overbalance and fall back into the room he was trying to leave. The angles here were tough. He maneuvered himself to a position where he was squatting in front of and with his back turned to his exit portal. His weight was evenly distributed between his fingertips and the balls of his feet, which were all aligned in the same plane.

Balance was key. Keeping his back straight and as erect as possible, he shifted his weight to his palms as he moved first one foot and then the other through the vertical hole. When his legs were through up to his thighs and dangling on the other side, he rocked forward and let his lower body slide through the hole up to his waist. The last eight or nine inches were the worst as his doodads passed over the ledge. He rocked his hips to the side to protect them as best he could, but the wire-stab in his ass cheek kept him from rocking over too far.

When his lower body was through, he pressed his belly against the flat sill and eased himself out.

He took one final look at the door through which Teddy had exited—and no doubt the one through which he would reenter—praying that this would not be the moment of the torturer's return. At this juncture, the only way to stop Graham from all the way across the room would be to shoot him in the face.

He didn't want to be shot in the face.

So he needed to keep going. Inching backward along his belly, he reached the tipping point where the weight of his dangling legs overcame his ability to hang on, and he allowed himself to drop.

The point of his chin clipped the far side of the sill as he tumbled a few feet to the floor. He landed hard on his heels—he felt the piece of glass that punctured his left foot in the middle of the arch—and his momentum carried him all the way over onto his back. When he came to rest, his feet were up in the air, and the back of his head was on concrete.

Graham rolled to his side, cleared the shard of glass from his foot with a swipe of his hand, and stood. Something was wrong here. It didn't feel like outside air. The floor was concrete. It took him two seconds to process the obvious—he wasn't outside after all. He'd wasted all that time and all that effort crashing through an interior window.

"Who the hell builds a window to the *inside?*" he whispered to no one. "Shit."

It didn't matter. There had to be an outside some-where. He just needed to find it.

Beyond the wash of light through the windows from the room he'd just exited, the rest of the building was dark. As in *cave* dark, the absence of light. Graham was sure that sooner or later his eyes would adjust, but—

In an instant, the darkness transformed to daylight, a blinding glare that dug at his eyes and made him feel unbalanced. By reflex, he covered his eyes with his bloody palms.

He heard a noise that sounded like people clapping and he dropped to a crouch, making himself as small as possible.

"That took you long enough," said Teddy's voice from somewhere beyond Graham's covered eyes.

Graham peeled his hands away, and as his eyes ad-justed, he saw the torturer approaching him. His head told him to run, but his instincts told him to wait.

"I wanted you to feel that adrenaline rush," Teddy went on, "because for every rush there is a crash. I think the most important thing that someone in your position must remember is that hope is imaginary. By breaking through that window and coming out into this space, you did exactly what I expected you to. That's why we've been waiting. Though I must tell you that we've been waiting for much longer than I thought we would. Sooner or later, you will give me what I want."

Graham could see people gathered behind Teddy—many of the same faces he'd seen in the room with the tub—but they seemed to be hanging back. Graham stood and took a couple of steps back, maintaining his distance from Teddy.

"I gave you an assignment last time we spoke,"

Teddy said. "Have you had a chance to think about the options I gave you?"

Graham knew that if he tried to bolt, they would hurt him, so he stayed put, unmoving.

"I expect an answer, Graham," Teddy said.

This was the big moment. He could declare himself to be sniveling, or he could show some pride. Graham stood to his full five-foot, nine-inch height and faced Teddy head-on. "Yeah, I've thought about it," he said. "I've decided you need to believe the truth—I don't know anything you want to hear."

Teddy planted his hands on his hips, the posture of a man who was sorely disappointed. "That's very sad," he said. "It's a decision that makes your life many times more difficult. In my opinion, too many people value bravery and defiance over common sense. We will do it the more difficult way, then."

His heart screaming for relief, Graham tensed and waited for the attack. He had no experience fighting, but he had plenty of experience running away from fights, and in this place, there was plenty of room to duck and dodge. That couldn't go on forever—certainly not against people with guns—but every delay brought him a new opportunity for a miracle.

Only, they didn't rush him. Instead, they sneaked up on him from behind. He sensed them before he saw them, and before he could react, a noose dropped over his head and pulled tight around his neck. He brought his hands to his throat to protect his windpipe, and when he did, the noose pulled tighter, lifted higher. He had to stand on tiptoes to keep his head from being pulled off.

"Hands to your side, Graham," Teddy said. His voice kept a relaxed monotone that sounded so easygoing and businesslike. "Relax them. We're not trying to kill you, we're trying to control you."

Graham did as he was told. He lowered his hands, and the man who controlled the noose loosened it.

"Good man," Teddy said. "And a good lesson in cause and effect. Now cross your wrists behind your back."

Graham hesitated. They were going to tie his hands, and once that was done, he'd be finished, his chance for survival over. The hesitation caused him to be lifted off his heels again and onto his toes. The rope—he couldn't see it, but he was certain that it was a rope—chafed the flesh of his neck. He battled every instinct to claw at the noose, and instead did as he was told, and crossed his wrists behind his back.

The pressure eased. He stood still and tried not to give into the tears that pressed behind his eyes as someone slipped a loop over his hands and pulled it tight. The plastic ratchet sound told him that they'd used the zip ties he'd seen on cop shows.

"Your future is in your own hands now, young man," Teddy said. "Failure to comply means pain. Doing the reasonable thing means less pain. It's that simple." Teddy started walking away, and Graham's minder followed, lifting slightly on the noose to encourage his captive to follow.

There was no doubt in Graham's mind as he danced through the broken glass on the floor to the amusement of his handler that they'd deliberately chosen the most painful path. To stumble at this point would be to hang himself.

When they were through the glass, Graham swiped the sole of each foot against the opposite calf to rub away any straggling shards, and then allowed himself to be led to wherever they were taking him. He knew he was in trouble the instant he saw the big freezer door. This was probably the very route they'd carried him into the building, but of course he hadn't been able to see anything then. As soon as Teddy pulled on the door latch, his suspicions were confirmed.

The first thing he saw was the hooks hanging from the ceiling, and then he took in the table that he'd tried to turn into his shelter. The room looked smaller from this angle, and somehow even more frightening. The meat hooks dangled from overhead like so many gleaming, blood-ravenous bats. The table mocked him as the slab on which to perform his autopsy. The floor still glistened with ice. Graham felt sick, but he was determined not to give his captors the satisfaction of seeing him puke.

"Remember," Teddy said, "this is all your choosing."

The goon on the other end of the rope led/dragged Graham to the center of the room, and positioned him in a precise spot. Graham didn't know what the spot meant, but apparently, it was important to whatever lay ahead. Only a few feet in, the frigid air enveloped him like a blanket of razor blades.

Equipment of some sort moved behind him, but his efforts to turn and see earned him a slap in the gut, so he resigned himself to being surprised.

Time and opportunity.

Graham felt a slight tug on his neck—nothing like the first ones—and then people moved away from him.

When he looked up, he saw that the far end of his noose had been tied around the J of a meat hook.

"Be careful," Teddy said as Graham's minder pulled away. "That noose is a one-way knot. Once it tightens, you need hands to loosen it. And, well, you don't have functioning hands anymore. Remember what happened last time you grew so cold?"

The asshole actually waited for an answer. Graham refused to give him one.

"Do you really want me to pre-tighten the knot?" Teddy asked. "When I'm in control, questions get answers. Now, again. Do you want me to pre-tighten the knot?"

Graham shook his head.

"Motion is not an answer," Teddy said. His voice was getting reedy. Graham didn't know what that meant for him, but he knew that it couldn't be good.

"No," Graham said. "I don't want you to tighten the knot."

"Very well, then. The question I asked is, do you remember what happened the last time you got very cold?"

Graham scowled. The God's-honest truthful answer was no, he didn't remember. He remembered being cold and frightened, and then he remembered being in the warm bath. Everything else was either nonexistent or a blur in his memory. But he sensed that Teddy wouldn't want to hear that.

"You're confused," Teddy said. "That's because you fell unconscious. And that, my young friend, is the point. If you fall unconscious now, I will not rescue you. What you know is important, but not so important that we cannot live without it."

"What is it?" Graham asked. He stood taller than was necessary, keenly aware of the nonloosening knot and the lack of slack in the rope. "What do the numbers mean?"

Teddy smiled. "So, you do remember," he said.

"I remember that there were numbers and letters," Graham said, "but I don't remember what they were."

Teddy made a clicking sound with his tongue and shook his head. "Such a shameful way for a good-looking young man to perish. I'm told that at first you feel a great pressure in your head and your face as the blood gets trapped above the level of the rope. As your windpipe crushes, it obviously gets harder to breathe, and as the pressure builds more, your gag reflex is triggered. If you have enough strength—enough wind—to vomit, then you make a mess down the front of yourself. If you do not, then the vomit will drown you. Either way, when people discover your body, your face will be bloated to two or three times its normal size—as will your legs and your scrotum—and you will be a deep purple in color. More times than not, hanging victims who have been unattended for too long have their tongues sticking out of their bloated faces."

It was a horrifying image, and Graham knew that it was 100 percent true. He knew it because he'd seen movies where that was nearly the exact image portrayed. The tongue was the most disgusting part. And the scrotum. Jesus, the thought of a swollen, purple ball sack was enough to ruin anyone's stomach. Terror welled from his gut. Was that whole vomiting thing about to happen now?

"I'll leave you to your shivering," Teddy said. "But first, I have a surprise for you."

On cue, the freezer door opened again, and Graham heard movement behind him.

"You may pivot," Teddy said. "Just be careful not to trip and break your neck. I don't want you to miss your surprise."

Graham quick-stepped a tight circle to his left, toward the sound he'd heard.

When he saw his surprise, there was no way to contain his horror.

CHAPTER TWENTY-FIVE

Jonathan launched the Raven with more or less the same motion he would have launched a Hail Mary pass with in a football game—a wide overhead pitch counterbalanced by an extended left arm. The electric motor was already up to speed, so once free of his hand, it was airborne and in controlled flight. LeBron and Georgie stood so close to him that it was difficult not to hit them in the head with his follow-through.

"So, what's that going to do?" LeBron asked.

"It's going to send us some awesome pictures," Jonathan said. He led the tiny parade back into the house, where Boxers was engrossed in the business of piloting the aircraft via a mini control panel and a computer screen, to which Dawn seemed 100 percent glued.

"Nice launch, Boss," Boxers said. "You didn't do that girlie throw-into-the-ground move. That would've been embarrassing for all of us." As he spoke, his eyes never left the screen, which showed very little of interest. If you used your imagination, you could see the ground passing underneath the drone's camera, but it required a suspension of disbelief.

Boxers was the pilot of the team, but Jonathan understood most of the rudimentary elements of navigation and aerodynamics, so he knew that Big Guy was guiding the Raven by instruments, coordinating the nonvisual elements of compass direction, altitude, airspeed, and even wind speed to bring the UAV on target. The camera was working, thus the near-images of the ground, but there was no definitive image to observe.

Twenty or thirty seconds later, the screen filled with an overhead view of the building they'd seen as a blueprint. Next to Boxers' navigation screen, Jonathan pulled up the plan view that Venice had uploaded for him. He also re-upped the blueprint package, just in case they needed it.

"That's amazing," LeBron said. "You can see everything."

It was a true statement, emphasis on *everything*. The days of grainy black-and-white or silver-and-white IR technology as the only way to see in the dark were gone. If you had the bucks to spend and the access to the developers of top-secret technology, modern optics had the power to transform night into day.

Boxers' eyes narrowed as his concentration increased. As the pilot, his eyes stayed on the computer images of a control panel, and he could afford only brief glances at the images that were beamed back. Jonathan recorded the images for later examination. Because everything was digital, they would be able to freeze any frame they wanted and zoom in on it as if it were a high-definition still photograph. Very cool technology.

Boxers flew the aircraft first in a wide circle around

the building, and then in a zigzag pattern over the top. Even before careful analysis, Jonathan took in the obvious—people stood at each of the doorways. The prudent assumption would be that they were armed guards. Each was positioned in such a way that they would be difficult to see from the street.

"What's your altitude?" Jonathan asked.

"About four hundred feet. Even if they looked straight up, they wouldn't be able to see or hear a thing."

After five, maybe seven minutes of cruising over the building, Boxers said, "I've seen everything I need. Ready to call it a night for the Raven."

"Affirm. Before we get hooked." Even in a tense situation, cool technology could become mesmerizing in itself, the coolness factor converting the equipment into a toy, and the recon mission into playtime.

"This is like Jack Bauer shit," Georgie said.

"Big Guy could kick Jack Bauer's ass," Jonathan said through a grin.

"And not even break a sweat," Boxers said. His eyes never left his controls.

"Can anybody buy one of these?" LeBron asked.

"If you've got enough money and you know the right people, I suppose you can buy anything," Jonathan said. He didn't add that he'd built an entire career around doing just that. "But you won't find it in RadioShack."

"Who are you people really?" Dawn asked. It was the question that she couldn't get past. "All these guns and electronics, throwing cash around like it's water. Who are you?"

Jonathan turned away from the screen and addressed her. She stood behind her husband and his brother, hugging herself. Tears balanced on her eyelids. She was scared.

Jonathan stood from his chair and gently nudged the young men to step out of his way. "Don't touch anything," he said. He approached Dawn slowly, easily. He set his face on what he hoped was a look of compassion.

As he closed the distance, Dawn took a step back and he stopped. He didn't want to invade her space. "Dawn, all I can tell you is that we're the good guys. I have no way to prove that to you, and I understand what a leap of faith it must be for you to believe that, but I swear to God it's the truth. We're here to help a young man and a young woman live to see tomorrow. Really, that's all we're about."

Dawn looked at him, assessed him, for a long time. Maybe thirty seconds. "This young man and young woman. How old are they?"

"Fourteen and twenty-seven." As the words passed his lips, he heard Boxers growl. More of the sharing that he detested.

"Which is which?" Dawn asked.

"The male is the younger."

"So he's a baby."

"Hey!" Georgie said. "I'm fifteen. I'm no baby."

Dawn smirked, and Jonathan got it.

"What did they do?"

"They were in the wrong place at the wrong time. They have some very dangerous information."

"Yo, Boss," Boxers said. "How about a little discretion here?"

"We're in their *home,* Big Guy. It's only right that we

share as much as we can." To Dawn, he said, "Don't ask what that information is. That would be a step too far."

Dawn stewed a little longer. "So, if I called the Detroit PD right now . . ."

She let the sentence hang in the air.

"I would prefer you didn't do that," Jonathan said.

"But if I did?"

"We'd be lucky if they got here in an hour," LeBron said.

Jonathan smiled, but otherwise ignored him. "I think you're asking me if the police would know if we were here," he said. "The answer to that would be no. And if you called the FBI, that answer would be no, as well. You may take from that whatever you wish."

"What are the chances that LeBron or Georgie or me will get in trouble with the law for any of this?"

Jonathan was impressed with the way this young woman thought. She was a wife, a mother, and a caring sister-in-law. Her first priority was to make sure that no harm would come to the people she loved. Jonathan had nothing but admiration for people who put family first.

"Let me put it to you this way," Jonathan said. "If you don't call them, the Detroit Police—and the FBI and the CIA and every other three-letter agency you can think of—will never know that we set foot in your lovely home. The only way that word could possibly leak out is if you or LeBron or Georgie leak it."

"So it's your plan to rescue the boy and the girl?" Dawn asked.

"It is," Jonathan said.

"Oh, come on, Scorpion," Boxers complained. "Just a little secret-keeping? You know, for old time's sake?"

Boxers had always been the OpSec purist, but Jonathan sensed that he was laying it on extra thick tonight to enhance Jonathan's aura as a good cop in his negotiation with Dawn. Jonathan looked at her and shrugged. "There's no way I can make you comfortable with all that is happening, but I hope this convinces you that you and yours getting hurt is nowhere in the plan." He waited till he had eye contact. "In fact, I promise that I will kill and I will die to protect you."

He knew that Boxers was going to bust his balls later for the melodrama. He saw Big Guy swivel his head to make eye contact, but he ignored him. This encounter was about selling Dawn on the mission.

"So, what are we supposed to do tomorrow?" she asked.

Jonathan cocked his head.

"Just looking at all the equipment you brought, I'm guessing that tomorrow morning the factory across the road is going to look a lot different," she said. "It's gonna have holes in it, and it's gonna have dead bodies in it. Am I right?"

Jonathan sensed all the heads turning to await his answer, so he turned to stone. There was simply nothing for him to say in response.

Dawn seemed to get that. "Okay," she pressed. "Let's just say I'm right. For all I know, you might be one of the bodies in there. But whatever happens, people are going to find out, and people are going to start asking questions. What do I tell them?"

"Whatever you think is appropriate," Jonathan said. "You can repeat every word of this conversation, if that's what you think is necessary. But by way of full disclosure, I have to warn you that that particular route will prove very frustrating for all concerned." He wiggled his gloved fingers, as if to wave to a child. "We've left no fingerprints, and even if we did, they would be untraceable. You know us as Scorpion and Big Guy, and you know we communicate with someone named Mother Hen. Pretend you're a cop and run that story through your head. How do you think that will go?"

Dawn looked at the floor. She got it.

Everyone always got it. The money he threw around didn't hurt, but that wasn't the deciding factor 99 percent of the time. Jonathan believed—and Boxers would fight him on this one—that people were inherently good. Many were assholes, and all of them lived every day primarily to advance their own agenda. But when the chips were down, the vast majority would endure significant risk for the benefit of a stranger. And if the stranger were a *baby,* as Dawn had referred to Graham, the willingness to take risks spiked dramatically.

"Hey, Boss," Boxers said. "We need to do some planning."

Jonathan kept his gaze on Dawn. "You know you're the linchpin on all this, right?" he said. "I don't mean to presume, but I sense that I've got LeBron and Georgie one hundred percent with me. I've got you pegged as about thirty-five percent. In relatively few minutes, Big Guy and I are going to step into the furnace. Can I count on you not to start another battle to our rear?"

Dawn started to answer, then stopped. "I'm not sure I know what that means, 'start another battle.' "

Boxers snapped, "It means he doesn't want you ratting us out to the cops who are run so ragged in this town that they'd shoot their Aunt Millie if she scratched her armpit, thinking she was going to draw down on them from a shoulder rig."

LeBron laughed. "We actually have an Aunt Millie."

"And if she reaches for her armpit, the smart move *would* be to shoot her." The two brothers laughed together.

Dawn remained unamused. "Here's what I promise you," she said. "I pray that you save those people, and I don't care what you have to do to make that happen."

Jonathan smiled.

"Don't be happy yet," she said. "If anything happens to my family—if there's so much as a scratch on my house—I will do everything I can to hunt you down and make you pay."

Jonathan looked to LeBron. He'd married himself one hell of a woman. Jonathan admired the passion. "It's a deal," he said.

They shook on it, but he never took his glove off. He had no idea if that made the deal less binding.

Jolaine looked terrible. They arranged her so that she was straddling a tall sawhorse, still fully clothed. Her hands were tightly bound and the goons strung them to one of the meat hooks overhead. She'd clearly been beaten. Blood glistened from her nose to her chin, and her face was bruised purple. Her left eye was swollen shut.

Graham didn't know what to say. He wasn't even sure that she was conscious, or if she was, that she knew that he was present. How could anyone do such a thing to her? A gorge of anger blossomed in his gut. Who the *hell* did these people think—

"I believe you two know each other," Teddy said.

At the sound of the voice, Jolaine's head rocked up. At first, she looked confused, but then she saw Graham and she smiled. One of her front teeth had been knocked out. "I'm sorry, Graham," she said. With her mouth trauma, "sorry" sounded like "thorry."

Graham's vision blurred. Nothing was worth this level of suffering.

"Look at me, Graham," Jolaine said.

They made eye contact.

"Give up nothing," she said. One of the silent goons lifted her T-shirt to reveal bare flesh and touched it with a stick that made a snapping sound. Jolaine's back arched and she screamed as she became rigid.

"That's an electrical torture stick," Teddy explained in his ear. "Some people call it a cattle prod in your country. It is certainly an attention-getter. Allow me to demonstrate." Teddy lifted the front of Graham's T-shirt and tucked the tail behind his head, effectively blinding him while exposing his entire torso. He felt contact high on his belly, just below his breastbone, and the world went purple.

A jolt of hot agony erupted from his core and shot from his teeth to his toes. The electric jolt seemed to pass through every cell in his body. He smelled blood in his sinuses, and as his knees sagged, a strong pair of arms grabbed him from behind and propped him up, but not before the noose tightened. He could still breathe, but he could feel pressure building in his head from the blood backing up.

"Impressive, don't you think?" Teddy said. He pulled Graham's T-shirt back down so that he could see. When he saw Graham's face, he smiled. "Ah, so you learned two lessons," he said, "not least of which was the wonder of the self-tightening knot." He displayed the cattle prod so that Graham could see it better. "That was but one brief contact to a relatively insensitive part of your body. Imagine that against a *very* sensitive part of your body. Is this really the life you want to live? Do you really want to inflict this kind of pain against someone who is close to you?"

Teddy nodded to the voiceless henchman, who smiled and nodded back. He touched the stick to a place on Jolaine's back. Graham couldn't see the exact point of contact, but the resulting scream was horrifying. It reverberated off the concrete walls and metal surfaces. When it was over, Jolaine sagged even deeper. When she rolled her glazed eyes up to look at him, she no longer looked human. It was as if that part of her— her soul, maybe?—had been driven out. Equal parts humiliation and pain, her expression told him that she was done. Her spirit had fled her body.

"Pain is such a terrible thing," Teddy said. "Look at what it does. Look at what *your* decision does to others. Perhaps we could touch the prod to her eye. I'm not sure what—"

Graham blurted, "3155AX475598CVRLLPBHQ44 6833D0Z."

Teddy looked stunned. "Excuse me?"

"Graham, no," Jolaine rasped.

Graham repeated the code. "That's what you're looking for, right? The code?"

"Graham! Please don't!"

Teddy's eyes narrowed to slit. "Say it two more times," he said.

Graham glared through Teddy's skull. He sensed that he'd created an opportunity for himself—he wasn't sure what it was, exactly, but he sensed that the stakes had changed, and for at least a little while, Graham now had a hand to play that might buy additional time.

"Get this thing off my neck," Graham said. "I've given it to you twice. For a third time, you get rid of the noose."

"Or, how about I just tighten it more?" Teddy countered. "Tighter and tighter until you give me what I want?"

Graham's heart could not race any faster without shredding itself. He was playing a dangerous game of who-blinks-first, and he was already in it too deep to stop. "Brain cells," Graham said. "They're very sensitive to oxygen."

Teddy turned to the goon who stood next to Jolaine.

"No!" Graham shouted before Teddy could give the order. No one moved, awaiting Graham's next step. "No more prodding," he said. "Let her arms down, and get her off of that . . . whatever the hell she's sitting on. That's sick."

That frightening look of amusement returned to Teddy's eyes. "So now you're telling me that I am sick?"

"You're a friggin' torturer, dude! Of course you're sick! Jesus."

Teddy leaned in closer, till his features blurred and their noses nearly touched. "You think you have control," he whispered. His breath stank of cigarettes. "You are wrong."

"I have the code," Graham said. "I have everything you want. Please step away from my face."

In his own time, Teddy moved back.

"Thank you." Graham cleared his throat again. "Whatever this code is—whatever it does—I figure it's got to be important. There's no pattern to it. It's a random cipher, so that means it's not the Kremlin garage code or something stupid like that. And given everybody's focus on me and my family, I figure that somehow we're the only ones who know it."

The change in Teddy's eyes told him that he was close to the mark.

"So, here's where I think I have a little control. It's a long code, with a lot of characters. If you shock Jolaine again, or if you don't do what I ask, I'll just change some of the elements. You'll never know."

"Oh, we will know," Teddy said. "We will test the code and we will know."

This was going exactly as Graham had hoped it would. These assholes had inadvertently taught him how to extract information through a diversionary conversation. He'd just learned that they had a way to verify what he told them. "Then what?" he pressed. He was so excited—so terrified—that his voice trembled. "You'd test and find out it didn't work. Then all you'd know was that I gave you the wrong sequence. You'd never know *how* it's wrong."

"That would be a very big mistake, young man. You do that, you'll see how *sick* I can be."

"So, let's make a deal," Graham said. "Take this noose off of me, get Jolaine a chair, and I'll tell you what you want to know. If I've lied, then we'll still be here. You can torture us till you've had your fill."

Teddy regarded him, clearly looking for the angle that could hurt him or his cause. "You are playing a very dangerous game, my young friend. If you toy with me, I will hurt you very, very badly."

"I'm not your friend," Graham said. This defiance game was not for the weak of heart, but once in, he had to go all the way.

"Okay," Teddy said. "Okay, we do things your way. But God help you." As he loosened the slipknot from around Graham's neck, he called over his shoulder and said something that caused the goons to loosen the ropes on Jolaine's arms. A folding chair arrived from somewhere. They lifted her off the horrible sawhorse contraption, and they put her on the chair. Her wrists remained tied, but they rested on her lap.

Graham ducked a little as the noose was lifted away. When he was free, he said, "And now my hands."

"Not part of the deal," Teddy said. "You should understand that my patience is now gone."

"I had to try," Graham said.

"It is time to give me what I bargained for."

Graham nodded. "You're going to want to write this down," he said.

From a few feet away, Jolaine tried one more time:

"Graham. They're terrorists. You're giving them something terrible. I can only imagine what it is, but please don't—"

"Look at me," Teddy said. "Not at her. You and I have deal." He snapped his fingers and spoke again to his buddies, one of whom produced a pen and a tablet of paper. "Say it slowly."

Graham enunciated every character.

Teddy wrote as he spoke. After he'd documented the cipher string, he said, "Now we'll see if you told truth. Say it again."

Graham didn't hesitate. This time he raced through the cipher, nailing every character. "Would you like me to do it backwards?"

He barely saw the man deliver the punch to his gut. The blow pushed the air from Graham's lungs and collapsed his knees. Spots exploded behind his eyes, and for the longest time, he could neither see nor breathe as his insides convulsed. He wondered for a while if he might suffocate. Finally, breath came, but his insides felt like they might have been run through a blender.

Unable to access his hands for support, and Lord knows unable to do anything that might resemble a sit-up, he rolled from his side onto his stomach, and from there inch-wormed to his knees, then found his feet and stood. He didn't know why, but it felt important to stand. By the time he was up, the goons were all gone.

The cold was beginning to work its way into him again.

"You shouldn't have done that," Jolaine said. "That code is for some kind of weapon. And for them to go to these extremes, it must be a weapon of enormous value." She spat a wad of blood onto the floor.

"I bought us time," he said.

"At a huge price."

"I couldn't just watch them do that to you," he said. "That wasn't right. I couldn't watch it."

Jolaine shook her head. "I can take care of myself," she said.

A laugh burst out of Graham before he could stop it. As she heard her own words, Jolaine chuckled, too. "Evidence to the contrary notwithstanding," she added.

Graham looked around the room for some way out. This place had the same wire windows as the room he'd broken out of. He could see the heads of two guards who now were stationed just on the other side. Movement through the window on the door told him that at least one guard was out there, too.

"This is our time and opportunity," he said. "What are we going to do?"

"Right now, it seems that dying is at the top of the list," Jolaine said.

"Not yet," Graham said. The bruises on her face seemed to be worsening as he watched.

"What, you think they're going to let us live now that they've got what they want? I've been telling you from the beginning—"

"I lied," he whispered.

A beat. "Excuse me?"

"The code," he said. "It's not the right one. I transposed some of the characters, and made up others."

Jolaine looked confused. "But how? He made you repeat them."

"So?" No matter how many times people *talked* about his memory, they always had a hard time grasping the reality.

"Could you have actually recited it backward?"

He smiled. "No. That was a bluff." The smile went away, however, as he thought about the misery that lay ahead when the assholes found out what he'd done.

"Well, shit," Jolaine said. "We need a plan."

CHAPTER TWENTY-SIX

The Raven crashed on impact and broke apart, just as it was designed to do. A soldier-proof system, it was built to be frangible on impact so that the wings and the horizontal stabilizers in the rear would separate easily from the fuselage. That eliminated the need for smooth surfaces to allow for long roll-out landings. Georgie found the crash to be particularly entertaining, laughing far too loudly for the otherwise quiet night.

"A little stealth would be good right now," Jonathan said to him as he collected the pieces and laid them across the bed of the Expedition. He locked the door when he was done and went back inside, where Boxers had cued up the recorded images.

"I've been looking at this, Boss," Big Guy said as soon as Jonathan entered the room. "Good news—this is definitely the target."

Jonathan smiled. "Confidence level?"

"Ninety-nine and change. Look here."

Jonathan kneeled next to the chair Boxers had commandeered.

Big Guy rolled the wheel on the mouse and zoomed

in on a sedan that was parked in the rear of the plant. "Look at that license plate."

"That's our guy," he said. The plate matched the one that transported Jolaine from the jail. He clapped Boxers on the back. Since this adventure began, they'd been chasing assumptions. Before any shooting started, it was good to know that they were really in the right place. "What tactical info do you have?"

"I know we've got at least six bad guys, but it's probably safe to assume twelve to fifteen." He pointed to the screen with a capped pen as he spoke. "We've got two on each of the three main entrances—the white, black, and green sides. The red side is the loading dock, where the blueprints show an overhang. The IR doesn't show anyone there, but no guarantees that's not guarded, too."

Boxers clicked the mouse, and the screen changed to the infrared view. The imagery transformed to black and silver and the details got fuzzy, nearly to the point of being a blur. "Here, we're limited by technology," Boxers said. "You can see on this section here"—he pointed to a spot against the black (back) wall that was twenty feet from the green (left) wall—"that it's much, much colder than anywhere else in the building. I think that means they've turned the freezer on."

"Which means they had a reason for doing it," Jonathan said, closing the loop. "Assuming they're not just cooling beers, the freezer holds something we want to see."

"That's where I was going," Boxers said. "So if we assume eight people on the doors, nobody's gonna work alone inside, so that's at least ten. No way we can have a hard count. The kids say twenty to twenty-five."

Before raiding a place, it helped to know precisely how many bad guys there were. It mattered less when the opposing force was massed together—say, in barracks, where mass-casualty tactics could do a lot of harm with relatively little effort or danger. But when the enemy was spread around like this, the team was looking at a lot of individual gunfights, and there was no way to know when the last bad guy had been dropped.

Enter the concept of the force multiplier. Through advanced fighting techniques, Jonathan and Boxers could tilt the odds away from the strengths of the enemy—cover and knowledge of the surroundings—toward their own strengths. Chief among those strengths were the ability to maneuver and shoot effectively in darkness.

"Superimpose the electrical feeds Mother Hen sent us," Jonathan said.

"I guess we've got to assume that they haven't jury-rigged something on their own," Big Guy said. "If that's the case, there appear to be two of them. The main box is here on the red side, on the loading dock. Then there's another one—a big one—on the black side, on the outer wall of the freezer."

Jonathan squinted, staring at the screen. It was so much easier to blow one source of power and move in. Now they would have to sequence two blasts. That wasn't a big deal, necessarily, but it meant more time on target, and time meant additional exposure.

"That's not the shit I worry about," Boxers said.

Well, of course not, Jonathan thought. Boxers was most self-actualized when he was playing with explosives.

"I worry about how we're going to get close enough to do what we need to do without being seen."

He raised a good point. Breaching a fence was barely a challenge, but then what? Getting in was only half the mission. Getting out quickly with precious cargo intact was the greater challenge. With the entire perimeter fenced in, and with guards stationed outside, they couldn't just crash the front gate and race up the driveway because it would take too much time and make too much noise. The key to an 0300 operation was to get the precious cargo out alive. With that kind of advance warning, the bad guys might panic and create a barricade situation that rarely ended well for anyone.

"Is there a back gate in the fence?" Jonathan asked.

Boxers shook his head. "We don't have plans for the fence, and it doesn't show in the imagery."

"Sort of," LeBron said.

Jonathan and Boxers turned in unison to face him. In his peripheral vision, Jonathan noted that Dawn's face wore a similarly intrigued expression.

LeBron grew uncomfortable with the attention. "There was stuff back there," he said. "Lots of scrap metal that nobody wanted, so maybe someone cut a hole in the fence."

Dawn was aghast. "You *stole?* How could you do that? You have a family to support now. The judge told you that one more—"

"I didn't steal," LeBron said. "It was just there. It's junk. Nobody wants it."

"Why steal it, then?"

"For money. I sold it for scrap."

"How did you get it to the scrap yard?"

"In Doobie's truck," LeBron said.

Jonathan raised a hand to interrupt the conversation. "Excuse me," he said. "My clock is ticking here. LeBron, how big was the hole you cut?"

"Big enough for the truck."

"No way that's still there," Boxers said. "These guys would have patched it up."

"But they didn't," LeBron said. "We kinda patched it back up ourselves because we didn't want to put up with a lot of shit from the cops if they found it—like they'd ever drive back there. We put the section we took down back up with a little wire to hold it in place. I was back there a few days ago, and nobody had changed nothin'."

"Why would you go back there?" Dawn pressed.

"Because we got to eat, and I got no job," LeBron said. "You never know when you might have missed something." He paused, and Jonathan could see the wheels turning in his head. Did he want to say more or not? "Okay, and there's one more thing. I don't like those people. I've never trusted them from the first minute I saw them. They got no business bein' here. I wanted to see what I could see."

LeBron looked into Jonathan's eyes. "And Scorpion, yes, there are guards at the loading dock. There are always guards at the loading dock. That's another reason I don't like them bein' in my hood."

Jonathan smiled broadly. "Well, God bless neighborhood watch," he said. "How did you get a truck around there? The map shows trees."

LeBron moved to the computer screen. "Zoom out

some," he said. "Get to where we can see the whole thing."

Boxers pulled away to about the two-hundred-foot mark.

"There." LeBron pointed to the woods line on the black side of the building. "There's like a clearing right in here." He squinted and leaned closer. "I don't see it here. Can you bring back that daylight picture?"

Boxers clicked and the satellite image reappeared.

"You can almost see it here," LeBron said, pointing. "And there's a road that runs just behind the fence. Doobie's truck is smaller than yours, though, and it barely fit through."

"That's okay," Jonathan said. "It's a way in."

"It's a way out, too," Boxers said. "I'm not thrilled with the open-field run, but it's doable if we stage the Expedition."

"I'll come with you, if you like," LeBron said. "I can show you the opening in the fence."

"No!" Dawn snapped. "You'll do no such thing."

Sometimes there was only one right answer to a controversial question, and in this case, it was obvious. "I'm with Dawn on this one," Jonathan said as he closed his laptop and slipped it back into his ruck. "I made a promise that you would not be placed in jeopardy. I'm sticking by that. You've already helped us more than you know. Now it's time for us to go."

Boxers had already begun to pack up the Raven's electronics.

"There has to be a way we can help. We're in it this deep. It's like it's too late to quit."

Boxers shot Jonathan a death glare. In the past,

Jonathan had included people he probably shouldn't have in the execution of 0300 missions, and almost always with massive complications.

"Big Guy and I have done this gig too many times as a duet to expand now." He extended his hand. "Really, though. I appreciate the offer." He shrugged into his ruck.

"Suppose we see something that shouldn't be?" Dawn asked.

The source of the question startled Jonathan. Clearly, that showed in his face.

"Watching is different than getting shot," she explained. "And a boy's been kidnapped. I can't stand by and just let that happen. Do you have a cell phone number or something?"

Boxers' glare screamed, *I'll kill you if you do.* Cell numbers were traceable, and therefore sensitive.

But the offer was one that intrigued Jonathan. They were working blind tonight. An extra set of eyes on the outside was a damned good idea. "Tell you what I'll do," he said.

"Scorpion." Only Boxers could put so much menace in a single word.

"Relax, Big Guy." Jonathan worked his way back out of his ruck and dug into its main pocket, from which he produced two standard, commercially available cheap walkie-talkies, the kind anyone could pick up in the mall. A well-learned lesson over the years preached that sometimes, as the shit hit the fan, the simplest technology worked best. He turned them both on, and keyed the mike for one of them. The feedback squeal told him that they were functioning.

He handed one of the radios to Dawn. "Just push

that button to talk," he said. "But please don't do it unless it's really, really important. I don't want to be sneaking up on somebody only to have your voice blast through the night telling me that the stars have come out. Follow me?"

Dawn turned the radio over in her hands, examining it. "I understand."

"Be sure you do," Boxers growled. Seeing their fearful reaction, he added, "I'm nowhere near as nice as my little friend." He shouldered his ruck as if it weighed nothing, and with the suitcase of Raven controls in one hand, and the empty aircraft sack in the other, he left.

"He means no harm," Jonathan said to the family. "But please do us all a favor and don't piss him off."

"So, what happened?" Graham asked. He examined Jolaine's wounds as best he could without the use of his hands. She wasn't particularly cut up, but man, was she bruised. Her left eye had swollen shut, and her jaw was swollen. "Who did this to you?"

"Who do you think?" She spoke through nearly clenched teeth.

"I mean, which one of them?"

"Does it matter?"

He took a few seconds to answer. "Yes, it does."

"Let's just say they took turns."

"Why?" he asked. "You don't know anything."

Jolaine closed her eyes against an obvious spasm of pain. "I kept telling them that," she said. "It wasn't what they wanted to hear. How did they get you?"

"They were transferring me to a foster home,"

Graham said. "They killed everybody but me." Until he said the words, he'd blocked the images of those nice people's murders from his mind. He couldn't even remember their names.

"I'm sorry," Jolaine said. "That's not right."

"That's why I had to tell those assholes something," Graham said. "This . . . *thing* has killed too many people. It's hurt too many people. It has to stop."

Jolaine gave a wry chuckle. "I don't know what their verification procedure is, but once they find out, my money says the end will be nearer than we want."

"You're giving up," Graham said. "You can't do that."

She rolled her eyes. "Come on, Graham. Sometimes reality has to trump hope. It's freezing in here."

"Give it time," Graham said. "This is nothing." He walked around to stare into Jolaine's face. "You can't go pessimist on me, Jolaine. Not now. We've got time."

"To do what?"

"I don't know! Goddammit, I don't freaking know, all right? *Something.* Our only other option is nothing, and that one sucks."

Jolaine fought another spasm.

"I'm sorry I got you into this," Graham said.

"And I'm sorry I didn't protect you better."

Graham kept walking to keep his feet from going numb.

"Why did Mom set me up?" he asked. He spoke the words without emotion.

"Now who's being pessimistic?"

"I'm serious, Jolaine. She gave me that code knowing that people would come to get me. Do you think she knew it would come to this?"

Jolaine inhaled, hocked once, and spat a wad of blood. "I think she was scared," she said. "I think she'd been shot and she was just trying to do something."

"But you said that the code was for some kind of bomb."

"Actually, I said I thought that's what it *might* be."

"Do you still?"

Another spasm, and she didn't even try to speak. She just nodded.

Graham stopped pacing and turned as it dawned on him: "And these guys are terrorists," he said. "Mom *wanted* them to have the code. That makes my parents terrorists."

Jolaine scowled as well as her battered features would allow as she considered what he'd just said. "Oh, my God."

Linus, the librarian in Graham's head, was moving like crazy to arrange all the logic cards so he could read them. "She didn't set me up for torture," Graham said. "She set me up to help terrorists."

How was that for a shit-sicle? How could she do that? How could *they* do that—Dad had to be in on it, too, right? Well, maybe not the part that directly involved Graham—Dad had already been killed by then—but the rest of it. The terrorism stuff. He paced again. He was thinking about his parents—the people who had brought him into the world, wiped his butt, and preached right and wrong. He knew he should be sad for their injuries, but all he could feel was anger.

"Holy shit, Jolaine, how could they?"

"I'm really sorry—"

"Wait," Graham said. "No, no, no, that doesn't make

sense, either. Why would the terrorists attack and kill them if they were all on the same side?"

"Maybe Uncle Sam found out," Jolaine offered, but her tone sounded more like thinking out loud than forwarding an actual theory.

"No," Graham snapped. It was a stupid theory. "You heard them yelling to each other. That wasn't English. No one yelled, 'Freeze, FBI,' or whatever they say in real life." He stopped pacing again. "Gregory," he said.

"What?"

"Gregory. That was the name of the man in the front door. Gregory. He kept saying, 'I'm sorry, they know. I'm sorry, they know.' Remember?"

Jolaine seemed to search her memory. "Okay."

"The people we ran away from were the people who knew."

"Knew what?" Jolaine asked. She looked like she was having difficulty keeping up.

"I don't *know*. Jesus, how could I know?"

"Graham, I'm not even sure I know what you're talking about anymore."

He wasn't either. He was trying to think his way through a problem. Finally, Linus dealt his last, most important card. "Oh, shit," Graham said. "There's another set of people trying to kill us."

"Who?"

"I don't know who, but I know why."

Jolaine saw it, too. "To keep these guys from getting the codes."

"Exactly," Graham said. His sense of triumph over solving a problem was quashed two seconds later by the obvious rejoinder. He shot a panicked look to Jolaine.

"They won't bother to torture," she said, connecting the dots for herself. "They just want to kill you."

In a rush, he realized the truth of Jolaine's earlier words. Sometimes, reality really did trump hope.

Tears pressed his eyes as he faced Jolaine. "We really are going to die tonight, aren't we?"

The door to the freezer slammed open. Teddy stood there with three of his friends. His right hand held a sledgehammer by its neck.

His eyes showed murder.

CHAPTER TWENTY-SEVEN

Jonathan almost regretted his decision not to let LeBron show him the clearing in the woods. Driving with the lights off and NVGs in place, it took two passes to find the spot.

"There it is," Jonathan said, finally. It wasn't the clearing he'd seen so much as the tire indentations that led to it. Once spotted, it was obvious. "Either they're not the only ones, or they come here a lot," he said.

"You ask me, every inch of this Godforsaken town is worn thin," Boxers said. He threw the transmission into park. "You're sure you want to go with full rucks?" he said.

Jonathan shrugged. "It's the neighborhood. If gang-bangers decide to break in, I don't care if they take possession of the Raven, but I wouldn't sleep well if we gave them explosives and detonators."

"Call it urban renewal," Big Guy said and he opened his door.

"Full soldier," Jonathan said. "We don't know what we're getting ourselves into." That was his term for full body armor, complete with chest plate and Kevlar helmet. It was unwieldy and heavy as hell. Boxers pointed to any opportunity he could find not to wear it, but the lack of push-back this time told Jonathan that he saw the risks, too.

When they were fully kitted up, they each carried their preferred rifles—Jonathan a suppressed M27 and Boxers a suppressed HK417—and a suppressed 4.6 millimeter HKMP7 holstered on their left thighs. Boxers also dangled a Mossberg twelve-gauge with a breaching barrel under his arm. No suppressor there, just a big bang.

With their four-tube night vision, the night had become day. Jonathan tied his gear in tight to limit any rattle, and then he was ready to go. "You all set?"

"Born ready," Boxers said.

Jonathan turned a knob on his radio and said, "Mother Hen, Scorpion. We're going hot and we're on VOX."

"I copy," she said. "Do a good job."

Jonathan smiled at that. He'd scolded her once for wishing them good luck when they were stepping out on an op because, as he said, luck was a thing to be managed, not victimized by. Since then, she'd been struggling to find the right phrase. For Jonathan, *do a good job* was just fine.

When they arrived at the fence, Jonathan understood why people had missed the presence of the hole. It had been wired up that well.

"Think there's a little OCD in young LeBron?" Boxers whispered. It took less than two minutes to undo the patch and lift the section away.

Jonathan assessed the size of the opening. "You'd better be careful, Big Guy. Turns out you're bigger than their truck." He pulled an infrared chem light from a side pouch on his ruck, snapped it, shook it to bring it to life, and then dropped it on the ground to mark the makeshift gate. Chances were good that there'd be a lot more activity swirling around them on the way out than there was on the way in. He didn't want to be feeling their way along the fence in the dark, looking for the back door.

They approached the black side of the building as a single shadow gliding through the dark, moving slowly and deliberately so as not to make unnecessary noise. Jonathan scanned continuously left to right walking forward, while Boxers moved in the same direction walking backward, scanning their six o'clock for bad guys.

"Contact at twelve o'clock," Jonathan whispered. The two guards stood at their stations, flanking the back door. The embers of their cigarettes flared in his NVGs. "MP7," he said.

The 4.6 millimeter round from the MP7 was a devastating bullet when shot well. Barely wider than a BB, it left the muzzle at over 2,400 feet per second, but because it was so small, it made far less noise than the larger, faster 5.56 millimeter round from his M27. With the suppressor in place, there was no discernible muzzle flash, and the noise was less than that of a ladyfinger firecracker. Jonathan didn't know how Heckler and Koch continued to get it so right every time in the manufacture of weapons.

All of the team's long guns and MP7s were fitted with infrared laser sights that cast a beam through the dark that only they could see, thanks to their NVGs. In

Jonathan's world, fair fights were for losers. "I'm right, you're left," he said.

"Roger."

"On zero," Jonathan said, as he settled his laser on his target's forehead. "Three, two, one . . ." He didn't bother to say the word because it was the cadence that counted. Their weapons fired in unison, and their targets dropped in unison, their bodies unplugged from their brains. "Two for two sleeping," Jonathan said for Venice's benefit.

They resumed their fore-and-aft advancing configuration as they closed the distance to the rear wall. Jonathan didn't bother to check the guards for pulses. The spatter told him everything he needed to know. "Okay, Big Guy. You're up."

Jonathan pivoted to cover the rear—their only exposed side, now that they were up against the building—while Boxers wrapped a loop of detonating cord around the electrical box serving the freezer unit inside. Detonating cord was every operator's best friend. Essentially a tube of PETN—an explosive with a detonation velocity that exceeded twenty thousand feet per second—a coil or two could drop a hundred-year-old oak. Just an inch or two would make ridiculously quick work of an electrical cable. While Big Guy did his thing, Jonathan holstered the MP7 and brought his M27 to his shoulder and continually scanned left to right and back again, one-eighty to one-eighty.

Thirty seconds later, he heard Big Guy's voice in his ear. "Done. Redundant electronic fuse set on zero then a hundred milliseconds." When the stakes were high, redundancy reigned as king. In this case, Boxers' first detonator would blow the instant he pushed the button on his controller. If it malfunctioned, then the backup would initiate one tenth of a second later.

"Ready to advance?" Jonathan asked. He fought the urge to look at Boxers because Big Guy posed no threat. At this stage, all he cared about were threats.

"Ready to advance."

"Advancing to Red." In recent years, the special operations community had moved away from the color-coded sides, but it was in Jonathan's DNA. White was front, black was back, and red was right. Compass points were far more precise, but who had a compass on them all the time?

They reassumed the same back-to-back posture as they approached the rear side, Jonathan leading and Boxers following. As they approached the end of the back wall, Jonathan said, "Corner."

That expanded Boxers' area of responsibility to a 270-degree radius as Jonathan concentrated on the threat that lay directly around the turn.

"Advancing right," Jonathan said, and he turned the corner. His senses told him that there had to be guards here. It didn't make sense otherwise. Why put sentries on some doors yet not on others? Since the loading dock was elevated, and the doors inset, it was difficult to get a line of sight. Advancing blind now, he moved much more slowly than before.

He heard voices from up on the deck. He didn't understand the language, but they seemed to be chatting, unaware of danger. Jonathan eased away from the wall for a better look. He whispered. "I've got two more targets."

They were standing next to each other, which to Jonathan's perspective put them in the same plane.

"I've got a bad angle," Jonathan said. "Swing out and tell me what you see."

He felt Boxers pivot, swinging his rifle in a horizontal arc over his head. "I've got a left target if you want me to take it," he said. "That would be the farthest from you."

"On zero, then," Jonathan said. He counted the cadence again, with the same result, except this time, because of the oblique angle and the backlight, he saw the aura of simultaneous brain-sprays. Both targets were neutralized. Jonathan had lost count over the years of the number of lives he'd taken, but it never got easier. To point a gun at Jonathan was a capital offense that that earned the perpetrator a guilt-free execution. But to die standing sentry—the most basic of soldierly duties—bore no honor or fanfare. In dispatching those, he always felt a burden of sadness. Nothing he couldn't handle, but a sadness nonetheless.

With the lifeless bodies collapsed on the deck, Jonathan and Boxers moved together up the steps to the loading dock, where Boxers affixed the second charge of det cord to the electrical service. While he did that, Jonathan moved to the personnel door next to the roll-up overhead to see if it was unlocked. It was not. "I'm going to set a breaching charge," he said. That meant pressing a GPC—a general purpose charge, which consisted of a wad of C4 high explosive triggered by a tail of det cord—into a three-inch trail where the door lock met the jamb. Typically, Jonathan preferred old-fashioned fuse (OFF) for the GPC, but to stay in concert with the charges Boxers had already set, he inserted dual electronic initiators into the detonating cord.

Jonathan asked, "Are you—"

An agonized scream ruined the night.

Teddy might have been on rails, he glided so quickly across the room, the short sledgehammer raised. His eyes were focused and hot. He seemed unaware of anything or anyone but Graham, who remained frozen in place. Teddy was still moving when he swung the sledge like a baseball bat.

Graham closed his eyes as the head of the hammer shattered his left elbow. The jolt of agony somehow unplugged his nervous system and he collapsed in a heap onto the icy tile.

"Remember," Teddy said. "This is your deal. This is what you asked for." With that, he launched a kick to Graham's belly. As he doubled up on his side, another kick nailed him in the kidney.

Someone was screaming.

He'd just realized that the screams were his own when the building shook with an explosion and blackness fell.

The splintered jamb was still burning when Jonathan and Boxers squirted through the door. As was their tradition, Jonathan went in first and swept low and right while Boxers swept high and left. Their IR laser sights drew crisscrossing lines through the lingering smoke of the explosions.

The smoke confused the NVGs, potentially obscuring targets behind a veil of heated gases.

Jonathan and Boxers moved as one, in a crouch, their weapons at the ready and pressed against their shoulders. As their ears recovered from the concussion of the blasts—hearing protection could protect only so much—they heard the sounds of confused bedlam. Shouting voices combined with more howls of agony. Most of the shouting was in the same dialect that he'd heard from the guards.

"The noise is coming from two o'clock," Boxers said.

"I agree."

They pivoted together a couple of points to the right and continued to advance. Jonathan saw movement in the smoke, but before he could react, Boxers' rifle barked twice and the silhouette dropped. Big Guy had switched to his cannon—the 7.62 millimeter HK417. Whatever his bullets touched instantly joined a parallel universe. Even with a suppressor attached, the gunshot rocked the building. With stealth no longer relevant, Jonathan holstered his MP7 and lifted his M27 from its sling. Similar in construction and weight to the venerable M4—but vastly superior in its performance, particularly in adverse circumstances—it wasn't the perfect weapon for close-quarters battle, but it felt like an old friend. Because it was chambered in 5.56 millimeter, the people Jonathan killed wouldn't be quite as dead as the people Boxers killed, but it would be close.

With their presence known, they stepped up the pace. The noise and the darkness had no doubt rattled their enemy, but the effects could only last so long. Close-in rifle fire had the tendency to focus the attention of the shot-at, and in a few seconds, if these guys had any clue what they were doing, they were going to mount some kind of defense.

"Threat left!" Boxers said.

Jonathan pivoted in time to see one of three approaching men drop when Boxers shot him. Jonathan took out a second, but the third disappeared behind the wall of an inner room that Jonathan recognized from the drawings as the meat freezer.

"Shit," Jonathan spat. He was about to pursue the attacker when another scream echoed through the factory. "That's coming from inside the freezer," he said.

"The door's on the other side," Boxers said.

Another scream.

"Leave him alone!" a female voice yelled. In English.

"We'll use the back door," Jonathan said.

Graham thought he'd been knocked unconscious. The darkness came so suddenly and was so absolute, he couldn't imagine another scenario.

But the pain kept coming, lightning bolts of agony that seemed to have no focus. Everything hurt, and he couldn't breathe.

Another explosion.

Gunshot? It sounded for all the world like the rifles that had become so much a part of his life these past days.

The assholes all started shouting in Chechen. He couldn't understand the words, but they were the sounds of panic, and they were accompanied by quick, heavy movement that likewise seemed to have no focus. Some-one either kicked him or fell on him, and that really lit up his injuries.

His scream hurt his throat.

Two more sharp explosions—maybe three.

Definitely guns.

More shouting, and someone grabbed him by his shoulder and lifted.

Jesus God.

"Leave him alone!" Jolaine yelled.

In darkness he couldn't be sure, but from the heavy *thud,* and the grunt that followed, he was pretty sure they'd hit her.

Amid a lot of discussion he couldn't understand, Graham was passed among several people.

In the movies, people in excruciating pain passed out and got relief.

He was ready to live in a movie.

The freezer was a room within a cavern, roughly twelve feet square, and it had both a front door and a back door, presumably to allow the free flow of cow carcasses in and out without creating a traffic jam. Jonathan remembered the detail from the plans Venice had sent them. He sent up a prayer that the drawing be correct.

Through the NVGs, Jonathan saw the hinges before he saw the latch. And then he saw the massive padlock that had been placed over the latch assembly. "Shit," he said.

"Outta my way, Boss," Boxers said. He had a GPC

in his fist, with a detonator already dangling from the det cord fuse. "Five-second delay," he said, "so we'll be inside in ten."

Jonathan pivoted to make room for Big Guy, and he scanned the inside of the factory for more targets. He saw movement in the shadows to his right and he fired a long burst, got a yelp of pain in return.

"Fire in the hole," Boxers said.

Jonathan turned away from the door and stooped to become a human soccer ball. The blast made the building bounce, and turned the heavy freezer door into a rectangular hole.

"All right, let's—"

Automatic weapons opened up from behind them— from the direction of the loading dock through which they'd entered.

Boxers coughed and fell. "Ah, shit. God*dammit.*"

Jonathan felt a stab of panic. "Are you hit?"

"Damn straight I'm hit. God *damn* it!" Boxers opened up with his 417, raking the area where the shots had come from. "Go!" he said. "Get the freaking PCs. I'll kill these assholes myself. God *DAMN it!*"

Jonathan's mind raced to push the panic away. *Mission first,* he told himself. He had to tend to the PCs. "I'll be back for you, Big Guy," he said, and then he slipped in through their newly opened door.

The opening was blocked with rolling racks and assorted shit, and floor was coated with ice. Through his green artificial light, Jonathan saw a scrum of activity ahead as beefy men tried to find their way to meaningful activity in the dark. Everyone he saw carried a long gun of some sort, and at least one had a sidearm.

Through the tangle of dangling meat hooks, he had difficulty separating the PCs from the bad guys, until he heard yet another howl of pain, and he focused in on the kid who was being manhandled by one of the thugs.

"PC One is in the grasp," he said over the air. Protocol mattered, even when your best friend had been shot. He let the M27 fall back against its sling and drew his MP7 again. "Switching to hollow point on the MP7."

He released the nearly full mag of ball ammo and switched it out with a thirty-round mag of hollow points that he pulled from its pouch on his vest. The advantage of hollow-point ammo lay in the fact that the mushrooming effect of the hollow point expended much of the round's energy on impact, thus making it less likely to overpenetrate and hit a good guy who might be standing behind the bad guy target.

He could tell that they were getting organized up there, and they had come to grips with the fact that their space had been breached. Two of the men had opened fire in Jonathan's general direction, but in their darkness, they didn't have the visual frame of reference to even come close.

He needed to disorient them even more.

Jonathan opened a Velcro fastener on his ballistic vest and removed a cylindrical stun grenade. Filled with magnesium and ammonium perchlorate stuffed into a cardboard tube, the grenade was designed to temporarily blind and deafen anyone within a few-yard radius, buying a few precious seconds for rescuers to work their magic.

Squeezing the safety spoon, Jonathan pulled the pin, then lobbed the grenade in the general vicinity of the bad guys.

"Flash-bang away," he said. He turned away, closed his eyes, and pressed his hands against his ears. Two seconds later, the building shook again. Even with his eyes closed and his head turned, Jonathan could see the blood vessels in his eyelids from the flash. One second after the blast, while the disorientation was still pure, Jonathan moved on the bad guys.

Behind him, fully automatic fire continued to rip the silence from outside the freezer. "Engaging multiple targets," Boxers said before an extended burst of gunfire.

Hearing Big Guy's voice calmed Jonathan, reminded him that he had a half dozen targets of his own to engage.

"Hostages get down! Hostages get down!" Jonathan yelled. "Get the hell down!"

Predictably, two of the thugs swung their weapons at the sound of Jonathan's voice and opened fire. Jonathan dropped to a knee and smoked the one on the left with three rounds to his chest. The one on the right dove for cover and saved his own life.

Goddammit.

Jonathan scooted to the left because some brainiac had done a study a while ago that demonstrated that absent evidence to the contrary, people assumed movement to their own left—Jonathan's right—and he wanted to be unpredictable.

Outside, Boxers' gun battle raged on.

As he moved, Jonathan's laser beam stabbed a shooter in the ear. Jonathan judged the distance at fifteen feet, ten feet short of the distance the sight was zeroed to, so he lowered the beam to the top of the guy's shoulder and pressed the trigger.

The head exploded.

Two down.

Boxers' gunfight raged beyond the freezer door. From the sound of it, he'd employed his 417, and he was not being shy in his application of firepower.

"I will shoot the boy!" a man yelled from nearby. "Put down your gun or I will shoot the boy!"

Had the bad guy not shouted out like that, Jonathan would likely not have seen him. As it was, the target was maybe ten feet away, and facing in the wrong direction, presenting his back as he looked toward a direction where Jonathan had never been. The target held PC One in front of him as cover, his elbow cinched under the PC's chin. The boy's arm flopped oddly—clearly broken.

Seconds ticked.

At this range, hollow point notwithstanding, a head shot or a center-of-mass shot would probably over-penetrate and wound the PC. That was not acceptable.

Moving quickly yet silently, Jonathan slipped the MP7 into its holster and drew his KA-BAR knife from its scabbard on his left shoulder. Uncle Sam had tried a lot of different fighting blades since the KA-BAR was first introduced in 1941, but as far as Jonathan was concerned, none had even approached the elegance and raw lethality of the wooden-handled Marine Corps favorite.

Jonathan held the knife as an extension of his fist, blade facing forward, hilt against his thumb, and he closed the distance in just a few strides. The fact that the bad guy had a full head of hair made it so much easier. Jonathan grabbed a fistful of hair at the crown and pulled back just as he thrust the razor-sharp steel blade in to the base of his skull at a thirty-degree angle, effectively separating the man's brain from the rest of his body. If he didn't die instantly, he'd be dead soon. Either way, score another for the good guys.

As the man collapsed, Jonathan caught Graham at his middle and lowered him to the floor.

Graham felt unhinged, completely disoriented. So much sound and light. So much pain. Violence swirled from everywhere and without meaning.

"I will kill the boy," Teddy yelled in his ear. And then a few seconds later, Teddy made a horrible sound and collapsed, bringing Graham with him.

And then Graham felt someone lower him gently to the floor.

"I'm here to take you home," the stranger said. "Lie on the floor and try to be invisible."

Graham was not prepared for the kind tone, and he certainly was not prepared for the kind words. While the manhandling was gentler, it was no less painful. Ten thousand questions formed in his head. Before he could form one well enough to ask, he'd been placed on the floor, and the stranger let go of him.

Lying on his stomach, he imagined himself dissolving into the concrete floor, becoming so small as to be an oil slick—not a target at all.

Then a bullet whipped past his ear and slammed into the floor behind him.

CHAPTER TWENTY-EIGHT

"**B**ig Guy, I need a status report," Jonathan said. As he spoke, he toured the bodies on the floor. All six were dead, or close enough to not to be a threat.

"I'm engaged with three OpFor," Boxers' voice said in his ear. Two gunshots fired in quick succession out beyond the freezer. "Make it two. The remainders are better at hiding than shooting."

"Graham and Jolaine, stay down!" Jonathan commanded. He couldn't see them, couldn't verify that they were even alive still, but with their threats neutralized, they could fend for themselves for a few minutes. Jonathan headed back for the door they'd created, back to join in Boxers' war.

He'd nearly made it to the opening when it filled with Big Guy's massive silhouette. "Four more baddies are sound asleep," Big Guy said. He listed to the side, but Jonathan couldn't see any blood.

"Jesus, are you okay?" he asked.

"No, I'm not okay," Boxers said. "Bastards freaking shot me."

"Where? Where are you hit."

Boxers pointed to a spot in the center of his chest. "Right here," he said. "Where I'm supposed to have a heart." He grinned. "My vest stopped it."

Jonathan's shoulders sagged as the tension drained.

"They had MP5s," Big Guy said. "Thank God for little nine mike-mikes." He looked past Jonathan to survey the carnage inside the freezer. "Whoa, you've been busy, too."

Jonathan's head filled with a thousand things he wanted to say, a hundred prayers he wanted to offer up to thank God for Boxers' survival. After dropping only a beat, he said, "Those vests aren't cheap, you know. And now I have to replace that one."

"Cry me a river, Billionaire Boy. Where do we stand?"

Jonathan switched out his partially empty mag for a full one and re-holstered the MP7. "You take PC One," Jonathan said. "Be careful. I think that arm's pretty badly broken." Everyone who served in the Unit had decent combat medic skills—Jonathan was no exception—but Boxers was particularly gifted. Where injuries were obvious, Big Guy was always the best choice.

Jonathan turned back toward the room. "Graham?" he called. "Speak up."

For five or six seconds, he heard only silence, and his heart sank.

"Here," the kid said.

"Jolaine Cage?"

"Right here," she said. She lay on the floor on her side, her hands tied in front of her. Her voice sounded weak. Jonathan walked over to her. He had to pull a corpse out of the way by its shirt collar to stoop far enough to speak softly. "Hi, Jolaine. We're here to take you home."

The H-word, home, was one of the most powerful words in the universe. He never tired of watching the realization dawn on the victims he rescued. That was the money shot—the few seconds that made all the rest of it worthwhile.

"Popping chem lights," Boxers said as he cracked a luminescent stick and shook it. When the stick shone green, he rolled it across the floor to Jonathan.

Now, the hostages were no longer blind, but seeing didn't necessarily put their minds at ease. Jonathan and Boxers both wore black hoods that revealed only their eyes, and with the NVGs in place, even those did not show.

"My name is Scorpion," Jonathan said. "My friend is named Big Guy."

"W-who are you?" Jolaine stammered. He caught the slurred speech.

"Just friends," Jonathan said. He examined her arms and the ropes that bound them. The loops were sadistically tight. "You're going to see a big sharp knife," he said. "I'm going to cut you loose, so don't panic or start jerking around. I literally could shave with the edge of this thing, and I don't need either one of us getting cut." As he put the KA-BAR into use, he hoped that she couldn't see the blood that remained on the blade.

Whoever tied her up was an expert. Rather than wrapping her limbs in one continuous loop as amateurs typically did, her torturer used six knots, which ensured that they wouldn't loosen until they were supposed to.

"How did you know?" Jolaine asked.

From behind, he heard Graham's yelps of pain, along with Boxers' soothing tone.

"I work in a weird business," Jonathan said.

"So Scorpion is a code name."

"Or my parents were really twisted. I won't tell you which."

With her hands free, Jolaine tried to sit up, but Jonathan put a hand on her shoulder to keep her down. "How hurt are you?"

"I think they broke my jaw," she said. "And I know they broke a tooth. I don't think I'm bleeding out anywhere."

The cogence of her response led Jonathan to believe her. "Can you feel your hands?" They'd been tied so tightly that there might have been nerve damage.

Jolaine wiggled her fingers. "They're tingly, but they work."

Jonathan cupped his hand under her biceps and lifted. "Let's see if we can get you on your feet."

"How's Graham?"

"Big Guy, how's PC One?"

"I'm splinting him up. He'll live, but this arm needs surgery."

Jolaine moved carefully as she rose to her feet. She wobbled a little, reminding Jonathan of a newborn colt, but then she seemed to find her balance.

"I'm okay," she said. "You called him PC One. Are you SOCOM?"

Jonathan recognized the acronym for Special Operations Command, but he opted to ignore the question. "Test out those legs," he said. "They're about to get some serious use." He turned his attention to Boxers and Graham. "Is he about packaged?"

PC One's arm had been stabilized with a ladder splint—a length of bendable wire that consisted of two long edges connected by cross pieces that together resembled a long ladder—and about a half mile of Kling wrap. Boxers was in the process of putting on the finishing touches to the immobilization by binding the splinted arm to the boy's chest with another long length of Kling.

"One more minute."

From behind, Jonathan heard the clattering sound of a gun's bolt being charged. He snatched his M27 to his shoulder and spun 180 degrees as he dropped to a knee.

"No!" Jolaine said. "Don't! It's me." She held out an MP5 as if it were a peace offering.

"God*dammit,*" Jonathan snapped. "What the hell?"

"I want a weapon," Jolaine said. "You might be John Wayne and the cavalry, but I still want a means to protect myself."

"She's really good with it," Graham said. It was the first time Jonathan had heard him speak.

Generally, it was a mistake to let PCs arm themselves, but Jonathan weighed this time as an exception. Given her past experience, an extra trigger might not be a bad idea. "Just don't confuse the good guys and the bad guys," he said.

"I'm set," Boxers announced. "Can you walk, kid, or do I need to carry you?"

"I'm okay," Graham said. His right arm cradled his shattered left as if it were a baby. "We just need to go slow."

Yeah, right, Jonathan didn't say. "Here's how it's going to work," he said. "We're going to become a human snake. I'm the head, Big Guy is the tail, and you two are the belly in the middle. Follow in lockstep, do everything I tell you to do the instant I tell you to do it, and we'll get you safely out of here."

"Do you know anything about my parents?" Graham asked. "Are they both dead?"

Jonathan hesitated, then let him have it. "Yes. I'm sorry." It would have been wrong to lie. "Now let's make sure you don't join them. Let's move."

Jonathan led the tiny parade to the freezer door, where he raised a hand to stop them while he peeked out and swept the space with his muzzle. "Clear," he said.

From behind, he heard Boxers say, "Put your safety on, young lady. And keep the muzzle pointed at the floor. I'll tell you if and when we need your help."

Jonathan hadn't realized the extent of Boxers' firefight out here. The walls and floor had been chewed to hell. One of the attackers had gotten disturbingly close.

He turned a hard right and started back toward the loading dock. They were in the middle of the open space when the throwaway radio broke squelch. "Um, Scorpion?" LeBron's voice said. "Were you expecting people by parachute?"

* * *

Anton Datsik continued to be impressed by the resources that the American government could make available when they were motivated. He'd requested parachutes for his team, an airplane, and a pilot who knew not to speak. All things were available to him with two hours.

Dangling from his harness, watching through night vision as the ground approached beneath his feet, his only worry was whether he was too late. With about three hundred feet to go before impact, he checked to his right and to his left to make sure his team was still together. They were, of course. They were six in total, plenty enough to confront a bunch of Chechen amateurs.

Datsik was gratified to see the cars still parked behind the factory, interpreting it as a sign that the interlopers had not yet accomplished their mission. Once the code was revealed, there would be no need for the enemy to stick around.

At slightly under one hundred feet, he saw two dead bodies sprawled astride the entry door on the loading dock. Startled and distracted, he nearly missed nailing his stand-up landing. On the ground, with his chute under control, he said to his team on the radio, "Gather on me. There is a complication."

Jonathan watched from a window at the rear of the building—the closest exit to the Expedition that would get them out of here. At first, Jonathan saw only two invaders land from the sky. Their technique was perfect, and even from this distance, he could see their night vision and their weaponry. This was trouble.

"I've got two," he said over the radio.

"I've got four," Boxers said. He was watching through the loading-dock windows.

Jonathan's two dumped their parachutes and scurried to the right. "Mine are coming your way, Big Guy."

"I see them. Let me know what you want to do."

It took all of two seconds for Jonathan to decide their next move. "Disengage," he said. "We're going out the rear." It made no sense to start a firefight, especially when the enemy seemed competent. Truth be told, those parachutes unnerved him a little. For all he knew, they could be a souped-up team of feds coming in to lend them a hand. He doubted that, but you never knew. Opening fire on the unknown without provocation was always a bad idea.

He knew that Boxers would disagree, but Big Guy was first and foremost a soldier, and he knew when an order was an order.

When they were all gathered by the back door, Jonathan delivered his instructions. "I don't know who these guys are, and they clearly haven't seen us yet. We're going to head out this door and move carefully to a car we have stashed about a hundred yards from here. There are a couple of dead guys on the other side of the door. Don't freak out.

"Graham, I know you hurt and this is going to be tough, but I need you to keep your good hand on my rucksack. Do not let go. As long as I can feel the tug, I know you're still with me. If there's shooting, do exactly what I tell you. If I tell you to drop to the ground, you become one with the dirt. Do you understand?"

The kid's eyes grew huge and he nodded.

"I need a verbal response. Do you understand?"

"Yes."

"Okay. Jolaine."

She looked up.

"Do not engage with your firearm unless we are engaged first. If it comes to that, remember the only ammo you have is what's left in your one mag. I'd make them count if I were you, and watch your background. Every miss goes somewhere, and I don't want to be responsible for any collateral damage."

"I understand," she said.

"Done," Jonathan said. "Mother Hen, we're moving."

"I copy," Venice.

"Hand on my ruck, Graham."

He felt the tug.

"Big Guy, IR Lasers off. They've got night vision, too. Here we go." Jonathan pushed the door open and led the short parade out into the open and into the night. He pivoted to face right as he confronted the threat at their three o'clock, using his body as a shield for PC One, and walking sideways in a kind of bastardized grapevine step. He glanced left periodically to stay in line with the IR glow stick he'd dropped at the hole in the fence.

All it would take at this point would be for one of the bad guys to glance their way and they'd be made, all advantage of operating in the dark lost. His one advantage over the OpFor was their use of the outdated two-tube NVGs. The tunnel vision they created all but eliminated detection of the periphery. To capitalize on that, Jonathan led the way at a painfully slow pace. Particularly in reduced light conditions, the human eye was much more likely to capture motion than it was to capture a single image. Throw in the fact that both his PCs were essentially blind, and one of them was crippled, it was a bad idea to run.

And then running became a very good idea.

"People have already been here," Datsik said to his assembled team in Russian. "See the bodies at the door."

"What does that mean?" a team member asked. His name was Leonid, and while always aggressive, he never seemed very bright to Datsik.

"I do not know," Datsik replied. "But this looks like professional work. The fact that we do not hear continuing gunfire means that we are either just on time or perhaps too late."

"The enemy of our enemy is our friend, is he not?" Leonid asked.

Datsik had learned years ago that all surprises were inherently bad. If the US was sending a team here for action, Philip Baxter should have told him. And if the shooters were not American agents, then who else would want to kill the Chechens? "We need to enter carefully," he said. "We don't know—"

"Look!" Leonid said. "To the right!"

Snatching his Kalashnikov to his shoulder, Datsik turned and saw what appeared to be two American Special Forces operators, one huge and one of average height and girth, moving slowly away from the factory with two other people, a lady and a boy. Beyond them, Datsik saw the glow of an infrared marker on the ground near the woods line.

His team assumed shooting positions and prepared to engage.

CHAPTER TWENTY-NINE

To run would mean turning their backs on their enemy. Jonathan had no choice but to engage. "We're made," Jonathan said. "Graham and Jolaine, on the ground, now."

Graham yelled as Jonathan pushed him to the deck face-first, but Jonathan didn't care. He didn't have time to. Jolaine likewise dropped to the ground, but she assumed a prone shooter's position. Jonathan and Boxers both dropped to a knee, weapons up and ready.

"Everybody hold your fire," Jonathan snapped.

"Are you friggin' kidding me?" Boxers said.

"Hold your fire," Jonathan said again. They were out in the open, with zero cover, and they were outnumbered by professional shooters. "We don't know who they are."

"I know they're pointing a goddamn gun at me."

"As we are them, but you'll notice they haven't fired, either. For all we know, they're good guys."

"That would explain the pigs I saw flying over frozen Hell this morning," Boxers said.

A voice called from the other side, "Put your weapons

down or we will open fire." The thick Russian accent did nothing to soothe Jonathan's doubts.

"Who are you?" Jonathan shouted.

"Does not matter," the Russian said. "You are out-gunned."

"Oh, for Christ's sake, Boss," Boxers growled. "It's Ivan. Are we really doing this?" Ivan was their generic term for any Russian. Any Eastern European, for that matter.

"Full-auto," Jonathan said, softly enough to be heard only through his microphone. "If it comes to it, I'll rake 'em left to right, and you rake right to left." If this went hot, the best they could hope for was to be hit in their body armor.

"Drop your weapons!" the Russian shouted again. One of the operators on the Russian's right started to pull away from their skirmish line to move on Jonathan's left flank.

"Don't move!" Jonathan yelled. "Get down now or I will open fire!"

The commander on the other side barked something in Russian and the flanker pulled back in.

"This is some weird shit," Boxers said. "Who are these guys?"

"We are not putting our weapons down," Jonathan said to the other commander. "For the same reason that you are not. If you shoot, we'll shoot. If you don't, we won't."

"You can trust us," the Russian said.

"Easy words for a Russian who just parachuted into the middle of my operation," Jonathan said.

"Would you like me to make some friggin' tea?" Boxers said.

In the distance, Jonathan could just hear the first tone of approaching sirens.

"Leash is getting short, Boss."

"Tell you what," Jonathan called to the other side. "If you're here for what I think you are, everything's fine. Your enemies are dead, and your codes were not revealed. You can go home and sleep well. Meanwhile, my friends and I are going to walk away from you." Under his breath, he said to his team, "Nobody move till I tell you."

"Do you have boy?" the Russian yelled.

"Twenty bucks says this does not end well," Boxers mumbled.

Jonathan ran the options through his head. The approach of sirens made quick action essential, and he couldn't very well lie about something Ivan was about to see with his own eyes. "I do," he said.

The Russian paused. "Okay," he said. "You leave, but go slowly. Give me no reason to shoot you."

"He wants the kid," Jonathan whispered.

Graham groaned. "Please, no," he begged. "I want this to stop."

"Wanting's not the same as getting," Jonathan said.

Boxers said, "They're waiting till we stand up, and then they're going to take their shot. I think we should go first."

"Not yet," Jonathan said. The two forces were separated by maybe seventy-five yards of open field. Napoleonic face-to-face battlefield tactics had faded away a long, long time ago.

Jonathan saw movement in the night, beyond the Russians. Seconds later, the motion revealed itself to be a dark panel truck, and it was moving way too fast. It skidded a turn into the long driveway, blasted through the chain-link gate, and raced toward them.

Two of the OpFor turned to face the new threat while the others kept their weapons trained on Jonathan and his team.

"Odds will never be better, Boss."

"Not yet."

"Shit."

The truck skidded to a halt a good sixty to seventy feet before hitting the assembled Russians, therefore no doubt preventing the driver from getting seriously ventilated. The driver's door flew open, and a female voice yelled, "Don't shoot! Nobody shoot."

As the driver emerged, Jonathan recognized her right away as Maryanne Rhoades.

"Oh, man," Boxers said with a laugh. "Ain't this some shit?"

"Oh, my God," Jolaine said. "That's Agent Rhoades."

Maryanne approached the Russians at a run, her arms extended from her sides, and her hands exposed. "Nobody shoot!" she called. "This is over. This is *over*. No one needs to shoot anyone."

Jonathan could vaguely hear the Russian commander speaking to his troops, presumably translating her words.

Maryanne passed through the Russian skirmish line to take a position between both parties. She extended her hands like a traffic cop stopping traffic in both directions. "Please," she said. "Put your weapons down. The police are coming, and we need to be out of here."

Jonathan broke his aim, but kept his M27 at low-

ready as he stood. The Russian commander said something to his troops, and they likewise lowered their
muzzles.

"So, this is what brinksmanship feels like," Jonathan
muttered. He moved casually to his left so that he could
see the entire enemy line, without Maryanne being in
the way.

"Don't trust them," Boxers warned. He, too, had
broken his aim, but he maintained a stable shooting
platform, up on one knee, his hand still wrapped
around the grip of his 417.

"What's going on, Maryanne?" Jonathan asked. "Why
are you here?"

"To interrupt the bloodshed," she said. "To make
sure that Graham is safe."

"And why are they here?"

"To stop the Chechens," she said.

"I already did that," Jonathan said. "You already
gave me that job."

"Can we talk about this later?" Maryanne pressed.
"The police are on the way."

"Hey, Ivan," Jonathan yelled. "What are your plans
now?"

One of them stepped forward. "If we are done, then
we are done," he said. "We will leave."

"Good," Jonathan said. "Then we're done, too.
Jolaine?"

"Right here."

"Help Graham to his feet, will you?"

The Russian said something to his troops.

"Remember the plan, Big Guy," Jonathan said.

"Uh-huh."

Jonathan listened to the boy's moans as Jolaine got him to his feet, but he never took his eyes off the bad guys, just as they never took their eyes off him. He slipped his finger into the trigger guard.

"I'm ready," Graham said. His voice was weak with pain. And he was posed in the open for a clear shot.

"Good," Jonathan said. "I'll be right—"

The Russian leader jerked his rifle up, but before he could bring it to his shoulder, Jonathan fired a five-round burst into his neck and his ear. At the same instant, Boxers opened up on the skirmish line. Jonathan raked the line from left to right. In less than two seconds the Russians were all dead.

Maryanne had dropped to the ground, her arms covering her head.

Jonathan walked over to her and patted the top of her head with a gloved hand. "Are you okay?" he asked.

When she looked up, she was confused at first, and then she went right to anger. "What the hell did you just do?"

"Can we talk about this later?" Jonathan said. He keyed the mike on the RadioShack radio and said, "Thanks, guys, for the heads-up on the parachutes. The Expedition is yours if you want it. The toy airplane, too, but I'd be careful not to show that off too much." Not wanting to engage in a conversation with LeBron and Dawn, he switched the handset off before they had a chance to answer.

Jonathan looked to Maryanne. "The police are on the way. And I could use a ride."

As she rose to her feet, Maryanne surveyed the carnage. "Oh, my God," she said. "You have no idea what you've done."

"Probably not," Jonathan said. "Now, about that ride."

Boxers drove the panel truck over Maryanne's objections, but he let her ride shotgun. There was a row of seats behind, and Jonathan sat there. Graham tried his best to find comfort on the floor, and Jolaine tried her best to help him.

"So," Jonathan said. "How big an international incident did we cause back there?"

"You'll never know," she said. "I just don't believe it went down that way."

"How was it supposed to go down?" Jonathan asked.

"Never mind," she said. Jonathan read discomfort in her body language.

"Yeah, okay." A beat. "You know what I don't get is why you were there in the first place."

She shifted in her seat. "There are some things you just don't have a right to know," she said.

Jonathan smiled. "Hey, Big Guy, do me a favor, will you, and pull over."

Boxers had hit the turn signal even before the question was out.

Maryanne shot Jonathan a panicked look. "What are you doing?"

As the vehicle slowed, gravel crunched under the tires. When they were stopped, Jonathan said, "Get out."

Maryanne looked appalled. "What? Why?"

"Because I can't stand the sight of anyone who betrayed me."

"What are you *talking* about? I just saved you."

"I confess there are holes in what I've figured out, but the one thing I know for certain is that you were there to exfil the Russian team, and that the Russian team was there to kill my PC—the very PC that you hired me to protect. I don't understand why, and frankly, I don't much care."

"You're wrong," she said. "It's not like that."

Jonathan shrugged. "I've been wrong before," he said. "Get out."

"But we're in the middle of nowhere."

"All the better," Jonathan said. "Please don't make me ask again."

Boxers drew his pistol and rested it against her head. "Think of it as a safety thing," he said. "The longer you're here, the stronger my desire to use this."

Tears came to her eyes. "I didn't know," she said. "I mean, I tried to—"

"I deeply don't care," Jonathan said. "Out."

Boxers pulled the hammer back on his Beretta. It now had a two-pound trigger pull. In trigger terms, that's a tickle.

Finally, she got it. The door handle clicked and she shouldered it open. It was still open, in fact, when Boxers stepped on the gas the instant her ass was clear of the seat. Jonathan climbed over the engine cowling that separated the two seats and settled into shotgun, reaching out to pull the door shut.

Boxers rumbled out a laugh. "Mother Hen is going to love this part of the story," he said.

CHAPTER THIRTY

Jonathan pulled another beer out of the fridge for Father Dom and poured himself another two fingers of Lagavulin. June had arrived, and the Washington Nationals were about to mix it up with the Baltimore Orioles. Neither team sucked yet—though there was plenty of time left in the season for that—so Jonathan's team loyalty was still up for grabs. The Orioles had been the de facto Washington home team for so many years that he couldn't turn his back on them quite yet. The Nats could make it a lot easier, though, if they could figure out a way to stitch a whole season together. "May they not humiliate themselves," he said as he delivered the drink.

"To coping with reduced expectations," Dom toasted. "I can't help but notice that you haven't yet turned on the television. That usually means you've got something on your mind."

Jonathan sipped the liquid smoke that was Lagavulin scotch. "A couple of things, actually. First, how is Graham Mitchell adjusting?"

"You mean Vincent Malone?"

Jonathan made a face. Under the circumstances, the new name was a lifesaver. Literally. "Yes," he said. "How's Vincent Malone?"

"Physically or mentally?"

"Yes."

Dom scowled as he considered his answer. "Physically, I think he's fine. He's out of the cast, and the restrictions have been lifted from his physical activities. He's cleared to perform to the *limits of his capabilities.*" He did finger quotes with his free hand.

"Why the emphasis?"

"That's the segue to his psychology," Dom said. "He's by no means stretching his capabilities. He's been through a lot, and as much as I and Mama Alexander and the rest of the staff try to be supportive, we'll never get his parents back for him. Every time he looks at that scar on his elbow, he's going to be reminded of some pretty awful stuff. Think about it. He doesn't even live under the same name anymore."

Jonathan inhaled deeply to prepare for his next question. "Every kid in Resurrection House is damaged goods. How is . . . Vincent on that scale?"

Dom's scowl deepened. "Well, I'm not sure how much I like the characterization of the kids in Rez House being damaged—"

"You know what I mean."

"—but I know what you mean. And I don't know how to answer you. There's no paradigmatic Rez House resident. Do they all come with baggage? Hell yes, their parents are criminals. Are some more damaged than others? Of course. But I have no way of comparing Vincent's damage against that of another student. Do I think that Vincent will come out of this experience as a functional adult? Yes, I do. But some damage will be permanent."

Jonathan took his time considering the answer. He supposed that would be okay. Jonathan felt a personal responsibility for Graham that he didn't feel for many others in Rez House.

"You said there were a couple of things bothering you," Dom said. Once he fell into psychologist mode, he could be tenacious. Especially so when Jonathan was his patient.

"Yeah," Jonathan said. "And they're related. How much do you know about this Maryanne Rhoades chick?"

"The FBI agent?"

"Right."

"The one you threw out of her own truck?"

Jonathan smiled. "That's the one. I had a chat with Wolverine today. It was about Maryanne. In fact, it was about that entire mess that landed Graham here in the first place."

"What did she say?"

"After a lot of ducking and dodging and denials, Maryanne confessed that she, Maryanne, was the information vector for the Russians. She was the one directing the Russians on how to kill him."

Dom recoiled as he test-drove the thought. "Why would she do that?"

"Apparently, she had a gambling problem," Jonathan said. "And a big one, at that. To the tune of something like eighty grand. And she was upside down with the Russian mob."

"Yikes."

"Exactly. I don't know all the ins and outs but the

bottom line was, if she could deliver the codes and the code-keepers to the mob, they'd let her off the hook."

Dom shook his head. "Good Lord. So, she sold out a kid?"

"No, not initially," Jonathan said. "At first, the targets were his parents, via their rebel friends. Somehow, she talked herself into believing that it would be bad guy versus bad guy. No harm, no foul. But when things went wrong, and Graham's mom passed along the code to him, he became the target."

"You mean Vincent's mom."

"Goddammit. Yes, right. Vincent's mom. I mean, think about that—she knows he's got this photographic memory, and she gives him this death sentence on purpose. While his dad was working with the FBI, his mom never had any intention of doing so."

"So, either way, he was doomed."

"Right. So Maryanne hired Security Solutions because she genuinely felt for the kid. She launched a footrace between the Russians and me to see who would get there first. That's a lot of gaming with people's lives."

Dom took another pull of beer and leaned in closer. "I'm sensing something out of you that I don't often see," he said. "You've seen the world as a dark place for a long time, yet this incident seems to have surprised you."

Jonathan waved that off. "No," he said. "Not surprised. Disgusted."

"So, why share this with me?"

"You're a priest and a shrink."

"Which I've been for a long time, and we don't often have conversations like this."

Jonathan sipped the Lagavulin. "I thought you should know," he said. "You make the call whether or not to share the details with Gr—Vincent. I thought you should know."

Dom nodded. "Okay."

Jonathan checked the clock and thumbed the remote.

As the picture arrived from the ether, Dom said, "Is it true what I hear about Boxers? He's got a girlfriend now?"

Jonathan smirked and made a rocking motion with his hand. "I'm not sure the G-word is appropriate, but Jolaine certainly has the hots for him."

ACKNOWLEDGMENTS

Nothing happens without the constant, undying love of my wife, Joy. She is my strength, my beauty, my . . . joy.

You dear readers who have been with me from the beginning remember stories of my great pride in my son, Chris, who was barely eight years old when *Nathan's Run* was published. Now he's twenty-eight, and my pride in him continues to bloom. Way to go, kid.

Jolaine Cage made a generous donation to the Youth Quest Foundation to have a character named after her, and for that I am grateful. For the record, she bears no resemblance to the character who bears her name, yet I still feel compelled to apologize for what I put her through.

Lee Lofland, the proprietor of the wonderful Writers' Police Academy, gave me a valuable lesson on how to steal a car. Thanks for that, Lee. Jolaine thanks you, too. (The fictional one, not the *real* one.)

Special thanks to Michelle Gagnon, who agreed to set aside her own very busy writing life to read an early draft of *End Game* and lend some well-needed advice. All along the way, my dear friends Art Taylor, Ellen Crosby, Alan Orloff, and Donna Andrews—collectively known as the Rumpi (ask them why when you see them)—have lent a guiding hand to the pile of pages that ultimately melded together into this book. Thank you all so much.

My team at Kensington is becoming more like family with every book. In Michaela Hamilton, I have the best, most supportive editor a writer could ask for, and none of that would be possible without the tireless work of publisher Laurie Parkin. Arthur Maisel is my production editor, Adeola Saul my publicist, and Alexandra Nicolajsen is my own Venice Alexander. She makes the computerized world work for me. They all work for Steve Zacharius, who has been a vocal supporter of mine from way back in the early days—long before I boarded the publishing vessel he runs so well.

Last, but never, ever least is my good friend and agent, Anne Hawkins. She's the guiding hand of my career, and I'm honored that she does it with such charm and grace and ferocity. Thanks. (Yes, Anne, I'm working on the next manuscript! Jeez.)

Don't miss John Gilstrap's ncxt breathtaking thriller
starring Jonathan Grave

AGAINST ALL ENEMIES

Coming from Pinnacle in 2015!

Keep reading to enjoy an exciting excerpt . . .

Jonathan Grave concentrated on his sight picture, forcing himself to ignore the heat of the afternoon sun that threatened to strip the skin off the back of his neck. In Virginia in July, the tropical sun was part of the deal. He lay on his belly on the mulchy forest floor, the forestock of his 7.62 millimeter Hechler & Koch 417 supported on a stack of three beanbags. He pressed the extended collapsible stock against his shoulder and split his attention between what his naked left eye could see and the 10-times-magnified circle from the Nightforce Optics that dominated the vision in his right eye. Somewhere out there in the woods, roughly a hundred yards away, a target would present itself.

Soon.

Jonathan told himself to watch his breathing and to relax his hand on the rifle's pistol grip. When the target showed itself, it would take only a slight press from the pad of his right forefinger to send the round downrange. After that, it was all physics. He watched the movement of the grass for wind speed, and the—

His naked eye caught movement left-to-right, and

he brought his scope to bear in time to see the black silhouette of a man streak from one tree to another. The target was back behind cover before he could commit to a shot, but at least now he knew where the son of a bitch was. If he moved again—

There! The target darted back to the left, taunting him, but Jonathan was ready for it. He led by a couple of feet and released a round. Then a second. The woods echoed with the rolling sound of the gunshot.

"Did I get him?" Jonathan asked.

"You were behind him by two feet on the first shot and probably four on the second." The critique came from his spotter, a giant of a man named Brian Van De-Muelebrocke—aka Boxers—who had saved Jonathan's ass more times than anyone could count.

"Are you sure?"

"Would you like me to show you the scars on the trees?" Boxers monitored the action from Jonathan's right, his eye pressed to a Leica spotting scope. "Would you like a warning for the next one?"

Jonathan felt his ears go hot. "No, I don't need—"

The target darted out again from behind a tree, and Jonathan fired two more times. He knew even as the trigger broke that he'd yanked the shots wide.

"If I'm ever a bad guy," Boxers said, "will you promise to be the sharpshooter who takes me out?"

"Bite me."

"No, seriously. I'm tempted to go ride the target piggyback," Boxers went on. "I can't think of a safer place to be." As he spoke he pushed the joystick in his hand to the right, sending the target out of hiding again.

This time, Jonathan didn't bother to press the trigger. He knew better.

"Hey Digger," Boxers said. "How 'bout I give you a baseball bat and you can beat it to death."

Jonathan released his grip on the weapon and squatted up to a standing position, leaving the 417 on the ground. "Okay, Mouth," he said, cranking his head to look up under Big Guy's chin. "Let's switch places. I'll take a turn at the stressful work of pushing buttons. Let's see you hit Zippy." The target—Zippy—was a converted tackling dummy that Jonathan had mounted on rails that could be laid just about anywhere. Powered by a remote-controlled electric motor, Zippy was a great training tool.

Boxers grinned. "Look at you sounding all threatening and shit. Do you want me to shoot with my eyes open or closed?"

Jonathan held his hand out for the controller, and Boxers handed it over. Big Guy settled on his belly behind the rifle. Jonathan smiled at the slogan on his friend's T-shirt: *Never run from a sniper. You'll only die tired.*

"Let me know when you're ready," Jonathan said.

"That's your call, not mine—"

Jonathan jammed the joystick to the left, and the target took off while Boxers was still speaking. The 417 barked twice. Half a second after each blast, Jonathan heard the faint *pang!* of a solid hit.

Boxers didn't bother to look up as he said, "Hey, Boss, did I hit it?" He rumbled out a laugh.

Jonathan pulled away from the tripod-mounted spotting scope. "I hate you," he said. Boxers was the most natural shooter Jonathan had ever known, and he'd been that way since the beginning. It was as if bullets responded to Big Guy's whims.

Boxers stood, brushed off the front of his T-shirt and jeans, and held out his hand for the controller. "I push the buttons because you need the practice."

As Jonathan handed over the box, his phone buzzed in his pocket. The caller I.D. said UNKNOWN.

He pressed the connect button and brought the phone to his ear. "Yeah."

"Yes sir, Mr. Horgan," a man's voice said. "This is Cale Cook at the western guard shack. There's a visitor here to see you. He identifies himself as a Colonel Rollins, and he says it's important that he speak to you now."

Jonathan didn't know the security team out here at the compound very well, so Cale Cook could have called himself by any name, but he sure as hell knew who Colonel Rollins was. "Take a picture of him and send it to my phone. I'll call you back when I get it."

Boxers' face showed that he'd been eavesdropping. "What's up?"

"Roleplay Rollins is here."

Boxers recoiled at the words as anger settled in his eyes. There was a time not to long ago when Big Guy would have hurried to beat the man to death, and Jonathan would have let him. The three of them had a history that involved Jonathan and Boxers' last days with the Unit, and it did not end well.

Jonathan extended his palm to settle his friend down. "Take it easy. Past is past. He saved our asses and we owe him a solid." His phone buzzed, and displayed a picture of the man the visitor claimed to be. Jonathan called the guard shack. "Send him up to the lodge and have him wait on the porch. We're on our way."

"Should we escort him?"

"Is he alone?"

"Alone and unarmed. I searched his vehicle."

"No," Jonathan said. "Let him go solo. It's hard to get lost when there's only one road." He clicked off and looked to Boxers. "This should be interesting," he said. "Let's pick up the weapons and ammo. We'll break the target down later."

Boxers pointed through the Hummer's windshield toward the front porch of the stylishly rustic structure that had started life a hundred fifty years ago as a log cabin, but whose original owners would recognize nothing but a portion of the western wall. "There he is."

Colonel Stanley Rollins, U.S. Army, stood from one of the porch's cane rockers as they approached. He wore jeans and a white polo shirt, and an expression that was impossible to read.

"Looks like Roleplay is a civilian today," Boxers said.

"He hates that name."

Big Guy chuckled. "I know. That's why I like it."

"Don't start anything," Jonathan said. "Not until we hear what he has to say."

"I'll call him Stanley, then."

"He hates that even worse."

Boxers looked across the console and grinned. "Yeah."

Jonathan opened the door and slid to the ground. "Hello, Colonel," he called as he approached the lodge. "This is a genuine surprise." He extended his hand as he closed the distance, and Rollins walked down the four steps to greet him.

"Hello, Digger," he said. His handshake wasn't the bone crusher that it used to be. "Nice to see you again."

"Stanley!" Boxers shouted, feigning delight. "Hasn't someone fragged your ass by now?"

Rollins didn't rise to the bait. "Big Guy," he said with a nod. "Pleasant as always, I see." He pointed to the Hummer. "And still the environmental conscience that you've always been."

Dubbed the Batmobile by Boxers, the lavishly customized and heavily armored Hummer H1 was literally irreplaceable. They weren't made anymore.

Jonathan smelled trouble in the air, so he placed a hand on Rollins's elbow to ease him back toward the porch and the inside of the lodge. "Let's talk inside," he said. "It's too hot out here."

Jonathan led the way up the steps. He turned the key and pulled the heavy wooden door out toward them. He stepped aside to allow the colonel to pass.

As he did, Rollins rapped on the door with a knuckle. "Impressive. What is that, oak?"

"Something like that," Jonathan said. "I believe in living securely."

Inside, the foyer led directly to a living room, fifteen-by-fifteen feet, beyond which a dining area led to a closed door that hid the kitchen from view. A stone fireplace dominated the eastern wall—the wall to the right walking in. In the far western corner, stairs led up to the sleeping levels. In decorating the place, Jonathan had leaned heavily on his experience at Colorado ski lodges. Woodsy artwork hung from exposed pine walls across the way on the north wall, while a rack of eight long guns took up much of the front, southern, wall.

"Wow," Rollins said. "I guess I keep underestimating just how friggin' rich you really are. What is this place?"

"Pretty much what it looks like," Jonathan said as he nudged a switch on the wall to wake up two dangling chandeliers made of antlers. "This is a place to escape to, to unwind. Two hundred twenty-five acres of seclusion."

"And a guard patrol?"

"When did you become a reporter?" Boxers asked as he pulled the door closed.

"Who would see this and not be curious?" Rollins said.

"Which is a good reason to have a guard patrol," Jonathan said. He motioned to the leather sofas and chairs near the fireplace. "Have a seat, Colonel. Suffice to say that things happen out here that are best not witnessed by curiosity seekers. Think of it as my company's testing grounds." He let the words settle in. "Can I get you something to drink?"

Rollins shook his head and waved the question away. "No, I'm fine, thanks."

Big Guy was already halfway to the wet bar in the back corner of the dining area. "I'm not," he said. "You want your usual, Boss?"

"Please." On his own, this would be the time of day for a martini, but since Boxers was tending the bar, that meant a couple fingers of Lagavulin scotch. Boxers didn't have the patience for the delicate chemistry that was a good martini.

Jonathan settled himself into a chair, crossed his legs, and locked in on Rollins's eyes. "You know, Colonel, I don't think either one of us wants the charade of small talk. What say you get right to what you have on your mind?"

Rollins leaned forward in his chair and rested his elbows on his knees. "I presume you still remember Boomer Nasbe."

"Of course I do." Boomer had joined the Unit shortly before Jonathan was on his way out, but it was a small, tight community. Plus, Jonathan had had some recent dealings with Boomer's wife and son. "Is he okay?" The scotch floated over Jonathan's right shoulder, clamped in Boxers' fingers.

"No," Rollins said. "He's gone rogue."

"What the hell does that mean?" Boxers asked as he took the sofa for himself.

"It means he's killing off Agency assets."

"Bullshit," Boxers said. "He was a good kid. No way would he do that."

"And yet he is."

"Why?" Jonathan asked.

Rollins shrugged. "Why does anyone do anything like that? Something went crosswise in his head, and he started wasting people."

Jonathan and Boxers exchanged looks. "I'm not buying it," Jonathan said. "I mean, I can imagine him whacking Agency guys—who among us hasn't considered that a time or two?—but I don't buy that he's crazy. He's got a reason."

"Lee Harvey Oswald had reasons, Dig," Rollins

said. "So did John Wilkes Booth and Charles Manson. But so what? Murder is murder."

"The Army is up to its nipples in shrinks these days," Boxers said. "*Somebody* has to have wondered the obvious."

"You already know some of it," Rollins said. "Those assholes who came at his family undoubtedly screwed him up at least a little."

"No," Jonathan said. "Well, of course it was traumatic, but I spoke with Boomer not long after that. He was okay."

"His deployments, then," Rollins said. With an acknowledging hand to Big Guy, he added, "Nipples-deep in shrinks as we are, there are no doubt hundreds of possible diagnoses, but none of them can be tested because we haven't been able to talk to Boomer because we don't know where he is."

"Why does it have to be Boomer?" Jonathan pressed. "You've got a couple of dead Agency guys—"

"Three," Rollins interrupted. "*Three* dead Agency guys, and they were all in the same AO as Boomer during his last deployment."

Jonathan recognized the acronym for area of operation. "So? After we punted on Iraq, Afghanistan was the only AO we had left. There have to be thousands of cross-links between the Agency dead and soldiers in country."

"And what makes you think they weren't killed by the Taliban?" Boxers asked.

"You're both getting defensive," Rollins said.

"Of course we're defensive!" Boxers yelled. Jonatha

could tell he was spinning up to a bad place. "And why the hell aren't you? Haven't you turned your back on enough of your brothers over the years?"

Jonathan extended a hand to calm his friend down. "Not now, Box."

"Screw you," he snapped, and his face instantly showed horror. "Not you. Him. Not only do you lay this on your own Army, you have to lay it on our Unit brother."

"If you'll calm the hell down, I'll explain it all to you!" Rollins shouted. He could get spun up, too.

Jonathan knew it was time to play peacekeeper. "Quit shouting, both of you. Colonel, I encourage you to make your case quickly, and with minimal bullshit, and as you do, keep in mind that you're talking about a friend who's given a hell of a lot for his country."

Some of the red left Rollins's face. None of it left Boxers'.

"Some bad things happened on Boomer's last tour," Rollins said. "I can't go into details, but he'd been working a source for quite some time, and then the source disappeared. We think he blamed his CIA counterparts."

"Why would he do that?" Jonathan asked.

"Because we blame the Agency for everything," Rollins replied. "Some things never change."

"There's a giant step between blaming and killing," Boxers said. "What proof do you have?"

Rollins looked to the ceiling and scowled, as if to divine his next words. "There's proof, and then there's *proof.* We don't have any of the latter. What we do ~~now~~ is, he came home, walked away from his mar-~~ge~~, and disappeared." His eyes bored into Jonathan. ~~d~~ I mean *disappeared.* Off the grid."

"You know, we're trained to do that, right?" Jonathan said. "In fact, we're *paid* to do that when we're in hostile territory."

"But domestically? Who would do that?"

Jonathan waited for him to get the absurdity of his own question.

Rollins acknowledged with a nod. "Okay, other than you, who would do that?" He didn't wait for an answer. "Within a few days of his disappearance, the first of the Agency guys was killed, shot with a five-five-six round from a long ways away. Over a hundred yards, as I recall. He was on his way to his car in the driveway, and it was a perfect head shot."

Jonathan felt tension in his chest. That wasn't the kind of a shot an amateur could make.

"Three days later, the second agent was taken out as he exited a coffee shop outside of Fredericksburg, Virginia, not far from your stomping grounds. Five-five-six again, center of mass, hollow-point round. Perfect shot and no one heard it."

Boxers' ire had transformed to concern. "Was this a coffee shop he went to regularly?"

Rollins nodded. "Every day. How did you know?"

"Was the first guy—the head shot—a hollow point?"

"No." Rollins smiled. He saw that Boxers got it.

"He was worried about collateral damage," Big Guy said. He looked to Jonathan. "He'd studied the guy's routine and used HPs as a safety."

"What about the third?" Jonathan asked.

"Another head shot," Rollins said, "again from long distance. The interesting thing there was that the shooter showed great patience. The agent had been standing for ten minutes with his kid at the end of the driveway, waiting for the school bus." He looked to Boxers. "Like before, this was a daily routine. He waited till the little girl was on the bus, and the bus was on its way before he shot. No one heard or saw anything. By the time his wife woke up and noticed he was missing— and then found the body—he was already stiff."

Jonathan took a pull on his scotch as he pushed the pieces into place. "That still doesn't mean Boomer did it," he said. Even he heard the weakness of his words.

"Doesn't matter," Rollins said. "The Agency thinks he did, and they'll move heaven and earth to find him and take him out."

"What about due process?" Boxers asked.

"Where have you been the past few years?" Rollins countered. "The alphabet agencies stopped caring about due process when the regime changed. That was about the same time when beat cops started riding around in tanks. This isn't your childhood America anymore."

"So, we've got a lot of conjecture and assumptions," Jonathan summarized. "Cut to the chase, Colonel. Why are you here?"

Rollins cast a nervous glance to Boxers as he said, "We want you to find Boomer and bring him home."

"Well, that's not gonna happen," Boxers said. "I don't hunt down my friends."

Jonathan said, "By 'bring him home,' do you mean alive or dead?"

"Preferably alive."

"But dead would be okay, too?" Boxers growled.

Rollins worked his jaw muscles. "No, dead would not be *okay*, Box. I'm not the monster you pretend I am. But don't forget that every wet-work contractor for the CIA is out looking for this guy. If they get him, he's toast."

"Then why not just leave it to them?" Jonathan asked.

Rollins recoiled from the question. "Now who's being the monster? You said it yourself, Dig. He's family. Boomer deserves better than a bullet. I don't care what he did, he deserves better than that. If you can get to him first, maybe you can talk him down. If he hears that you're the one hunting for him, maybe he'll surrender. This is serious shit."

Jonathan leaned back into his seat and crossed his legs. The math here wasn't working for him. "You said bad things happened to him over there on his last tour. I won't even ask you for those details—at least not yet—but if the bad stuff is traceable to specific interactions with specific Agency assets, then I presume the remaining assets have become much harder targets."

Rollins looked to the floor.

"*Are* there any more targets, Stanley?" Boxers asked.

Rollins took a deep breath. "No," he said. "All the targets have been eliminated."

Jonathan exchanged a confused look with Boxers. "Then what's done is done," he said. "Good reasons, bad reasons, that's for others to decide. I'm not a cop. I'm not going to traipse all over hell's half acre to bring a colleague into custody."

"It's more than that," Rollins said. "The killings are real—they really happened—but that's not the punch line."

"Good Christ, Stanley," Boxers said with a derisive

laugh. "Can't you just for once in your life deal from the top of the deck? Why does everything—"

"He's a traitor, guys," Rollins said. "He's selling secrets to the world."

Something stirred in Jonathan's gut. "What kind of secrets?"

"The most damaging kind you can think of," Rollins said.